F   Spencer, Katherine.
SPE
           All is bright

All Is Bright

Thomas Kinkade's Cape Light

All Is Bright

KATHERINE SPENCER

BERKLEY BOOKS, NEW YORK

THE BERKLEY PUBLISHING GROUP
Published by the Penguin Group
Penguin Group (USA) LLC
375 Hudson Street, New York, New York 10014

USA • Canada • UK • Ireland • Australia • New Zealand • India • South Africa • China

penguin.com

A Penguin Random House Company

This book is an original publication of The Berkley Publishing Group.

Library of Congress Cataloging-in-Publication Data

Spencer, Katherine, (date–)
All is bright / Katherine Spencer. —First edition.
p. cm. —(Thomas Kinkade's Cape Light ; 15)
ISBN 978-0-425-26432-4 (hardcover)
1. Cape Light (Imaginary place)—Fiction.   2. Clergy—Fiction.   3. Fathers and
daughters—Fiction.   4. Man-woman relationships—Fiction.   5. Christmas stories.   I. Title.
PS3553.A489115A78 2014
813'.54—dc23
2014017782

FIRST EDITION: November 2014

PRINTED IN THE UNITED STATES OF AMERICA

10 9 8 7 6 5 4 3 2 1

Cover image: *Winter Evening Cottage* © 2012 Thomas Kinkade.
Cover design by Lesley Worrell.

To readers of Cape Light, with gratitude
—K.S.

DEAR READER

Sometimes it seems to me that one of the best parts of Christmas is reminiscing about the many holidays that have passed. As if each Christmas season is part of some larger work in progress, like pearls on a string. One precious bead added each year. Every decoration, taken from its hiding place, speaks to me, telling its particular story. Each ornament, music box, wooden bear, or snow globe summons vivid memories.

When I was very young, my father worked for a company that imported Christmas ornaments from Europe. These handmade decorations were very fine, made of hand-blown glass, painstakingly painted and decorated—skiers and ice-skaters, ballerinas and angels. An entire set of Snow White and the Seven Dwarfs. A blue candle with a miniature nativity scene inside, a fragile glass shadow box. As Christmas drew closer, my father would come home each night with mysterious packages, and we would sit in awe as the newest treasures were unveiled. I still remember those slim brown boxes tied with string coming through the door, and feeling so eager to see what was inside.

When my parents sold the family home, they passed these family heirlooms on to me and my sister. No matter how carefully preserved, only a few have survived. When I hang them on our tree, I am instantly transported back in time to golden hours. But now these antique ornaments hang alongside newer treasures, definitely made of sturdier stuff, but with no less claim on a place in my heart's scrapbook.

In this book Reverend Ben is also transported back into the past, to his very first Christmas in Cape Light. He recalls the many challenges and joys the season brought to him, while in the present, his daughter, Rachel, wonders if she can open her heart and trust the gifts that this Christmas brings.

So it is with all of our Christmas traditions and memories. As the beloved carol "Silent Night" reminds us, "All is calm. All is bright." The beauty of Christmas past and Christmas present, shining together, with one steady light.

And while I fully intend to relish my memories this Christmas, as I do every year, I will also be mindful and grateful for the present moment—the memories in the making. And so many blessings received at Christmas and all year through. I truly hope you will, too.

With all best wishes,
Katherine Spencer

CHAPTER ONE

Present day, December 3

REVEREND BEN HAD FORGOTTEN ALL ABOUT THE MEET-
ing. It was already late afternoon when he emerged from
his office, coat and briefcase in hand. He had planned to leave the church
early and look in on Dr. Elliot, who had been home with bronchitis over
Thanksgiving weekend.

"Are you leaving for the day, Reverend?" Mrs. Honeyfield abruptly
looked up from her keyboard. "What about the meeting?" Before he could
ask the obvious question, his secretary added, "About the church history?"

"Oh right . . . was that today?" He noticed the rising sound of voices
in the conference room. The group must have started without him.

"Wednesday at four. I left a sticky note on your calendar." Mrs.
Honeyfield politely looked back at her computer.

"Guess I missed it." That was true. Though he wasn't sure how. His
secretary's sticky notes were growing progressively brighter as he grew
older. The little squares had started off a bland, pale yellow and now
fairly screamed at him in neon pink and roadwork orange.

"I'd better get in there." Ben set his coat on a chair. "Would you call Mrs. Warwick . . . I mean, Mrs. Elliot," he quickly corrected himself. "Please tell her I've been delayed. I can stop by after five. Or tomorrow. Whatever she prefers."

It went without saying that Lillian Elliot would not hesitate to state her preference. He would always think of her as Lillian Warwick, though her surname had changed a few years back when she and her longtime friend, Ezra Elliot, were married. The well-earned triumph of a patient heart—Dr. Elliot's, that is . . . not Lillian's, to be sure.

But it was now clear to all that Lillian's devotion equally matched that of her husband. With Ezra fighting off the flu, Ben thought he should visit. Lillian liked to give the impression that she didn't care one way or another about such attentions from her minister. He could almost see her shrugging a thin shoulder. But Ben knew—after nearly forty years as Lillian's pastor—that the great lady did care. And felt it was her due.

"Of course, Reverend. I'll call her right away."

"Thank you, Mrs. Honeyfield. Where would I be without you?"

She answered with a small smile. "I can't say, Reverend. But probably not at your meetings."

Ben laughed and headed to the conference room. Meetings—and more meetings—the chugging engine that kept his little church moving down the track. Often slow and ponderous, prone to sudden stops and unsettling puffs of steam. But sooner or later, all the passengers were carried where they needed to go, their progress slow but steady.

This afternoon's meeting was about producing a church history, a book that would be sold to raise funds for the church's many service projects in the community: the community garden in the spring, free books and school supplies given out to schoolchildren in the fall, the gifts and toys for struggling families at Christmas, the food pantry, open all year long, and so many other worthy efforts made by his congregation.

Even without that benefit, the book would be a wonderful way to preserve the church's long, colorful story and the contributions of so many generations, dating back to the seventeenth century.

The history had been Sophie Potter's idea, and a good one, though it would take long hours of complicated work to see it through. But despite the challenges, the group was eager to try their hand at it.

"What is now proved was once only imagined," the poet William Blake had written. It was one of the amazing things about this world, Ben often reflected. How God inspires us to create, bestowing an idea and a vision and the energy and means to follow through if we only have the faith to try what appears at first to be difficult . . . or even impossible.

He entered the conference room, a few doors down from the office, and greeted the members of the committee. "Hello, everyone. Sorry I'm late."

He glanced around the table and took the nearest empty seat, noticing his wife, Carolyn, seated directly across the table. He met her bright blue eyes with a smile.

Sophie Potter, the committee chairperson, sat at the head of the table, an impressive array of papers and folders spread around her.

"We've just been discussing what needs to be done and sorting out the jobs, Reverend. Vera and Claire have volunteered to write the text," she added, referring to longtime church members Vera Plante and Claire North. "Carolyn and I will work on the research, and Grace Hegman is going to put the whole thing together, figuring out where the pictures go and all that. She's made some beautiful scrapbooks and collections of vintage photographs about town history and the fishermen of her father's day. Have you ever seen them?"

"I've never had the pleasure," Ben admitted, glancing at Grace, who tilted her head in her modest way. She was a quiet and sensitive soul, but very observant. Ben didn't doubt her scrapbooks were wonderful. And Sophie sounded so sure of her assignments. But so much was done on computers these days, especially making a book of this kind. Did Grace Hegman, an expert on all things antique and vintage, know enough about the necessary technological shortcuts? Before he could voice his concerns, Vera Plante spoke up.

"Dan Forbes offered to edit the manuscript and put everything on the computer for us so we can have it printed at the lowest cost."

"Wonderful. He can keep his eye on the historical facts, too," Ben added. Though he trusted the group to do an excellent job researching the church's story, he was happy to hear that the former reporter and editor-in-chief of the town newspaper was on board as well. Dan would doubtlessly lend a professional touch. After handing over the *Cape Light Messenger* to his daughter Lindsay, he had written and published several books about local history. Working at home, he had been doing most of the child care for his younger daughter, Jane, while his wife, Mayor Emily Warwick, ran the town.

"I think Emily persuaded him to take part. She wanted to help, but has her plate full, as usual," Claire explained.

Sophie made a note on a yellow pad. "He's also going to check the newspaper archives for articles about the church."

"That will be a huge help for the researchers," Carolyn said. "Meanwhile, we have a job for you, Ben."

"For me?" Ben fumbled to hide his surprise. He was happy to give his opinions and oversee, but didn't expect to be doing any hands-on work. Maybe they wanted him to write an introduction or a letter to the reader?

"It's an important job." Sophie stood up and took a large brown box with a lid from a table near the door. Ben hadn't even noticed it until that moment.

"Can I help you?" he asked quickly. Sophie was healthy and strong, but she was well over eighty. It was only polite to offer.

"Thank you, but it doesn't weigh much. About half a bushel of McIntosh, maybe less." Sophie had run an orchard all her life and tended to judge the world in terms of apples. Reverend Ben couldn't help but smile.

He sat down again and she set the box at the end of the table. It looked like the kind used to store files, though he could tell by the way she carried it that it was not filled with piles of paper, but something lighter.

She removed the lid and Ben inhaled a musty scent, even at a distance. "We found quite a few boxes of photographs stored around the church. We're taking turns sorting them out, trying to identify who's in the pictures and when and where they were taken, and selecting any that could be included in our book."

"I can help with that. I love looking at old photos," Ben said sincerely.

"We were hoping you would say that. You've been at the church a long time, Reverend."

"Yes, I have," he replied with a laugh. He'd been called by the congregation over thirty-five years ago. He'd been just thirty-one years old, relatively young to head his own church. But he arrived with great confidence and faith that he was ready for the job—and was soon disabused of those illusions. Ben smiled to himself, thinking back to that rocky first year in Cape Light when both his maturity and his faith had been tested.

."Most of you have been here even longer," he pointed out.

"No argument there," Sophie agreed. "But there are a lot of photos. Why don't you start with this box, and we'll put a few more in your office later this week?"

A few more? There must have been about a thousand photos in the single carton on the table. He could see his wife suppress a laugh.

"I'll take this home and we can look at it tonight, Ben." Carolyn slid the box toward her end of the table. "It will be fun. Better than watching television," she promised him.

His wife had such a graceful way of smoothing over an awkward moment. It was a quality he had always loved in her.

He nodded and forced a smile. "Anything for the cause. I wasn't sure about this project when you suggested it, Sophie. But I think this book is going to be wonderful; a chance to honor the past and everyone who helped build our church. And a very special gift to the members who enjoy it now."

"That's our mission, Reverend," Vera replied. "So many people down through the generations have had a hand in making the church what it is now. There are so many fascinating stories. It won't be dull reading, to be sure."

"We aim to be truthful, too," Claire added. "A real history, including the rough times. There were a few."

"I agree. Let's not gloss over the facts. Though that's not nearly as easy as it sounds," he warned. "I've tried my hand a few times at writing nonfiction accounts, and capturing the truth of a matter can be very elusive."

Like an optical illusion that can transform before your eyes, he had learned.

"Another reason we're glad Dan is working with us," Claire noted. "He'll keep us on the straight and narrow."

Ben agreed—and also hoped the former newspaper editor would help sort through all the photos. For one thing, Dan would be far better at picking the best pictures for the book. And for another, it appeared the group could use all the help they could get with that task.

He glanced at the large box, which all but obscured the sight of his lovely wife. They would hardly make a dent in it tonight, he predicted, even if they looked through the photos for hours.

It turned out Ben was accurate with that guess. It was nearly eleven that night, and he and Carolyn still sat together in the living room, their reading glasses perched on their noses, shielding bleary eyes. Piles of old photographs were mounded on the dining room table. They had devised a system for sorting them, though Ben kept forgetting the categories and had to ask Carolyn each time he wanted to put one down.

"Let see . . . a Christmas pageant. Oh, there's a date on back, 1967. The wise men are all wearing Beatles haircuts," he added, looking up at her.

"It took me a while to get used to that style. But I think it seems very cute and harmless now," Carolyn murmured. "Oh, look at this." She bounced up in her seat and held out a large sepia-toned photo that looked more like a formal portrait than a casual snapshot. Ben guessed it had been taken with an old-fashioned box camera.

"Looks like this baby was just baptized. There are the parents and godparents . . . and the minister." Carolyn pointed, but didn't touch the delicate old photo.

Ben took in the beautiful clothing of the era: the long, draping dresses of the women, with their bobbed hair and soft eyes; the stiff, high-necked shirts and vested suits on the gentlemen. "Babies wore long gowns for a christening in the old days—girls and boys," he added, noticing the lace edges on the baby's flowing, snowy white gown. "It's a beautiful photo, a real masterpiece."

"And definitely has possibilities for the book. If we can just figure out who's in it . . ." She turned the photo over, then held it under the lamp on the end table. Ben noticed some pale, scratchy writing. "June sixth, nineteen twenty-five. Baptism of Dennis . . . Hegman. Reverend John Bingham presiding." She looked over at Ben. "Dennis Hegman . . . Some relation to Grace?"

Ben laughed. "Indeed he is. That's Digger," he said, identifying Grace's father by his well-known nickname. "Dennis is his given name."

Carolyn looked shocked, then stared back at the photo. "That adorable infant . . . is Digger? Where did those plump, dimpled cheeks go?"

"They might have been hidden under his beard all these years," Ben suggested. "You could check next time you see him."

"I'll take your word for it." Carolyn examined the photo again. "I never heard anyone call him Dennis. In all these years, I've never heard anyone call him anything but Digger."

"And you probably never will," Ben guessed. Perhaps at the old fisherman's funeral, whenever that might be, he thought. Maybe once, as a formality. "This one can definitely be set aside for the book." Ben took the photo very carefully and laid it down in a special spot on the table.

"I vote for it, too. But that will be my last effort for tonight." Carolyn rose to her feet and stretched, then picked up her shoes. "I'm feeling beat. I'll try again tomorrow."

"All right, dear. But before you go, take a look at this one. Anyone you know?" It was hard to keep the laughter from his voice as he held out the small photo.

She glanced at it curiously, then her entire expression lit up. "Ben . . . where did you find that?" She took the photo from his hand and stared at it. "The day we moved in here. I don't remember posing."

"Neither do I," he admitted. "Someone from the church who came to help us must have taken it."

"Yes, must have been . . . Look at us. We were so young."

She leaned over his shoulder, her hands resting on it with a gentle touch. Ben stared down at the sight of a fresh-faced young man with fair skin, blue eyes, and a thick head of curly, reddish-brown hair that made him sigh with envy. He was wearing glasses with wire rims, a style he had not deviated from all these years. But he didn't wear a beard; that came later, along with a paunchy middle.

Carolyn was simply stunning—her soft blond hair lifting in the breeze, her beautiful smile and bright eyes as she held their baby daughter, Rachel, in her arms.

"Look at you. You could have been a model," he told her.

"Oh, Ben, not quite. Not with all that baby drool on my dress," she added, laughing.

"I don't see any baby drool." He saw his arm around Carolyn's shoulder as she cradled Rachel. Carolyn had been so very beautiful it made his heart skip a beat sometimes just to catch sight of her. Still did.

It was a fair spring day, the middle of May, he recalled, though he didn't remember the exact date. But he did remember the white puffy clouds in a blue sky and the trees and bushes around the parsonage just starting to sprout tender buds and small green leaves.

"How old were we here?" he asked her quietly.

"You were thirty-one and I was twenty-nine. I thought I was so old to be having my first baby. These days, women are waiting into their forties. Look at Rachel. She looked like a little angel."

Ben sighed, staring at the sight of their firstborn, only one month old at that time. "She did look like an angel. And cried like a banshee."

"Yes, she was a fussy baby," Carolyn admitted. "She grew out of it, though."

"She did," Ben added. Of course, to young parents it seemed like it would always be that way, no matter what people told them.

"She doesn't cry at all now," Carolyn remarked softly. "Sometimes I wish she would, just to blow off some steam. She holds everything inside. As if she might crack if she lost control for a single moment."

It was nearly two years now since Rachel had lost her husband, Jack. He had died from a heart attack; no warning, no sign. A seemingly healthy young man, only forty, who ate right, jogged, and even played one-on-one basketball with his son for hours on Saturday afternoons.

What could Ben say that had not been said before, a thousand times or more? His daughter was still grieving. It was just that way.

"She couldn't help it," Carolyn said, glancing back at the photo. "Crying when she was a baby, I mean. The heating pipes were so noisy, they woke her up all night long."

"Noisy pipes were the least of it." Ben shook his head as he set the photo down. "Do you remember this place? It was practically falling down around us."

Carolyn laughed. "I think a chunk of plaster did fall off the kitchen ceiling once while we were eating . . . But we fixed it up, little by little."

"Yes, we did. But you were a good sport, dear. You never complained."

She laughed at him. "Come now, Ben, ministers shouldn't lie."

He laughed, too. "Well, not much. A lot of other women wouldn't have put up with it at all."

"That's true. But I knew what we were together; that's what mattered to me." She squeezed his shoulder and kissed his cheek.

"Lucky me," he replied. He meant it, too.

Carolyn picked up an empty mug that had held some tea and a plate with cookie crumbs. "That's enough reminiscing for me. I'm going up."

"I'll be along in a little while. I just want to look at a few more."

Carolyn didn't answer. He heard her in the kitchen, and by the time she climbed the stairs, he was focused on the photographs again, lost in the stories that the pictures told him.

Many were very old, from the 1920s and 1930s, with a few more recent photos sneaking in somehow. There had been no rhyme or reason to the storage. He sifted through several without recognizing anyone, then suddenly stopped.

He saw his own image again, dressed in his long white robe, a green stole draped around his neck, along with his wooden cross, of course. He stood in front of the big wooden doors to the sanctuary. It looked as if the Sunday service had just ended. The doors were decorated with a garland made of twisted grapevines and autumn leaves. Beside the doorway, stacks of corn sheaves were tied with orange ribbon.

A man stood next to him, posing for the picture. He was tall and broad-shouldered, with thick black hair and bright blue eyes. Certainly a handsome man—"movie-star looks," they used to say back then. In this case, it was true. His suit was worthy of a movie star or a millionaire. Which, in this case, was true as well.

It was Oliver Warwick, of course, Lillian Warwick's first husband and, at that time, the wealthiest member of Ben's congregation, and probably the richest man in town.

Ben turned the picture over. A date was scrawled on back.

Sunday, November 26, 1978, Thanksgiving Weekend. Ben's thoughts drifted back, and he realized that the photo must have been taken just before Oliver's troubles began. And even before the rumors of those troubles, which gathered like dark clouds only days later, heralding the storm that broke over the Warwick mansion and forever changed the lives of the family who lived within.

Did Oliver have any inkling at all on that sunny Sunday morning of what was to come?

Ben examined Oliver's expression but could not find a hint of worry in his easy smile. Maybe a bit of weariness in his eyes? Ben couldn't tell now if he was just imagining that. For all his admirable traits, Oliver had been able to hide his true thoughts well.

But when did I first hear about it? Ben wondered. *Where was I? What was I doing?* Ben set the photo aside and traced back the slim thread of memory to that long-ago autumn.

He recalled a meeting of the church trustees—it must have been the day after the photograph was taken, because they used to meet on Monday nights. He could picture the members of the board seated around the table: Lester Plante, who was the moderator, Walter Tulley, Joe Morgan, and, of course, Ezra Elliot. All of them in their prime at the time.

Oliver was late to that meeting and had not even called . . .

November 27, 1978

"WHERE IS OLIVER?" LESTER PLANTE DEMANDED. LESTER TOOK HIS responsibilities as church moderator seriously, which Ben was all in favor of. But there was something about his overly serious, even pompous, manner as he presided over a meeting that got under Ben's skin. It was a small church with a small budget and even smaller issues to decide. Lester acted as if he were running the U.S. Congress—or, at the very least, General Motors.

Ben knew he shouldn't judge. He silently asked God for forgiveness and for patience—and found himself repeating the prayer several times during the evening.

"We need to settle this heating-oil business tonight," Lester went on. "I put it at the top of the agenda. But we can't evaluate the bids without the records. Which Warwick was supposed to bring." Lester emphasized the church treasurer's name in an annoyed tone, then glanced at his watch. "Do you think he still's coming?"

Ben felt pinned by the dark eyes that peered out from under the moderator's heavy brows and thick glasses. Of course, he might be imagining it. Ben was still fairly new at the church, and Lester had not warmed to him. Not like some of the others—Oliver Warwick in particular, who had been on the search committee and had been a strong advocate for calling Ben as their minister. Oliver had remained an aide and an ally ever since.

Lester had not been much in favor of offering Ben the position. And now the older man's tone and expression seemed to suggest that Ben was to blame in some way for Oliver's unexplained absence. Everyone had been reminded this morning about the meeting by phone. Ben had already told the group that Oliver had promised to attend.

"I guess he's been delayed," Ben offered. "I'll try him at home. Perhaps he forgot, after all."

"Probably," Lester mumbled.

"Yes, try the house. He can be in here in a few minutes if you catch him," Dr. Elliot said. "Why don't we just table the heating-oil issue for now and go on?" Dr. Elliot spoke quickly, smoothing the situation over, as he often did, Ben had observed. He liked Ezra Elliot very much. His sharp mind and straightforward, if often brusque, manner masked a kind and generous heart.

Ezra and Oliver had known each other since childhood, and they were friendly competitors, as far as Ben could tell. It was a complicated relationship, but the bonds were deep.

Ben went into his office and dialed the Warwicks' home number. Most of the time, a servant answered—a butler or a maid. He pictured the residence now: Lilac Hall, a towering stone mansion set on a large estate just outside of town.

Just as he expected, a man answered in a practiced tone. "Warwick residence. Who's calling, please?"

"This is Reverend Lewis. Is Mr. Warwick in?"

"He is not, sir."

"Mr. Warwick was expected at a meeting at church tonight. Do you know if he's still in his office?"

"I couldn't say, sir. Would you care to speak to Mrs. Warwick?"

Ben briefly considered the question. "That's all right. Don't disturb her. I have Mr. Warwick's work number; I'll try him there. If he comes in, please tell him I called."

"I will, sir. Good evening."

Ben ended the call and quickly dialed Oliver's office. He glanced at his watch. It was already past eight. He didn't expect anyone to pick up at this hour. But after only a few rings, Ben heard Oliver's familiar voice.

"Warwick," he answered in a low tone.

"It's Reverend Ben. The trustees are meeting tonight. My secretary called to remind you this morning?"

Oliver sighed. "Oh blast. Yes, of course. It's been one of those days. I shouldn't have gotten out of bed this morning." Oliver laughed, but it was a harsh, forced sound. Ben thought he sounded tired, and even distressed.

The man owned two big canneries and a lumberyard, all in all employing several hundred workers. He doubtless had a lot of business affairs of his own to handle. Ben was often surprised he volunteered to help run the church at all.

"Sorry to bother you, Oliver. Is everything okay?"

Ben waited a moment for Oliver to answer. "Just a paperwork mix-up," Oliver said finally. "It will sort itself out. What can I help you with, Reverend?"

"We're looking over bids for heating oil. Lester wanted to compare them to the last few years' records."

"Right . . . I did pull those invoices. I have them somewhere." Ben heard Oliver put the phone down, and then the rustle of paper. "Can't seem to locate them . . . and I see a call on the other line. I have to take this, Reverend. I'll bring the files to church tomorrow morning, on my way to the office. Good night."

Before Ben could reply, Oliver hung up.

Ben stood in his darkened office, staring at the phone, listening to the dull sound of the disconnected line.

Many people might have ended a call in that rushed way. But not Oliver. His smooth manner and sense of etiquette were impeccable. Ben could only assume that the problem in his office was more pressing and unsettling than he had let on.

Oliver has probably faced many long nights in his office sorting out business situations, Ben told himself. He would sort this one out, too.

Oliver was a smart man, a veteran who had attended an Ivy League college after the war. Ben had heard that his father, Harry Warwick, had built the family fortune from practically nothing. Oliver's older brother, Harry Warwick II, had also served, and had died on a battlefield in Italy, leaving Oliver the sole heir to his father's empire.

Many in town envied Oliver Warwick, even resented him, for the life he had been born to. But Ben knew that no life is without trouble, rich or poor, old or young. Oliver and his wife, Lillian, were probably the wealthiest family in town, but they did a great deal of good with their money, including supporting the church.

Lester Plante was someone who resented the Warwicks, Ben knew, and he would not be happy to hear that the records he wanted tonight were not available. Ben headed back to the meeting room, preparing himself for Lester's reaction. But Ben was sure Oliver would soon make it right. He obviously had more important matters on his plate right now.

The next morning, Ben sat at his desk, debating whether or not to bother Oliver at work again. It was almost ten, and the records had not arrived as Oliver had promised. Ben also had some documents that the church treasurer needed to sign. Lester had passed them to Ben during the meeting with explicit instructions that they needed to be completed and mailed no later than tomorrow. Lester would have taken care of the situation with Oliver himself, but Ben had offered, expecting to see Oliver at the church in the morning.

As the day wore on and there was still no sign of Oliver, Ben decided he should bring the documents over to the cannery during his lunch hour. He would have Oliver sign them and also pick up the files. It seemed a good solution, especially if Oliver was still in the midst of his business problem. It would also be worth the trip to keep peace on the board, Ben decided.

He dialed Oliver's line, and a secretary picked up on the first ring. "Mr. Warwick's office."

"This is Reverend Lewis. May I speak with Mr. Warwick?"

"I'm sorry, Reverend. Mr. Warwick is out today."

Ben found that surprising. Oliver's office problem must have been settled quickly. "Do you know where I could reach him? I have some paperwork from the church that he needs to sign."

"You might try him at home," she suggested. "He came in for a little while this morning but said he wasn't feeling well."

"I see. I'll try him there. Thank you."

Ben stood for a moment with his hand on the phone receiver, about to dial Lilac Hall. Then he put the phone down, put on his coat and hat, took the large envelope of tax documents in hand, and headed out to his car.

He needed to go out anyway, to get some lunch and pick up a few items at the drugstore that Carolyn needed for the baby. He remembered the list in his pocket as he drove down Main Street.

He would do his shopping on the way back to church, and maybe call Carolyn beforehand to make sure there was nothing to add. He wondered how his wife's day was going. The baby was still so fussy at night, though she was almost seven months old. Carolyn was worn out. He had gotten up early that morning to change and feed Rachel so Carolyn could get a few minutes' extra sleep. Not a huge help, but it was something. All the books told new mothers to sleep during the day, when the baby did. But of course his wife couldn't do that. She had to cook, clean, and keep working on the parsonage.

Their new house was calling out for all sorts of repairs. Many members of the congregation were willing to help them, but Ben hadn't had much time since they arrived to do more than the basics. With the holidays coming, Ben knew he wouldn't have any time at all to make improvements until the new year.

His first Christmas season in his new church—he was so looking forward to it. He had so many ideas for the Advent and Christmas services. The deacons and music director had mostly seemed pleased with his plans. He might be young to have his own church, but he had worked hard to earn this opportunity. He certainly felt more than capable and ready. Christmas, a high point of the church calendar, was going to be an important moment for him, a moment when he would feel truly bonded with his congregation, fully stepping into his role as their spiritual leader.

Ben had lived in Cape Light since May, a little over six months, but he still enjoyed the drive through the village and out to Beach Road. Tall trees lined the route, their branches gracefully arching overhead. Most of the trees were bare now, with only a few brown leaves clinging persistently, defying the change in season. This part of New England often had snow by this time of year. But it hadn't snowed yet. It still seemed a limbo sort of season, with autumn clearly over but winter not quite overtaking the landscape.

The entrance to Lilac Hall was easy to miss. The estate was surrounded by a brick wall covered with ivy and vines that blended in seamlessly with the wooded growth along the road.

The wrought-iron gates were open today, luckily. Ben steered his car through and headed down the long gravel drive toward the mansion. The drive was lined with lilac bushes. Well, lilac trees, you'd have to call them; they had grown that tall and full over the decades since Oliver Warwick's mother had planted them. She had designed several gardens on the property, and had also been an avid collector of art and antique furnishings.

Ben had only been inside the mansion once or twice. As he pulled into the circular drive and stared up at the massive stone structure, he had the same feeling in the pit of his stomach that he'd had on those earlier visits. The place was intimidating. To Ben, it looked more like a castle or a museum than a place a family would call home. There was nothing homey about it.

It was simply grand. And that had been the founding principle of Oliver's father when he built it, Ben assumed, copying the great houses in Europe—and not only importing the stones from France, but the stonecutters as well.

Grand it was. About that there could be no debate.

Ben walked up to the massive front door, tucked the envelope a little tighter under his arm, and rang the bell. He heard the chimes within, but had to wait a few minutes before a maid in uniform answered the door.

"Hello. I'm Reverend Lewis. I'm here to see Mr. Warwick," he explained.

The maid quickly stepped aside and let him in. "Is he expecting you, sir?"

"Well . . . no." Ben suddenly realized he probably should have called after all. "We had sort of an appointment this morning, at the church. But I understand he's home from work today. Not feeling well? I just spoke to his secretary."

The maid stared at him, her expression neither confirming nor denying this report. "He's in his study. I'll tell him that you're here, Reverend."

She turned and left him in the large foyer. A round pedestal table stood in the middle of the space. Ben guessed the wood was mahogany, though the surface was so shiny, it might as well have been made out of glass. A porcelain bowl on top was filled with fresh flowers. A large mirror with an ornate gold frame hung over an antique cupboard that stood against a wall, and a set of high-backed chairs with matching silk upholstery stood on either side. The chairs looked too delicate for use, Ben thought. He wouldn't dare sit on them.

He heard footsteps and looked up at the long, curving stairway. Lillian Warwick walked down slowly. She fixed Ben with a curious stare but didn't call out to him or smile in greeting. Dressed in a dark blue woolen suit and pearls, she looked like she might be on her way out for some appointment or meeting.

He waited, rocking back and forth a bit, feeling nervous, though he couldn't say why. Something about Mrs. Warwick never failed to intimidate him. She was older than he was, but that wasn't it. He dealt with plenty of church members, men and women, who were even older than Lillian without feeling off balance.

It was something about her aristocratic and elitist air. She kept herself at a distance, judging all she observed. Lillian Warwick was an assertive woman, not easily pleased, and free with her opinions. In fact, he had learned to assume she was nearly always displeased or disapproving.

He tried hard not to judge her temperament and to be as positive and patient as possible. Perhaps in time, she would come to trust him and treat him with respect, instead of with a veneer of proper manners.

"Good afternoon, Mrs. Warwick," he called out as she reached the bottom of the steps. His voice echoed off the high ceilings and paneled walls.

"Reverend Ben, I didn't know you were here. No one told me." She walked toward him, her chin tilted at an imperious angle.

"I'm waiting to see your husband. I have some papers for him to sign, and he needs to give me a file. Church business," he added quickly. "He was going to drop by my office today. I wanted to save him the trip."

She didn't answer at first, just eyed him curiously, as if, for some reason, she didn't believe him. "Oliver's not feeling well. I can take the papers and make sure he signs everything. I'll have our chauffeur, Howard, bring everything over to the church this afternoon." She held out her hand, ready to take the envelope.

Ben was about to hand it to her, seeing as how she had left him little choice, when Oliver Warwick walked into the foyer, coming out of the same open doorway where the maid had disappeared.

He didn't look sick, exactly, Ben thought, though he didn't look entirely well. He was not his usual, carefully groomed self. He was in his shirtsleeves, his necktie loosened and his hair mussed. His eyes were shadowed and red-rimmed. He looked very tired; even a bit older, Ben noticed.

But when he met Ben's gaze, a familiar smile fell over Oliver's face, like a curtain.

"Hello, Reverend. What brings you here today?" Oliver held out his hand and Ben shook it.

"I was given charge of some papers you need to sign, tax documents. Lester said they need to be mailed by tomorrow. And I wanted to pick up the heating-oil records."

Oliver laughed and tapped his forehead. "So sorry. I promised to drop them off this morning, didn't I? Slipped my mind entirely."

"That's all right. Your secretary said you weren't feeling well and had to head home. I didn't mean to disturb you."

"Yes . . . a very bad headache. I must be coming down with something," Oliver explained in a tired voice. "Come into my study, Reverend. I have the files, and I can sign all that stuff right now."

Ben was pleased to hear that plan. He felt like he had chased Oliver down and was being a nuisance, but this was church business and had to be done. Oliver seemed to understand that. Lillian, however, was giving Ben a look that suggested just the opposite.

"Well, I'll leave you two to take care of your business matters. Good day, Reverend," she said curtly. She gave her husband a look as she swept by.

Oliver took Ben's arm and led him through the large parlor and then down a short, dark hallway. Ben had a quick impression of dark wood moldings, wainscoting, and walls covered with old photographs and small oil paintings.

They came to a paneled wooden door. Oliver opened it and allowed Ben to walk through first. Ben suddenly smelled liquor. Had Oliver been drinking this early in the day? That would account for his bedraggled appearance. Ben kept his gaze down and entered the room without glancing back at his host.

The large room had long windows on one side, offering a view of the wide-open property behind the mansion. Most of the other walls were covered with tall wooden bookcases that rose from the floor to the high ceiling, filled with hundreds of volumes. Two small sofas flanked a fireplace with a large stone hearth, and opposite that, some soft leather armchairs faced a wooden desk that was covered with papers and files. Though it was sunny outside, the room was shadowed, and even a bit damp and chilly.

A dark green banker's lamp shone over the desk, and Oliver took a seat behind it. Ben noticed a table with a crystal decanter filled with whiskey or brandy and several crystal glasses. One had a few drops of amber liquid in the bottom, confirming Ben's impression.

"Have a seat, Reverend. The fuel bills are here. I just saw them this morning . . ."

Ben sat in an armchair that faced the desk. Oliver did not seem very organized, and he wondered how he managed so many businesses. But of course, Oliver had many employees to handle the details. He just made the big decisions. And this was his home office. Ben imagined that his office for the canneries and lumber mill was much more organized.

"Here it is. Beecham Oil nineteen seventy-three to nineteen seventy-eight." Oliver read out the title on the file folder and handed it over to Ben.

One task down, one to go, Ben thought.

"Now, let me take a look at these documents . . ." Oliver opened the envelope and removed the sheaf of papers, his pen in hand. "Forgive me for making you wait, Reverend. But people tell me it's best to read everything you sign your name to, even if it is just routine church business." Oliver's tone was, as usual, half-serious and half-joking.

"Good advice. Take your time; I'm in no hurry."

The phone on Oliver's desk rang. He watched it for a moment without picking it up, then looked back at the documents. Ben wondered at that, then realized that, of course, the Warwicks had servants to answer the telephone if they didn't feel like being interrupted.

A few moments later, a sharp knock sounded on the door. "Come in," Oliver replied.

The Warwicks' butler, dressed in a black suit and white shirt, opened the door and stood in the doorway. "Mr. Hastings is on the phone, sir. I told him that you have a guest, but he said that it's urgent."

Ben saw Oliver's complexion go pale, and his ever-present smile went slack, like a sail on a boat that had suddenly lost the wind. "Is he still on the line?"

"Yes, sir. He said he would hold."

"All right. Thank you, George." Oliver looked over at Ben. "I'm sorry, Reverend. I need to take this call. It's my attorney—important business."

"Of course. Would you like some privacy? I can get those papers back from you later," Ben offered.

Ben began to rise from his seat, but Oliver waved at him with one hand, picking up the phone with the other. "No reason to go. This will just be a minute."

Ben still wasn't sure if he should leave, but Oliver had already pressed the receiver to his ear, his attention shifting to his caller. After a brief greeting, Oliver simply listened, his gaze staring at some distant point out the window, his expression tense.

"Uh-huh . . . uh-huh. I see," he murmured, the furrow between his brows growing deeper. "I have a guest in my study right now. I'll have to call you back in a few minutes . . . Yes, I understand the gravity of the situation. I will call you right back," Oliver promised.

Oliver let out a long, slow breath as he returned the receiver to its cradle. Ben couldn't help but lean forward in his seat, trying to catch Oliver's eye.

"Is everything all right?" Ben asked.

"It's nothing, really." Oliver shook his head. "A tempest in a teapot. But you know these attorneys, once they get their teeth into something."

Ben nodded, sensing Oliver wanted to talk.

"There's a sticky situation at the cannery right now. An audit of some kind . . . They've found some sloppy bookkeeping, that's all."

Oliver leaned back in his chair and tossed his hands in the air. "I just sign what these managers put in front of me. I assume they know what they're doing. That's what they're paid for. I can't be expected to read every bloody word of every document. Now everyone is blaming me for these . . . these inconsistencies." He sounded annoyed and frustrated, even angry. Ben was about to ask a question but Oliver continued, "It will sort itself out. I'm not worried. But it's a big headache in the meantime."

Ben took that as a sign that Oliver didn't want to go into detail. He felt as if he had overstayed his welcome anyway.

"I'm sure it will. I'd better leave you to it," he added, rising from his seat.

"I suppose so. Though I'd much rather chat with you, Reverend." Oliver offered a smile as he tapped the church documents into a small pile, then slipped them back into the envelope. He handed it to Ben, then rose and walked Ben to the study door.

"I'll see myself out," Ben said.

"Good day, Reverend. My apologies again for making you drive all the way out here."

"No problem. I can see you have more serious issues on your mind."

"Yes . . . I do."

Ben didn't think much of the comment at the time. It seemed the sort of innocuous reply anyone might give. But later, that quiet answer came back to him.

Ben didn't take the church tax documents out of the envelope again until the next morning. He was about to give them to his secretary to copy, but noticed that Oliver had not signed in all the necessary spaces. He had been interrupted by the call from his attorney, Ben recalled.

"Oh blast," he said out loud.

"What's the matter, Reverend?" Mrs. Guilley, his secretary, stared at him. He rarely exclaimed about anything.

"Nothing that earth-shattering. Mr. Warwick was supposed to sign in three places. He only signed in two. And these forms have to go out in today's mail," Ben explained. He stared at the blank line as if he could somehow will it to fill itself in. Little chance of that happening.

"Would you like me to call him?" Mrs. Guilley offered.

"All right," Ben replied. "Try his office, please."

He went into his own office while Mrs. Guilley made the call.

"Mr. Warwick's secretary said that he was in a meeting. She'll give him the message that you called," Mrs. Guilley reported a few minutes later.

"Thank you," Ben replied. He picked up the document, folded it, and put it in the breast pocket of his jacket. "I think I'll just run over there."

Lester Plante was stopping by the church in the late afternoon, and Ben wanted to report that the documents were already in the mail.

"All right, Reverend. If he calls back, I'll say you're on your way."

"Please do. I'm reluctant to bother anyone during their business day. But church business is important, too."

"Very true." Mrs. Guilley nodded in agreement as Ben shrugged on his coat and headed out the door.

Warwick Cannery was a short drive just north of the village, about halfway to Newburyport. Ben turned off the main road and then down Crooked Hill Lane. The cannery had been built near the water with its own docks, where all types of fishing ships and trawlers unloaded their precious cargo.

The old brick building was three stories tall with loading bays on the first level and small, dark windows on the second and third. A few tall stacks emitted puffs of steam into the clear blue sky.

Ben had been at the cannery once before. Now, he pulled his car around to the lot closest to the executive offices. He recognized Oliver's dark green Jaguar in a reserved space next to the glass doors. But he was surprised to see an Essex County sheriff's car parked there as well; the red light on top spun slowly, and a uniformed officer stood nearby, talking with two men in dark suits.

Ben parked his car in the first spot he could find and walked toward them. Had there been an accident in the factory? Maybe the ambulance hadn't come yet.

Just as he said a silent prayer asking for help for anyone injured, the sheriff's deputy suddenly turned to him. "Sorry, sir. No access to the building right now."

"Has there been an accident? Is anyone hurt?"

"The area is closed. For a police action," the officer said in a stronger tone.

"I'm a minister. Maybe I can help . . . I'm a friend of Mr. Warwick's," he added, wondering if that would help.

One of the other men turned and met his gaze. "Then you'd better say a few prayers for your friend. He's going to need all the help he can get."

Ben was alarmed by the reply. And confused. But before he could reply, the glass doors of the building swung open.

Another officer and another man in a dark suit were walking out with Oliver, leading him, one on each side.

Oliver held his hands out in front, his wrists bound together, a pained expression on his face. Ben could hardly believe his eyes. Oliver Warwick was in handcuffs. He was being arrested and led down to the sheriff's car.

Ben took a few quick steps toward him. "What's happening? What's going on, Oliver?"

Oliver shook his head. "A huge misunderstanding. A travesty. My attorneys will work this out. I'll be home in an hour," he insisted. He had reached the police car and stood with the officers.

"No more conversation. Get into the car, Mr. Warwick," one said brusquely.

"Tell Lillian. Please, Reverend . . ." Oliver called. One of the officers covered his head with a big hand and coaxed him into the backseat.

"Of course. I'll go right now," Ben called back just before the police car doors slammed shut.

He stared into the car, trying to tell if Oliver had heard him, then just watched it pull away. A siren sounded and the light on top spun faster. The men in dark suits had all jumped into a second car and followed close behind.

A crowd had gathered in the doorway—employees at the factory, Ben assumed. A few had come out to watch the spectacle. The grimy windows were also filled with faces, their expressions shocked.

Ben stood shocked as well. He could barely collect his thoughts.

Oliver Warwick had just been arrested and escorted from his factory in handcuffs. Did this have something to do with the bookkeeping mix-up he'd been complaining about yesterday? Ben couldn't be sure. All he knew now was that he had been charged with bringing Lillian this dreadful news.

Ben stumbled back to his own car, headed toward Beach Road again, and soon arrived at Lilac Hall. His mouth went dry as he stood at the front door and rang the chimes. The butler answered.

"I'd like to see Mrs. Warwick. It's a very urgent matter."

If the servant was alarmed or even curious, he didn't show it. "Mrs. Warwick is out for the day," he said evenly.

Ben wasn't sure what to say. Should he try to get a message to her? That seemed too intrusive, even considering the circumstances.

"If she calls, or returns home early, please tell her to call me right away."

"I will, sir." The butler nodded gravely. "Good day."

Ben nodded back, thinking it was not a good day. Not a good day at all for anyone in this house, though they didn't seem to know it yet.

He walked back to his car with a heavy heart, his black shoes crunching on the gravel. As he searched his overcoat pocket for his car keys, he glanced up at the windows just above the stone portico.

A curtain stirred, and he caught a glimpse of a woman's profile. It could have been anyone—a maid, or one of the Warwick's daughters, Jessica or Emily. But Ben felt sure it had been Lillian.

He felt sure that she was home and somehow already knew of her husband's trouble. But she had not wanted to see Ben, even though he was their minister. The realization was deflating, as if he had failed twice on this mission.

CHAPTER TWO

Present day, December 4

RACHEL ANDERSON WAS NO STRANGER TO A CROWDED school gymnasium—the heat and echoing din and endless activity. The shrill whistle on the basketball court, the pounding feet and screech of rubber soles against shiny wooden floors. She sat hunched up, her chin resting on her hands, trying to pick out her son, Will, from the mass of moving, grunting bodies and bouncing basketballs.

Four different scrimmage teams were on the floor, each boy playing his heart out, trying to win a place on a team in the travel league.

"How much longer, Mom? I'm really hungry." Rachel's daughter, eight-year-old Nora, gently tugged on her sweater, then stared at Rachel with large brown eyes.

"I know, honey. I'm hungry, too," Rachel replied, stroking Nora's hair. "It won't be much longer."

I hope, Rachel added silently. She glanced at her watch. How much longer could this go on? It was already the second day of the rigorous tryout. Will had been thrilled to be called back after the first round. His excitement had almost quelled Rachel's feeling of dread at having to watch another afternoon of rough competition.

It wasn't the bother of sitting in the gym again. It was just that Rachel worried about him so much that watching him play was a nerve-racking marathon. Will had had his first bout of asthma at age three, and ever since, the asthma came and went, never gone for long. Sometimes it was brought on by pollen or dust, but stress or exertion could also leave him gasping for breath.

Although Will was cleared by doctors for sports and always traveled with at least two inhalers, as a physical therapist, Rachel knew only too well the risk he took out there. A simple asthma attack could quickly evolve into cardiac arrest and take her son away from her in the blink of an eye.

Of course, such a dreadful outcome was rare, she reminded herself. But how many women were widowed at age thirty-four, as she had been? That was rare as well.

So she sat and watched . . . and worried. And tried not to show it. She tried to be just another mom, wondering what to give her kids for dinner tonight and how to get all the homework done before bedtime.

While all the time her eagle eye searched for telltale signs of Will's fatigue or labored breathing. If she kept her unblinking eye on him, kept her eye on both of her children, no harm could come to them. They couldn't be hurt or get sick. Or leave her. The way Jack had. She knew it wasn't reasonable to feel that way, but she couldn't help it. She just did.

A whistle blew three short, authoritative blasts. An older coach in the midst of it all held up one hand as if he were directing traffic. "All right now, squads, coaches. That's it for today. Nice job, boys."

The action on the floor slowed and finally stopped; a few stray basketballs still bounced or even rolled away from their owners. The boys, sweating and panting, glanced at their coaches and at each other. A few pulled off the colored vests that topped their T-shirts, looking relieved to leave. Others, more relaxed, fooled around and teased each other. To Rachel, most looked bigger and stronger than her son. Even though Will was tall and agile, he was only fourteen. Most of these boys looked as if they were in high school. It was another reason she wasn't wild about him joining this league.

"Gather around. We have a few instructions," the head coach said.

The boys massed around him. The parents and siblings slowly made their way down the bleachers, which shook precariously with so many trying to climb off at once.

Nora hopped like a little goat, balancing her backpack on one shoulder. Rachel took slower, more careful steps, even though she wore running shoes. Under her down jacket, she still wore her dark blue uniform.

She searched the floor for Will and finally found him sitting on the floor next to his basketball, listening to one of the coaches.

She and Nora waited on the sidelines, and he was soon dismissed. She waved, and he jogged toward them. When he drew closer, she noticed that his cheeks were flaming red—he was overheated—but he was smiling. That was a good sign.

"How do you feel?" was the first question she really wanted to ask. Instead she took a breath. "How did it go?" she said instead.

He shrugged, shoulders bony under his T-shirt. He slicked his hair back with his hand. "I thought I did okay. I won't know for sure until they call me."

Good point. Will had a straightforward way of expressing himself that sometimes sounded as if he was sassing her. But Rachel knew he wasn't, not most of the time. He was just telling things the way he saw them, just the way Jack did. She often wondered if that was a learned trait or genetic. Either way, he reminded her of his father more each day.

"I guess we'll see. Let's get out of here. I can hardly hear myself think."

It seemed even louder now that the families had reunited.

"What's for dinner?" Will asked.

"Can we have pizza?" Nora added.

Rachel had expected that question. She resisted on principle and on the basis of the pizza rule: only once a week, including school lunches.

"I don't know . . . Let's figure it out in the car." Rachel had turned to talk to the kids, who were walking behind her. It was hard to stay together in the milling crowd that was now trying to squeeze through the two doors to the school parking lot, like a herd of cattle going through a small chute.

A boy about Will's age rushed by, pushing through the crowd and pushing Rachel straight into a body directly in front of her. She just had the sense of a tall man with a broad chest. He stood facing her, like a wall, as the tip of her nose touched his sweater.

"Sorry . . . !" She tilted backward, nearly falling over in the other direction.

But he reached out and grabbed her arm just in time, holding on until she caught her balance. "Excuse me. I didn't mean to get in your way."

"That's all right . . ." Rachel stepped back, getting her balance. "It's so crowded in here. I think someone pushed me." She looked up and forgot what she was saying, totally distracted by his dark blue eyes.

He wore a black V-neck sweater and jeans, along with a whistle on a cord around his neck. Rachel realized he was one of the coaches who had been on the court. She felt Will practically hiding behind her and heard him swallow hard.

"I was just trying to catch up with Will," the coach explained. "Hey, buddy . . . I think you forgot something."

The coach held out the basketball he was carrying, and Rachel realized it belonged to her son. It was the special, super-lucky basketball that had been Jack's last gift to him.

Will stepped forward, and Rachel saw the awe in his expression, then heard it in his voice. "Thanks, Coach Coop. I can't believe I forgot this."

The coach laughed, deep dimples appearing in both cheeks, bracketing a brilliant smile. "I think you were just so in the zone for a while. Better hang on to that," he added, handing over the basketball. "You're going to need it."

Before Will or Rachel could reply, the coach waved and headed in the opposite direction. Rachel couldn't help watching him; his tall, lean form and broad shoulders were easy to spot in the crowd. Rachel noticed a boy about Will's age walking by his side. The coach slung his arm around the boy's shoulder in a way that made her guess the boy was his son.

"That was Coach Coop," Will said in a hushed tone. "I hope I get picked for his team. He's really cool."

"Coop, like chicken coop?" Nora asked. Rachel could tell that she wasn't even trying to tease Will, for once. But it was an odd name.

"It's Cooper. Coop is just his nickname. He knew my name, Mom," Will pointed out. "That's a good sign, don't you think?"

"Could be." Rachel was careful to keep her reply brief and balanced. She didn't want Will to get his hopes up only to have them come crashing down if he wasn't chosen. They had been through this before with other teams. But she did think Coach Coop knowing Will's name was a good sign. And maybe so was his saying that Will would need his basketball? But anyone might have said that, she reminded herself.

She put her arm lightly on Will's shoulder and urged him forward again. "Put your fleece on, please," she said, handing it to him.

Once outside, she caught site of the coach and his son again, walking through the lot. Their car was parked nearby, and she couldn't help looking at him as she and her kids climbed into her SUV and pulled out of the parking lot.

Coach Cooper, huh? He was certainly the best-looking coach in the gym, that was for sure. Though Rachel was surprised she had come to that conclusion. She had taken no notice of men for the last two years—as if some switch deep inside had been disconnected when Jack died. But this man just smiled at her and . . . Well, it was very disconcerting. She felt herself blushing.

It must have been the surprise contact. She did walk right into him. And he was quite good-looking. She certainly couldn't deny that.

But this sudden light-headed rush . . . Where in the world did that come from? Rachel didn't like it. It disturbed her. It made her feel guilty. As if she had been disloyal to Jack. Though she knew rationally that wasn't a healthy way to think about it. But it was her heart, her loss, her grief. Her father had told her that there was no set time for mourning. She had to go at her own pace and take one day at a time. And so she had. It was a long, slow road, to be sure.

But that sudden rush of out-of-the-blue attraction . . . That had rippled through her like a crack in an icy lake. As Rachel steered out of the crowded lot, she wondered if she had imagined it. It was almost too strange to be real. She shook it off, happy to be distracted by her children arguing in the backseat.

"Calm down, guys. I can't see out the back window . . . When will you hear if you're on a team, Will? Did they say?"

"Over the weekend. Everyone will know by the time we get back to school next Monday."

Rachel nodded, turning onto the main road. That was another thing—the peer pressure. As if the competition on the court wasn't tough enough.

"You had some great plays out there. You showed them your best stuff. That's what counts. If you aren't chosen for this league, there will be other chances. You just have to stick with it." She knew that was true, but she also knew she sounded like Jack now. She was trying to say what her husband would have said to cushion Will's confidence if he wasn't chosen.

"It's a more competitive level than I usually play on," Will said. "A lot of guys are older than me, and bigger." Was he pointing out the reasons why he might not make a team?

"That's true. But you never know unless you try, right?"

"Yeah. Right. Even Michael Jordan didn't make varsity at his high school the first time he tried out," Will quickly replied.

"I've heard that." Many times, in fact. Another Jack-ism. And now Will sounded just like his father, too.

It was hard sometimes being both Jack and herself. But Rachel knew it was a fallen flag that was hers to pick up and carry into battle now. Watching Will's games, coaching him, giving him pep talks and post-game feedback, even playing one-on-one in the driveway—that had all been Jack's territory. Now it was her job to carry out the plans Will had made with his father. This was the part of her that really wanted Will to be chosen for this league. While the other part of her—the mother part that worried about his health and safety—was secretly hoping he would be passed over.

Just for this year, she told herself. When he was a little older, this wouldn't be so challenging for him. He would be bigger and stronger, too.

Now she could almost hear Jack arguing with her.

You're right, she replied in her head. *He wants this chance, and he did hold his own out there. Maybe you can put in a good word up there somewhere for your boy?*

Rachel didn't wait for an answer. She knew if there was any possibility of that, the task was already done.

As the week wore on, Rachel watched her son's pumped-up mood gradually deflate, like a helium balloon left over from a birthday party. By Saturday, Will was quiet and distracted, watching too much TV and snapping at everyone over the least little thing.

Ah, adolescence. Rachel sighed and shook her head. It was moments like this that she deeply missed sharing with her husband. The wonder— and misery—of raising their children. She knew very well what was bugging Will. There had been no call yet from the basketball league.

And he had heard in school that several boys had been called on Thursday and Friday.

They talked about it a little on Saturday night, about how the process might be slowed down. She sat on the edge of his bed while he stared at his laptop, pausing a movie just long enough to hear her out.

"You never know how these things work. Maybe the person who's supposed to call you is out of town, or busy with something. Maybe you'll get called tomorrow," she told him.

"Yeah . . . maybe." He nodded and sighed. She kissed his forehead and said good night. "Don't stay up too late. Church tomorrow," she reminded him.

But he was already lost in the film again.

At least he wasn't on Facebook, watching to see if more boys he knew had been called. Each self-congratulatory message sank his spirits even lower.

On Sunday morning, as Rachel expected, Will didn't want to wake up; he had stayed up too late the night before. He balked at coming down for breakfast and getting ready for church. His excuses ranged from too much homework to a headache.

"Too much screen time last night," Rachel said flatly. "It's the first Sunday of Advent. We can't miss it. You can bring your homework to Grandpa and Grandma's house afterward. They won't mind."

She delivered her answer with a smile and closed his bedroom door on his frown. She had made pancakes for breakfast and knew he would be down soon without more coaxing.

After the service, Rachel and her children were going to her parents' house for lunch, as they often did on a Sunday. She hoped the visit would be distracting for Will—and she hoped her father would talk to him a little. Will had always been close to his grandfather, and with Jack gone, that relationship had deepened.

But her father was always so busy with the church, especially at this time of year. After growing up in the parsonage, Rachel knew well the demands on his time.

She wished that her brother, Mark, lived closer. He also had a great rapport with Will, but Mark was in the Northwest now, raising his own family. His visits were a treat, but far too rare. Will really needed a male role model, someone to look up to. That was another reason team sports were good for him, she reminded herself, despite all the drawbacks that worried her.

Rachel found the Sunday service both soothing and renewing, especially her father's sermon. She enjoyed welcoming the Christmas season with the Advent candle-lighting ceremony at the start of the service. David Sawyer and his wife, Christine, were up there today with their two-year-old son. The Sawyer family still ran the Christmas tree farm and nursery outside of town that David's father, Jack, had first planted.

Seeing the young couple and their little boy made Rachel think back to a Sunday when she stood there herself, with her own Jack and their children. Nora had been so little, Rachel had lifted her up in her arms. Funny how she hadn't appreciated the moment at the time. Of course, she had been proud of her family and happy to take part. But it had also seemed a bit stressful to get everyone dressed nicely and learn their parts of the liturgy.

How silly those worries seemed now; silly and wasteful. She would give anything today to have Jack back beside her and do it over again.

When she was growing up, Rachel hadn't appreciated church that much. Since her father was the minister, she had taken it for granted, like the child of a baker who always has fresh bread and cake in the house. The spiritual nourishment of their family life just seemed normal to her.

Now that she had a family of her own and had faced such great heartache and challenges, she experienced church and her own personal faith in a much deeper way. She knew she would belong to a church like this one even if her father were not the minister. And she valued and felt grateful for the faith both her parents had instilled in her.

After the service, Rachel hustled her children back into her SUV. Her father would be a while longer at church, but her mother had already headed out to her car, and she rolled down her window as she drove past. "Don't forget the dessert. I didn't have time to bake anything. Get something the kids will like."

"I didn't forget, Mom. Don't worry." After leaving church, Rachel drove to Willoughby's Fine Foods and Catering, right across the village green. The line was always long on a Sunday, the cakes and breads well worth waiting for.

She was soon leading her children up the familiar path to the parsonage, the little gray Cape where she had grown up. The door was unlocked, and she let herself in, feeling an immediate rush of comfort and ease. The small foyer, where she helped her children take off their winter coats and hang them up neatly, was just large enough to hold a lamp table and a coat tree. A dark, polished wooden banister curved upward to the second floor.

Little had changed under this roof since Rachel's childhood. The walls were the same warm sandy-gold color, and the same pictures hung in the same frames. It even smelled the same, like her mother's cooking. She heard her mother in the kitchen and called out to her.

"Something smells good. What are you making, Mom?" Rachel carried the box of cake back to the kitchen, along with a bouquet of flowers she had brought for her mom.

"Just a pot roast . . . Those flowers are lovely. Thank you, dear. I'll put them in a vase in a minute."

"With noodles?" Nora had followed Rachel and now faced her grandmother with a beguiling expression. If noodles were not already on the menu, they soon might be.

"Yes, noodle-girl." Carolyn briefly touched her granddaughter's cheek. "You can help me cook them, too. Watch the water and let me know when it boils."

"No worries. I know what to do." Nora took her orders seriously and stood next to the pot, staring at it.

"That's the only thing left to cook. I made everything yesterday. It just has to heat."

Rachel was glad of that. These family dinners were a lot of work for her mother, who was not that young anymore and had suffered a stroke eleven years ago. Thankfully, Carolyn had recovered with only a trace of after-effects. She looked wonderful today, her blond chin-length hair in its usual style and an apron over her Sunday outfit—a cream-colored sweater set and a brown wool skirt, along with tasteful pearl earrings and low heels.

Rachel had not always understood the pressures her mother faced as the minister's wife, always on view for scrutiny and expected to represent her husband. Her mother was a professional musician who had never had much chance to pursue her gifts in this small town and within the framework of the life set out for her. She had taught piano for many years and had seemed to enjoy that. But Rachel often wondered if her mother had dreamed of something different for her life, some larger goal or ambition.

Carolyn had great charm—legendary Southern charm, having been raised in North Carolina—and wonderful people skills. Whatever challenges or disappointments she had faced over the years, she had handled it all with grace. Rachel could see that now.

"What can I do? Set the table?" Rachel picked up an apron and glanced around.

"Good idea. I've set out the dishes and silverware. Maybe Will can help you," Carolyn suggested as she worked on a salad.

She and her mother shared a look. Both of her parents knew that Will was waiting for news about the tryout—and being sulky and difficult because of it.

"Where is he, anyway?" Carolyn asked.

"Watching sweaty men in matching uniforms chase a ball around. Where else would he be?" Nora said, rolling her eyes.

"That sums it up nicely." Carolyn smiled as she lifted a pot cover and checked the contents.

Had he escaped to the family room already? "I'll get him. He didn't even say hello. He should be helping, too."

Rachel's mother touched her arm. "Let him be. We'll be ready to eat as soon as your father gets home. Will can help clean up."

Rachel didn't recall her parents being so easygoing when she was a child. But that's what grandparents are for: to let children break the rules. This was a difficult day for Will. It was hard to wait for important news—news that seemed a life-or-death matter to him. No wonder he was looking for distraction.

Her father returned while Rachel and Nora were setting the table, and they all soon sat down to eat. "It was nice to see the whole Sawyer family in church today. David and Christine look so happy."

"And his father is fairly bursting with pride, being a grandfather, and with a namesake, no less," Carolyn added.

"Yes, he is," Rachel agreed. "We love to get our tree at Sawyers'. The kids wait for it every year."

"But we didn't go last year," Nora pointed out, between bites of her dinner.

"No, we didn't go there." Rachel kept her tone even and matter-of-fact.

Last year they all agreed on a little tabletop tree, and no lights on the house or in the windows. It seemed too soon to be celebrating after their loss. It had been just about a year.

But they would probably visit Sawyers' this Christmas—another tradition they would have to carry on without their father.

If Will had been saddened by the conversation, Rachel couldn't tell.

He didn't even seem aware of what they were talking about. He sat hunched over his plate, chewing his food and staring blankly into space, then down at his food again.

Tilting her head to one side, Rachel realized he had his phone out, balanced on his lap, and was monitoring his messages.

"How's the pot roast, Will?" her father asked him. "Grandma said it was your favorite. I really wanted roast chicken."

Rachel knew her father was just teasing, trying to engage his grandson. Will suddenly looked up, nearly spilling his water. "It's good . . . real good, Grandma."

"Thanks, honey. You can take some home. There will be plenty of leftovers."

"How is school? Do you have midterm exams now?" his grandfather asked him.

"Yeah, and a lot of stuff is due. I have an English term paper and a big test in Earth science."

"Earth science, one of my favorites. Fascinating stuff." Rachel saw her father's face light up. "I still remember the names of the continental plates, and the way volcanoes form under the Earth's crust."

"That makes one of us," Will mumbled.

Nora started laughing. Carolyn smiled, too.

Her father didn't seem offended. In fact, Rachel could not recall if she had ever seen anyone ruffle her father's feathers with a snide comment, or even an outright insult. He only grew hot under the collar over more important matters—matters of principle and justice.

"If you need a study partner, I'm your man," her father offered with a wide smile. "When's the final coming up? We can schedule our get-togethers."

Rachel liked that idea. She liked to see Will and her dad spending time together. And she did worry about her kids being home alone after school when she had to work late.

"Good idea, Dad. Will's afternoons are mostly open right now." She looked at her son, who didn't seem that sold on the idea.

"Thanks, Grandpa . . . but I might not have that much free time. If I get on the travel team, I mean. I think there are a couple of practices a week, plus a game."

Rachel had forgotten about that. Will apparently had not. She glanced at her watch. It was almost four o'clock. If someone was going to call, wouldn't Will have heard by now?

She could tell from her father's expression that he was thinking the same thing. But he said, "Oh, right. That will be a consideration. Your mother tells me it's a competitive league—lots of pressure."

"I can handle it." Will's tone was firm. Not defensive, but confident. The attitude Jack had taught him.

"Yes, I'm sure you can." Will's grandfather nodded encouragingly. "What's for dessert? I thought I noticed a box from Willoughby's in the fridge."

Rachel knew her father had a sweet tooth. But she also knew when he was trying to change the subject. She guessed he didn't think Will would get chosen at this point. It was getting too late for a positive call.

"A delicious-looking chocolate cake. It looks absolutely illegal," her mother said. She rose and picked up some dishes. "If we all clear together, I'll make some coffee and tea."

Will got up from his seat and started helping without any prodding, which Rachel was happy to see. But as soon as he set one dish near the sink, he slipped out his cell phone to check his messages again.

"Any word?" Rachel asked him quietly.

He shook his head. "No, but . . . it's only four. You said the person who has to call me might be out of town or something. Or might have some delay."

She had said that. But now she was beginning to doubt the theory. Her heart went out to him. "They might. But it is getting late."

She couldn't bear to say anything more, seeing the expression on his face at those words. Was it better to let him keep hoping? Or to help him start facing the disappointment?

Her father stepped over and rested a hand on Will's shoulder. "Let's play chess. It will take your mind off all this waiting and staring at your phone."

Will just shook his head. "Thanks, Grandpa. I have a lot of homework. I brought it with me."

"Oh . . . right. Another time, then," her father said gently.

Will headed for the doorway, his back to them. Rachel thought he might be crying and not want anyone to see.

"No chocolate cake?" Carolyn called after him. "I'll bring you in a slice with a glass of milk."

Will nodded without turning. Now Rachel felt sure he was either crying, or just about to break down. She started to follow him when her father touched her arm, then shook his head. "Leave him be awhile. He needs some time alone," he whispered.

She stared at the empty doorway and could still hear Will's footsteps heading for the study.

Wouldn't they also call the kids who didn't get on teams? That seemed the humane way to handle it. But Rachel knew these sports leagues weren't always that sensitive.

Poor Will. She hated to see him disappointed again, but there was little she could do to shield him. He had tried for the team two years ago, with Jack at his side, and been rejected. Last year, still shell-shocked from his father's death, he hadn't even mentioned the tryouts. So she had been proud of him for trying again and knew he wanted to make the team for his father. She hated to think that now, in his heart, Will might feel he had let Jack down.

CHAPTER THREE

~~~

*R*ACHEL HEADED FOR THE DINING ROOM WITH A SIGH AND began gathering the dirty dishes and glasses again. She heard a cell phone ring. It took her a few minutes to recognize the sound as her own and to remember where she had put it.

She practically dropped the pile of dishes on the table, then ran to the foyer, where she had left her coat and bag. "Nora, help me! I can't find my phone . . . where'd I leave it?"

Nora and Carolyn raced over to help track down the sound of the ringing. Nora was the winner, pulling the cell phone out of a sweater pocket. "I got it! I got it!" She waved the phone overhead, and Rachel snatched it.

"Rachel Anderson," she said breathlessly. She didn't recognize the number. A good sign, she hoped.

"Hello, Mrs. Anderson. This is Ryan Cooper, from the Cape Light Travel League. We met at the tryouts on Thursday night?"

As if she wouldn't remember him. *I walk smack into tall, extremely handsome men every day.*

"Yes, I remember," she replied smoothly. "And I hope you're not calling to say Will didn't get on a team and better luck next time."

"I'm calling to offer your son a place on the Falcons, the team I'll be coaching. He was a strong competitor. A bit younger than most of the other players," he added honestly. "But we do have a place for him. I think he'll do very well with this group of kids, too."

Rachel didn't know what to say. She felt a ball of emotion well up in her throat. She was so happy and relieved for Will, she could hardly speak.

"That's very good news, Mr. Cooper. Thank you. Will is going to be thrilled."

"We're happy to have him. I want to talk to him in a second, but I also wanted you to know that there's a team meeting with players and parents tomorrow night, at my house. And our first practice is this Tuesday. I'm sending out an email with all the information right now."

Rachel suddenly noticed her mother and father standing right beside her, as quiet as two kindly mice. Then Will came jogging down the hallway, with Nora following. She had obviously run to get him. He ran up to Rachel, looking tense as he listened to the end of her conversation.

"We'll be there," she promised quickly. "Here's Will. I'll put him on."

Rachel held out the phone, smiling so wide at Will, her face hurt. "It's Coach Cooper. You made the team. He wants to speak to you."

Will looked shocked and pale, almost afraid to take the phone. She could tell that he had been crying, and now his mouth hung open in wonder. He blinked and swallowed hard. "Hey, Coach . . . I did? Wow, that's totally awesome, man. Thank you so much . . ."

Will fist-pumped the air. Then he turned away, and Rachel could barely hear what he was saying.

She turned and smiled at her parents, her body sagging with relief. "Better late than never," she whispered.

"I'll say," her mother agreed.

"Let's go inside. He'll find us," her father said quietly as he put his arm around Nora's shoulder.

Rachel followed, offering up a silent prayer. *Thank you, God, for making Will so happy. Please help him do well . . . and keep him healthy. And help me with my fears and worries.*

She wished Jack were with them now to share the glory. To see the look on Will's face when she had handed him the phone.

Deep in her heart, she felt he was there and had shared in that moment. She hoped so, anyway. *He made the team, Jack. You were right. He's got the talent and the dedication.*

When Will returned to the dining room, there were more congratulations for him and conversation about the new basketball team while everyone had their fill of chocolate cake.

"That's very exciting news, Will. We can't wait to watch you play," her mother said.

"Yes, we'll definitely be cheering you on," her father added. "When is the first game?"

"Next weekend, I think," Will replied around a mouth full of cake. "I can't wait to get my uniform. I think it's really cool."

Rachel just smiled. Will's entire personality had done a one-eighty from the past few days. She hoped he would remain in this cheerful mode for the rest of the week.

Meanwhile, Nora was growing bored with all the basketball talk. She had found a pile of old photographs on the sideboard and brought one over to Carolyn. "Is that you and Grandpa?"

Carolyn nodded. "One and the same."

"Wow, Grandma. You were a real babe." Nora's awestruck and honest tone made the adults laugh.

"And she still is," her grandfather quickly added. "And that little girl is your mom."

"I figured that," Nora replied, looking back at the photo. "She still looks the same."

Rachel laughed. "Hardly . . . Let me see." Nora handed her the picture, a snapshot with faded colors. Carolyn looked young and strong, happy and beautiful. She was pushing Rachel on a swing. Rachel noticed how she herself looked so happy and free, as if she yearned to fly. "I loved that playground," Rachel said, remembering.

"I used to take you there every day. The swings were in that little park up the street. The town took down the playground equipment a few years ago. It was getting worn out."

"You liked to get that swing going really high and jump off. Do you remember?" her father asked her.

"Mom used to jump off a swing?" Will stared at his mother and grandfather in shock.

Her father laughed. "Oh yes. She had a mischievous streak. She would have to spend a time-out in her room."

"Mom got in trouble? I don't believe that."

Rachel laughed at her son's reaction. "The truth is out. Yes, I did have a lot of time-outs at a certain stage. But I guess I learned my lessons."

"I'll say." Nora rolled her eyes. "You never do anything fun like that now."

"Oh yes, I do," Rachel insisted, though she couldn't think of any good examples at the moment.

She did have a more playful, risk-taking side when she was younger . . . and before her husband died. But she felt like she had been walking a fine line ever since just to keep her emotions and her life under control. Maybe Jack's passing had closed some door in her heart forever. "I just got older, honey," she said finally.

Rachel and her children were soon putting on coats and saying good-bye to Ben and Carolyn.

"I can stay with Nora while Will has basketball practice," Carolyn offered as she fussed over her granddaughter, tucking a strand of wavy brown hair behind Nora's ear. "There's no reason for her to sit in a noisy gym for hours, too."

Her mother already knew that Rachel would be at every practice and game—just in case Will's asthma acted up.

"Thanks for the offer, Mom. There's a team meeting tomorrow night and a practice on Tuesday. Nora has gymnastics that day, so maybe you could pick her up there?"

"No trouble. I'll pick her up and bring her to your house, and we can cook dinner together."

Nora clapped her hands together. "Thank you, Grandma."

Rachel was relieved to see everyone happy with these arrangements. The team schedule was demanding and would take some juggling, that was for sure. A lot of juggling, actually.

"Thanks, Mom. I'll get the schedule tomorrow night. Then we can figure out the rest."

"We're happy to help. On the weekends, too," Carolyn added with emphasis, giving Rachel one of her special looks. Rachel knew her mother wished she would go out more with her friends and even start dating. At least she had avoided that conversation tonight, she thought, taking the container of leftover pot roast and what remained of the cake, which her mother had carefully wrapped.

There were more hugs and kisses and wishes for a safe drive home. An entire five miles, Rachel reflected as she slipped behind the wheel and saw her folks still watching from the golden square of light in their front door.

Though she made fun of their fussing, Rachel was not sure what she would have done without her parents after Jack died. She couldn't imagine how she would have made it through.

*　*　*

The house seemed suddenly quiet as Ben closed and locked the front door. Carolyn was straightening up the living room, picking up stray cups and glasses, and plumping up throw pillows. She turned when he walked in. "I think I'll just go up and read for a while. I love them dearly, but they do knock me out," she admitted with a laugh.

"Because you go all out," he reminded her. "But I'm glad you offered to watch Nora while Will is at practice. Maybe Rachel will skip the gym one night and take a little time for herself—see a friend for dinner or go to a movie."

"I wish she would. But you know how she gets if we even suggest it. Or say anything about her social life—or lack of it. She keeps saying she feels guilty leaving the kids because she works so much during the week. But I think she feels . . . well, disloyal to Jack. To his memory," Carolyn said quietly.

"She's just not ready. She needs to heal at her own pace. There are no set rules for the grieving process."

"Nor should there be," Carolyn agreed. She touched his arm and kissed his cheek. "You must be tired, too. Don't stay up too late again with those photos."

He couldn't put much over on Carolyn. She already knew what he planned to do for the rest of the evening—sift through more photographs from the big box. Sophie's assignment had initially made him querulous, but once he started, he couldn't stop. He was enjoying this stroll down memory lane—was even eager to get back to it.

"I just want to get through the stack I took out on Friday night," he explained. "I found some newspaper articles saved in a folder. I haven't even looked at those yet."

"You can pass them to Vera and Claire, for their research."

"I will. After I look at them," he added. He kissed Carolyn good night and took the box of photos into the living room. He was more comfortable in his armchair than seated at the dining room table.

He took the folder of newspapers from the box and took out the first sheaf of pages, yellowed and brittle. Unfolding it carefully, he found the front page of the *Cape Light Messenger*. The headline read, "Cannery King in Hot Water. Warwick Arrested on Felony Charges."

Since this had happened long before the day of cell phones, nobody had had a camera handy, ready to take an unflattering photo of Oliver being stuffed into the back of a police car. Instead, the paper ran a very decent picture of him standing in front of the Cape Light Yacht Club in a dark blue blazer, open-necked shirt, and white pants. It was a picture they must have had on file.

Ben took a breath and quickly read the article. Memories of that time came rushing back to him. But the facts cited in the newspaper story were at odds with the account Oliver himself had given him.

The facts . . . Who can really know the facts of any situation? *Except for God,* Ben reflected. He glanced at the date, remembering how the news of Oliver's arrest swept through the village like wildfire before this news article was even printed.

He could have written that part of the article himself, having witnessed the arrest firsthand. He remembered racing over to Lilac Hall, as Oliver had requested. But what had he done after that? He recalled how his hands had been shaking as he took the wheel of his car, driving down Beach Road, back to the village and to his church.

He had felt too shaken up to go straight back to his office. Instead, he decided to stop at the Clam Box to pick up some lunch. It wasn't a fancy place, but there was something friendly and comforting about the Clam Box.

That's right. I stopped at the diner.

He remembered that day, the cold breeze off the harbor and the bright sunshine and clear sky that belied the clouds of scandal and gossip moving in like heavy weather, covering the village with a cold, dark shadow.

He had felt quite upset when he walked into the diner. As usual, the eatery was quite crowded at that hour. Dr. Elliot sat alone at a table near the window. He had been reading a magazine, a medical journal perhaps, but had looked up and waved. Ben had waved back but made no motion to join him. Instead he walked to the take-out counter.

His heart felt heavy. Yet there was no one he could talk to about it, not without feeling that he was gossiping. No, he wouldn't be the one to break the sad news, he decided. Such talk certainly wasn't befitting a minister.

Otto Bates, who owned the diner, was working behind the counter, alternating between cooking at the grill, where he flipped burgers, and serving the customers who sat on the swivel seats. It was no small feat, considering he didn't have full use of his left arm, ever since he was wounded in the war. But Otto never complained. He was an even-tempered fellow and had built his business with his easygoing manner.

"Hello, Reverend. Ready to order?"

Ben glanced at the chalkboard menu. "Grilled ham and cheddar on a roll would be fine, Otto. Some lettuce and tomato. And a coffee, light with one sugar," he added.

"Coming right up." Otto didn't bother to write it down. He always remembered the orders by heart. He hadn't mistaken one since Ben had been eating there these past six months.

"How's the weather out there? Looks pretty fair for December," Otto noted.

Ben was distracted. He had hardly been listening. "It's a little windy," he murmured. How long would it be before people heard about Oliver's troubles? How long before the newspaper got ahold of the story? The *Boston Globe* might even pick it up.

"Are you all right, Reverend? You look a little peaky. Want a glass of water?" Otto asked, packing up his sandwich.

Ben looked back at him. Before he could reply, the door of the diner flew open with such force it bounced against the wall.

A rough-looking man staggered in. He wore yellow rubber overalls with suspenders and high black boots, a ragged but thick woolen sweater underneath. A black knit cap was pulled down to his eyebrows; not much of his face showed between the cap's edge and his full, dark beard. He gazed around at the crowd but didn't move toward the tables.

Ben recognized him. His last name was Hatcher, though Ben wasn't sure of his first. Fred Hatcher, maybe? Lobster fishing was his main profession, but he worked at the boatyard in his downtime. Ben guessed this at least partly accounted for his tough demeanor. It was a hard way to make a living; highly competitive. A lobsterman always had to be ready to protect his traps and defend his territory.

"Hey, did you all hear the news?" Fred Hatcher shouted, like a town crier. "His royal highness, Oliver Warwick, got himself arrested. The cops came to get him at the cannery. Dragged him off in cuffs, like he'd been in a bar brawl." The messenger paused for a hearty laugh. "I hear they got him in the county jail, cooling his Italian loafers in the tank." Hatcher wiped his mouth with his hand. "Serves him right, that stuck up son of a—"

Otto had been staring at the man in shock all this time, but now he whipped off his apron and shouted back, "Hey you! What do you think you're doing, coming into my place talking like that?"

Ben jumped back as Otto lifted himself with one hand and jumped right over the counter. He landed squarely in front of Hatcher, facing him down like a bulldog protecting his home.

Fred Hatcher tilted his head back but didn't give ground. "You calling me a liar? A guy on the dock seen it with his own eyes. Down at the cannery, he seen the whole thing. Says Warwick's been caught red-handed. Says he was crying like a baby when they took him away."

Now Ben wanted to step forward, too. Oliver had been greatly distressed, but he had not been crying.

Otto snagged Fred Hatcher's collar with one hand and practically lifted his feet off the floor. The red flush that had filled Otto's cheeks climbed to his bald scalp. Ben thought the man was about to explode.

Otto pushed his face into the fisherman's. "I don't care what you heard, Hatcher. That man nearly died saving my life and those of nine other soldiers. He's worth ten of you. Now get out of here, before I throw you out."

Otto set the man on his feet with a push. Hatcher stumbled backward a few steps, staring at Otto with a belligerent expression. Ben thought there might be more trouble. He stood up, ready to intervene. But finally the lobsterman just laughed harshly and shook his head.

"What do I care what you think, Bates? It will all be all over the newspapers tomorrow. Then let's see if you can keep the whole town from talking trash about your buddy."

Ben saw Otto's good fist clench at his side, but before he could take a step forward, his antagonist was gone.

The diner was so quiet, Ben could hear the tinny sound of a spoon hitting the edge of a coffee cup as someone stirred their coffee. Otto turned slowly and looked at his customers. "Anyone else want to talk about Oliver Warwick? If so, you'd better take your business down the street," he advised.

No one answered. They turned to their companions and began talking again—softly at first, though the volume gradually rose.

Otto walked around the end of the counter. He put on his apron again and checked the meat on the grill. Most of it was charred and spoiled. After a moment, he walked over to Ben and packed up his coffee.

Otto shook his head. "You believe that guy, Reverend? Coming in here talking like that? Where do people come up with this stuff?"

Ben sighed. It was hard to tell Otto the truth. But holding back about what he had seen was just as bad as lying, Ben believed.

"I don't know what Oliver did," Ben said carefully. "It could all be a big mistake. I do know that he was arrested today."

Otto's head snapped up. He stared at Ben with shock. Before he could speak, Ben added, "I was there, Otto. At the cannery. I drove over about church business and I saw the sheriff's cars. Then the deputies led him out of the building and took him away."

Otto stared at Ben and let out a long sigh. "Geez . . . I can't believe it. What did he say? Didn't you try to help him?"

After seeing Otto in action just moments ago, Ben could only imagine what he would have done to defend his friend. Tackle the sheriff's officers, probably.

"There wasn't anything I could do, Otto. He wasn't able to talk to me, either. Except to ask that I go to Lilac Hall and tell Lillian what had happened."

Otto looked upset, his square jaw set, his knobby chin sticking out. He lifted his head and stared at Ben. "What did he do, Reverend? Why did they have to do that to him—shame the man like that?"

Ben shook his head. "I don't know . . ." His words trailed off. He had a guess, looking back at Oliver's complaints the last few days about his business problems—the sloppy bookkeeping, which he had called a big headache. But Ben knew it wasn't right to talk about his speculations. He might be wrong, and it would just cause even more gossip.

Otto had his own ideas and didn't hesitate to share them as he set Ben's lunch and coffee on the counter. "Maybe it's something stupid. Like too many speeding tickets. Oliver could be reckless when we were young, no denying that. Got himself into a few jams. Trouble with girls, too. His father always smoothed things over with the cops or some judge."

Ben had never heard about Oliver's early escapades. The disclosure contrasted sharply with the image he conveyed—business leader, devoted father, pillar of the church.

"Once he met Lillian, he put all that wild stuff behind him," Otto went on.

Ben took the brown bag with his lunch and handed Otto some bills. "Many people, men especially, act impulsively when they're young. Oliver seems altogether different now."

Ben believed that, too. He knew that people could change and mature. Just because a person took a few missteps in his youth, it didn't mean he was capable of a crime.

"Oh, he is, believe me. Oliver might not seem like a serious guy, always mocking and taking things light. But deep inside, he's rock solid. I think some upstart politician is just trying to get his name in the paper," Otto said gruffly. "Oliver's family has always been a lightning rod in this town. People are eaten up with envy about their money. Know what I mean?"

"Yes, I do." Ben had not been here all that long, but had noticed that. He dropped a tip in the jar of bills and coins on the counter and pocketed the rest of his change. "Oliver is lucky to have a friend as loyal as you, Otto."

"Thanks, but . . . what other kind is there?"

Ben paused a moment. "Good question," he replied. "I'll see you soon."

"Sure thing. See you in church," Otto called back.

Otto rarely missed church, even though the diner was open and Sunday morning was the busiest time of the week for his business. He always made time for the service, along with his wife, Mary, and their children, Charlie and Sharon.

Ben decided to leave his car parked in front of the Clam Box. It was a short walk to the church, just a block or two down to the village green and harbor that now filled his sight, with the old stone church set off to the right. As he walked across the green, he hunkered down in his overcoat and flipped up the collar, a stiff, chilly breeze off the harbor nearly lifting off his hat.

He often wondered why the early settlers of Cape Light had picked this spot for their sanctuary. They could have chosen most any other spot in the village. At the far end of Main Street, on higher ground and away from the water, would have made more sense to Ben. Or even up on one of the hilly streets that led down to the harbor: Providence or Fairview. Why right there, on the harbor, exposed to the battering winds and tides that often rose right over the docks and stone seawall? So far, he had not seen that high a tide, but he had heard of the storms and could easily see the watermarks on the dock and building.

In fact, he had heard a story from his predecessor, Reverend Bingham, of how one of the first ministers of this congregation had been trapped in the church for days during a raging hurricane, with nothing to sustain him but a bushel of clams. He managed to walk out under his own power, and the church had been left standing, too.

He wondered if the church founders had been testing or even challenging God's powers of protection, even in the face of raging storms. Or maybe they just wanted to show everyone—and God—how deeply they trusted Him?

He had also heard from his predecessor that a fire in the early 1800s had burned down most of the original structure, right down to the stone foundation. Once again, the congregation had rebuilt on the waterfront, choosing it not once, but twice. Now, so many decades later, the church still stood, as solid as the rocks it had been built upon.

Ben entered the quiet building and headed to his office. How would Oliver Warwick's troubles affect the congregation? Doubtlessly, there would be gossip and speculation. There would be friends like Otto speaking up for Oliver. And others tearing him down. And many might feel caught somewhere in the middle, not eager to contribute to the Warwick family's pain, but questioning Oliver's innocence.

Still feeling shaken from the scene he'd witnessed at the cannery, Ben felt that way, too. It was possible that Oliver was indeed innocent, or at least unaware, of any wrongdoing. But then again, if he didn't know Oliver and had witnessed the situation as a stranger, he would have to say that people are not usually arrested for no reason at all. Investigators have to show probable cause, some evidence that a law has been broken, in order for the court to issue a warrant for arrest.

It was still entirely possible that this situation was mistaken or confused in some way, as Oliver seemed to claim. But Ben had to consider the possibility that it was not confused, and that Oliver, whether he did it willfully or not, had done wrong.

Ben knew that a fair share of gossip circulated at any church. He had frequently seen it in his former church in Gloucester, and in the church he had attended as a boy. Gossip was simply part of human nature, and no church community was free of it, despite what Scripture said. This news about Oliver was certainly more serious than most situations people talked about. Ben wasn't quite sure what to expect of leading this congregation except that, like the gusty winds blowing off the harbor, it would surely be a test.

Ben spent a quiet afternoon in his office. He checked on Carolyn and told her about Oliver's arrest, how he had been there at the cannery and seen everything—the desperate, shocked look on Oliver's face and how the man in the dark suit had said that Oliver needed his prayers.

"Oh, Ben, that's awful. And you had to stand there and watch and couldn't do a thing to help him, besides. But I have to tell you, I already knew, before you called."

"You did? Who told you?" Ben couldn't fathom that. Carolyn was isolated at home all day with a baby. She didn't even have a car of her own yet to get into town.

"I had to call the doctor's office. Rachel has that little rash on her neck again. And the receptionist told me. I guess bad news travels fast."

"Faster than good news; that's what they say." And it was true, Ben thought. He heard voices in the outer office and saw Lester Plante and Walter Tulley. His secretary, Mrs. Guilley, was dealing with them, though she glanced into Ben's office, looking like she wanted some help. ". . . he's on the phone right now," he heard her saying. "I'll tell him that you're waiting . . ."

"Got to go, dear," he told Carolyn. "I've got some surprise visitors."

Ben came out from behind his desk and waved the board members in. "Lester, Walter . . . Good to see you. Come right in."

"Sorry to bust in on you like this, Reverend. Without calling first," Walter Tulley said.

"We didn't want to waste time," Lester added. "I'm sure you know why we're here."

Ben guessed it had something to do with Oliver's arrest, but he wasn't sure exactly what.

"Is this about the tax documents? Unfortunately, they're still missing one signature. I was trying to—"

But Lester waved his hand, interrupting him. "That's the least of our troubles right now, Reverend, wouldn't you say?"

Ben didn't know how to answer. What was going on here?

Lester stared at him, looking frustrated that Ben was not able to read his mind.

Walter stepped toward the open door. "I'd better close this, give us some more privacy to talk."

Once the door was shut, Lester turned back to Ben. "I'm sure you've heard that Oliver Warwick's been arrested?"

"Yes, I have . . . I happened to be at the cannery this morning when it happened. I'd gone over to get the missing signature on the tax documents."

"That's not all that might be missing around here," Lester huffed.

Ben suddenly realized what Lester was talking about. Before he could reply, Walter said, "We think an immediate audit of the church accounts is necessary. Since Oliver has been handling all the money . . . and considering what he's accused of." He added the last part reluctantly.

Ben was not really surprised. It was a predictable reaction and even a valid one, all things considered. If Oliver had mishandled his business accounts, he might have mishandled church funds, too. But Ben did recoil from the way the message had been delivered, as if the accusations against Oliver had been proven.

"We can call a board meeting and vote on it," he said evenly. "Perhaps the members can even meet tonight."

Once more, Lester didn't seem to like that answer—even though the church was run on a democratic model and all decisions, big and small, were voted on.

"I've already spoken to the rest of the board by phone. This morning, as soon as I heard the news. It was unanimous . . . Well, with one exception."

Either a vote was unanimous or it wasn't, but Ben didn't stop to educate Lester on that point. He could guess who the abstainer was: Ezra Elliot, most likely.

"I understand your concern, Lester," he replied, seeking to bring some perspective to the situation. "But we have no reason to suspect that Oliver has handled the accounts inappropriately in any way. In fact, Oliver recently presented all of last year's accounts in preparation for the church's annual meeting."

"That's true, Reverend." Walter, who had been standing behind Lester, now stepped forward to give his opinion. "But some people can be clever with numbers. How do we even know those figures are valid? Has anyone checked them against the bank statements and accounts?"

Ben had to concede that was a valid point. But before he could answer, Lester said, "The answer is, 'No one has checked.' We trusted whatever Warwick told us. Now we find out he's playing around with the books of his own company. Who's to say it isn't going on here, too?"

"As I said before, I understand your concern, Lester. It's a valid one. We are all concerned about the church. But I might point out that the specifics of Oliver's situation haven't even been disclosed yet. So far, it's all hearsay and gossip. For another," he added before Lester could counter, "last time I checked, the law says a man is innocent until proven guilty. And so does the Bible."

"We're not trying to judge the man, Reverend," Walter said, his voice soothing. "But it does make you wonder."

Lester glanced at Walter, as if embarrassed by his statement, then looked back at Ben. "I didn't come here for a Bible lesson, Reverend. And I don't think the district attorney could get a warrant to arrest a man if they didn't have a solid case with plenty of evidence."

"And yet many people are brought to trial and proved innocent, even with such 'solid cases,'" Ben couldn't help pointing out.

Lester's face was getting nearly as red as Otto's had been. "With all due respect," he said, barely containing his anger, "I'd think our minister would be more interested in putting this church before Warwick's reputation."

Ben took a moment to gather his patience. Despite his disclaimer, Lester's tone had not shown due respect. It had been downright disrespectful. But it would do no good to react and only escalate the situation.

"I understand your concerns and the seriousness of these events. I agree that, under the circumstances, we should review the church accounts. But I don't see it as a choice of one over the other, Lester. I think both protecting the church and withholding judgment on Oliver until we know more are important . . . But there's no sense in debating about it," he added.

"Yes, there's no sense at all in debating it," Lester echoed. "I don't know why we've even been standing here talking for so long. This is going to take time, and we'd like to get started."

"Of course. All the files are in that first cabinet," Ben said, stepping aside. "I'll get the ledgers and checkbook."

Ben walked over to a storage closet and took out his key ring, searching for the key to another cabinet, where the church checkbook and ledgers—and sometimes cash and checks from church offerings—were stored before they were brought to the bank.

He was relieved to find everything there. Not that he suspected Oliver, too. But he knew how Oliver often brought the church accounts home to work on in his spare time. Ben didn't want to have to go through the trouble of asking Lillian to look around for the ledgers. It would seem as if they were rubbing salt in the wound.

He carried the heavy records into the meeting room, where Lester and Walter were already set up at the table with pens, pads, and calculators. Ben wondered if Lester expected him to help. He was terrible with numbers and would probably slow them down. But he didn't want to seem as if he were unconcerned, as Lester seemed to think.

"Here are the ledgers and checkbook. How can I help?"

Lester was already adding up a long column of figures and barely looked up at him. "Thank you, Reverend. We'll take it from here."

Walter looked up and forced a smile. "Just a lot of adding and subtracting, Reverend. If we need some reinforcements, we'll call you."

"Please do," Ben said to them.

He returned to his own office and closed the door. He sat behind his desk but felt restless and disturbed. Had he really done the wrong thing by trying to at least slow down the rush to judgment? Lester already had Oliver tried and convicted . . . and involved in other crimes. Ben knew that he was as concerned and protective of his church as he ought to be. He didn't understand why it was necessary to slander Oliver Warwick to prove that—necessary to Lester Plante, anyway.

Lester had been on the search committee that had interviewed Ben for his position. Ben had known him a bit longer than many other congregation members and was fairly certain that Lester had not been in favor of calling him. He would have preferred an older minister, with more experience. Whatever the reason, Lester didn't respect him much. Ben could sense that but wasn't sure what he could do about it, except maintain his own self-respect and not let himself be cowed by the force of Lester's personality.

It was certainly a slippery slope. It wouldn't do him any good to antagonize the church moderator. Ben still felt very new to the congregation and knew that his relationship with the members, though mostly positive, had still not taken root completely. Someone like Lester could undermine and even uproot him very easily.

Ben wasn't sure where that thought had come from. He brushed it aside, scolding himself for being so insecure. He was new at this church, but people liked him; his relationships were growing stronger every day. Their last minister had been here over thirty years; families had known him for generations. One doesn't come in and fill those shoes overnight.

Oliver's situation is sure to ripple through the church community and the community at large, Ben told himself. *But you can use this event, however unfortunate, to make your connections to church members stronger. Let this difficult meeting with Lester remind you of how some people will react, how unsettled and frightened they'll feel.*

Underneath Lester's self-righteousness and puffed-up heroics— sweeping into the office to defend the church finances—there was fear. The news had changed his world, something he'd known for sure, taken for granted. That had scared him, Ben realized, and threatened his security. Many others would feel the same.

You need to be sensitive to that, he reminded himself, *and not just to Oliver's plight.*

He wondered when Oliver would be released by the police. Would he be kept in jail overnight—or even longer? Ben hoped not. Oliver's family must be in turmoil now. He could only imagine their pain and confusion. He picked up the telephone and dialed Lilac Hall. Maybe Lillian would speak to him, even if she didn't want to see him.

The phone rang and rang, the effort proving as fruitless as his visit earlier in the day. So many people must be calling, he guessed, that Lillian had probably taken the receiver off the hook. He wished he could help them, but he didn't know what else to do.

There was only one thing he could do right now for Oliver Warwick and his family, Ben realized. He closed his eyes and prayed.

CHAPTER FOUR

Present day, December 8

$\mathcal{R}$ACHEL AND WILL WERE AMONG THE LAST TO ARRIVE AT Ryan Cooper's house on Monday night. They had to park halfway down the street, and Will jogged up to the house. "Come on, Mom. We're late."

Rachel picked up her pace. He was a little nervous tonight, eager to make a good impression on the coach. And she was a little nervous, too, hoping she could find a way to talk about Will's health issues privately. She didn't want to seem like a hovering, overprotective mother, but it was hard to hit just the right note.

As they rushed up the path to the front door, Rachel took in a quick impression of the house. It was a traditional Colonial, but newly built, with a big porch in front, cedar shake shingles, and classic gray-blue shutters and trim.

The front door was open. They walked into a large foyer, where a wooden bench overflowed with jackets and coats. Large rooms opened on either side of a center hall that led to a kitchen and a great room in back. Rachel could just glimpse a second floor at the top of a wide stair-case with a polished wooden banister.

Parents and their sons were still finding seats in the large living room to the left. Comfortable-looking couches with dark blue upholstery, big armchairs, and some folding chairs were centered around a rustic stone hearth. The room was decorated in an easy, warm style with area rugs and large kilim pillows. Family photos, along with paintings, mostly of the coast, hung on the walls.

Rachel recognized a few familiar faces as she and Will found two empty folding chairs. She hadn't caught sight of Ryan yet and glanced at handouts that had been left on her chair—the coach's welcome state-ment and playing philosophy, team rules, and schedules of practices and games. There was also some information on how to order the team uni-forms, league registration, team dues, and payment for a team trainer and assistant coach, Jason Keller.

Get out your checkbook. Let the games begin, Rachel silently teased herself. She would gladly pay the fees and more to see Will so happy. He had been walking on a cloud since the phone call the night before.

All eyes turned when Ryan walked in, followed by a few more parents.

As he took his place at the front of the group and scanned his audi-ence, Rachel looked down at the handouts again. She doodled on a piece of paper to avoid meeting his eye. She wasn't sure why. He was just . . . unnerving.

She was almost sorry to see that Ryan Cooper was as attractive as she had first thought. Maybe more so. He wasn't wearing anything special— a dark blue V-neck sweater made of thin wool that outlined his broad shoulders and fit physique, and a pair of worn jeans and running shoes. It all worked together on him like some advertisement for men's cologne—or sheer male charisma.

Another man walked in and stood beside Ryan. He was younger, with buzz-cut, fair hair, and a wide, friendly face. He, too, was very fit-looking, but smaller in height and stature than Ryan Cooper. He was also dressed casually, in jeans and a hooded sweatshirt that said UMASS. Rachel guessed that he was Jason Keller, the trainer and assistant coach. He seemed to know a few of the boys, and spoke to them in a friendly way while everyone waited for Ryan to start.

She wasn't consciously trying to eavesdrop but couldn't help overhearing two women behind her talking about Ryan.

"—he was divorced about three years ago. His wife lives in town. They share custody of Andy, though Andy is with him more during basketball season, for all the games and practices—"

"He's such a nice guy. Can you believe he's still single?"

So he was not only amazingly attractive . . . but definitely single.

Rachel sighed aloud, and Will looked at her curiously. "What's the matter?" he whispered.

"Oh, nothing. I just wish they'd get started. I have some paperwork to do tonight."

Just then Ryan started speaking. They both looked up at him, but Rachel hardly heard a word he said as he introduced himself and Jason.

Okay . . . so after nearly two years, there's a blip on the radar screen, she told herself. *A tiny blip. Let's get over it and go on from here, shall we?*

She forced herself to focus as Ryan talked about his coaching philosophy. She liked his balanced, upbeat attitude. He sounded positive but not like a macho "winning is everything" guy. She felt Jack would have approved of him, too.

"—and if you look at professional sports and who's winning the World Series, or the Super Bowl, or even the NBA title," he told the group, "it's not the teams that rely on one or two superstars. It's the teams with strong, dedicated players who work together. And that includes reserve players who can come off the bench and deliver."

"Look, Mom. There are fifteen guys on his team. I might not get to play that much," Will whispered, showing her the roster.

Rachel had noticed that—and was secretly relieved. "We don't know for sure. You have to do your best," she whispered back. She already knew that only five would be starters, five would be second-string replacements, and the rest would be reserves.

Which was fine with Rachel. The less Will was on the court, the less chance of an asthma attack. That's how she saw it, anyway.

After the handouts were reviewed and Ryan had answered some questions, he came to a moment that always arrived at such meetings: the call for a parent volunteer to help manage the details.

"We need someone who will make sure the team has updated schedules and directions to the games, and knows which color uniform to wear. This lucky person will also collect fees and help out with the uniform orders. Basically, I'm looking for someone willing to be a regular support and presence."

"Like a Class Mother?" someone called out, making everyone laugh.

Ryan smiled that melting smile of his. "Something like that . . . but not too many cupcakes. We want these boys eating healthy food," he added, eliciting another laugh. "More like a team manager, I guess. Though I hesitate to use that word. It makes it sound too much like work," he admitted with a charming wince.

It did sound like work—a lot of work. Work that Rachel knew she didn't have time for. Neither did anyone else, apparently. Despite the banter, no one volunteered.

Rachel took a breath, willing herself not to raise her hand.

You're kidding, right? You barely have time to keep up the house and get meals on the table, let alone manage a basketball team, she reminded herself. *You'd only be doing it to hover over Will. Just a sneaky helicopter-Mom trick, the way you chaperone field trips, host all the sleepovers . . . You have to give the kid some space. Even your father said so. He'll be all right. Will knows how to use his inhaler and can carry one or two extras . . .*

"No one has to decide right now," Ryan said, cutting into her thoughts. "I'll send an e-mail this week and—"

Rachel felt her hand shoot up involuntarily. "I can do it."

Everyone turned to look at her, and she felt her face get warm.

Will rolled his eyes and groaned. "Mom, please *don't*."

But she ignored him, especially when Ryan met her gaze with a wide, warm smile. "Great. Thank you . . . Mrs. Anderson, right?"

Rachel nodded, noticing he already knew her name. "Yes, that's right."

He scribbled a note on the pad he was holding and looked back at her. "Can you come to the practice tomorrow night? I'll explain everything you need to know."

Rachel nodded again, instantly regretting her impulsive act.

You spoke up and now you need to follow through. If you don't want to do it, you can back out gracefully in a day or two. That's some sort of plan, she consoled herself.

Jason spoke for a few minutes on conditioning, and then Ryan had a few reminders before he thanked everyone and wrapped up. "I know we've brought together a great bunch of players and parents. And the Cape Light Falcons are going to play some great basketball, and learn a lot, too."

The group applauded briefly, then quickly filed out of the living room. Rachel and Will gathered up their belongings and followed.

"What do you think?" Rachel asked her son as they left the living room.

"I'm, like, totally psyched to be on this team. Coach Coop is amazing."

Rachel wasn't sure the coach had done anything so far to justify that accolade. But she was glad Will thought so.

"Did you really have to volunteer to be the helper?" Will made a face, squinting at her.

Rachel squinted back. "Yeah, I know. Totally uncool to have your mom around, right?"

"Like, totally," he replied.

"Don't worry, I'll stay out of your way. I figured I'd be at all your games anyway. Let's just see how it goes."

"Okay, but that's what you always say when you think me or Nora are going to just forget about something and give up."

Rachel laughed. "You're wise to that ploy? It only took, like . . . twelve years," she teased him.

She had to reach up to ruffle her son's hair with her hand, and was rewarded with an irritated but amused reaction.

When she looked up, Ryan Cooper was standing nearby. He had been watching her interaction with Will and looked pleased. Rachel felt self-conscious and looked away. But he stood by the door, saying good night to everyone, and she knew she had to speak to him.

"Thanks again for stepping up," he said to her. "Team manager isn't a hard job, but it does mean a lot of afternoons and evenings in the gym. I hope you have the time, Mrs. Anderson."

Rachel laughed. "I don't really, but I like to be involved in my children's activities, if I can." *Especially Will, because of his health issues.* She knew that was true but didn't want to admit it. Not here, anyway. "By the way, please call me Rachel," she added.

"Thanks. Please call me Ryan."

Not Coop? That was a relief. The nickname seemed fun and friendly coming from the boys, but she would have felt odd using it.

"Well, good night. See you tomorrow at the practice."

"I look forward to it," he answered with a small smile, meeting her gaze and holding it.

She felt another spark of attraction and forced herself to look straight ahead—and ignore her silly reaction.

She walked out to the SUV and climbed in, listening to Will with only half her attention as he rattled on about the other kids on the team and what a great guy Coach Coop was.

"Seems nice so far," Rachel said evenly.

And the type who knows he's good-looking and likes to catch a woman's attention, she silently added. *Not my type at all. If I was even looking for a "type" . . . which I definitely am not.* Rachel felt very clear about that— and intended to remember those priorities when she saw Coach Coop at the practice tomorrow night.

Rachel had a full day of patient visits on Tuesday and hardly gave Will's practice a thought. But as the evening approached, she found herself dreading it. Dreading hanging out with Ryan Cooper for an hour and a half.

She dressed in jeans, a sweatshirt, and sneakers, and brushed her long hair back into a ponytail, purposely not wearing any makeup or earrings. She did not want to give the coach any encouragement.

She heard her mother and Nora come in and greet Will. Carolyn was going to stay with Nora during the practice. Rachel stopped in her home office, grabbed a clipboard, and attached the sheets with the team roster and rules.

It always made her feel more grounded and official to have a clipboard in hand. They used them all the time in the PT clinic, charting each patient's progress. It made her feel efficient and businesslike, even if she didn't know the first thing about managing a school basketball team. Still, her stomach was filled with butterflies as she trotted downstairs, grabbed Will, and gave her mother a few last-minute instructions.

"Don't worry, we'll be fine. Two peas in a pod," her mother promised. "Should I fix dinner for you and Will, too?"

"Oh, don't bother. We'll get some takeout. Will had a humongous after-school snack. He shouldn't be hungry until . . . next week."

Just in case, though, he'd taken along some energy bars and plenty of water for the workout. He was at that teenage-boy stage where he could eat an elephant and stay thin as a blade of grass.

Rachel so hated that.

Of course she had his inhaler. Two of them, in case one failed. She had checked her tote bag about three times, but checked again in the car, before pulling out of the driveway.

"Mom, we're going to be late," Will groused from the back seat.

"No worries, the gym is five minutes away." *Luckily,* Rachel thought.

By the time they got into the gym, half a dozen boys were already on the floor, running laps around the perimeter of the court. Jason was working with them; he'd set up some traffic cones and now dragged a huge net bag of basketballs onto the court.

Ryan was on the sidelines, talking to parents and also watching the boys. He wore dark blue track pants with stripes on the legs and a short-sleeved blue T-shirt that said CAPE LIGHT FALCONS in yellow letters. He crossed his arms over his chest, and Rachel couldn't help noticing the biceps bulging in them.

Okay, he works out. You're a physical therapist. You've seen a biceps or two before, Rachel.

He smiled briefly at her as she set her belongings on the lowest bench. She smiled back, but took a seat at a distance. She took the clipboard and pen from her bag, then stared straight ahead at the court, watching the boys work out.

She looked for Will, who was already on the court sweating up a storm, an intense look on his face as he waited for his turn to dribble around the traffic cones.

Once the other parents had left, Ryan walked over and greeted her.

"I'm going to let them warm up. Then we'll scrimmage and practice foul shots. I pretty much know who the starters will be on Saturday, but I want to switch it around a little, see who steps up."

Rachel nodded. She was used to sports jargon from hearing Jack and Will talk, but it was hard to keep up with a steady flow of it when she was expected to respond—a little like studying a language in school, then being dropped in the foreign country and having to speak to the natives.

"Sounds good," she said. "How about the jerseys? When do you want me to give them out?" Rachel had looked around but hadn't seen a sign of the uniforms yet.

"Oh . . . right. The jerseys . . ." He grinned and smacked his forehead. "See why I need a team manager? I'd have those kids arriving at their first game in Angry Bird T-shirts."

Rachel laughed. She couldn't help it. He was . . . cute.

"Jerseys are in that box over there, small, medium, and large—yellow and dark blue together in one bag. Shorts in another. You need to record the number on the jersey that each boy takes."

"Right, got it." She made a little note on her clipboard just for something to do. It wasn't exactly rocket science.

"You seem very organized, Rachel."

"I try to be. It makes life easier."

"It will for me. We have a ton of paperwork to give out . . . and then collect. We can go over the folder after the practice, okay?"

"That will be fine." Rachel didn't let her gaze linger this time, but quickly looked back at the clipboard, glad again that she had brought it with her. It was turning into a very useful prop.

A few moments later, Jason and Ryan called the boys in for a drink of water and some feedback on their play.

Rachel sat a few benches higher so she wouldn't be in the way. Will seemed to be winded, but most of the boys were. They gulped from their water bottles while Ryan spoke and demonstrated a few moves he wanted to see more of—and a few he didn't want to see at all.

The boys soon went back out to scrimmage, breaking into four squads that played one another on the half courts. Jason worked on one side, and Ryan coached the side where Will played. Ryan instructed them in a firm but positive tone, rarely raising his voice, not like some of the coaches Will had encountered.

"Nice pass, Kyle . . . Ben, keep it moving. Watch out, look around. Move it down the court . . . now pass, man open. Nice . . ."

Rachel soon realized his coaching style was a lot like her own when working with patients who were building strength and mobility after surgeries or strokes. He had a way of pairing a compliment or positive feedback with a bit of instruction for improvement.

His tone was one of authority, but also of good humor, and most of all, he was respectful of their efforts. Rachel liked that. Will had been with a few coaches who seemed to think that boys only understood tough and even humiliating talk—or the threat of it. She didn't like that approach at all. It seemed very clear to her that in sports, physical therapy, and life in general, positive encouragement was the surest way to motivate performance.

But her main concern was not Ryan's coaching style; it was her own son's stamina. As she expected, most of the boys on the team were older, bigger, and more competitive. Even if Ryan wasn't emphasizing crushing the competition, boys will be boys, Rachel very well knew.

Will was playing point guard, racing around after a boy who was quite fast and agile for his height. Will was, as usual, giving it his all, just as Jack had taught him, even though it was just a scrimmage. Rachel watched him gasp a few times as he ran and put his hands on his hips to get a deeper breath whenever he had a chance to stand still, waiting for a time-out or a foul shot.

Rachel suddenly wondered if Ryan had actually read Will's medical report. Was he aware of Will's asthma, or had he just skimmed those details? She sat on the edge of the bench, then slipped down two levels to be closer to the court. She grabbed her tote bag and felt for the inhaler. Just in case she had to jump up and bring it out to Will.

She glanced at Ryan, wondering if she should tap him on the shoulder and tell him to let Will sit out awhile. She didn't want to embarrass her son. But she didn't want to see him get sick either.

Why did I ever volunteer for this job? This is torture for me. Rachel took a few deep breaths of her own and forced herself to get perspective. *Will is fine. He's doing what he needs to do, what he should be doing. Don't spoil that for him, Rachel. You're just scared, because of Jack. Nothing bad is going to happen to Will.*

The practice would be over in fifteen minutes, she noticed, checking the big clock on the gym wall.

She jumped up and started to distract herself by sorting the jerseys by size on one of the benches—much more efficient than having each boy sort through the big box—though she was still able to see Will on the court.

She was done with her task about the same time that Ryan and Jason blew their whistles again. The boys dropped down on the gym floor, most just collapsing in a sweaty heap. Will was breathing heavily, but it was nothing unusual. Rachel felt relieved—and glad she hadn't given in to her nerves and said anything.

Ryan let the boys get some water and talked more about their skills and strategies. Then he had them split up for layups. "Three shots each. Then go over to Mrs. Anderson and pick out your jerseys."

Okay, you're on. Finally. Rachel grabbed her clipboard and jumped into action.

The boys came up a few at a time, and she helped them pick the appropriate-size jersey. Some were looking for lucky numbers, and she helped them find most of those, too.

Finally, everyone had two set of jerseys and shorts—colored and white—and she had a complete list of their jersey numbers. She put the extra uniforms back in the box as Ryan ended the practice.

"That was an amazing first practice, guys. You're all looking very strong. There are a few areas I want to work on at the next practice, so let's make the most of it before our first game this weekend. See you Thursday," he said, sending them off.

Parents were already waiting, and the team quickly dispersed. Rachel felt very hungry. She had managed to grab an apple after work, but it was already seven thirty, an hour past their usual dinnertime.

She knew that Will had to be ravenous by now, too. She didn't even want to ask him. He didn't seem in a huge rush to leave, though, hanging on the court with Ryan's son, Andy. They were still fooling around, playing one-on-one, and taking some outrageous—and hideous—shots.

Ryan looked over and laughed at them. "I bet we could shut off the lights and they'd still be out there."

"I bet we could," Rachel agreed. "You wanted to give me a folder with forms to give out?" she reminded him, hoping to make a fast getaway.

"Oh right. We'd better go over that stuff. The parents need some more info before Saturday's game and for the other games, too . . ." He riffled through his gym bag, which was brimming with folders, whistles, air pumps, water bottles, rolls of sticky tape, instant ice packs, and other coaching necessities.

He suddenly looked up at her. "Hey, I have an idea. Did you guys eat yet? We could all get some pizza and look at this boring stuff over dinner."

Rachel wasn't sure what to say. Her first impulse was to make some polite excuse, but Will and Andy had already overheard and were highly in favor of the idea.

"Can we, Mom? I'm starving. I feel like I'm going to faint." Will made a pleading face as he gulped down more water.

When Rachel looked back at Ryan, his expression was almost as coaxing. She felt cornered. "All right . . . We'd like to join you," she added, realizing she had not sounded very polite. "I just need to check in with my mom. She's watching my daughter."

Rachel knew her mom would happily stay as long she was needed. But it gave her a good excuse to keep the outing short.

Ryan smiled, looking pleased at her answer, and making her pulse race again, as if she, too, had just scrimmaged for half an hour.

Spending any more time with this guy than absolutely necessary would not be conducive to her peace of mind, Rachel knew. She was already regretting agreeing to it.

They decided on Village Pizza, a small, no-frills restaurant in Cape Light, on a side street off Main. The place was packed on the weekends, but since it was a weeknight, they found a table easily, a booth where Will and Rachel sat on one side and Ryan and Andy on the other. They quickly put in their order and the boys wandered off to talk to some kids on the team who had found the same solution for dinner.

Left alone at the table with Ryan, Rachel felt self-conscious and suddenly wished she had put on some makeup. Even a little lip gloss would have been better than nothing.

"I noticed from Will's registration form that you're a physical therapist. That must be a rewarding career."

So he had read the forms. If he knew that, he also knew that she was a single parent. And about Will's asthma.

"Yes . . . it is. It's a lot like coaching," she added. "I never thought of it that way before. But I was noticing tonight, the way you talk to the boys. You give them some positive reinforcement and follow up with a pointer on how they can improve or push themselves to a higher level."

He laughed and sat back, flashing that dazzling smile again.

"Am I that obvious? Please say no."

"You are to me," she said honestly. "I'm not sure they've figured out the recipe yet. Praise gets better results in learning new behavior. It's a proven fact."

"Actually, the best results come from random reinforcement. Giving praise some of the time, when it's unexpected," he pointed out. "But I can't coach like that. When I see kids trying their best on the court, I want to encourage them, not be a withholding Scrooge-type of coach. But not a pushover either."

She could never see him in the Scrooge role.

"It's a fine line," she agreed. "But I've seen a lot of coaches. You do a good job. So far, at least."

He smiled at her praise. "Thanks . . . Are you going to offer some suggestion for improvement now? That's the formula, right?"

It was her turn to laugh. "Give me a minute. I'll think of something."

A large salad and two pizzas were brought to the table. The food instantly drew the two boys back, but they soon decided they wanted to take one of the pies and sit at their own table. Rachel didn't mind. The booths were not very big, and Will would have been poking her endlessly with his elbow.

Once the hungry basketball players had disappeared to eagerly pounce on their pizza, Rachel and Ryan began their meal at a much more leisurely pace.

"What do you do for a living, Ryan?" she asked, curious.

"I'm an architect. I build new homes mostly. I have a small firm of my own in town—Cooper & Associates, Architectural Design." He paused, cutting into a slice of pizza. "I don't have many associates, but I thought it looked good on the sign."

She laughed again. "Did you design the house you live in?"

He nodded. "Yes, it was one of my first projects in town. I'd make some changes if I had it to do over again. But you get used to a place. The little quirks and imperfections make it more your own."

"I know what you mean. I feel that way about my own house. It's no architectural masterpiece, but there are so many memories of raising my children there." *And all the happy years with my husband,* she nearly said.

He glanced up at her, as if sensing she was about to say something more. Before he could speak, she added, "Where does all the basketball knowledge come from? Did you play in college or high school?"

He sighed theatrically. "How I tried . . . I didn't even make junior varsity, as much as I loved it. I played a lot of driveway basketball and in noncompetitive leagues, teams that would take any kid who signed up. Even so, I was usually on the bench. I got my height early, like Will and Andy, but I wasn't nearly as strong or coordinated as they are at this age." He sighed again, but was smiling pretty widely. "I was pretty much a geeky beanpole, and a math nerd to boot. So high school and even college were not my glory days."

Rachel laughed with surprise. She had him pegged for varsity and the most popular boy at school. Certainly the most handsome.

"I'm sure it wasn't that bad." She took a sip of water, avoiding his glance again.

He grinned and thought a moment. "Yeah . . . it was. But there are perks to being a late bloomer . . . Did Will gravitate to the sport because of his height?"

"Not exactly." Rachel paused. "My husband, Jack, played in college. He really encouraged Will and worked with him a lot."

Ryan nodded, looking suddenly serious. "Andy told me that Will lost his dad. I'm sorry."

"Thanks," Rachel said quietly. She was sorry to ruin the light mood but glad to tell Ryan this essential truth about herself. "It will be two years at the end of January. But it's still difficult for the kids."

"And for you, I'm sure. I can't imagine it," he said sympathetically.

"Yes, for me, too. In ways you'd never expect," Rachel confided. "Jack died very suddenly. He was perfectly healthy and then *wham*, he had a heart attack out of the blue. That was it," she tried to explain. "Ever since . . . well, I worry a lot. Especially about the kids. I don't mean to. But I can't help myself."

"That's understandable," he replied quietly.

She shrugged. "I suppose. But it's not always a good thing, especially for Will. You know that he has asthma, right?"

"I read it on his medical form. But he's cleared for sports, right?"

"Oh, he is. Totally. It's really under control. Except when he gets stressed. Like when we lost Jack. But I still worry about it. I mean, I'm like a walking drugstore," she added, making him smile again. "And . . . the truth is . . . that's why I really volunteered to be team manager. To keep an eye on him." She practically winced making the admission, but somehow, she needed to. "I'm just a helicopter mom in disguise. Not even that well-disguised. I'm every coach's nightmare, right?" she asked with a small, self-conscious laugh.

Ryan met her gaze and shook his head. "I get it . . . and thanks for your honesty. I admire that," he said sincerely. "And you are not my nightmare, Rachel. Far from it."

Rachel didn't know what to say. She sat staring back at him, wondering what had made her disclose all these secrets—but not feeling nearly as awkward as she thought she should.

"Do I still have the job? Even though I volunteered under false pretenses?"

"Are you kidding? Of course you have the job. Mostly because you're the only one who wanted it," he added, making her smile. "Which reminds me, we never got to go over all those forms."

Rachel had forgotten all about the main reason they'd come here, too. He was so easy to talk to, she had no idea of the time.

He pulled out the folder and put it on the table. "These are the forms. And there's also a league website. We have to send out information to the team from there, too. Why don't you look at all this when you have a chance, and we can talk about it on Thursday."

"All right. I can probably figure it out."

"I'm sure you can," he said, signaling for the check. "But I'm glad we got together. Outside of the gym, I mean. I enjoyed talking to you."

Rachel had enjoyed talking to him, too, but didn't feel comfortable admitting it.

"Well . . . thanks. And thanks for the pizza," she added, noticing how he gave the waitress a credit card without even reading the bill. She had expected to split the check with him, but that was obviously not his plan.

"My pleasure," he said politely. She had a feeling he was about to say something more, but the boys suddenly returned to the table. Will looked wound up and exhausted at the same time. Rachel knew she had to get him home to shower and do homework, hopefully before he fell asleep with his head in a schoolbook.

They all said good night again outside and were soon on their way. Rachel didn't have much time to think about the practice or her pizza dinner with Ryan Cooper until much later that night, after her mother had left and Nora and Will were both in bed.

She checked her emails and found one from Ryan.

Rachel—Sending you one more boring form. It's for ordering team gear, sweatshirts and all that. It needs to be sent out to all the parents sometime this week.

I'm glad we were able to spend some time together tonight. I look forward to working with you—and getting to know you better—in the weeks to come.

All best, Ryan

Rachel read the message over a few times. She could almost hear his voice and see his face, as if he were saying the words aloud to her.

It wasn't really personal. But it wasn't impersonal, either. What did he mean by "get to know you better"? Like . . . go out on a date? Or just, be a pal? A teammate?

Rachel, don't even go there, she advised herself. *For one thing, a man that attractive is not roaming around the world unattached. He's probably already dating someone. He was just being nice to you. You're just not used to spending time with men.*

And spending even a tiny bit of time with him made her even more certain that she was not ready for the dating scene. Nohow, no way. Even with someone as easy to talk to as Ryan Cooper.

He was definitely attractive . . . and seemed to be a really nice guy, smart and funny and everything she might like. But just a "teammate" was all she could handle right now.

If he asks me out, I'll just have to explain it to him. It's as simple as that, Rachel decided.

CHAPTER FIVE

December 3, 1978

*D*O YOU REALLY THINK THEY'LL COME TO CHURCH TODAY?"
Gus Potter, the head deacon, stood with Ben in the church
office on Sunday morning. He was stacking neat piles of programs and
held one open, pointing to the first page. "The Warwick family. They're
supposed to light the Advent candles."

Ben had forgotten about that; these things were scheduled so far in
advance. He hadn't even noticed their name on Friday when Mrs. Guilley gave him the draft of the bulletin to proofread before she ran off
copies.

"I tried the house this week," he told Gus, "but I wasn't able to reach
anyone. I suppose it would be a good idea to look for another family
willing to step in—if that's even possible at this point."

Ben was doubtful. He might have to read the liturgy and light the
Advent candle himself. Which seemed awkward and totally beside the
point. His first Christmas season service was getting off to a rocky start,
wasn't it? He hadn't even put his robe and scarf on yet.

"I'll see what I can do, Reverend. There are some early birds here for choir practice. I'll ask around," Gus promised.

Ben thanked him as Gus gathered the bulletins and headed out for his search. Ben headed back into his office to don his vestments.

Gus was an even-tempered soul. Some would have balked at that errand. It would not be easy to find a replacement family at the last minute. It was not just lighting the candles but taking turns reading the liturgy aloud. And the families always liked to be well dressed, with all their braids and bows in place.

The Advent wreath was a beloved tradition of Christmas in the church and, like all church traditions, steeped in meaning. Centuries ago, the pine wreaths were vast and held twenty-four candles, one lit each day in December to mark the light of the world growing stronger in anticipation of Christ's birth. The circle of evergreen boughs were a symbol of the promise of everlasting life and the everlasting love and steadfast promises of Christ.

Nowadays, the wreath held four blue candles, each one marking a week in the Christmas season. But it was no less beloved or significant.

Well, God, we have a small glitch. Please step in and handle this? Ben thought, offering up the problem for some divine solution. *Help me keep focus on starting off this Advent season with joy and anticipation; anticipation of celebrating Christ's birth and Your promise fulfilled. That's the most important thing.*

Ben sat at his desk, the pages of his sermon laid out before him. He liked to review and then practice in the sanctuary, if time allowed. As he mentally rehearsed the words on the page, he felt himself reaching for the Advent spirit, but a heaviness lay in his heart. The troubles of the Warwicks had cast a long shadow, even though they would most likely not attend this Sunday.

The story of Oliver's arrest was still fresh in everyone's mind and on their tongues. Both the *Cape Light Messenger* and the *Boston Globe* had run front-page stories on Thursday with details of Oliver's alleged crimes. He was accused of stealing funds from the pension accounts of cannery and lumberyard employees. Prosecutors also claimed he had used the money to gamble at the racetrack and in high-stakes poker games. Oliver's attorneys claimed their client was innocent. Oliver himself had made no direct statement to the press. He had spent one night in jail before being released on bail to await his next court appearance and trial.

The newspaper stories had come out the day after the skirmish at the Clam Box and the emergency audit of the church financial records, which, so far, had not shown any irregularities. For that, Ben was grateful, though he had not made much of it when Walter Tulley told him, acting instead as if he had assumed no problems would be found. Walter had seemed relieved, too, but Ben didn't know what Lester's reaction had been.

As the start of the service drew closer, Ben gathered the pages of his sermon and smoothed his scarf—bright blue, the color of hope, for the weeks of Christmas—over his white hassock. He swept out of his office and headed for the sanctuary, greeting some congregation members on the way. The deacons had been at church on Saturday putting up Christmas decorations: a pine wreath on the big wooden doors and a Christmas tree in the sanctuary. Everyone who greeted him seemed to be in a cheerful holiday mood.

He didn't see the Warwicks. He did wonder if Gus had found a family to take their place. As the music director, Quentin Digby, struck the chords of the opening hymn and the choir lined up just outside the sanctuary, Ben took his place behind them and peeked in. He saw the Bates family standing up at the altar and breathed a giant sigh of relief.

Otto; his wife, Mary; their teenage son, Charlie; and their daughter, Sharon, were walking up to light the candles on short notice. Gus must have explained the problem, and Oliver's true friend had been willing to step up.

Right after the opening hymn, the candle-lighting proceeded as scheduled. The Bates family read the liturgy very smoothly, Ben thought, considering they had only had a few minutes to practice.

He thanked Otto with a smile, not only grateful for the help, but also heartened to see that the Warwicks had friends here eager to stand by them.

It was later in the service, during Joys and Concerns, when another friend of the Warwicks spoke up. Ezra Elliot stood and looked about the sanctuary. "I'd like to ask for prayers for the Warwicks. As we all know, they're going through some dark times right now. They need God's help and His comforting hand. And our help, too," he added.

Ben nodded in agreement. "Thank you, Ezra. We will certainly remember them in our prayers this morning."

It took Ben a moment to notice that some of the congregation members looked uneasy at these words, shifting in their seats or frowning. Lester Plante leaned over and whispered to his wife, Vera, and Ben had a feeling it was not an endorsement of Ezra's sympathy.

After all the requests were heard, Ben offered Morning Prayers for all those mentioned. When he came to the Warwicks, his voice rose a bit more emphatically. ". . . and please reach out to the Warwick family, Lord. Help them through these difficult times, and support them with Your comfort and love. Please help us to stand by these members of our church family . . . and refrain from harsh judgment and criticism."

He rarely added to the prayers in such an editorial way, but this morning it seemed necessary.

After the service, Ben stood in the narthex, greeting the congregants. Lester and Vera Plante were among the first in line.

"I enjoyed the service, Reverend," Vera said. "I always like to see the families lighting the Advent candles. Too bad the Warwicks had to miss their turn. But God moves in mysterious ways," she added with a shrug.

Ben forced himself to maintain a bland expression. He knew what

Vera meant. Maybe the Warwicks "had this coming to them" for some reason. Maybe this fall was divine retribution of some sort. It was hard for Ben to abide the way some people used Scripture to justify a miserly spirit and a very unchristian perspective.

"Mysterious? Yes, I agree. God has provided a perfect opportunity for us to make the right spiritual choices here. To refrain from judging Oliver and his family and to extend our sympathy and comfort to them in their hour of need . . . Is that what you mean, Vera?" He met her puzzled expression with a calm, questioning look.

Vera seemed about to answer, but her husband, Lester, took her arm. "I'm sure that's what she meant to say, Reverend," he replied curtly. "Come along, Vera. You're holding up the line."

The Plantes disappeared before Ben could reply. He silently and sincerely wished them a good day. Wasn't it a good day when your eyes were opened to a truth you didn't see before? When you took a spiritual step in the right direction? And wasn't it his place—his duty, truly—to lead members of his congregation onto that path?

Ben knew he needed to salvage any crumbs he could from this sad situation, if only to frame it as a teaching moment for his flock. Perhaps that, too, was one of God's mysterious intentions.

TUESDAY BROUGHT MORE HEADLINES AND DAMAGING NEWS ABOUT Oliver. Both the *Globe* and the *Messenger* were delivered to the parsonage. Ben picked up the newspapers from his driveway and tucked them into his briefcase. He didn't open them until he had reached his office, where he spread the pages on his desk.

He scanned the latest headlines and reports: *Cannery king pleads "not guilty" to embezzlement charges.*

A knot of tension tightened in Ben's stomach at each censuring phrase. Oliver had appeared in court on Monday, Ben read, and entered a plea of not guilty to charges of embezzling money from the pension funds of cannery and lumberyard employees, and not guilty as well to forging signatures and other reprehensible acts. The court was expected to hear the case in a few weeks, though the date for the trial had not been set.

Ben sat back in his chair. The details were unnerving, to say the least. And the alleged facts of the matter seemed, on the surface anyway, to build a strong case against Oliver. Once again, Ben had to consider that, if he didn't know Oliver personally—had not experienced the man's goodness of heart, his generosity and loyalty to his friends, family, and fellow church members—all these accusations and newspaper stories would persuade him that Oliver was guilty of these crimes.

He sighed aloud and pushed the papers aside. Feeling restless, he rose from his desk and glanced out the office window. In his heart, he still gave Oliver the benefit of the doubt. Innocent until proven guilty. Isn't that what he had told Lester that first day?

Newspaper reports are not infallible, he reminded himself. The name "Warwick" sold a lot of newspapers, and both the *Messenger* and the *Globe* were taking advantage of that. They portrayed Oliver as some heartless, rich despot, a tycoon from the Gilded Age. "Cannery King," they called him.

The *Cape Light Messenger* had, anyway. Jonathan Forbes liked a clever headline; Ben already knew that of the publisher and editor-in-chief. The *Boston Globe* was a little bit more circumspect, calling Warwick simply "a prominent Essex County businessman."

Prosecuting attorneys claimed that Oliver had been propping up the failing company with his private fortune for a time. But when that came to be too great a strain, he dipped into the retirement accounts—using some of what he took to keep the businesses running, and using some to gamble, trying to replace the missing money. When that desperate scheme failed, he had wound up with gambling debts as well.

Ben rubbed his hand over his chin. Every revelation was still shocking—and at odds with the man he'd come to know these past months. It was all so different from the face Oliver presented to the world.

Prosecutors can make all kinds of claims. It still doesn't mean Oliver is guilty of any of it. Ben recalled again how Oliver said it was a big mix-up. He had signed some papers without reading them. Though the more information came out, the more Ben wondered.

We are all being tested not to judge and condemn, he reminded himself. *It's not just Vera Plante. I'm being tested as well. I pray for the wisdom, patience, and self-control to hold fast to God's word: "Judge not and ye shall not be judged."*

Ben began drafting some letters and tried to put the latest Warwick news out of his head. Mrs. Guilley appeared in his doorway at half past ten. "Time for your meeting, Reverend. With the Christmas Fair committee?"

"Oh right . . . Please tell them I'll be right in."

He put his correspondence aside and grabbed a pad and pen. Sophie Potter, one of the more active members of the church, had come up with a fund-raising idea—a Christmas bazaar where they would sell baked goods, knitted items, pine wreaths, garlands, and handmade ornaments. There would be games for children and strolling minstrels. It would take a lot of work, but everyone seemed willing to see if it was worth the bother.

The meeting was being held in Fellowship Hall, adjacent to the kitchen. Ben noticed that not all the members had arrived yet, and also noticed a pot of fresh coffee and some sort of apple cake with large, tantalizing crumbs on top; one of Sophie's specialties. Her meetings were always sweetened by her home-baked cakes and cookies. As he stopped in the kitchen to pour himself a cup of coffee, eyeing the cake and trying to resist, he couldn't help but overhear the conversation in Fellowship Hall.

". . . now he claims he was trying to save the companies. More like he just grabbed all that money to gamble. He had already wasted too much of his own cash. Horse races, card games, you name it," a man's voice said.

"It's in the blood. His father owned racehorses. Don't you remember?" a woman replied.

Ben stood up straight, listening. He didn't recognize the speakers. He didn't know everyone in the congregation that well yet.

"Old Harry Warwick. A son of gun. At least he didn't put on airs, like Lord Oliver. He made his millions during Prohibition. Sneaking in whiskey from Canada on fishing boats. Then he bought them canneries and became respectable." It was a third person speaking now, filling in the history.

"But he always had a few tricks up his sleeve. He was just too smart to get caught," another voice pointed out.

The older woman spoke again. "The apple doesn't fall far from the—" The words stopped abruptly as Ben slowly walked in.

"Hello, everyone." Ben put down his pad and coffee and looked around at the table.

"Hello, Reverend."

Ruth Hegman was sitting across from him. He smiled at her, and she shyly smiled back, looking a bit embarrassed, he thought. But he knew her voice. She hadn't been the one talking, but she sat next to her mother-in-law, Doris, who may have been one of the speakers. Muriel Krupp, who owned a dress shop and knew all the gossip in town, was also the table. Ben was fairly certain she had been the one person talking about Oliver. And at the end of the table, Skip Belmont, who owned the barbershop in town, had a lot to say, too.

"Have I interrupted your conversation?" Ben asked.

"We were talking about Oliver Warwick," Skip said. "Just like everyone else in town is this morning."

"Yes, I know. I was in the kitchen. I could hear you," Ben said plainly.

"It's true what I said about Harry Warwick," Muriel spoke up. "He was a bootlegger. Everyone knows that."

"It's true what I said about his son," Skip added. "Oliver Warwick is a gambler."

"Oh, you don't know that." Ruth Hegman shook her head, her voice practically a whisper. Ben knew she was painfully shy and could see that it was difficult for her to voice even these few words, and almost unbelievable that she would contradict someone as outspoken as Skip.

"I don't think this conversation is helpful . . . or appropriate," Ben interjected. "Let's leave all these reports and speculation—and quite possibly the tearing down of an innocent man's character and reputation—for the newspapers. That's their business. This is a church. We have a higher standard and important work to do. Didn't the Lord tell us, 'By this everyone will know you that are my disciples, if you love one another'?" he reminded them, quoting from the Book of John.

A quiet settled over the group. Skip looked about to say something, then twisted his mouth in a frown. Muriel shook her head a bit, staring down at her pen and pad. Ben could see he had not changed their minds about Oliver. They would continue sharing their opinions, he predicted. They would just wait until they were out of earshot of their minister. He wondered what else he could do about it, but no inspiration came to him.

Sophie arrived then and started the meeting, and everyone acted as if nothing special had happened while she had been out of the room.

BEN WAS RELIEVED TO RETURN HOME THAT NIGHT. THE SIGHT OF THE parsonage, a sparkling white rim of snow on the roof and lights glowing in the windows, was a welcome one.

"Hi, honey, I'm home." He stomped the snow off his boots and hung up his coat and hat.

"We're back here," Carolyn called from the kitchen.

He found her sitting at the table, holding Rachel in her arms and waving a bottle of formula like a small plane looking for a landing strip. Rachel turned her little face away, her expression squashed into an unattractive but adorable frown.

"I'd really like her to take a little more of this bottle," Carolyn said with a wistful sigh. "Otherwise, she won't sleep a wink."

"And neither will we," Ben added. He walked over and kissed Carolyn's cheek. Her hair was pulled back with bobby pins, her T-shirt was stained from the day's baby-care battles, and a smear of green baby food . . . or green something . . . streaked across her cheek. But she looked as beautiful to him as the summer day they had met.

Ben slipped off his suit jacket and tie and washed his hands at the sink. "Let me give it a try. She might take it from her daddy."

Carolyn gave him a doubtful glance, but shrugged. "Worth a try. She's being stubborn with me today, aren't you, darling girl?" she cooed at Rachel as she handed her over.

Ben cradled the baby on his shoulder and strolled her around the kitchen. She smelled so good, all baby powder and lotions. He loved the brush of her hair against his cheek. It felt like feathers. Carolyn must have just given her a bath.

"I'm going to distract her a little, get her mind off it. Maybe she just has to burp," he said, patting her back.

"Possibly. Though she didn't seem to eat enough for that to be a problem." Carolyn closed her eyes and rubbed the middle of her forehead in small circles.

Ben already knew what that gesture meant. "Headache?"

Carolyn just nodded.

"I'm sorry, dear. Did you take anything for it?"

"I ran out of my medication. I had to call the doctor's office for a new prescription. You can't pick it up until tomorrow."

She had always been prone to migraines, but ever since Rachel came along, the condition had flared up. Her doctor said it had to do with the hormonal roller-coaster ride her body had been on during and after the pregnancy. The lack of sleep and stresses of mothering an infant all contributed to the problem. All Ben knew for sure was that he felt so helpless when the headaches came. He could see they were horribly painful, though Carolyn never complained.

"I'll get you some more medicine tomorrow. First thing," he promised. "And I'll stay home and watch Rachel if you're still in pain."

It was inconvenient for Carolyn to be without a car, but they really couldn't afford two cars right now. Ben was going to work on that, find her a good used car she could use around town. Feeling stranded with a small baby all day was probably adding to her stress.

"Can I get you an ice pack, dear? It helped last time, remember?"

"Maybe later." She opened her eyes and forced a smile. "I feel better just having you here. I'll go to bed early. That usually helps."

"Yes, good idea. Right after dinner."

"I'm sorry, Ben . . . I never got around to cooking dinner. There's a chicken in the fridge. But I lost track of time and it got too late to make it."

"Don't worry about it. I can fix something for us." Scrambled eggs, canned soup and the occasional grilled cheese sandwich were the extent of his kitchen repertoire but were good enough in a pinch. "I had a big lunch. I'm not very hungry." He shrugged, still strolling with Rachel and patting her back.

"I'm not hungry either. But you're just saying that to be nice." Carolyn smiled at him.

Ben laughed. "Ministers don't lie, dear. Even to spare their wife's feelings," he promised her.

Carolyn seemed about to debate that statement when suddenly Rachel let out a loud, deep burp. They both stopped and stared at her— then started laughing.

"See, I was right. She needed to clear her pipes."

"Beginner's luck." Carolyn eyed him. "Give her here." She held out her arms. "I'll work on the bottle again if you're going to cook."

"Good plan." Ben handed back the baby and put an apron on over his shirt and suit pants.

A short time later, he was serving Carolyn scrambled eggs with cheese, toast, and a green salad on the side. Rachel had eaten her fill and dozed in a baby seat at the end of the table.

Ben had dimmed the lights so the baby would sleep more soundly. It was better for Carolyn's headache to have less light, too. The truth was, when the little imp wanted to sleep, you could run a vacuum cleaner right next to her crib. And when she didn't, the silence of a soundproof room wouldn't help.

"She looks like an angel now, doesn't she?" Carolyn didn't wait for him to answer, gazing at Rachel with pure love and devotion. "I should bring her up to her crib," she added in a hushed tone. "But I know if I pick her up, she'll start wailing."

"She's fine. Let her stay here with us. I don't get to see her all day." He gazed fondly at his sleeping little girl.

"True, but . . . you do get to see her in her best light. I'll tell you that," Carolyn said with a laugh.

Ben nodded and took a bite of toast. "Yes, I know. And I know I haven't been much help since we moved here. After the holidays, I'll have a lot more free time. I'll start fixing this place up, helping you more with Rachel."

Carolyn put her hand on Ben's. "I know you're busy. You just started a new job, and it's not like an office job, either. I understand, Ben. I really do," she promised him. "I was talking to my folks today, and they'd like to come up earlier for their visit—to spend more time with the baby and help me."

Ben was chewing a bite of food and forced a smile. "How nice of them to offer . . . What did you say?"

"I said I'd love that, but I wanted to ask you if it was okay. They want to fly up. They can get here on Saturday. And they would stay about three weeks, through Christmas."

When Ben didn't answer right away, she added, "That's too long, right? It's a small house. We'll get on each other's nerves. I know how you like your privacy and quiet."

All true. But Ben quickly brushed his concerns aside. He could tell Carolyn yearned to see her parents; her mother especially. Sometimes he did feel guilty about the way he had uprooted this delicate Southern flower and transplanted her to rocky New England soil.

"Of course it's fine. You want them to come. I can tell by your voice," he teased her. "You hardly ever see them. And they've only seen Rachel once since she was born. I think they should come and stay as long as they like," he said quickly, hoping to please her. "You need some help, dear. Your mother will take good care of the baby and make sure you get more rest, too."

"I know she will. She'll just love taking over." Carolyn was joking, but it wasn't that far from the truth. Her mother had a very strong personality. So did her father, for that matter. "You know how disappointed my folks were to be so far away from their first grandchild," she added.

"Oh yes, they remind me of that every time we meet. They would have been perfectly happy if you had married that fellow who lived down the street . . . what was his name again? The accountant . . . Millard Fillmore?"

He was teasing her. He knew that was a president. Though the guy did turn out to be some kind of success story in Carolyn's hometown, Shadygrove, North Carolina.

Carolyn gave him a look. "Willard," she corrected him. "Willard

Fallen. And he's a tax attorney. A very successful one." Her accent always got thicker when she talked about her hometown, Ben had noticed. But he did love her voice—one of the many reasons he found her so enchanting.

"Your parents thought he would be a much better husband for you than me. They still do," he said bluntly.

"Oh, Ben . . . let's not go through that again. If I had wanted to marry Willard Fallen, I would have," she said with a nonchalant shrug. She reached over and took his hand. "I wanted to marry you."

He smiled and lifted her hand to his lips. "Lucky me." He sat back and sighed. "I could never be worthy of you, sweetheart. But I try."

Carolyn laughed at his romantic declaration, but Ben knew it was true. He smiled and picked up their empty dishes. "I'll empty out that spare room next to Rachel's nursery for your folks, maybe slap on a coat of paint," he said, thinking out loud.

"Oh, you don't have time to paint, Ben. Besides, you don't have to go to all that trouble for them. They know we just moved in. They'll just have to rough it along with us."

Oh yes I do, Ben wanted to answer. Not that painting one room would help all that much. The parsonage was a pretty house with lots of possibilities, but it had been left to wear down and needed repairs. He knew Carolyn's parents would notice every flaw and inconvenience—and comment on them. But what could he do? They hadn't lived here long enough to do anything but the basics. Home repair had been especially hard with a new baby.

Carolyn took a few more dishes to the sink and put on some water for tea. "So, how was your day? Were you busy?"

"I had a meeting or two, one of them about the Christmas Fair. It's coming along. Sophie Potter's in charge. She's very organized. But something happened before the meeting even started that was . . . disturbing," he confided.

"Really? What was that?" Carolyn sat back at the table and handed him a mug.

"The meeting was in Fellowship Hall. I stopped in the kitchen for some coffee, and I could hear everyone talking. I didn't mean to eavesdrop, but it was clear that they were talking about Oliver Warwick. The latest news on his legal troubles appeared in the papers today, stirring everything up all over again."

"This isn't likely to die down anytime soon," Carolyn observed.

"I know. But that's no excuse for the gossip and the groundless speculation and . . . outright slander. With absolutely no evidence. Well, just what the newspapers say," he conceded. "I was very upset. I knew I had to stop them but . . . it was hard to do," he admitted. "I'm new here. I don't want the congregants to see me on some bully pulpit and dislike me."

It was a secret fear, coming from a small side of his character he didn't like to admit or give much credence to. But he couldn't deny it. Not to his wife whom he trusted with his life and who he knew never judged him.

"Of course you don't," Carolyn said, looking concerned. "But what did you do? What did you say to them?"

"I told them gossip had no place in our church. Then I quoted Scripture, from the Book of John: 'By this everyone will know that you are my disciples, if you have love for one another.'"

Rachel stirred in her seat and Carolyn reached over to rock her with one hand. "Yes, very true. I don't understand some people. How can you come to church every Sunday, then go out in the world and ignore all those promises you made to God? It just doesn't make sense to me."

"Exactly, dear. But we're not here to judge those congregants either. I'm just afraid I didn't really reach them. All they learned was not to talk about the Warwicks in front of me."

"I see." Carolyn nodded sympathetically.

Rachel's fussing got louder, and she suddenly let loose an ear-piercing wail. Carolyn took a breath, looking almost as distressed as the baby.

"There she blows," Ben joked, trying to get Carolyn to smile.

She did smile a little. "She just needs to be changed," she said wearily.

"Don't worry. I'll get her." He scooped up the baby and cradled her against his shoulder again. "It's my turn tonight, I already told you. You should get to bed. These headaches take a lot out of you."

"I guess I could. If you think you can handle her."

"Of course I can handle this little dumpling. We'll all go up together. I'll do the diaper, and then Rachel and I will tuck you in," he teased his wife.

Carolyn laughed as she led the way. "That will be a switch."

Ben wished he and Carolyn could talk more about the situation he faced at church. She always had good advice for him, even when she gently pointed out that he was wrong. But she was so tired, along with that headache. He didn't want to burden her.

After changing and washing the baby from head to toe—her pajamas had gotten soaked through—he carefully carried her into the bedroom he shared with Carolyn. The small lamp by the bedside was on, but Carolyn was fast asleep. He shut out the light and pulled the blanket to her chin, the way she liked it, then tiptoed out with Rachel again.

Down in the living room, he sat in his favorite armchair, his daughter on his lap. "You wore your poor mommy out today, didn't you?"

Rachel gurgled, looking very pleased with herself.

"Let's watch some TV. That might make you drowsy again. It's been a hard day for everyone. A good night's sleep will make everything look better in the morning."

Rachel stared at him and blinked, seeming to agree. Ben turned on the television and balanced her on his lap, not really noticing the flashing images on the screen. The cares of the day seemed to slip away as he observed his darling daughter, and he knew no matter what, he was truly blessed—by his beautiful wife and daughter and all the love in his life. Every day brought new challenges. But he had been blessed with a loving home where he could rest and renew himself. That was saying a lot.

"How's the headache?" Ben asked Carolyn when he came down to the kitchen the next morning. She sat at the table in her bathrobe, Rachel tucked in the crook of her arm.

"It's all right. It will go away in a while. They always do."

Ben knew it must be painful for her to even admit that she still had it. He could tell from the tight look around her eyes. He poured himself a cup of coffee and added milk and sugar. "I'll stay home and take care of the baby today. You can't take care of her, feeling sick."

"Don't be silly, Ben. There's too much going on at church right now, what with Christmas coming. I'll be all right." Carolyn sat Rachel up on her lap and waved her favorite toy, a floppy cloth rabbit.

Ben sighed. He felt torn. "Just for the morning. Maybe the headache will go away if you rest some more."

"Too much sleep isn't good, either," she replied. "I guess it would help if you could pick up my medication. Maybe during your lunch break or on your way home tonight? The drugstore here in town doesn't have it. You have to go all the way to Newburyport. Dr. Elliot said he would call in the prescription this morning."

"Then I'll go to Newburyport right now and bring it back to you," Ben said gallantly. "I can get to church a little later today."

"If you really want to. No need to rush back. Lunchtime would be okay, honestly." Carolyn had followed him to the front door, and he kissed her quickly on the cheek as he pulled on his coat and muffler.

He was happy to run this small errand for her. Grateful to find something he could do to help her feel better.

It was a quick drive to Newburyport at that time of the day. He picked up the pills at Eaton's Drugstore, at the corner of State and Pleasant streets. The only parking space he could find on busy State Street was in front of Fowles Diner and News, a large store that was split down the middle, with a long counter serving breakfast and lunch on one side, and every type of magazine and newspaper imaginable on the other. Ben decided he could use another cup of coffee before heading back to church and went inside. He always loved coming into Fowles. The interior was just as old-fashioned and classic as the sign out front, which dated back to the 1950s, or even earlier. Wooden floors creaked under his steps, and a tin ceiling echoed the clatter of dishware and voices. The buttery scent of eggs and toast rose from behind a white counter and a row of chrome-trimmed swivel seats, the tantalizing odor perfuming the air.

He was heading over to the counter to order some coffee to go when he noticed a familiar figure seated at the far end. Ben thought he had to be imagining things. But no, he wasn't.

It *was* Oliver Warwick.

CHAPTER SIX

OLIVER SAT WITH HIS COLLAR TURNED UP AND THE BRIM OF HIS hat turned down. The rest of his face was obscured by an open newspaper. His brow was furrowed with deep thought—or maybe just with the effort of avoiding eye contact with all who passed by.

Ben walked down to the end of the counter and stood near him. "Oliver?"

Oliver looked up, his eyes startled. Ben thought for a moment he might jump up and run out of the store. Then he took a breath and relaxed.

"Reverend . . . I thought for a moment you were another reporter. They've been tracking me like bloodhounds."

"I'm sure they have," Ben said sympathetically. "Mind if I sit down? I could use a cup of coffee."

"Please do. I'm just killing some time, a little early for an appointment with my attorney. His office is down the street."

Oliver looked tired, as if all the coffee in the world could not erase the dark shadows under his eyes and deep lines around his mouth. In the dimly lit corner, he looked much older than he had even a week before, Ben thought. His trademark charming and ironic smile was nowhere to be seen, replaced by an anxious, even frightened, expression.

A waitress passed and filled Ben's cup. "I tried Lilac Hall a few times. I know it must be impossible to keep up with all the calls. I just wanted you and Lillian to know I've been thinking of you and your family. You've been in my prayers. Everyone's prayers," he added.

Oliver's smile flickered. "Thank you, Reverend. Though I doubt *everyone* has been praying for me, I appreciate the overstatement. I know it's well intended."

That was true on both counts. Ben knew he had been exaggerating. He might wish it were everyone, but it was clearly not. Still, he wanted so much to give comfort and encouragement.

"There are many people in town who support you," he insisted. "Who believe you are innocent. And that will be proven in court."

"I hope so, Reverend. The DA is ready to lock me up and throw away the key. This is all a huge misunderstanding. They say I mishandled funds, but . . . whatever I did, I did it to save the company, to save all the jobs," Oliver insisted quietly. "It was *never* for my own benefit. I was pouring in my own capital for years to keep people working and to keep those factories going. Don't I get any credit for that?"

Ben could see that Oliver was exhausted and distraught, practically rambling now. He had been through a lot these past days, staying overnight in a jail cell and being pummeled by the newspapers.

Still, Ben found some of his disclosures quite unsettling. What did he mean "whatever I did"? It could only mean one thing, Ben reasoned: that Oliver had taken some actions that were not completely on the up-and-up. He had bent the rules. But for good intentions, he believed.

Ben sat a moment, considering this. But he knew what he had to say, moving his mind and heart to a higher place.

He gently touched Oliver's arm. "I understand. You had good intentions. No matter what your transgression, you can get through this with God's help. Tell the truth and ask for God's forgiveness, which He will surely grant to you and grants to you already. The truth is always the easiest path, Oliver, though it doesn't always appear to be."

"God might forgive me, Reverend, but I don't know if the district attorney can." Oliver's eyes looked glassy; his voice was somber. "Even if the court doesn't find me guilty, the newspapers already have. The entire town is against us. They've been waiting for this moment, to see the Warwicks fall. Some people are delighting in this spectacle. If I could sell tickets and popcorn, I'd make a handy profit."

His joke sounded desperate and sad, though Ben knew it was true. But he couldn't be washed away in Oliver's wave of despair. He had to stand firm and throw the man a line, or at least try to.

"The town is not against you, Oliver. You have many loyal friends. People like Ezra Elliot and Otto Bates, Digger Hegman and the Potters. And me," he added. "We aren't judging you. We stand with you solidly. Focus on your friends, our love and loyalty. We're the living, breathing expression of God's love and support."

Oliver nodded, but stared at his empty plate. "Thank you, Reverend. It's easy to forget that. We've practically had to barricade ourselves at Lilac Hall these last few days. A few people have called, but . . . we weren't able to call back. I haven't spoken to anyone but lawyers for days now."

"You feel isolated, abandoned," Ben said, understanding. "But you're not. Believe me." Ben paused, watching Oliver's expression. "I think it would do you all good to come back to church. To light the Advent candles with your family this coming Sunday. Or just attend the service. No pressure," he added. "No matter what's going on in your life, no matter where you are on your spiritual journey, you are always welcome by your church family."

Oliver glanced at him and sighed. "I'd like to come, Reverend. But the truth is, I'm afraid to face everyone. I doubt Lillian will want to do that right now either."

"How is Lillian?"

Oliver sat back and let out a long breath. "Oh, up and down. She took it very hard at first. But she's come around. She's a strong woman. She's the type that gets stronger in hot water. Like a tea bag," he quipped with a small smile.

Ben smiled back. "Please talk to her about it. See what she thinks. I would be happy to visit you at home and talk with you both anytime." He slipped off his seat, took his coffee, and left some bills on the counter. "I have to go. But I'm glad I ran into you."

"I am, too, Reverend. I appreciate . . . well, what you said."

Ben just nodded and touched Oliver's arm again. As he turned and left, Oliver glanced at his watch, then hid behind his newspaper once more.

It had been hard to see the man so reduced in spirit, so shaken. Ben's heart went out to him. Although a few things Oliver had said made Ben wonder now if he was indeed entirely innocent. It was so difficult to sort out the truth. Even an individual directly involved could not always get a firm grip on it, their reports colored by their own perceptions and considerations. Sometimes, even a court of law could not establish the facts. Only God knew the real truth.

That was another reason why the ultimate judgment of men like Oliver was not for other men and women, but only for God, Ben reminded himself.

THE MUSIC DIRECTOR, QUENTIN DIGBY, SOUNDED THE OPENING chords of the first hymn on the organ, and Ben followed the robed choir members into the sanctuary at a stately pace. "There's a Voice in the Wilderness Crying" was a favorite of the Advent season. The service for this second Sunday of Advent had been carefully planned, the one exception being a commitment from the Warwicks to light the candles. Oliver's driver had picked up the liturgy and instructions on Friday, but Ben knew that was still no guarantee.

As Ben sang along with the choir, he scanned the rows of pews. He saw Carolyn sitting to the right of the pulpit, just behind his seat, with Rachel in her arms. He would see how long that would last. Louisa and Charles LaFonte, his wife's parents, sat right beside her. They had arrived last night at Logan Airport, their presence so far adding to the general mayhem in the household on Sunday morning, as he tried to get to church before eight and be prepared to run the service.

Carolyn beamed with pride as he caught her eye. His in-laws looked interested, but far less than impressed. Especially his father-in-law, who sat back with his arms crossed over his chest in his typical "been there done that" attitude. Ben was not surprised. Still, he was sure they would appreciate the service on some level. They were both people of great faith. Though they didn't have great faith in him as the best choice as their daughter's husband. Not yet, anyway.

He was really looking for the Warwicks. He checked their usual spot: front and center in a row close to the altar. Those seats were filled by the Tulleys today.

He felt deflated, but at least this week he had a fallback plan. The bulletin said ADVENT CANDLE LIGHTING, but a family name had been left off. He had discreetly arranged with Gus Potter to step in with his family if the Warwicks failed to come or simply didn't want to take part.

As the choir filed off to the left and took their places on the risers, Ben looked up at the altar, expecting to see the Potters. There was no one there. He took a breath, glad he was still facing the back of the sanctuary and the congregation didn't see his exasperated expression. He couldn't imagine that Gus and Sophie had forgotten. Were they running late? That wasn't like them, either.

Carrying out a service was like a theatrical performance, Ben often reflected. The stage must be set exactly right, the actors must come in and out on cue and, above all, remain deadpan, no matter the glitches or surprises.

What now? He glanced quickly to the back of the sanctuary, where Gus Potter usually stood at his station by the big doors. Gus wasn't there, and neither were any of the other deacons.

Ben's gaze swept over the rows of expectant faces, looking once more for the Potters. Instead, he saw the Warwicks. They were, against all expectation, walking up the side aisle, ushered along by Gus.

Lillian led the family, her gaze fixed forward, her hair swept up in her trademark sophisticated style, her chin tilted at its usual imperious angle. If she felt any effects of her husband's crisis, or any self-consciousness about the storm of gossip, her expression and demeanor revealed none of that.

She hadn't time—or perhaps, the inclination—to remove her long fur coat. It swung open as she walked, revealing a gray suit and cream-colored satin blouse, tied at the neck with a looping bow, and over that, a double strand of pearls. All in all, she looked her usual grand self. As if nothing in her world had changed. Because she willed it so.

She held her youngest daughter, Jessica's, hand with a firm grip as they approached the altar. The little girl, who was about eight, wore a bright red wool coat with black tights and patent-leather shoes. Her brown hair was fixed in a long, tight braid, with small curls springing out around her sweet face.

Emily, their older daughter, walked alongside her father. Holding his arm, Ben noticed. Her entire energy seemed focused on him, supporting him somehow. Dressed in a brown tweed suit that might have been borrowed from her mother's closet, she looked much older than her years—she was a mere high school junior. But Emily was a levelheaded, mature girl, Ben knew. At the top of her class, too. She had plans to attend an Ivy League college. What would happen now? Ben wondered. Would her father's troubles derail her future, too?

Oliver looked somewhat better than he had the other morning at

Fowles, partly due to his daughter's support and partly to his fine suit: navy blue wool with thin pinstripes, a formfitting vest, a high, starched white collar, and a burgundy silk tie. It was a suit he might wear to lead a board meeting—or to appear in court, Ben thought.

Lillian lit the candle and was the first to speak, her voice clear and strong. "O God, we light the second candle of Advent."

She glanced at her husband, who spoke with his eyes downcast. "We seek your comfort. Both mighty and tender, You come. Prepare our hearts to be transformed by You." Oliver's voice had been much softer than his wife's, but the timbre of his tone touched Ben's heart, as if he was praying in his most private moment.

The girls read the next section, Emily leading Jessica through the verses.

Then it was time for the congregation to pray along with the readers. But Ben noticed that many members sat stone-faced, staring straight ahead or down at their programs, their lips motionless as the group prayer was read, as if boycotting the Warwicks' right—or spiritual fitness?—to lead this prayer.

Ben felt puzzled . . . then upset . . . and found his own voice growing louder as the verses concluded. "Saving God, look upon Your world and *heal* Your land and *Your people.* Prepare us to be *changed.* This Advent, *teach* us to be *tender* and *just,* as You are," he said emphatically. He stood silently for a moment, gazing out the congregation. "Amen," he added loudly, though he still did not hear a strong response.

The Warwick family made their way down the side aisle, and Ben saw Gus touch Oliver's arm in encouragement as he found them seats next to the Hegmans and Dr. Elliot.

Ben noticed how many faces turned away as Oliver tried to nod a few greetings. These were people whom Oliver and Lillian socialized with regularly, and even some of the employees at his factories. They had all treated Oliver with warmth and respect just days ago, it seemed.

Now many wore disdainful or distressed expressions, and others bent their heads together, whispering as the family passed. Ben felt disappointed and unnerved. He had expected better of this congregation. A chill seeped into his heart as he forced himself to concentrate on the service.

The second candle of Advent was lit for hope, and Ben had based his sermon on that theme. The hope of Christ coming into the world, he explained. The eager anticipation of God's greatest gift to man.

"But for Christians, hope has a special meaning. It is not mere wishing or daydreaming. Or even an optimistic attitude," he tried to explain. "Our hope is solidly grounded in our faith in God. In our certainty of His love for us and our certainty that His promises will be fulfilled through our faithful prayers. 'Ask and it shall be given; seek and ye shall find; knock and it shall be opened unto you,'" he reminded them. "Our hope is backed by faith that nothing is impossible for Him. No matter how dark or difficult our lives might appear at any given moment, there is always a light—His son, the Light of the World, who is always there to show us the way."

As the sermon ended and the choir began to sing, Ben wondered if his words had touched the hearts and minds of his congregation—especially the Warwicks, and particularly Oliver. The words could have been written expressly for that single member of this church, and Ben realized, not for the first time, what an amazing coincidence it was that the Warwicks would light the second candle instead of the first and be present for this message. For he had outlined the sermon weeks ago and had no idea at all how relevant it would seem today. Of course, he knew how that had happened. It was just another example of God gently arranging the jigsaw puzzle of our lives.

When the service ended, Ben took his usual place outside the doors of the sanctuary, ready to meet and chat with the congregants. He kept an eye out for the Warwicks. Although they had sat toward the back of the church today, they were slow leaving their pew. He noticed Oliver heading for a side exit and Lillian firmly twining her arm in his, leading him toward the main aisle. Lillian Warwick was not about to sneak out the side door.

She wore a small, stiff smile and nodded graciously to people who greeted them—and many who did not. There were a few who paused to say a kind word, Ben was heartened to see. He guessed others felt sympathy, but were too self-conscious to reach out. It happened that way sometimes. A person's pain and suffering makes many people feel embarrassed.

Sophie Potter was not one of those. Though she and Lillian didn't share a close relationship, Sophie was now walking alongside Lillian as if they were dearest friends. The women were completely opposite in appearance, Lillian looking even taller and more elegant flanked by the plump, red-cheeked country woman. But Sophie was undaunted, chatting away about the Christmas Fair or some other charity project, Ben guessed. Did the subject matter? Her stout, strong presence and cheerful attitude stood like a bulwark between the Warwicks and the waves of disdain projected by so many others.

Oliver walked with Digger Hegman. They were genuinely friends, though Ben could not imagine a more unlikely pair there, either, than the dashing captain of industry and the scraggly, eccentric clammer who often believed the shellfish were speaking to him.

Ben lost sight of the Warwicks for a few minutes as he conversed with those near to him. Suddenly, he heard a grunt and quick footsteps. He saw Oliver stumble and nearly lose his balance while another man— Ben never saw his face—walked past at a quick clip.

"Excuse me," Oliver mumbled, even though he was clearly the injured party.

The other man mumbled under his breath. Ben couldn't quite make out the words, but they were something vile, like "Dirty liar."

Ben wasn't sure if Oliver heard. He hoped not. Oliver didn't stand up immediately. He stood hunched over a moment, as if the wind had been knocked out of him. Lillian put her arm around his shoulders. "Oliver, are you all right?" Her voice was warm with concern. In fact, Ben had never heard her speak so kindly to anyone, even her daughters.

Digger was alarmed. He stared after the man who had bumped his friend. "I'll be . . . Did you see that?" he asked his wife, Ruth. "Fellow didn't even stop or say 'I'm sorry.'"

The man had not been sorry. The slam looked intentional to Ben. It made him so angry, he wanted to go after the hit-and-run walker himself. But he calmed himself and held his ground, knowing it would do no good to make a scene.

Oliver had straightened to his full height again, his expression sad and exposed. Lillian quickly took his arm. "Are you okay, dear?" she asked quietly. Oliver just nodded.

"What a silly thing . . . people rush so much," she said in a louder, theatrical tone. "Can't they see this is a church, not an athletic track? For goodness' sake." She laughed lightly, looking at Oliver again, encouraging him to share the joke.

Ben could see her sympathy and protectiveness—and her strength. Lillian Warwick was determined to show a brave face for both of them. Oliver forced a smile. "I'm fine. Nothing to fuss about," he said finally. He turned to Ben and extended his hand. "Fine sermon, Reverend."

"Thank you, Oliver. And thank you for lighting the candles today. You all did a wonderful job," Ben praised them.

"It was our pleasure," Oliver replied politely.

"An honor," Lillian added in a gracious tone.

"If you'll excuse me, I'd like to have a word with Dr. Elliot before he leaves." Oliver slipped away, and Ben was left with Lillian.

Ben wondered if Oliver was really going to seek out his friend, or simply slip out to his car, as he had originally planned.

"It was a good sermon, Reverend. An important message, well said," Lillian said, paying him a rare compliment. "We do have hope. Real hope," she insisted with a smile. A determined, teeth-gritting smile, Ben had to call it. "We will come through this . . . test. No life is without problems and setbacks. Oliver will be proven innocent. Then we'll see who stood by us . . . and who didn't."

She sounded as if she were making a list. Ben didn't doubt that she might.

He hoped with all his heart Oliver was proven innocent, though it seemed that so much damage had already been done. Could it ever be the same for him and his family?

"Many friends are standing by your husband and will continue to."

"And just as many are not." Her tone was quiet but sharp-edged.

Before he could answer, Emily walked over, holding Jessica's hand. They had obviously been to the coffee hour already—Jessica was eating a cookie.

"Daddy's waiting in the car. He asked me to find you."

"Here I am. Mystery solved." Lillian shrugged and pulled on a soft leather glove. "Good day, Reverend," she said curtly before sweeping off with her children.

Ben watched them go, wondering if he had done the right thing after all by encouraging the family to come to church, to expose themselves to the harsh feelings and derision they had found here. Ben's heart felt heavy. It didn't seem right that such a long-standing member and supporter of the church, now burdened with troubles, could not find some compassion in this place. Some refuge. No matter what his transgressions had been. Wasn't that what a church community was all about?

Was he just a naive idealist to think it should be different? To think any church that he led would be different? Ben felt the blame for this lapse of charity fall squarely on his shoulders. He did believe his church members could do better . . . but first he had to do a better job of leading them.

CHAPTER SEVEN

Present day, December 13

HE GYM WAS SO CROWDED, RACHEL WORRIED WHETHER her parents would even find seats. She had dropped Nora off with them earlier, since the team had to arrive an hour before the game for their warm-up. It was their first match of the season, and the boys were so pumped with excitement, they were practically unbearable. If they could put all this energy to good use on the court, they would be invincible.

It was her job to take attendance, and a few boys were late. She already knew that their tardy arrival would cut into their time on the court. Ryan had some strict rules.

Will was on the court practicing layups. He was already red-faced but was moving with an easy gait. He wasn't a starter; that was an older boy. Right now Will was a second-string shooting guard. Rachel was grateful for that. As long as Will got some time on the court . . . but wasn't out there endlessly, exhausting himself.

She saw her parents wandering in on the other side of the gym. They found seats not too far up the risers and waved to her. Nora looked as if she wanted to run down and say hello, but Rachel's mother held her back.

The referees, in their striped shirts and black pants, talked together in the middle of the court, then told the coaches to call their teams in. Ryan handed Rachel a stopwatch. "It would help if you could keep an eye on the time-outs and periods, even though we have the clock."

"Right." Rachel nodded. She could imagine that in the excitement of the game, it would be easy to lose track of the number of time-outs taken by each team.

The boys sat on the bench, and Ryan crouched down to talk to them. "You look great out there. Remember what Jason and I have been telling you in practice. Play your position. Look for an open man. Really look. Don't try to do it all by yourself." He looked directly at one boy who had impressive skills driving the ball down the court but tended to hog the ball.

He gave a few more tips and called out the roster. The starters ran out happily to their positions. The other ten boys were left on the bench, watching intently, waiting for their turns to play.

Both teams scored quickly. It was clear they were evenly matched. Ryan made a few changes on the court at the time-outs, but Will was not called off the bench. Rachel could tell he wanted to be out there, and that it was hard for him to just sit and watch.

Rachel caught his eye and smiled. But Will sat looking straight ahead, wearing a serious expression, watching his teammates.

The buzzer for halftime sounded. The boys on the court returned to the bench. They were sweating buckets and looked exhausted. "Drink some water, everybody," Rachel reminded them as she and Jason handed out water bottles.

"Everyone have a drink and relax," Ryan added. "You're playing awesome out there. This is a top-tier team and you're playing right up to their level, guys. I just want to talk to you a little about strategy, so gather round." Ryan had his clipboard and a marker in hand, ready to review plays.

Rachel's parents had wandered down from their perch and walked over to the team. "Great game," her father said. "Very exciting."

"Will's team is very good. I have a feeling they're going to win," her mother added.

"Isn't Will going to play?" Nora asked innocently. She gazed over at her brother, who was still in the team huddle.

"He might go in during this half," Rachel said. "The coach has to call him. It's not like baseball where everyone gets a turn at bat." Nora had heard this before but could never quite remember how it worked. On her soccer team, everyone got to play, and they all tried different positions. It was more about learning than competing. *As it should be at that age,* Rachel thought.

Ryan walked over and asked Rachel for the stopwatch. Her mother smiled at him—one of her Southern belle smiles, Rachel noticed.

"Is this Will's coach, Rachel? Please introduce us," Carolyn urged in her gracious way.

"Yes . . . of course. Ryan, these are my folks—Ben and Carolyn Lewis."

Ryan smiled and shook Ben's hand. Carolyn offered her hand as well, and Rachel was almost positive she saw her mother search for a wedding ring on Ryan's hand—and then look very pleased when she didn't find one.

"I understand from Will that you're a minister," Ryan said to her father.

"Yes, that's right." Her father smiled and nodded.

"Maybe you could put in a word for the Falcons? I think we can win this if a few foul shots go our way."

Ben laughed. "I'll see what I can do."

Another buzzer sounded, signaling halftime was over.

Her mother took Nora's hand. "We're headed to the snack stand. Ben, you'd better guard our seats," her mother said. "Nice to meet you, Ryan."

"My pleasure. Hope to see you again soon," Ryan said politely.

"Oh, you'll be seeing plenty of us. We rarely miss a game." Carolyn led Nora away, but not without smiling and nodding at Rachel, sending a silent "he's very attractive . . . and has nice manners" sort of look.

Rachel pretended not to notice.

The second half of the game was even more intense than the first. Both teams were tired, and there were many sloppy passes and even a few turnovers. Rachel could see Ryan holding on to his patience to stifle a harsh reaction when one of the Falcons was stripped of the ball and the other team quickly scored.

But the plays came so fast, the Falcons quickly recovered and managed to score as well, chasing their rivals by only a few points. A few minutes into the third period, one of the guards on their team, a boy named Damion, stumbled and fell, then rolled into a tight ball, grunting with pain and holding his leg.

The refs blew their whistles as Rachel and Ryan ran out to him. Rachel gently turned him over. "What hurts, Damion? Did you twist your knee or your ankle?"

He shook his head, but could barely speak. "It's a cramp. In my calf. Really bad."

"Let's get him over to the bench," Ryan said. "Can you help me?"

"In a moment. Let me check his leg first." *I am a physical therapist,* she wanted to remind him, but her quelling look sufficed.

Rachel had the boy lie on his side, then gently massaged the muscle to relieve the knotted spasm. She could feel his leg relax under her touch and saw him suddenly take a deep breath of relief. "A little better?" she asked.

He nodded. "A lot."

She glanced at Ryan. "Let's get him up. But he still shouldn't put any weight on it. I'll set him up with some ice."

As Rachel set Damion up on a thin blanket on the gym floor with an icepack, she heard Ryan call Will in to play.

"You're on, pal. Remember what we talked about in practice."

Rachel turned and watched Will run onto the court. She didn't even get a chance to wish him luck. That would have embarrassed him anyway. She had been so focused on Damion, she had forgotten Will would be called to replace him.

Will played hard, hitting a few outside shots, blocking a pass, then racing back down to the Falcons' basket to shoot again. Rachel watched him carefully. As the minutes ticked by and the third period melted into the last, Will was starting to look more and more winded each time he came down the court. He was definitely tiring, his shots going wide of the basket. Rachel worried but didn't want to say anything.

She was just about to quietly point out to Ryan that maybe Will should be called back to the bench when a time-out was called by the other team. Ryan signaled to Will to come off the court and sent Noah, one of the starters, out.

Rachel met Will and stood by him as he sat down. "Are you all right? You don't look well."

Will started to answer her but could hardly speak because he was so short of breath. She heard him wheeze as he tried to catch his breath, and she ran to her bag to find the inhaler. "Here, take this." She sat next to him and put the inhaler in his face.

He shook his head but didn't answer. She could see he was embarrassed. Meanwhile, he was suffocating himself. "Will . . . for heaven's sake, just use the inhaler."

He shook his head, staring at the gym floor. She saw his bony back rise and fall, and heard him gasp. When he still didn't respond, she took his arm and pulled him up. "Come with me . . . we'll do it in the locker room."

"Mom . . ." he croaked. He glowered at her but was too short of breath to argue.

In the corridor, just inside the tunnel to the locker rooms, Will finally took the inhaler and sucked in a dose of medicine. Rachel stood staring at him, feeling angry and frustrated.

She was about to scold him when Ryan appeared. "What's going on? Is Will all right?"

"He just had an asthma attack . . . and he wouldn't take his inhaler. Too sissy for him or something."

"I'm sorry." Ryan looked surprised and concerned. "I didn't realize he was that tired . . ."

"I'm not tired," Will insisted. "I'm fine, I can still play—"

"You played him much too long," Rachel said angrily. "I thought we spoke about this. I thought you would remember . . . I don't know . . . I'm not sure this is going to work out . . ."

"What are you saying?" Ryan stared at her in disbelief. "You're taking him off the team?"

"Mom!" Will pleaded, his throat hoarse. "I just needed the stupid inhaler for a minute . . . I'm like totally and completely fine. Okay?"

Rachel threw her hands up. "Now he talks. Two seconds ago, I was about to call an ambulance."

"Come on, Mom. It's no big deal, okay?" Will looked at Ryan with a sorry expression, as if he was afraid he would never get played again. Rachel suddenly felt bad for losing her temper and being so over the top.

Ryan rubbed Will's shoulder. "No worries, pal. You did great. You were a real stopper. Let's get back and see what's going on. Maybe we're winning . . ."

Ryan led Will back to the court and glanced over his shoulder at Rachel. She still felt upset. She needed time to cool off. She went to the restroom and splashed her face with water.

She was just patting her hands with a towel when she heard a roar from the stands. Then the buzzer sounded. She had missed the last minutes of the game.

She returned to the gym sheepishly and glanced at the scoreboard.

The Falcons had lost by two measly points! *A bad break,* she thought. But they had played their hearts out and done themselves proud.

As the boys staggered back to the bench, heads hanging low, Ryan and Jason applauded them. "Great job, guys! You were awesome! That team is way higher ranked than we are and you nearly beat them."

Rachel applauded, too, walking toward the team. "Great job, guys," she called out.

Ryan looked up at her. He met her gaze and held it. She expected him to be angry, or at least offended, at the way she had spoken to him. Rachel secretly winced. She had sort of freaked out, hadn't she? But his look was soft and caring, as if he only wondered now how she was feeling. That made her feel much better—and even share a smile with him.

RACHEL MET HER PARENTS IN THE PARKING LOT WITH NORA. HER father grabbed her heavy tote bags filled with team gear, and they walked toward her SUV together.

Will was walking just behind her with Andy and Ryan, still pumped up from the game. They were reenacting some "awesome moves" players had made and their own glorious—or not so glorious—moments.

"A tough loss, but Will's team played very well," her father said. "Tell Will we thought he was wonderful."

"We so enjoyed watching him. When's the next game?" her mother added.

"Next Saturday. In Andover. It's a long ride; you really don't have to come," Rachel replied.

Her mother smiled and kissed her cheek. "I guess we'll decide next week. We can still take Nora, either way. I know she loves watching her brother play. But she likes making Christmas cookies, too."

"I'd rather go to Grandma's and bake cookies," Nora said definitively.

"I'm sure you would." Rachel laughed. "We'll see."

Nora pouted. "You *always* say that . . ."

Her parents laughed and kissed Nora good-bye, then set off to find their own car. Nora was easily distracted by her brother's approach. "Hey, Will, you played really good," she praised him. "Grandpa was yelling his head off. Did you hear him?"

Will laughed. "Thanks . . . Here's a pass. Think fast." He softly tossed his ball to her. It bounced once between them and she caught it with two hands in a little-girl style that made Rachel smile.

"Good catch, Nora," Rachel heard Ryan say. He and Andy had caught up to them, and Rachel turned to look at him.

Ryan met her gaze, smiling warmly. Rachel felt flustered. She felt like a frazzled mess and just wanted to get home . . . and back to her real life. She didn't like all this excitement. The basketball game suddenly seemed the least of it.

"Hey, Mom, can Andy come over tonight? We just want to hang out," Will said.

Rachel never liked it when her children asked for playdates right in front of the friend in question. She always felt put on the spot. And her fallback—"We'll see"—wouldn't quite cut it right now either, she realized.

Before she could reply, Ryan spoke up, looking over at his son. "We have our tree to decorate tonight, Andy. I guess you forgot."

"Can't Will help us?" Andy asked his father.

Will liked that idea. "Can I, Mom?" he asked before Ryan could answer. "Andy has a Wii," he added.

"He does?" Now Nora was sounding interested.

Ryan looked at Rachel. "Why don't you all come? I'll fix some dinner. I think that extremely close, definite-almost win over the Salem Whalers deserves some sort of celebration."

Rachel felt cornered by the four sets of eyes pinned on her. Even Nora seemed in favor of the invitation. "All right," she said finally. "I can bring something. Salad? Juice?" she offered.

"I've got it covered; no worries."

Rachel had a feeling the menu would be pizza. But it was nice of Ryan to invite them, since Andy had more or less painted him into a corner. Will and Andy had already been friendly in school, but the team was quickly cementing their bond. She could see that it was good for Will to have a pal on the squad, since most of the other boys were older.

"Some dessert would make you very popular, though," Ryan added, eyeing their children. "How does six o'clock sound?"

"Sounds good. We'll be there . . . and thanks for the invitation," she added.

The boys said good-bye again, giving each other high fives. As they drove home, Rachel wasn't so sure about what she had been talked into. But she framed it in her mind as a neighborly thing. She sometimes socialized with the parents of Will or Nora's friends so the kids could get together. Especially when Jack had been alive.

This isn't any different, she told herself. Except that she and Ryan were both single . . . but that didn't mean anything. Or need to lead to anything. She liked him. He was a good person, a good father, and a great coach. But . . . she wasn't ready to start dating. And that was that.

Rachel repeated this promise to herself all the while she hustled the children into their showers, baked a fast pan of brownies, and got ready herself. And again while she changed her sweater three times, and still wasn't satisfied with her choice as they drove over to Ryan's house.

Just before they got out of the car, Nora leaned over from the backseat. "You look pretty, Mom. I like those earrings." She flicked one of Rachel's dangling earrings with her fingertip.

Rachel smiled wistfully. "Thanks, honey."

Oh no . . . was it too much? She considered taking the earrings off, but it seemed too late. The kids were making a beeline up the driveway, and Ryan and Andy were waiting in the open doorway.

Rachel grabbed the brownies and followed. Ryan smiled as she came up the porch steps, looking very happy to see her. And looking very handsome in a denim shirt and jeans, his hair still wet from a shower, emphasizing the strong lines of his face and dark blue eyes.

Rachel smiled back, then looked away. He looked almost too handsome to her at times. It was unnerving. She handed him the foil-covered dish and took off her coat.

"This smells good," he said, eyeing the plate.

"Just brownies . . . and I brought some ice cream," she added handing him a shopping bag. "Something smells *really* good in here."

She was surprised. It smelled like real food, not just pizza or Chinese takeout.

"I made some shish kebab, beef and chicken . . . with rice and a salad. It's the one adult meal Andy will eat," he added with a laugh.

He can cook, too? Rachel couldn't quite believe it.

She followed him back to the kitchen and adjoining family room, a part of the house she had not seen before. The Coopers' Christmas tree was set up in a stand just to the left of a big stone hearth where a fire blazed, bright and warm. The room was decorated much like the living room, where the team meeting had been held, with more Mission-style furnishings and big, soft couches. Bookcases lined one wall, and a big-screen TV was framed by cabinet doors.

Ryan had already strung lights on the tree branches, and open boxes of ornaments were spread out underneath it.

There was a long granite counter in the kitchen that partially separated the two spaces. Rachel saw that everything was already set up for dinner, except for the hot food.

"I thought I'd just put all the food out and we could eat while we decorated. I'm really not up for the challenge of keeping Andy and Will in one place for any length of time—even though they should both be exhausted after the game they played."

Rachel laughed. "Sometimes I think when Will works out like that, it gives him even more energy."

Ryan had walked over to the stove and was checking on something in the oven. He laughed. "True. It's scary. As a former teenage boy, I must admit, I forgot all about that part."

"Can I help you with anything?" she asked.

"You can grab the salad bowl in the fridge. There's some dressing there in a bowl, mustard vinaigrette. And a bottle of Ranch for the kids."

Rachel set to her small task, thinking, *He does have it all covered, doesn't he?*

As Ryan spooned the rice pilaf into a bowl, Rachel watched, falling silent. She suddenly felt she should apologize for the way she had acted at the game. He seemed to have brushed it all aside, but she didn't want Ryan to think she was a person who flew off the handle like that all the time. The truth was, she very rarely did—and now that she had, she felt she owed him an apology.

She walked a few steps closer to the stove. "Can I take that to the counter for you?"

"Sure." He smiled and handed her oven mitts. "You'd better use these. The bowl is hot."

She took the mitts. "Listen . . . I'm sorry about the way I acted at the game, when Will was wheezing and needed his inhaler. I just get very upset when he struggles to breathe. And he was being so stubborn about taking it. It drove me a little crazy. I blamed you, and that wasn't right. I really didn't mean to freak out like that—"

Rachel would have said more, but Ryan stopped her, shaking his head. "Thanks for saying that. But it's all right, honestly. I probably should have been watching him more closely. I definitely will in the future . . . but I'll still let him play," he added quickly. "He's really good. We can use him more."

Rachel was relieved to hear that. She knew Will was worried now that she had brought too much attention to his asthma and Ryan might be afraid to put him on the court.

"He'll be glad to hear that," she confided. "I don't mean to be such a hoverer. But this asthma thing pushes my buttons," she admitted with a sigh.

"Sure it does. There are plenty of worries I have about Andy that push my buttons. We've all been there. I always try to remind myself that our worst scenarios rarely come true." He glanced at her, catching himself. "I'm sorry . . . I guess that's not always true. I mean, it wasn't for you."

She knew he was talking about Jack. She was thinking about that, too. "No, it wasn't," she admitted. "But I know that for the sake of my kids—and myself—I have to stop looking for all the ways life can go wrong. I have so many things to be grateful for still," she said sincerely. "Nora and Will, for starters."

He smiled at her and nodded. "That's very true. It's a good way of looking at things."

"I'll call the kids for the dinner," she said, noticing that Ryan was bringing the last tray of food out of the oven, a platter of delicious-looking shish kebabs, beef and chicken, with grilled vegetables, which he set beside the bowl of rice.

"I think they're up in Andy's room."

Once the kids came down, there was no more heavy talk—only fooling around and reasons to smile as they all enjoyed Ryan's tasty dinner and took turns putting ornaments on the tree.

"Can we go downstairs and play Wii now?" Andy asked his father eagerly.

"Don't you guys want some dessert? Mrs. Anderson made some awesome-looking brownies . . . and there's ice cream."

"My mom makes really good brownies," Will promised, making Rachel smile. She was already in the kitchen taking out the dessert, along with plates and spoons.

"While we're having our brownies, I thought we could all play a game together." Ryan was at the bookcase and took out a big box. "Let's play Clue. What do you think?" he asked Rachel.

"It's been a while. I hope I remember how."

She wasn't big on board games but was impressed by his effort to keep the kids involved in an activity that didn't involve a screen.

"You'll be fine. It's all logic and deduction. And you seem very logical to me." He glanced at her and smiled. She wasn't quite sure that was a compliment, but she smiled back.

"Do we have to, Dad?" Andy gave his father a look.

Will shrugged. "I like Clue. It's okay."

"Good, we'll just play for a while. Then you can all go downstairs and Wii away," Ryan promised.

"I like Clue, too. My friend Emily has it." Nora sat on the couch next to Rachel with her ice-cream-covered brownie.

"Good, you can help me, then." Rachel leaned over and kissed the top of her head.

Ryan handed everyone their question sheets and pencils. "Can I be Mrs. Peacock?" Nora asked him hopefully.

"Absolutely. Will, you can be Professor Plum. I'll be Mr. Green," he said.

"You always pick him," Andy groused. "I'm Colonel Mustard," he said, taking a yellow marker.

Rachel looked at the characters who were left. "Miss Scarlet for me, I guess." Nora gave her a red marker. "I forgot we get cards and characters. I seem to be the only one who hasn't played Clue lately," she joked as Ryan dealt the cards out and Nora carefully placed the tiny weapons in each room of the mansion that was mapped out on the board.

"You have to get out more, Rachel. Have a little fun," Ryan teased. "Or should I call you Miss Scarlet now?" His expression was serious, but his eyes were sparkling.

Rachel didn't answer, just looked down at her cards and wondered what she was supposed to do with them.

"You check what you have off the sheet, Mom. And then you ask people about what's blank," Nora reminded her quietly.

"Oh right . . ." Rachel was remembering now. "It's elementary, my dear Watson," she added in a British accent.

"Easy does it, Mom. I think you had too much sugar." Will gave her a look. She could tell she was embarrassing him. That meant she was having fun, she realized with a grin.

Will won the first round quickly. It was Colonel Mustard in the study with the wrench. They played two more; Nora won one, and Rachel, amazingly, won the last time. "Mrs. White . . . with the dagger, in the kitchen," she announced in a decisive tone.

Ryan looked around the table. "Can anyone prove otherwise?"

When no one spoke up, he handed Rachel the tiny brown envelope and she slipped out the cards—Mrs. White, the dagger, the kitchen. "Yes!" She pumped her fist in victory.

"Good job, Mommy." Nora patted her shoulder. Will just groaned and dropped back against the couch pillows.

"Can we go downstairs now?" Andy asked his father.

Ryan glanced at Rachel, and she nodded. "All right. I guess you put in your time with the old folks."

Rachel laughed.

"Thanks, Dad." Andy was already halfway to the basement door. He glanced at Will, who also jumped off the couch. Nora tugged Rachel's sweater, catching her attention with a pleading look.

"Don't forget Nora," Rachel called after them.

Will looked over at Nora and waved his hand. "You can play. It's okay," he said kindly.

Rachel watched them wistfully, and Ryan caught her glance. "I remember when my little sister and I were growing up," he said. "I wasn't half as nice to her . . . But I'm really nice now," he insisted, making Rachel laugh again.

"Will wasn't always either." She pushed aside the abandoned ice-cream bowls and dessert dishes. "When we lost Jack, it made them closer. He's been a lot more protective of her. And me."

"He's had to grow up quickly, losing his father like that. But he seems remarkably mature and steady. I see a lot of kids," Ryan added. "You've got two really good ones. You've done a great job with them."

"Thanks." *Jack should get equal credit for that,* she wanted to say. But she didn't want to talk about her loss all night either.

"So you have a younger sister. Does she live around here?"

"In Bennington, Vermont. We don't get to see each other all that much, but we talk at least once a week on the phone. My dad passed away a few years ago, and my mom lives near my sister now. Bonnie and her husband have three children—one around Andy's age and two younger. She also works full-time as a nurse. She helped me a lot after my divorce," he added. "Bonnie was really there for me and Andy."

"Did you grow up around here?"

"No, we grew up in Hingham," he said, naming a lovely town on the South Shore of Boston. "But I always liked it around here, especially Cape Light. How about you?"

"Oh, I've always lived here. My folks moved from Gloucester when I was about a month old. My father has been the minister at the old stone church on the green for almost forty years."

She suddenly realized she had almost told Ryan her age. Not that it mattered, but it wasn't information she gave out too easily anymore.

"Almost? So that makes you about . . . thirty-five?" he asked politely.

"I was thirty-six in May," she admitted.

"I'm thirty-nine," he said. "And you look about . . . twenty-eight."

Rachel blushed and shook her head. "How did we get on this topic anyway?"

"You were talking about your father being a minister?"

"Oh right . . . Yes, he is. And I have a younger brother. Mark is the adventurous one in the family. He's traveled enough for all of us. He's married now and lives in Portland, Oregon. I wish he lived closer—to do things with Will. And I just miss him. My father and Will have a great relationship," she added. "My parents have really helped me these last two years."

"I just met them for a minute, but they seem like really nice people," Ryan said.

"Thanks." Rachel had a feeling Carolyn would say the same about him.

The fire had burned down to glowing embers and Ryan put more logs on, making it flare up again. Now that the children had disappeared, Rachel felt self-conscious with him. She was honestly afraid of what more she might say if they sat and talked all night. He had a way of getting her guard down.

Rachel picked up the tiny plastic weapons on the game board and the extra markers the children had left. "Now that I've brushed up, care to play another round, Professor? For the championship?"

She had to laugh at the way his eyes lit up. "Are you actually challenging me? You had some beginner's luck, Miss Scarlet. But that would be like you taking on . . . LeBron James in a one-on-one," he joked, naming one of the NBA's strongest players.

Rachel took the cards and began shuffling. "We'll see . . . Maybe I'm a Clue hustler. You never know," she teased him back.

He laughed, looking pleased by her comeback. "Okay, then. Bring it on."

They played another three-game match. While there was some conversation, Rachel liked the distraction of the board game. It made their time together feel much less like a date, she realized.

Ryan won two out of three . . . but only because she had marked her evidence sheet incorrectly. "Look, right there. I made a mistake. I thought you said you had the card for the gun."

He shrugged. "Turnovers happen. We'll have a rematch sometime."

"Indeed we will. In the meantime, congratulations," she added, not wanting to sound like a spoilsport. She had been surprised to see how competitive he was—and how competitive she could be at times, too. She gathered up some dirty ice-cream dishes and cake plates.

"Just leave that stuff. I'll take care of it later." Ryan followed her into the kitchen with some more glasses and cups.

Rachel picked up a sponge to wipe the countertop. When she turned from the sink, she found him standing very close to her. It suddenly reminded her of the tryouts, when she had run straight into him and smashed her nose in his sweater. He was even wearing the same cologne . . . and she was amazed that she had remembered it.

That moment suddenly seemed so long ago. Could she have possibly gotten to know him that well so quickly? They had spent a lot of time together the last week or so, sometimes in intense situations.

But you really don't know him, a voice inside her said. *Don't get too close . . . and don't look up at him.*

Rachel knew she should move away but suddenly couldn't make her feet obey her mind.

She felt his hand lightly touch her shoulder. "I had a lot of fun tonight. Not just playing Clue. Getting to know you better," he said in that strong, quiet voice that made her feel something inside was . . . unraveling.

Rachel took a breath and finally raised her gaze to his. "I had a good time, too," she admitted.

Before she could say more, she heard heavy footsteps coming up from the basement. Ryan heard them, too, and smoothly stepped away, leaving a more appropriate amount of space between them. Rachel turned back to the sink and put the sponge away. She was in such a dither, she hadn't even realized she was still holding it.

She was grateful to have a moment to take a deep breath and compose herself. She had nearly kissed her son's basketball coach. With a big fat wet sponge in her hand. Boy, was she out of practice with this stuff.

"How did it go, guys? Did you wear out the rug in front of the TV?" Ryan joked with them.

"Almost," Andy admitted.

Now all three kids looked totally exhausted. *Finally,* Rachel thought. Nora's eyes were drooping as she walked over to Rachel and buried her head in Rachel's leg. "Can we go home now?" she asked quietly.

Rachel laughed softly. "Right now. Too much fun?"

"Almost," Nora murmured.

"I know how you feel." Ryan glanced wistfully at Rachel.

She felt herself blush as she led Nora out to the foyer and looked for their coats. Will had followed without any argument.

A few moments later, she stood by the door with her jacket on. She smiled, feeling safe now to meet Ryan's warm gaze. "Thanks so much for having us over. We did have too much fun. And your dinner was awesome."

"The pleasure was all mine. You'll have to come back very soon."

Rachel wasn't sure how to answer. She just said good night again as she slipped her arm around Nora's shoulder. Her little girl was practically asleep on her feet as they walked down the driveway. Andy and Will traded high fives, and Will bounded down the porch steps ahead of them.

As Rachel started her SUV, making sure everyone's seat belt was secure, she caught sight of her reflection in the rearview mirror. She looked . . . better. More alive or something, her eyes brighter and her skin glowing. Not from the chilly night air either, she realized.

Miss Scarlet, get a grip, she warned herself. *Sure it was fun to get out and talk to an adult on a Saturday night. A handsome, intelligent, male adult,* she added. *But this can't go anywhere. For one thing, whatever else Ryan Cooper might be, he is your son's basketball coach. And that could get messy.*

For another—and more importantly—you're just not ready to date.

And thank goodness you didn't let him kiss you while you were holding a sponge. Talk about an awkward moment . . .

CHAPTER EIGHT

~⫘~

December 11, 1978

WHEN BEN WALKED INTO THE TRUSTEES' MEETING ON MONday night, all the board members were already seated. Lester Plante sat at the head of the table, of course, with Walter Tulley to his right. Ruth Hegman, who sometimes sat in as the board secretary, was on his left.

Joe Morgan, the youngest of the trustees, sat about halfway down, across the table from Ezra Elliot. Joe was a cook who worked in hotels and sometimes on cruise ships. He had a demanding job and a big family. Ben knew it was not always convenient for him to serve on the board, but he took his position seriously and usually had a very calm, practical view of troublesome situations.

The seat at the far end of the table, opposite Lester, was left empty for Ben, who was glad to see Ezra there. The doctor was so dedicated and overworked that though the meetings didn't start until eight, he was often late because he was still seeing patients.

"We'll begin with a prayer, as usual." Lester glanced down to the other end of the table. "Reverend?"

Ben was glad to oblige. He bent his head and closed his eyes, and the others did the same.

"Heavenly Father, please join us at this table tonight. Help us carry on the business of this church with a fair-minded and openhearted spirit. Help us carry out our duties as officers of the church, as true disciples of Christ, and in all that He continues to teach us. Amen."

"Thank you, Reverend," Lester said curtly. He started to pass out his agenda and the minutes from the last meeting.

"Before we get into tonight's business," Ben said, "I have a letter I'd like to share with all of you." He reached into the breast pocket of his jacket. "It's from Oliver Warwick. I suppose it should be entered into the minutes."

"Warwick?" Walter was writing something on a pad and briefly looked up. "What's he have to say?"

"I'll read it aloud. It's brief."

"Please do," Ezra said curiously.

" 'Dear Trustees,

'I regret that I am unable to carry out my elected term as church treasurer. Pressing business and family matters now require my full attention and prevent me from giving church matters the time and com-mitment they so deserve. Of course, I remain at your service to answer any questions about records or transactions made under my term, or to advise on any other issues.

'With all best wishes for the continued success of your work, I am yours, respectfully,

'Oliver Warwick.' "

Ben looked up. No one spoke for a long moment. Ezra sat back in his chair, looking as if his team had suffered a setback. But one couldn't blame Oliver for trimming his sails right now, Ben thought. Clearing his name demanded his full effort and attention. There could be no other way.

Lester leaned back in his chair. "That's a relief to me. I was going to make a motion tonight to vote him off."

"He doesn't have to give up his term altogether. He can just take a leave," Ezra insisted. "We'll find a replacement for a few weeks."

"It will take him longer than a few weeks to sort out his problems," Joe Morgan said. "That man's in deep."

"All things considered, I'd say it's for the best," Walter Tulley said evenly. "Let's let sleeping dogs lie, eh, Ezra?"

Ezra was not in the habit of letting a sleeping dog lie. Not if he believed the dog should get up.

Before he could reply, Lester said, "I will sleep easier knowing Oliver Warwick is nowhere near church money now, whether he's been found guilty in a courtroom or not. You can put that in the minutes, too," he told Ruth Hegman.

Ben had expected a debate of this sort, but he couldn't remain silent while Lester slandered the man with his mean-spirited innuendoes.

"You have no grounds to say that, Lester. The audit that you and Walter performed did not reveal a single irregularity. Oliver Warwick left the church financial records in perfect order. Let's put that in the minutes, as well," he stated clearly.

"I wouldn't sound the all clear so soon, Reverend," Lester countered. "If Warwick was able to dupe his own accountants, we may still discover some problems here . . . So yes, I will sleep better knowing he's no longer within reach of church funds. I think we all will," he added, gazing around the table at the other men.

"Well, they haven't proven anything in court yet," Joe Morgan reminded Lester. "We still have to see how it all pans out."

Ben felt the same, but he knew that his arguing with the board members had gone far enough. He had made his point. It would do no good to go back and forth on this. He and Lester would never see eye to eye. Not tonight, anyway.

"You get a good night's sleep, Lester," Ezra urged him. "You've protected the church funds from Oliver's reach . . . It's funny how you didn't mind when Oliver was *handing* the church money. When we needed a new boiler last winter and Oliver made up the gap in the collection with his own checkbook—and more times before that than I can remember."

Lester stared at Ezra with narrowed eyes. "What's that supposed to mean?"

"The Warwicks have been active, openhanded members of this church for decades. Even longer," Ezra reminded him. "Oliver grew up in this church and deserves the same respect as you or I or anyone. I won't sit still and listen to any more of your snide, unfounded insinuations."

"See here, Elliot . . . I know you two go way back. But this is church business," Lester insisted. "We need to be objective. Not sentimental."

"Sentimental? . . . It's bullying, plain and simple, to hit a man when he's down . . . and insult him when he's not here to defend himself. And not very Christian either," Ezra added.

The men were trading barbs so quickly, Ben couldn't jump into the fray. But he felt it was his place to keep the peace, to remind them they were still members of the same church.

"Gentlemen, please . . ." He stood up and held his hands out to each of them, like a referee in a boxing ring. "This is a complicated issue. And an emotional one. But a shouting match will not help us sort things out. I think there is room for us all to be both responsible and conscientious about church business . . . *and* to show compassion for a fellow church member who is facing a dire life crisis."

Lester sat stone-faced, his mouth twisted to one side, as if he wanted to argue but knew he shouldn't. Ezra was still upset; Ben could tell by the set of his shoulders and tight frown, his thin knee bobbing under the table. But he also managed to hold his tongue.

Walter Tulley was the first to speak. "I agree with Reverend Ben. We don't know yet what Oliver's done—or not done. He's given up his post as treasurer voluntarily, and I, for one, am relieved not to have to vote him out. Though I'm also relieved to be on the safe side there as well," he added, glancing at Lester. "I don't think there's anything more to say. We should move on to new business."

Lester nodded, seeming satisfied with that solution. "Let the letter from Warwick be entered into the minutes." Lester handed the document to Ruth Hegman. "Next item, estimates for the roof repair have come in. I'll pass around copies . . ."

Ben felt relieved that the tension was dispelled. He knew he could not win over hearts and minds by arguing with people determined to vilify Oliver. Still, he had been secretly grateful for Ezra's heartfelt rebuttal to Lester's accusations. How could he help them—and the rest of the congregation—see that Oliver deserved their compassion and not their cold censure—and that this was vital? It wasn't a matter of sentimentality, but a matter that defined the heart of being Christian.

The rest of the agenda was covered quickly. The trustees seemed to have talked themselves out on the first item—Oliver Warwick.

Ben offered a general, polite good night to the group as he gathered his papers. He met Ezra Elliot's gaze briefly but left the room alone.

As he gathered his coat and briefcase from his office, he heard the other board members leave the church. The building was empty when he left his office and checked that all the lights were shut off and the doors locked.

The parking lot was empty, too, he was relieved to see. He knew it would test his temper if he met Lester there and the church moderator wanted to have the proverbial "meeting after the meeting," as so often happened.

Ben walked to his car, his thoughts distracted and emotions simmering as he considered what he might have said or done differently. Was he standing up enough to the unfounded judgments and unforgiving attitudes? Not just for Oliver but for the Christian teachings that this situation put to the test?

Ben sighed as he unlocked his car door. He knew that he had tried . . . but he just hadn't been persuasive enough, or even forceful enough, in his rebuttals. People like Lester weren't paying attention to him. He felt brushed off and disrespected.

Put your ego aside. Thinking about your own feelings won't get you anywhere, a small voice inside scolded him.

Then another voice—a real voice—said, "Reverend Ben?"

Ben looked up as a figure stepped out of the shadows. It was Oliver Warwick, walking on a path from the side of the church that faced the village green.

He walked with his long overcoat open, though it was quite cold. A wool muffler was slung around his neck. His hands were sunk deep in his coat pockets, his chin hanging low.

"Oliver? Are you all right?" As Ben drew closer, the expression on Oliver's face seemed alarming. His step was unsteady, and he swayed from side to side. Ben suddenly wondered if he had been drinking. It seemed very likely.

"I'd like to speak to you, Reverend," Oliver said. "Excuse me for surprising you like this. I knew you would be at church for the meeting . . . but I didn't want to come inside."

For obvious reasons. Ben wouldn't want to either, in Oliver's place.

"I got your letter today. I gave it to the board," Ben said, thinking that might be what Oliver had come to talk about.

Oliver's mouth formed a thin, self-deprecating smile. "They accepted my decision, no doubt. I don't blame them. I'm sure they were about to kick me off anyway."

Ben didn't want to confirm that guess. Was that a lie of omission? Maybe. But to spare the man's feelings, he thought, was reason enough.

"Why don't we go back inside? It's cold out here."

Oliver shook his head. "This won't take long . . . I've been thinking, Reverend. About something you told me that morning we met at Fowles."

"Oh? What was that?"

"You said, 'Tell the truth.' You said it was always the easiest path, eventually. You said God would forgive me."

Ben felt his heart sink to his knees. He could guess now what Oliver had come here to say. "Yes. That's true. He will forgive you. He forgives you already."

Oliver took a deep, steadying breath, staring at the ground. "I'm not sure of that yet. But I must tell you, I lied. I lied to practically everybody . . . Lillian, my daughters . . . good friends like Ezra and Otto." He looked up at Ben, his eyes wet with unshed tears. "I took money from those accounts and gambled with it. Because the canneries were failing, month after month." He shook his head. "I tried to shore things up with my own money at first. But some is held in trust. My father knew what I was better than I ever did," he said sadly. "So I went into those retirement accounts, thinking I would be able to pay them back once business improved. When that didn't happen, I tried to make up the losses at the racetrack, at card games. Betting on anything, actually . . ."

He covered his face with his hands. Ben reached out and touched his arm. "Oliver . . . please . . ."

But Ben had no words after that. He felt shocked. Overwhelmed. So many emotions washing over him. Of course, he had wondered and even suspected that this could be the case; that the accusations against Oliver were true. But Ben had always returned to the idea of Oliver's claim of innocence and Oliver's essential goodness. Now he felt as if people in town had warned him about Oliver, and he had been too naive to see the truth. And he felt betrayed. Deeply betrayed.

"I've shocked you."

"Yes, in a way you have," Ben said frankly. "But not really."

Oliver took a pack of cigarettes and a heavy gold lighter from his coat pocket. He took a long draw, then released a puff of smoke.

"I still believe I did it for good reasons. Not to save my own pathetic skin, but the jobs of so many people who depend on me. I never used a cent of that money for my own gain. Or comfort. Honestly . . ."

Oliver stopped, looking suddenly perplexed by his confession. He flicked ash from his cigarette, a dismayed, almost deranged expression of amusement dropping over his face. "I say 'honestly' . . . and expect you to believe me. I can't expect anyone to believe anything I say anymore, can I?"

"That's the trouble with lying," Ben said quietly.

"I'm sorry for lying to you, Reverend. I appreciate the way you've stood by me and my family. I never meant to . . . make a fool of you. I'm a desperate man in a desperate situation. I hope you can find it in your heart to forgive me . . . if not right now, then someday." Ben stared up at Oliver, trying not to betray his true emotions. But Oliver had hit the nail squarely. He, and other stalwart friends, had stood up for Oliver all over town, defended him and prayed for him. Or at least had asserted that Oliver could be innocent, as he claimed, and shouldn't be tried and condemned in the newspapers, or in debates at the Clam Box, or even in church meeting rooms.

But the spiritual principles are still the same, a voice reminded him. *You must forgive Oliver because God forgives him. Your own hurts and disappointments are hardly the point. Oliver should still not be judged and rejected. He should be embraced; now more than ever.*

You're like a doctor, Ben, arriving at the scene of an accident. The victim is hideously injured, and you must put aside your personal reaction—your knee-jerk revulsion—and put your training on automatic. This man needs spiritual CPR, a life-or-death intervention. You must put your ego aside and help him.

"I forgive you, Oliver. And I believe you," Ben said finally, with all the emotion he could muster. "And I know you're doing the right thing to put all pretense aside and face the truth squarely. It's the most difficult but also the most courageous choice. The choice that will serve you and your family the best in the end."

"I hope so, Reverend. My attorneys have advised me to stick to my story. To plead not guilty. But I've been thinking of changing my plea to . . . to guilty." Ben could tell it was hard for him to even say the word out loud. "There's a chance I can bargain with the court and stay out of jail. My attorney said I could throw myself on the mercy of the court and offer to make amends, to pay back those I wronged. My military record might help me, too."

"Once you take that first step and show sincere regret for what you've done, that will all work in your favor."

Oliver didn't reply. He shook his head. "I'm not sure . . . I'm afraid," he admitted. "I'm not even thinking about myself. I want to make the best choice for my family. How would it help to plunge them even deeper into public humiliation? How will they ever come out of this?" Before Ben could answer, he added, "But if the prosecutor makes his case, he can put me behind bars for twenty years . . . or more. How will Lillian and the girls survive? How will I, for that matter?"

Ben was silent a moment. Then he said, "With the help of almighty God. 'Fear not, for I *am* with you . . . I will strengthen you, Yes, I will help you. I will uphold you with my righteous right hand.'"

Oliver took a deep breath. "Isaiah."

"That's right."

"Don't look so impressed, Reverend. I marched all over France with just a Bible and letters from home to read. I ended up memorizing both."

Ben was touched by the admission. Oliver had made a serious misstep in his life, but he wasn't a bad person. He was, overall, a good man, with weaknesses and frailties—just like any other man or woman, or any creature made by God's hand. Yes, he gave in to a certain weakness of character at times, but he was also capable of rising to a moment. Ben knew that was true. And he knew this was a moment when Oliver needed to call upon all his inner resources, all his better qualities and higher instincts.

"You were a hero on the battlefield," Ben reminded him. "Your bravery saved lives. You didn't just give up and give in. Think of this moment as another battle. The battle of a lifetime. It takes real courage to step forward and tell the truth. To admit you've done wrong and ask for forgiveness. That takes more courage than anything."

"Those days seem like a dream now, Reverend. Maybe I'm just not the same man I was back then," Oliver said softly. "You know, it's not very hard to be brave in combat. Everything is happening so fast, you don't have time to think, to reflect. To let the fear take over and paralyze you. It's all reflex and adrenaline . . . I'd rather face bullets and bombs right now than this nightmare I've made for myself."

Ben sighed and nodded. He knew that was probably true. Still, he tried to rally Oliver's spirit. "You are on a battlefield, Oliver. Fighting for your life. Your spiritual survival," he clarified. "Tell the truth. Show sincere regret for what you've done. Ask the judge for mercy and promise to make amends. That's the best choice. I think you know that in your heart, too."

"It's hard, Reverend. As soon as I set my mind on one course, I waver and think I should take the other. If I bull it out, I might have a chance of getting through the trial. My attorney says the evidence can be discredited, and he might find some legal protocol that lets me off the hook. They say the case against me isn't airtight. It's a gamble, of course. But one I might win," he conceded.

Gambling . . . that's what got him into this mess in the first place, Ben thought. He held back from pointing that out to him.

"The judge may not find you guilty at a trial, that's true. But you know the truth. So does God. Why not be honest and put it all behind you? Make amends to the people you've hurt and make a clean start with your family? If you try to duck and fake your way through this, you'll be living a lie—and might find yourself in jail anyway."

Oliver dropped his cigarette to the ground and stubbed it out with his shoe. "Yes, I know. I have to consider the consequences for everyone, not just myself. Either choice seems impossible. My life is ruined either way, Reverend. All of my relationships tainted, irrevocably altered. No matter what the outcome is. Even my most loyal friends can't look me in the eye. They look at me as if I've just announced some terminal diagnosis. And if I admit my guilt, who will stand by me then? No one," he answered, shaking his head. "If I survive a trial, everyone will still look at us differently. And I'll still lose everything. My factory is closing down in a few weeks. I'm so ashamed of the mess I've made of my life. Sometimes I think the best thing I could do for everyone is to get in my car . . . and not come back."

Run away—or end his life? Ben was shocked by the implication either way.

Ben gripped Oliver's arm with a force that surprised both of them. "Don't say that. Don't even think it. I know this is a dark hour, maybe the worst in your life. But take it step by step. Ask God to show you the way. He won't abandon you. You can't abandon your family and leave them to struggle with this problem alone. It won't go away. Even if you do," Ben said bluntly.

Oliver's jaw tightened and he looked down at the ground. Ben wondered if he was ashamed of what he had just admitted.

"What will you do now? Where will you go?" Ben asked him quietly.

"Back to the harbor. To sit by the water and think. Then I'll go home," he stated, in the tone of a promise. "I'm not sure yet what I'm going to do about the plea. But thank you for talking to me, Reverend."

"I'm here for you. Always. No matter what," Ben stated emphatically.

Oliver nodded and backed away. "I know that. Now better than ever before. Good night."

"Good night," Ben called after him.

He watched Oliver retreat into the darkness, in the direction from which he'd come. Then Ben turned back to his car and got inside. His hands were shaking as he put the key in the ignition. He couldn't drive yet. He was too upset; overwhelmed by this conversation. As much as he wanted to rush home and talk this all over with Carolyn, he knew it would be difficult to get her alone with his in-laws there now.

He sat and stared out at the darkness, feeling as though he might burst. Then he closed his eyes and prayed.

Dear heavenly Father, please give Oliver the strength to make the right choice, to tell the truth and make amends to those he's injured as best as he can. Please protect him and his family and guide them through these dark, difficult days.

Please give me the wisdom to guide him . . . and guide my church, rocking now unsteadily in the wake of Oliver's troubles.

Present day, December 14

EVEN THOUGH SHE AND NORA HAD ALREADY TAKEN OUT A FEW Christmas decorations on Saturday, when Sunday arrived Rachel found more excuses to avoid a visit to Sawyers' Tree Farm. A thick blanket of snow had fallen during the night. The main streets in the village were plowed, but Beach Road could be snowy and slippery, she reasoned. Then there was the problem of getting the tree into the house. She and the kids had shoveled a bit on Sunday morning, but really just enough to get the SUV out in order to get to church on time. They would definitely need to shovel more for a Christmas tree. She liked to set up the tree in the family room, around the back of the house, and didn't like dragging it from the front door, shedding needles, and maybe even snow, everywhere. Will had missed church in order to do homework. She had asked him to shovel a few paths outside and some of the back deck. But she doubted he had done much of anything yet—except play video games online with his friends.

Rachel walked out of church with her mother and Nora, arriving at her mother's car first. She was still debating the wisdom of the tree outing in her head when her mother invited them all over for dinner, as she so often did on Sunday.

"I don't know what came over me, but I bought a turkey on Friday and cooked it yesterday. Your father and I hardly made a dent in it last night. Why don't you and the kids come over today, and I'll heat everything up?"

"With stuffing and cranberry sauce?" Nora's eyes lit up at the mention of her favorite dinner. Rachel had forgotten that Nora was standing right beside her.

"There's tons of stuffing," her grandmother reported. "And I'll send your grandfather for more cranberries on his way home from church."

"We were thinking of getting a tree today," Rachel admitted, "but I guess we can do it during the week. It's still so snowy, we'll have to shovel the back of the house just to get it in."

"Whatever you like, dear," her mother said mildly. "I can pack up the turkey and bring it over for you, too," she offered. "You won't need to cook tonight."

A tempting offer, Rachel had to admit. But a chilly wind off the water decided the matter for her. The sky was clouding over again and there had been some talk of more snow today. She felt a slight chill in her heart as well—not quite in the mood to get a Christmas tree. Or even to pretend enough for her children.

"Oh, don't bother, Mom. We'll come tonight. It will be fun. I love a turkey dinner. I never understood why it's reserved for one day a year."

"It isn't really, dear. You just have to buy a turkey," her mother said quite logically. "Come by whenever you like. I thought we would eat around five."

"Can I go with Grandma now?" Nora whispered, tugging on Rachel's jacket.

"I'm not sure, honey . . ." Rachel glanced at her mother, wondering if having Nora over again was too much trouble.

But before her mother could answer, Rachel heard an insistent beep on her cell phone. She pulled it from her coat pocket, expecting it to be Will. He was probably wondering when she and Nora would be home and what was around to eat for lunch. Rachel picked up without checking the number.

"Hi, Rachel. It's Ryan. Am I catching you at a bad time?"

Rachel was thrown off balance by the sound of his voice. "Uh . . . no, not really. I'm just leaving church. What's up?" Maybe there was some emergency with the team, she thought; one requiring parent phone calls.

"Everything's fine. I just want to say I had a great time last night. I'm glad you were able to come over. And I was wondering if you want to get together some night this week. Aside from basketball practice, I mean."

Rachel caught her breath. She hadn't been in any kind of romantic relationship since she met Jack in college. She wasn't used to this sort of conversation.

"Um . . . like a date?" The words came out before she even knew what she was saying.

She heard him laugh, but it was a warm, affectionate sound. "Yes, like a date. But we don't have to call it that. How about having dinner together again . . . without children . . . in a restaurant a little nicer than Village Pizza?"

He *did* mean a date. The clarification made her even more nervous. Before she could reply, Nora tugged on her jacket again.

"Mommy, can I go with Grandma? It's cold out here," she whispered more urgently.

"Nora, just be patient. Your mother is on the phone." Rachel saw her mother take Nora's hand. But not before meeting Rachel's eye with a small, but telling, smile.

Rachel looked at both of them, then realized this was not the time or place to figure out this momentous question.

"That sounds very nice. But, you know, I'm just in the middle of something with my mom and Nora and . . . Can I call you back? Maybe tonight?"

"Sure, no problem. I was thinking Wednesday night," he said. "But I'm free Friday, too, if you already have plans."

Washing her hair and watching *The Wizard of Oz* for the millionth time was her expectation for both nights.

"I'll check," she said politely. "Talk to you later."

"Was that Will's coach, Ryan Cooper?" Carolyn asked after Rachel ended the call. Her happy expression reminded Rachel of the time she had won second prize in the science fair, back in fifth grade.

Rachel nodded. "Uh-huh."

"Sounds like he was calling to . . . to make plans," her mother said in code, glancing at Nora.

Rachel, too, glanced at her daughter, who always seemed to be in her own dreamy world but was totally tuned in to adult conversations. "Nora, honey, you can go home with Grandma if she says it's okay."

"Of course it's okay. Why don't you get in my car, sweetie? You look cold." Her mother opened the back door for Nora. "Jump in and put on your seat belt."

Once the door was closed, Carolyn turned back to Rachel. Rachel didn't really want to talk about Ryan but felt cornered. "Yes, he asked me out to dinner, maybe this Wednesday night."

Her mother smiled. "How nice. I'm free to stay with the children. No problem."

"Mom, I'm not even sure I want to go out with him. It's . . . it's complicated," she added, digging her hands into her jacket pockets.

"Yes, I'm sure." Her mother's expression was sympathetic. "But it's almost two years, dear, since we lost Jack. And Ryan's such a nice man. You already seem to be friends. What's the harm of going out and social-izing a little? Having some adult conversation?" When Rachel didn't answer, she added, "You don't need to feel guilty, honey. Jack loved you. He would have wanted you to be happy, not wait until the kids are in college to have someone in your life again."

Rachel sighed. "I know. But it's still hard, Mom. I don't think I'm ready yet."

The truth was, she felt safe this way. Maybe not happy, but safe. Dat-ing again . . . well, it seemed to make Jack's passing so final. Maybe that wasn't logical, but it was just the way she felt. It was hard to explain, even to her mother.

"I know, dear. It's a process, and it's different for everyone. There are no set rules or timetables," her mother acknowledged. "But there is a fine line between grieving and not moving forward with your life. I think it would be good for you to at least try. Sometimes if you take a step, it makes you ready," she added. "Think about Nora and Will. What mes-sage are you sending them?"

Rachel knew that was true. Sometimes she did feel stuck. Or maybe just as if she weren't summoning up enough courage. It did take courage to rebound after a setback. She saw it every day with her patients. The ones who healed quickly and got on with their lives often seemed to summon some extra grit, a willingness to accept change. Maybe they weren't returning to the same life they had left, but to a new version. Then there were those who lingered in a sort of limbo of recovery, absorb-ing the label of patient into their identity. Did she want to end up like one of them?

"I'm sorry, dear . . . did I say too much?" Her mother suddenly took her hand. "Your father told me not to say anything to you," she admitted.

Rachel smiled and squeezed her mother's hand with affection. "It's all right. I know you're trying to help, and . . . I know what you're trying to say. I told Ryan I'd call him tonight. I'll think about having dinner with him," she added.

"Good enough. But please don't tell me 'we'll see,'" Carolyn said with a laugh. "I'm the one who invented that ploy, remember?"

"I do." Rachel laughed, too, then gave her mother a hug—which was abruptly interrupted by the sound of a honking car horn. Nora's irritated little face appeared in the passenger-seat window.

"Guess I'd better go. Someone is getting antsy," her mother said. "See you later, dear."

Rachel watched her mother drive off and waved to Nora. Maybe her mother was right. She did need to at least try. She took out her phone and decided to call Ryan back there and then.

He picked up on the first ring. Before she could lose her nerve.

"Ryan? Hi, it's Rachel. I had a minute to call you back."

"Great . . . What do you think? Are you free on Wednesday night?"

She realized he was giving her a graceful out. She could easily say she wasn't free and put him off.

"I am free. And I'd like to see you. That will be fun," she added, though she wasn't sure of that. It would be nerve-racking; she knew that much. But it seemed like something she just had to do.

"It *will* be fun," he promised, sounding genuinely happy to hear her accept. "You know, after our last call, I realized that this must be hard for you. I haven't been dating that long either, since my divorce," he admitted. "I know it feels a little . . . strange at first."

Strange was definitely a word she would use to describe it. "Yes, it does feel strange." It was a relief to admit that out loud. "It's hard because of Jack and . . . because it makes me feel like I'm back in high school or something."

"Exactly . . . and I'm so relieved that you didn't make me feel like that geeky, gawky guy who sat behind you in math class. I'm sure you turned him down," he teased her.

Rachel had to laugh. There really had been a geeky, gawky guy in high school—though Ryan hardly fit that description.

"Actually, I met him recently at a class reunion. He's gone on to live a happy, successful life," she teased him back.

"Glad to hear it," Ryan said in a mock-serious voice. "There's hope for us all, then. I'll make a reservation someplace and get back to you about the time. And we'll see each other this week anyway," he added, referring to the team practices.

"Yes, we will." The expectation made her feel happy inside.

They talked for a few minutes more, then Rachel heard a text come in. Now that was Will for sure, tracking her down.

She said good-bye to Ryan and felt herself smiling as she answered Will's text. The skies above the harbor had clouded over, but the skies above her heart seemed to have cleared. She pictured a deep, clear blue color within, the sun inside, shining brightly.

RACHEL GOT HOME AND FOUND WILL IN THE KITCHEN WITH TWO sandwiches and a stack of chips piled high on his plate. She was about to tell him not to spoil his appetite for his grandmother's turkey dinner, but realized that wasn't possible. Will could eat ten sandwiches and still be able to polish off a turkey dinner five minutes later.

"Did you get your homework done?" she asked as she took off her coat.

"Almost. There's more Earth science. I have a test this week," he said with dread in his tone. "Maybe Grandpa can help me."

"I'm sure he'll want to try." Rachel opened the fridge to check the pan of brownies she had made the night before, wondering if there were enough to bring to her parents' house.

There was exactly one brownie left, stuck in a corner, and an assortment of crumbs. Will must have eaten them for breakfast.

"When is the test?" she asked him.

"Wednesday. I have some time."

"Yes, but there's practice Tuesday, and you're usually tired afterward. You'd better study today and tomorrow night, too."

The mention of basketball practice quickly brought Ryan to mind. Rachel suddenly wondered if she should tell Will about her date with him. She would have to tell both the kids sooner or later. She didn't worry about Nora; she seemed to like Ryan already. But Rachel did wonder about Will. He was older and had different issues about Jack's death. Maybe he wouldn't mind, but . . . maybe he would.

She glanced at him. He was munching on the last piece of sandwich and reading a sports magazine.

"I spoke to Mr. Cooper this morning," she said.

"Oh yeah? About the team?" he asked, without looking at her.

"No . . . not exactly." Rachel walked over to the kitchen table, to be closer to him. "He invited me out for dinner. On Wednesday night."

Will blinked and looked up from the magazine. As if he was wondering if he had heard her correctly. "You mean, like a date?"

Rachel realized she had said practically the same thing to Ryan. She shrugged, trying to be low-key. "We've become friendly. Because of the team, and you and Andy being friends," she explained.

"You're going out to talk about the team?"

She wondered if he was being sarcastic now. Or just really didn't get it. Or didn't want to get it.

"I'm sure we'll talk about the team a little. But that's not why." She paused. "I guess you would have to say it's a date. Yes, that's what it is. How do you feel about that?" she added, already sensing he didn't like it.

He looked down, seeming confused. "It seems weird. You and . . . *my coach?*"

Rachel understood how that must feel strange to him. Will probably didn't want to—and couldn't—picture her with anyone who wasn't Jack.

"We're just going to dinner," she explained. "To talk a little, socialize. The way I go out to dinner sometimes with my friends."

She didn't really do much of that anymore either. She actually couldn't remember the last time she had a girls' night, though her friends kept inviting her. *It was just a chance to step out of her 24/7 Mom role,* she wanted to say. But she knew that would hurt his feelings.

"Sure . . . okay." Will kept his gaze down on his magazine. She could tell it was not okay with him. Not at all.

Rachel touched her son's shoulder. He sat very stiffly, just tolerating her.

"Listen, I don't have to go out with Mr. Cooper if it upsets you. It's not that important. I'm sure he'll understand."

Will shook his head, but still didn't look at her. "No sweat. It's cool. I just didn't think you guys liked each other that way. It's sort of . . . weird, that's all."

His comment did make Rachel feel "weird" . . . but she suddenly remembered how old Will was. Everything made him feel weird, especially things having to do with relationships.

"I'm not exactly sure what that means," she said evenly. She sat at the table, tilting her head as she tried to catch his gaze. "Mr. Cooper and I get along. I consider him a friend, and we're both single parents, and we have a lot in common," she tried to explain. She paused, wondering if she was getting anywhere with him. "There's no need to be afraid of anything, Will. I still feel sad sometimes about Dad. But it's been almost two years since we lost him. I think I can start socializing now." She was very careful not to say "go on dates." "It doesn't mean I don't still love your dad . . . or you and Nora."

Will finally looked up at her. "I know. It's just . . . weird. Like that

time you permed your hair and I didn't recognize you when I came out
of school?"

Rachel sighed, but had to smile a little, too. Would they ever let her
live down that hair disaster?

"It's not like that, Will," she promised. "I'm still me. I'm still your mom."

But she knew what he meant. It did change something. And she was
sure she did "look" different to him suddenly, just by admitting she would
go out on a date. And now their loss had been churned up all over again.
Like the big signs that loom over the highway when you cross into a new
state. WELCOME TO MASSACHUSETTS. Or VERMONT. This one said her life
as Jack's wife was really over. She was moving on to some other place.

As much as she knew that what her mother had said was true—it
was important to move forward and not stagnate—it was hard to leave
this place. Even though Jack was long gone and she was alone here.

Will was reading his magazine again. Or pretending to.

Rachel thought she should take it as a sign he was finished with the
conversation. But she still didn't feel resolved about it.

"I don't want to make a big deal out of this, Will. Mr. Cooper and I
will probably have a bite to eat, and I'll be home by nine."

*I might go out with him and have a terrible time and realize it's too soon
for me, too,* she wanted to add. But, of course, she couldn't confide that
fear.

He didn't answer for a long moment. She waited. Finally he said.
"Okay . . . I get it." He stood up and picked up his dish and brought it
to the sink. "Can I go upstairs? I have to do more homework before we
go to Grandma and Grandpa's."

"Of course. Go ahead. I guess we'll leave in about an hour. If you
want to talk more, I'm right here."

Rachel watched him leave the kitchen, knowing he would probably
not ask her to talk again. Will had to process this on his own. They
both did.

CHAPTER NINE

Present day, December 15

$\mathcal{S}$OPHIE POTTER, VERA PLANTE, AND CLAIRE NORTH HAD
come to church early to work on the history project. Ben
found them in Fellowship Hall, sipping coffee from their travel mugs as
they strolled around several long folding tables that were covered with
photos, newspaper clippings, and old church bulletins.

Ben felt overwhelmed as he took in the display, but the women
seemed quite calm—including Sophie, who was also running the Christmas Fair again this year.

"This history project has turned out to be a lot more work than anyone expected," he said honestly. "Maybe we should put it on hold until
January. I don't see how you can keep track of all this and organize the
fair, too."

"I've been running that fair since nineteen seventy-eight, Reverend.
I could do it in my sleep. Sometimes I am doing it my sleep." Sophie
laughed. "I was the one who thought it all up, you know."

"Yes, I remember. That was my first Christmas at the church," he reminded her. "I just don't want you to run yourself ragged and not enjoy the holidays with your own family."

They had both had a lot more energy and stamina back then, Ben knew. He had, at any rate. In her eighties now, Sophie seemed as active as most people half her age. She still lived on her own out at her orchard, though she often had children and grandchildren visiting.

"Don't worry about me. Claire and Vera are doing most of it. I'm just the manager," she insisted.

"I feel like we're setting up a rummage sale right now . . . a paper one," Claire remarked with a smile.

It did look like a paper rummage sale, Ben realized. The annual rummage sale was another church event that always overwhelmed him, but one the hardworking women of the congregation cut through like a hot knife in butter.

"I brought in some photos and articles I picked out of that box you gave me," Ben said, "though you don't seem to need more."

"We aren't using all of these in the book," Vera said with a laugh. "We thought it was a good chance to sort things out and label them, and store everything properly when we're done."

Of course these women would do that. They would always leave any situation they encountered in better shape than they found it.

"Dan said if we give him the most important photos, he'll scan them into a computer and save everything on little sparkle drives for us," Vera said.

"Flash drives, dear," Sophie said.

Vera waved away the correction. "What I mean is, we'll never have to worry about mold and termites and all that. It will all be preserved safely for the future."

"Quite a project," Ben said. "I've found several interesting articles about Oliver Warwick that are worth saving. About his business troubles . . . and legal problems." Ben showed her the folder and set it on the nearest table. "I was wondering how you planned to handle that event in the church history," he admitted. "We have to include it, of course."

"Yes, of course. We can't leave it out. It was a very difficult time for the church," Vera recalled.

"And for the Warwick family," Claire added.

"Yes, it was. Reading about it stirred up lots of memories for me," Ben admitted. "I was very close to the situation."

"In the thick of it, I'd say." Vera looked up a moment from her sorting work, a pile of photos in hand. If she had any hard feelings from those times, she didn't show it.

Claire glanced at Vera. "It's a very delicate matter, with Lillian and her daughters still members here."

"And Dr. Elliot," Vera added.

"I was thinking that myself," Ben said.

"I was thinking that you should write about it for us, Reverend," Claire suggested. "You know the whole story, from all sides, and I believe you would be the most evenhanded."

"Not that it has to be a long section," Vera told him. "We were thinking just a paragraph or two."

"But we can't exclude it," Sophie countered. "We want a real history. Oliver Warwick's situation is part of our story."

"Yes, it is . . ." he replied. All of the women were looking at him now, waiting for his answer. "Well, if you all feel that way, I can try my hand. Maybe Dan can fix it up once I get something down."

"I'm sure he'd be happy to help. Though you're a very good writer, Reverend. Don't sell yourself short. I always enjoy your essays in the bulletin, and your sermons, of course." Claire was sorting out piles of old bulletins, and Ben suddenly realized how many little essays he had written over the years—enough to pile up to the roof of the building, probably.

"I'll keep the news articles, then. For the time being." He reached out and took the folder back. "And I'll try to draft a page or so for you soon," he promised.

Back in his office, Ben sat behind his desk and took a sip of coffee. The latest edition of the *Cape Light Messenger* was on his desk, but instead, he took out one of the older issues he'd been about to pass on.

It was one he'd noticed last night but hadn't even read. The date was Wednesday, December 13, 1978. Bold black letters, all caps, read *WAR-WICK PLEADS GUILTY.*

Ben remembered that morning as if it were yesterday. He had opened his copy of the newspaper at the Clam Box, stopping there on the way to church for a quick breakfast.

December 13, 1978

"Hello, Reverend. We don't usually see you here at this hour," Otto greeted him as Ben took a seat at the counter. Otto took a cup from one of the metal shelves and filled it with coffee without Ben even asking.

"I needed a little quiet time before I head to the office," Ben confessed.

"The baby?" Otto asked knowingly. He had two children, a boy named Charlie, who was a teenager, and a girl named Sharon, who was still in elementary school.

"Not exactly. My in-laws are visiting, and the house is a little busy in the mornings." *Chaotic* would have been a more apt description. His father-in-law, Charles, liked to watch morning news on the television, something called *The Today Show*. He had a little hearing problem and turned the set up quite loud, using his electric razor in the middle of the living room while he watched.

This upset the baby, of course. Or maybe she would have been fussy anyway. Carolyn and her mother took turns trying to soothe her.

"Dr. Elliot says the baby is teething. She can't seem to get comfortable, poor thing."

Otto nodded knowingly. "You take a washrag, soak it with water, and put in the freezer. When it's good and cold, let her chew it. Cools the gums right down."

"Thanks, I don't think we've tried that yet."

Otto nodded. "Don't worry, it will pass."

"That's what Dr. Elliot said."

Otto laughed. "I'll tell you a secret about raising kids, Reverend. Soon as you learn how to handle one situation—diaper rash, teething, whatever—they've grown out of that problem and are on to something else altogether."

Ben smiled wanly. "I had a feeling it was going to be that way."

Ben ordered a dish of scrambled eggs and toast. He didn't have to be in his office until nine. There was a meeting of the Christmas Fair committee in the afternoon, but he was otherwise free and planned to work on next Sunday's sermon. The fair would take place on the weekend, and this was the group's last meeting. Ben was thankful for that. So far the event had taken a lot of planning and work. He hoped it was worth it. But the first time was always the most difficult. If they held it again, it would be easier, he thought.

Otto cracked open a few eggs, whipped them up, and dropped them sizzling on the grill. Ben opened his copy of the *Messenger* and felt his heart skip a beat as he read the bold headline.

WARWICK PLEADS GUILTY. A slightly smaller headline read, *Cuts a deal with DA to forgo trial.*

Ben knew Oliver had done the right thing, but it was still hard to see the reality of it in black-and-white. He wondered if Otto had seen the paper yet, and realized at once that he hadn't. Otto wouldn't be nearly as chipper if he had seen it. Ben's heart felt like lead. He knew he was the one who had to show it to him.

Otto had disappeared into the kitchen but soon emerged carrying Ben's dishes: eggs and bacon on one, toast on the other. "Here you go," he said, setting the plates down and adding a little bowl that held pats of butter. "More coffee?" He filled the empty cup before Ben could reply.

"Thank you," Ben said. "Otto . . . I guess you haven't seen this yet . . ." He held out the paper.

"What's up?" Otto smiled as he wiped his hands on a rag, tilting his head to read the front page.

Ben watched Otto's smile disappear. His brown eyes grew glassy as he took the paper in two hands. He stared at it, quickly reading the story underneath.

When he looked up again, his face was angry. He smacked the paper with the back of one hand. "Yeah, well . . . I bet his lawyers made him do that. To get out of the jail time. It was the only way. He had to make a deal with the DA. He couldn't take a chance on losing the trial and leaving his family to fend for themselves. He did it for Lillian and the girls. That's got be it, don't you think, Reverend?"

Ben didn't reply, even though he knew the truth. Oliver was guilty and had confessed to him face-to-face. He doubted Otto would believe even that. Such a steadfast, loyal friend, he wasn't able to hear it.

"I'm relieved to hear Oliver won't go to jail," Ben said sincerely. "He and his family still have a very hard road ahead."

Otto nodded. "Poor guy. He doesn't deserve this, Reverend. He's a good man."

Ben didn't reply. He wasn't sure what to say. Was anyone truly good? Weren't most people a mixture of both good and bad? It really just depended on which side of themselves they chose to express and cultivate—the dark or the light. It seemed that way to Ben at that moment, anyway.

Two men in business suits had taken seats at the counter near Ben, and Otto walked over and began pouring coffee.

They had both carried in big cases and looked like salesmen about to start their calls. Ben noticed that the man closest to him also had a copy of the *Messenger* and was snapping it open.

"Look at that—'Warwick pleads guilty.' Surprise, surprise," he said to his companion.

"Yeah, what a shock. The guy's a total con artist, a lowdown, thieving chiseler. He must have blown all his millions at the racetrack, so he starts stealing from the poor suckers who work in his factories. I don't know why they don't lock him up and throw away the key."

Ben saw Otto's jaw drop and his face grow red. He stared at the two men, his lower lip trembling. Ben braced himself for another leap over the counter—or worse.

The two men stopped talking and stared up at Otto with puzzled expressions. "I'll have some cream for the coffee," the man with the newspaper said, "and two eggs over easy, bacon on the side. And rye toast."

"Same for me, skip the bacon," the other fellow added.

Otto kept staring at them, his head lowered and eyes bulging, as if he were a bull about to charge. He suddenly reached out and snatched their cups, sloshing coffee on one man's shirt and tie.

"What the . . . What are you doing? Are you nuts or something?"

The shocked customer jumped up from his seat, his hands raised as he stared at the stain.

"You guys better eat someplace else," Otto shouted at them. "We're all out of eggs today."

Then he pulled off his apron, threw it on the counter, and stomped into the kitchen, the double doors swinging wildly in his wake. Ben watched him, along with the two shocked customers. The man with the stained shirt was already grabbing his sample case and hat.

"Let's get out of here. That guy flipped his lid."

"I'll say . . . Geez, all I wanted was some coffee and eggs. Wonder what set him off."

Ben took a few last sips of his own coffee, most of his breakfast left on his plate. The newspaper headline had stolen his appetite.

He stared at the kitchen doors. He could only guess at what Otto must be going through. No matter how completely he was denying the truth, on some level, Otto must feel betrayed by Oliver. *As I did,* Ben thought. Perhaps in time, Otto would return to a place of compassion. Ben hoped so. Oliver couldn't afford to lose any more friends right now.

As he walked out of the diner, Ben heard several women sitting in a booth also talking about the news. And as he walked down Main Street toward the village green and the church, he felt as if the entire town was talking about it: in the aisles of the variety store; in the post office, bakery, and bank; in the beauty salon and pharmacy. He could imagine the voices, the harsh remarks and cruel jokes about Oliver. The echoes of the salesman's "I told you so" tone.

A short time later, Ben sat in his office. He glanced once more at the newspaper, then picked up the phone and dialed Lilac Hall. If ever there was a time to reach out to Oliver, it was now. Ben felt more than a little responsible for Oliver taking the dramatic step of reversing his plea and declaring himself guilty. He wanted to support Oliver in the aftermath of his confession in any way he could.

As he expected, the phone rang and rang. Ben was sure it was off the hook again, between too many reporters calling, and too many townspeople affected by Oliver's desperate blunders—who were even angrier now.

If the tone in the diner was any indication, the family was probably receiving a lot of hate mail by now, too. He pictured Lillian in the lavish foyer, screening each day's mail to protect her husband as much as she could.

I'll write him a letter, Ben decided, *and just hope it gets through.*

Dear Oliver,

I just read the news that you changed your plea to guilty. I know it was a very hard decision for you—very likely, the most difficult you have ever faced, or will ever face, in your lifetime.

Please know that you have done the right thing by taking responsibility for your mistakes in man's sight. And, more importantly, in God's. God did not create us as perfect beings but endowed us with the understanding to know right from wrong, and to make the spiritual choices that align us with His divine perfection. That choice is truth. In the difficult days ahead, I hope you will take comfort in the courage you've shown. Please remember that God is always with you, always at hand to renew that courage, to give you strength to face the trials that lie ahead.

Remember Isaiah 41:10. "Fear not, for I *am* with you; Be not dismayed, for I *am* your God. I will strengthen you; Yes, I will help you, I will uphold you with my righteous right hand."

If I can be of any service to you in any way, please let me know. You and your family remain in my heart and in my prayers.

Yours sincerely,
Reverend Ben Lewis

Ben read the letter over once, signed it, and slipped it into an envelope, addressing it to Lilac Hall. He wondered if Oliver would receive it. He hoped so, though he did not expect a response.

He dropped the letter on his secretary's desk on his way to a meeting in Fellowship Hall. The fair would take place in just a few days, on the upcoming weekend, and Ben hoped the many last-minute glitches would be solved before then.

"Reverend . . . on your way to the meeting, I hope?" Sophie appeared at his side carrying two baskets covered with checkered cloths, which he suspected were protecting home-baked confections.

"I didn't forget," he promised her.

"It shouldn't take long. Most of the plans are set. But we still need a few more volunteers to run the booths. Could you ask around, make it known at your other meetings? Folks always hop to it when the minister asks them," she noted.

Ben wasn't so sure of that. "I'll try my best," he promised. "I can ask one of the trustees to make some phone calls for you, too."

"Oh good, that will help," she said, smiling widely.

He had noticed that Sophie often faced little challenges like this with her church projects, but she never seemed stressed or disorganized. She seemed to trust that some higher power would arrange everything perfectly . . . and amazingly enough, she was always right.

Ben heard voices as they approached the room. More talk about Oliver Warwick, of course. He had expected that.

"Of course he came clean. You'd have to be blind not to see he was guilty as sin," a woman said. "He shouldn't get any special deals. He should go to jail and stay there."

"They ought to take all his money and give it to the people he robbed blind," another woman chimed in.

"My neighbor Arnold worked in the cannery for over forty years, all set to retire first of January. Now he's got nothing to fall back on in his old age," an older male voice reported. "He doesn't know what he's going to do. His wife is crying day and night. She's making herself sick over it."

"He couldn't even keep working if he wanted to. The canneries are going to close," another said quickly. "And probably the lumberyard, as well."

Sophie glanced at Ben as they approached the doorway, her expression sad and disturbed. He met her gaze and looked away. He felt a chill deep in his heart. The level of rancor and disgust had risen considerably.

"Hello, everyone. Sorry I'm late," Sophie said, announcing their arrival from the doorway.

The group abruptly stopped talking. Everyone watched Sophie and Ben enter and find places at the table.

Sophie placed the baskets on the table and took the covers off. "A little thank-you for your hard work," she told the others with a smile. Though her mood seemed subdued, Ben noticed.

"So . . . you've been talking about the latest news about Oliver Warwick," Ben said, taking the bull by the horns. "The whole town is talking about it."

"What's to talk about?" A man named Peter Blackwell waved his hand with disgust. "You had to be born yesterday to believe a word he ever said."

"I know he made some awful mistakes, but I don't think he was trying to steal that money for himself. Why would he? It just doesn't make sense," Sophie said reasonably. "I think he was just trying to keep the factories running, as he claims. The paper says he's promised to pay everyone back. As much as he can," she added.

Doris Hegman sat next to her daughter-in-law, Ruth. The older woman shook her head. "Who can trust a thing he says now? And it looks like he's not even going to jail." She looked at Ben as if to say, "What do you think now?"

Ben looked around the table. All eyes were upon him, waiting for his response. "I think that everyone affected by this situation needs our prayers, now more than ever. The cannery workers and their families, the innocent, hardworking people who have lost their pensions . . . and the Warwick family. Even Oliver."

Ben offered his hands to those seated next to him. Sophie, sitting to the right, took his hand eagerly. Doris Hegman, on his left, was less eager, but she did take hold and bent her head, wearing a dour expression. The rest of the group did the same, until the entire table was joined hand to hand, in a circle.

"Dear Heavenly Father—" Ben began.

His words were interrupted by the sound of a chair scraping on the floor. Peter Blackwell stood up and shook his head. "I can't sit here and be a hypocrite, Reverend, praying for Oliver Warwick when my son is about to lose his job. I'd rather go home and pray for my son and my grandchildren . . . and the ones that need it most."

Before Ben could answer, another member of the group, Helen Donahue, stood up. "I'm sorry, Reverend, I feel the same. My brother has been working at the cannery for twenty years, and now he has nothing to show for it. I doubt the Warwicks deserve, or even need, any of my prayers. They'll be fine with all their money."

"I understand," Ben said evenly. "I wouldn't want you to take part if your heart wasn't in it. That wouldn't be right. But before you go, consider what Jesus taught us in the Sermon on the Mount—the teachings that became the basis for the Lord's Prayer, so essential to our beliefs. He said to forgive your enemy; to pray for those who persecute you."

"Yes, we all learned that in Sunday school, Reverend," Doris replied in her low, rumbling voice. "But if you don't mind me saying, real life is a lot different. It's hard to forgive someone who crosses you in a little way, like someone who dents your car in a parking lot, much less, someone who steals all your money."

The rest of the group seemed to agree. A few laughed nervously; others shifted in their seats.

"There's no question it's hard, Doris. I don't mind you saying that at all," Ben replied quickly. "Jesus knew that. He said it's easy to love those who love you back. Anyone can do that. But he urged his followers to aspire to a higher law. A higher path in this world." Ben glanced around the table, trying to discern if they were listening and understanding.

"He showed us the example of God sending rain to fall on all—kings and beggars, criminals and priests in the temples. Or the way God created the sun to shine every day, bringing everyone warmth and light. No matter who you are, or what you've done, that is the way God forgives and loves us all. Like the sun. Like the rain. He didn't say we had to love the harm people did to us. Only to see that under their confusion and twisted motives, we are all essentially the same. We are created infused with a divine spirit.

"Jesus knew it would be hard for us to love those who have wronged us. In fact, he knew it would be impossible. But he told us that with God's help, through God's spirit, we could do it. In the Book of Matthew, Chapter 19, we read, 'With men this is impossible, but with God, all things are possible.' All things," he repeated.

He paused a moment, wondering if they were taking his words to heart. Or at least considering them. Then he found himself telling them the very same thing he had told Oliver on that dark night when he had urged him to confess.

"It's really very simple. God loves and forgives all of us. No matter what. He knows we are all frail and weak, all capable of making mistakes. All of us are in need of forgiveness from time to time. From Him—and from each other. He asks us to treat one another according to this divine, unconditional model. It is divine to be forgiven. It is divine to forgive. We know that's not always easy. But as Christians, we know it's right. We know we must at least try to do it. That is why I believe we should pray for everyone affected by this dire situation." He paused and looked around the table again. "For those of you who sincerely can't find it in your hearts to take part, I understand."

He waited a moment. Peter Blackwell got up from his seat and left. Helen Donahue glanced around, looking nervous and confused. Then she grabbed her purse and left, too. "I'm sorry," she said quietly.

No one answered. Not even Ben. He felt the color rising up the back of his neck and into his face. He had never had anyone walk out of a prayer circle like this before.

Finally, he held out his hands again. Sophie took hold of his right. She leaned over quickly. "Well said, Reverend," she whispered.

Doris Hegman stared at his hand a moment. He waited, looking straight ahead. Finally, she took it and bowed her head.

When everyone had joined hands, he led them in a heartfelt prayer, asking God to bring courage and strength to all of those affected by Oliver Warwick's mistakes. To bring comfort and support where it was most needed, especially to those who had lost jobs and lost their savings.

"We also ask that you bring strength and comfort to the Warwicks, and help us treat them with compassion and forgive their frailties, as You forgive us. We ask this in the name of Your son, Jesus Christ. Amen."

When he looked up, he felt very drained, and a bit saddened. Maybe just two leaving wasn't such a bad score, but Ben felt as badly as if they'd all rejected him—and God's word.

"Before we begin, Sophie, I have an idea to propose," he said.

"Go ahead, Reverend. The floor's all yours," she answered.

"Sophie came up with the idea of this Christmas Fair as a fundraiser. I was thinking that if the committee agrees, we might donate all the funds from this fair to the families from our church who are affected by the canneries closing . . . and those who may have lost pensions. I know it may not be all that much. But if we also dedicate a special offering on Christmas, it could be some help to them."

Sophie's eyes lit up at the idea, and Ben saw approving expressions on the faces of the others. "I think that's a wonderful idea, Reverend," Ruth Hegman said. "Once we tell the congregation where the money is going, I'm sure they'll all be very generous."

Her mother-in-law, Doris, nodded in agreement, though she was still frowning, Ben noticed.

"I'll chip in . . . and I'm going to put a little can or something in my barbershop. I'm sure a lot of guys will drop some change in," Skip Belmont said.

"Good idea, Skip. I'll put one in the dress shop," Muriel Krupp replied.

When a few other business owners offered to help with the collection, Ben felt encouraged that the fund would amount to something more substantial than the profits from the fair.

"You've got me thinking, Reverend. I can put a can in the shop at the orchard. Though we don't have many customers right now," Sophie admitted. "But what about helping those families who are losing their jobs with some toys for their kids? It would be just one worry off their shoulders, wondering how Santa will visit their house on Christmas Eve."

"But how will we know what children have asked for?" Vera Plante asked.

Sophie thought a moment. "I'm not sure. Maybe we could collect a whole lot of stuff and set up some sort of a store? Parents could come and choose for free, and pick something their child would really like."

Ben smiled. "That's an excellent idea, Sophie. I think you're onto something." Yet another project to add to her list.

There was more discussion about ways to collect funds for those affected by the Warwick factory closings, and more talk about the toy collection, too, before Sophie was able to bring up anything to do with the Christmas Fair.

But the group's sidetrack had been a very constructive one, Ben reflected. The church members around the table seemed to project a different attitude entirely once they focused on helping others instead of on judging and tearing down Oliver Warwick.

Ben listened to the plans for the fair with only half an ear. He still felt unsettled by the way Peter Blackwell and Helen Donahue had walked out on his prayer. He had to give them credit for being honest. The truth was, there were probably others in the circle who felt the same but weren't bold enough to follow them.

He also wondered if they would have walked out on their former minister. Or would they have tried harder to understand and accept his message? Perhaps it was just his own ego, but Ben couldn't help it; he felt disrespected, and, more than that, as if he was being tested by this situation and somehow failing.

When Ben got home that night, he wanted nothing more than some time alone with Carolyn to tell her what had happened at the meeting and get her opinion . . . and her sympathy.

But he was greeted at the door by his father-in-law, Charles. "There you are. We left two messages at the church for you."

Ben felt alarmed as he slipped off his coat. "Is everything all right? Is the baby sick? Is Carolyn?" Had she come down with another headache?

"Everyone's fine." Charles waved his hands, urging him to simmer down. "If you don't count freezing half to death," he added. "That old boiler is about to call for last rites, so I hope you have a Bible handy. Carolyn says you don't call a plumber around here either. You have to ask someone from the church to fix it?"

"That's right. We have so many able members at church. They take care of all the repairs here." Which also saved the church considerable money in upkeep for the parsonage.

Charles squinted at him from behind his thick glasses and folded his arms over his chest. "They don't charge. It's a donation, you mean."

Ben suddenly noticed his father-in-law was wearing one of his own sweaters, a thick fisherman-knit cardigan with leather buttons that he bought on a trip to Ireland when he was a student . . . and now only wore on special occasions. "That's right." Ben nodded.

"You get what you pay for," Charles mumbled under his breath.

Ben picked up the phone extension in the hallway and tried to think of whom to call. He would normally call Peter Blackwell, who was a master plumber. But that would be awkward tonight of all nights. Ben opened the church directory and finally found another likely member,

Harold Wexler. He caught him eating dinner, but Harold promised to come over in a little while.

Charles had gone into the living room and turned on the TV. Ben headed back to the kitchen, summoning a smile for his wife and daughter. But he didn't find them there. His mother-in-law was alone in the room, standing by the stove in her tweed wool coat with an apron over it.

She turned from the pot she was stirring and smiled at him. An appetizing aroma filled the room.

"That smells good," Ben remarked.

"Chicken gumbo. It will warm us all up. Carolyn's upstairs with the baby."

"I'm sure it will," Ben said agreeably. His mother-in-law was an accomplished cook, her dishes made with Southern flair. And while he greatly admired her culinary skills, his stomach had been raised on plain New England fare—baked fish, boiled potatoes, and straightforward chowder. One or two nights of her cooking was more than his stomach could bear. Three weeks of it was going to be a true test. "I'm sorry about the heat, Louisa. I've called someone to come look at it. He should be here in a little while."

"Oh, it's not your fault, Ben. We'll survive. Don't pay any attention to Charles. He puts on a sweater if the mercury dips below seventy."

Ben knew that was true. Still, he felt sorry for his in-laws. They had never been to New England in the winter and had had no idea what they were getting into.

Just as he was going upstairs to look for Carolyn, she came down, meeting him in the foyer and greeting him with a kiss.

He was relieved to see that she didn't have a coat on, too, though she was wearing a heavy sweater. Now that his own body temperature had acclimated from the outdoors, he had to admit it was quite chilly.

"How was your day, Ben?" she asked him.

"My day was . . . difficult. Did you see the news about Oliver Warwick?"

"Yes, I did." She sighed. "I know he did the right thing, but my heart goes out to his family. At least they won't send him to jail."

"Yes, that's some blessing." He wanted to tell her what had happened at the meeting, but didn't feel comfortable discussing it here, with his father-in-law in the living room watching the evening news.

And they couldn't go back to the kitchen and talk privately there either, with Louisa busy cooking. "I'd like to take a peek at Rachel," he said instead. "Is she sleeping?"

"Just went down."

"She isn't too cold up there, is she?" he asked with concern.

"She has on her heavy sleeper and lots of blankets. It's not nearly as cold up there as it is downstairs, for some reason."

"Heat rises," Ben said. "I'd like to go up and just look at her. Will you come with me? I'd also like to tell you about something that happened at church today," he added in a hushed tone. "It'd be nice to have some privacy?"

Ben glanced into the living room again. Charles gave them a cross look. "Why are you two standing so close to the front door? The draft is terrible. You'll catch a cold."

Carolyn met Ben's gaze and nodded, then led the way back upstairs. When they reached the top, she took his hand and led him back to Rachel's room.

"There she is, our sleeping angel," she whispered. "She was a handful today. But my mother took over for a while. She has so much patience with her."

"Yes, she does." Ben had observed that as well. "I'm glad your parents are here helping you."

Carolyn smiled. She didn't look as if she entirely believed him. "You're not irritated, being thrown off your little routines?"

Ben laughed. "Little routines? You make me sound like an old man."

"You know what I mean. I know it's not easy to have them underfoot. Especially when you're so busy getting ready for Christmas."

"If you're happy, I'm happy," he said honestly.

"I know we haven't had much privacy. Maybe we could go out for dinner one night, just the two of us. My parents will watch the baby."

"That's a great idea," Ben agreed, realizing he should have thought of it.

"If you're not too busy at church, I mean," she added.

"I'm not too busy. I mean, I am busy, but I can make time for a date with my beautiful wife." He put his arms around her and held her close. "I missed you today. I felt so . . . overwhelmed with this bad news about Oliver. I was in the diner when I saw the newspaper. Otto Bates practically started crying when I showed it to him. He came up with all kinds of excuses and rationalizations. He just couldn't believe it."

"I'm not surprised," Carolyn said. "He's been such a good friend to Oliver."

"Yes, he has; the very definition of loyalty. Oliver pleading guilty was a blow to him. It doesn't help that everyone in town was talking about it, even strangers coming into the diner. And it was just as bad at church, at a meeting for the fair. Some very harsh statements were made. I had a difficult time—"

Before he could get into his story, his father-in-law called from the foot of the stairs, "Hey, you'd better get down here, Ben. Something's gone haywire in the basement. There's water all over the place."

Ben ran to the top of the stairs and looked down at Charles. "What's going on? What happened?"

"Pipe broke, probably. Didn't you call the plumber yet?"

"He said he'd be by in a little while. I'll call him again," Ben said, running down the steps.

"I'll call. You'd better go downstairs and see what happened. Who was it?" Carolyn called after him.

"Harold Wexler. He's in the church directory."

"Got it," Carolyn shouted back. "I'll be down in a minute. There are so many boxes down there . . . I'd better put some rubber boots on. You, too."

"I know . . . Don't worry . . ." Ben raced past his father-in-law, hoping he wasn't too late to rescue their belongings.

All the boxes from the guest room had been moved down to the basement to clear the way for Carolyn's parents. Many of his favorite books, photos . . . all their summer clothing. Their Christmas decorations and lights. He hadn't gotten to that task yet either.

He didn't want to think of what else.

Not to mention the fact that they now had a major plumbing disaster on their hands and would probably be without heat and hot water for hours, if not longer.

He pulled open the basement door and headed down the next flight. He could hear gushing water but couldn't tell where it was coming from.

Where was the main valve? Under the staircase? He couldn't remember. He saw his father-in-law following down the wooden steps, a bucket dangling from each hand.

Charles is going to bail dirty water off the basement floor in my best sweater. And I don't know how to tell him to take it off . . .

He sent up a quick prayer. *Dear Lord, give me patience. I know things could be worse. No one is sick, no one is hurt. But this is about all I can handle in one day . . .*

CHAPTER TEN

Present day, December 16

EVEN THOUGH RACHEL HAD ACCEPTED RYAN'S INVITATION ON Sunday, she had gone back and forth in her mind ever since then about whether to go through with their date.

At Tuesday night's practice, she watched the boys run up and down the court, performing their drills, all the while silently rehearsing polite excuses.

When the practice was over and the team had been dismissed, Ryan stood packing up his duffel bags beside her. "Good practice. The kids looked sharp today," he said. "They're going to play well against Lexington next weekend."

Rachel had been too distracted to notice. "I think they looked great," she said anyway.

This is the perfect moment to tell him I can't go out tomorrow night, she thought. He hadn't even mentioned the date. Did he forget? That would really let her off the hook . . .

"I hope we're still on for tomorrow night?" He stood up, his wide, hopeful smile crushing her slim hope.

Rachel didn't answer for a moment. She finally nodded and smiled back. "Oh sure . . . yes, of course."

"Great. Is six thirty okay? I'll come pick you up. I was thinking of this new restaurant in Essex, the Boathouse. It's gotten some great reviews."

Rachel was completely out of the restaurant reviews loop these days. But even she had heard of the Boathouse—very hip and elegant *and* expensive. This was going to be a *real* date. She almost winced.

"Yes, I've heard of that place. That sounds . . . lovely," she said finally.

Will and Andy had been sent to collect the extra basketballs that were scattered all over the court. But they were mostly fooling around, playing a one-on-one game of dodge ball. They finally staggered up to the risers and grabbed their sweatshirts and string bags.

"I'd better get going. I need to pick up Nora," Rachel said quickly. "Good night."

"Good night, Rachel. See you tomorrow night," he said.

Rachel smiled but didn't reply. As they crossed the parking lot, she wondered if Will had picked up on their conversation and if he would make some comment about it in the car. He wasn't making eye contact with her but was dribbling his basketball, so it was hard to tell what was going on with him.

They got into the car and he sat in the front seat. Rachel pulled out, and they passed Ryan and Andy, who waved good-bye again.

"So, you're still going out on a date with Coach Coop?" Will was looking out the driver's-side window as he spoke.

"Yes," Rachel said evenly. "We're going out for dinner tomorrow night . . . Do you still feel bad about that? Would you like to talk about this some more?"

He didn't react for a moment, then shook his head. "I just wanted to know what was going on."

"That's what's going on," Rachel replied, glancing at him. "Grandma is coming over to stay with you."

He nodded and took out his phone. "Okay, cool." He started checking messages, and then put on his earphones to listen to music.

Rachel would have liked to talk more with him, but she knew she shouldn't push him. She sighed and focused on her driving. A quick glance at the dashboard clock told her that it was almost six thirty. *You still have twenty-four hours to go to Plan B, the carefully crafted excuse.* The realization made her feel a bit calmer . . . while the other part of her brain started planning an outfit.

A LITTLE OVER TWENTY-FOUR HOURS LATER, RACHEL FOUND HERSELF seated across from Ryan at a small, candlelit table. The Boathouse was quiet and elegant, located in a very old building near Essex Harbor. The furnishings were spare and modern, with a low ceiling and wide plank floors that looked like the original wood refinished to a soft glow. The lighting was low and the decor all cream and oat colors with touches of warm brown.

Rachel was wearing a sweaterdress with a cowl neckline and high brown boots. She wasn't sure if she had dressed up enough. But at least the heather color of her outfit blended in with the decorating. Ryan had on a dark gray suit, a blue shirt, and a black tie. He looked very handsome. It was hard not to keep looking at him.

Rachel kept from staring by gazing out the window. Their table by the long row of windows framed a view of the dock and the marshy inlets. It was already dark outside, but small lights on a few boats and distant houses glowed like distant stars.

And the aromas from the kitchen were totally tantalizing.

"They change the menu every day," Ryan explained as they looked over the intricately described offerings. "It's all very fresh farm-grown ingredients."

"Yes, I noticed that. The type of menu that lets you know exactly where your food is coming from."

He smiled at her. "At least they don't include the names of the farm animals. Like, Hester the free-range chicken, roasted and served alongside fingerling potatoes from Windsor, Maine?"

Rachel laughed. She was thinking almost the same thing.

"Did I sound snide? I didn't mean to. I'm a little nervous," she admitted.

"Me, too," he said. "Maybe I shouldn't have picked such a fancy place. It is a little formal. We can go someplace else if you'd feel more relaxed."

Rachel shook her head, thinking it was sweet of him to offer. "This is lovely, honestly. I just don't get out much."

"We'll have to do something about that," he said with a smile.

Rachel looked back at her menu, feeling herself blush. Finally, their waiter came and took their order. They both decided to start with the organic greens and roasted beet salad with goat cheese, made at a local farm.

They talked a little about the Falcons, and when that subject ran out, Rachel asked Ryan some questions about his work, questions she had actually prepared in advance just in case the conversation lagged. She still felt nervous but there seemed little she could do about it. Why was it so easy to talk to him when they were on a noisy basketball court or just hanging out with their kids? Now that they were alone together, her brain seemed to have frozen.

He seemed to be feeling the same way, too. Just as the silence between them grew, their waiter appeared with their salads. *Saved by the locally grown organic arugula, radicchio, frisée, and fern greens,* Rachel nearly said aloud.

She sat back in her seat, preparing to be served, when suddenly the greens were airborne . . . including the little silver pots of vinaigrette dressing.

Rachel jumped up, but that only made the collision of food and clothing worse. Ryan reared back, the salad landing in his lap, and his suit, tie, and shirt splattered with dressing.

They stared at each other as the waiter profusely apologized, trying to brush salad greens off them with a napkin. "I'm so sorry! I don't know what happened. The heel of my shoe must have caught on something . . . a nail in the floor," he tried to explain.

Rachel was dabbing herself with a napkin. "It's all right. Honestly."

She wondered if this was a blessing in disguise. They would have to end their date early. They were both dripping with salad dressing.

As Ryan wiped off his clothing, some goat cheese smeared on his beautiful black tie. "Oh boy . . . game over with the neckwear." He yanked open the knot and pulled it off.

The manager ran over to their table. "I'm so sorry. What a disaster. Please let us give you this dinner on the house."

Ryan glanced at her. He could tell from her expression she wasn't up for sitting there with soggy stains all over her dress. "I don't think so. We'll just take a rain check," he replied. He glanced at Rachel and she nodded.

A few moments later they were seated side by side again in his SUV. Ryan looked upset and she didn't know what to say.

"Well, thanks for planning such a nice evening," she said, feeling secretly relieved. "We'll have to try again sometime."

Ryan glanced at her. "Just because we both smell like a salad bar? Is that any reason to give up? It's barely even . . . seven thirty," he added, checking his watch.

She wasn't sure if he was joking or not. His car did smell like a salad bar; that part was true.

"What could we do? We're both a complete mess." Rachel didn't even feel comfortable enough to go into a pizza parlor.

"Totally true . . . just give me a minute. I'm not giving up on this date that easily, even though I'm down by ten points and there's thirty seconds left to play," he quipped.

Rachel had to smile. Coach Coop was not a quitter, that was for sure.

"Drive-through burgers?" she suggested, trying to be more positive. That would be quick and relatively painless . . . and then he could drop her off and she wouldn't even feel guilty about going home too early.

He didn't answer for a moment. Then he shook his head and smiled and started the car. "I've got the perfect idea. An inspiration, honestly. I have my gym bag in the back with fresh clothes to change into, and there are a few boxes of Falcon sweatshirts and sweatpants that are left over from the team sale. So if you don't mind changing in a restroom, we can go over to Summit Rock Climbing, in Beverly. They stay open late, and it should be really empty on a weeknight."

Rachel wasn't sure she had heard him correctly. "You want to go to an indoor climbing-wall place?"

"That's right. Ever been?"

She knew where Summit was. Will had been invited there for a birthday party once. But she hadn't let him go; it seemed too dangerous. She didn't even know adults did it. She had never been remotely tempted.

"I'm not great with heights," she admitted. "I mean, I can look out of a window. But I hate those glass elevators in hotels that go up really fast, and then you're looking down twenty floors and there doesn't seem to be anything underneath, holding you up . . . is it like that?"

He laughed and she realized she'd been rambling.

"Well, you're not up that high. It's challenging . . . and exhilarating. I think you'll really like it," he told her.

He had a certain idea of her that she didn't share, Rachel realized. A complimentary one, it seemed.

When she didn't answer, he added, "I'll hold the rope for you. I'll let you down really slowly, I promise."

Rachel sighed. This was definitely crazy. She had on her good jewelry . . . and mascara, for goodness' sake. She only wore makeup for weddings or trips to Boston. "All right. I'll try it, I guess," she said finally.

His smiled grew even wider. "You won't regret it, I promise."

ABOUT AN HOUR LATER, RACHEL FOUND HERSELF CLINGING TO A BIG, gnarly, make-believe mountain, balancing on colored pegs and hand-grips. She wore a helmet and a harness with some sort of rope and pulley arrangement around her body that kept her from falling straight to the floor.

And finding new meaning in the words "bad first date," she quipped to herself.

She had changed into sweatpants and a sweatshirt that said CAPE LIGHT FALCONS, along with a pair of Will's sneakers, which were way too big. She prayed that they didn't fall off and hit someone on the head, in addition to praying that she got home in one piece—and also asking God to please not let her meet anyone she knew. Even remotely.

Thankfully, there were only a few other climbing customers— mainly a group of college kids who seemed to be timing each other as they flew up and down the walls as if they had wings.

Ryan was below, holding the rope that held her aloft and shouting instructions she could barely hear above the blasting rock music. "Don't think so much, Rachel. Just climb. Figure out just one more handhold and foothold. You can do it," he told her.

Ryan had already done his climb, going up first to give her the idea, while a staff member of Summit controlled the safety rope. Ryan was so fit and agile, he made it look very easy, climbing to the top and coming down again in about as long as it had taken her to go ten feet.

"Are you okay?" he called up . . . for about the umpteenth time.

"I'm fine . . . but I feel sort of stuck." *And why am I doing this again?* she wanted to shout back.

"No such thing, Rachel. You always have a move. You just have to figure it out," he advised.

"Easy for you to say," she grumbled quietly. There was at least one benefit of being so high in the air: Ryan couldn't hear her complaining. Her hands were hurting, and this section of the wall seemed to slant backward, making her doubly dizzy if she looked down.

"I can't see where to go. It's sort of uncomfortable," she admitted.

He didn't answer. She wasn't sure if he had heard her.

"What about grabbing that blue rung with your left hand? Then putting your right foot on the yellow peg?"

Rachel eased her nose away from the wall as much as she dared, to figure out what he was talking about.

Are you kidding me? she wanted to shout back. *What do you think I am, a rain forest frog with suction cups on my feet?*

She sighed, not knowing what to do. She did feel stuck, but she couldn't stay where she was, either. Her hands were really hurting now. It was either go up or come down—no in-between choice here.

"What do you think?" he called up. "Do you want to come down now?"

She looked back down at him but didn't answer.

"You're almost to the top. More than halfway," he added.

"I am?" She was so close to the wall, she couldn't gauge her progress.

"A few more moves and you'll have made it."

"Are you telling me the truth . . . or just trying to *coach* me, Coach Coop?" she shouted back.

Ryan laughed. He had such a deep, warm laugh. She was getting used to the sound now. It always made her smile.

"I'm *not* kidding. You are really close . . . but yeah, I'm coaching you, too."

At least he was honest.

"So . . . up or down? Your wish is my command. I think you did really well for your first time," he added, giving her an out.

"Not so fast . . . I'll try the blue ring and the yellow peg . . . even though I feel like . . . a spider doing yoga." Ryan started laughing so hard, she thought he might let go of the rope by accident. "Hey, stop laughing down there. Are you ready?"

"I'm sorry. Sure. Go for it."

Rachel gritted her teeth and her resolve. She had to make a big effort and was actually hanging by just her hands for a very long time—probably only seconds, but it felt longer—until her feet in their floppy sneakers could find the right peg.

But once she was settled in her new spot and looked down, she realized she had come a long way. She had made a huge climb up the wall and maybe she really was close to the top.

"Bravo! Awesome!" Ryan cheered, as if she'd just won an Olympic meet.

She smiled, feeling exhilarated. "That was fun," she shouted back. Then she realized what she'd said. *Yeah, it was fun,* she had to admit to herself. She finally did understand why people liked doing this. Though the rest of the wall was perhaps the hardest part, she summoned her remaining bit of courage and found herself climbing steadily until she finally reached the top.

"You made it. You're up there. You did it, Rachel!"

Rachel was afraid to look down. Afraid she would get dizzy and let go of the wall. Finally, she took a breath and peeked over her shoulder.

And felt amazingly exhilarated. Ryan looked so . . . small.

Holy mackerel, I never in a million years thought I'd make it halfway. But I'm all the way up here. I really am . . .

"Want me to take a picture with my phone?" Ryan called up to her.

"That's okay." Part of Rachel wanted a picture, and the other part didn't want him to let go of the rope. Besides, she was sure she looked pretty funny from the ground. Not a very flattering view, she imagined. "Can I come down now?" she called to him.

"No problem. You earned it. Now, this is the really fun part."

She wanted to trust him, but his answer made her nervous all over again.

"Let go of the wall and kick away with your feet. I'll let the rope loose a little at a time. Gravity will do the rest."

Gravity? She didn't like hearing that. "Not too much gravity, right?"

"Ready?" he said, without answering her question.

Did she really have a choice in the matter? She didn't see any staircase hidden behind the rock.

"Okay . . . but not too fast."

"I hear you," Ryan promised.

She followed his instructions, let go, and kicked back from the wall. And the express ride to the ground floor began.

She knew he was trying to let the rope out slowly, but she felt as if she'd been dropped from an airplane without a parachute.

Was she screaming? Well, maybe a little, she realized. Sheer survival instinct, like on a roller coaster.

A few seconds later, her body hovered over the floor and she softly landed in a squat, and then a sitting position.

Ryan dropped the rope and ran over to her. "That was great! Do you feel okay?"

"My legs are a little wobbly . . . but I survived."

Rachel pulled off her helmet. Her long, wavy brown hair tumbled out of its clip, and she pushed it back with her hand. "I'm not going to cash in my gym membership yet. But I guess I'm glad I tried it."

"That's enough to make me happy. More than happy." He stretched out his hands. "Let me help you up. You must be tired."

She hesitated a moment, then took hold of his hands. Ryan pulled her up as if she were as light as a feather. Pulled her so quickly, in fact, that the momentum nearly landed her in his arms. Which perhaps was his intention. Rachel stopped just short of a real embrace and they stood face-to-face.

He met her gaze and held it. She had the feeling he was going to kiss her. And she didn't step back or even try to pull her eyes away.

Then she noticed someone walk up behind Ryan and tap him on the shoulder. It was one of the college kids who had been waiting for the wall. "Hey, man, done with the equipment?"

"Yes, we are. Just a minute and we'll be out of your way," Ryan answered him.

Rachel unsnapped the harness as Ryan gathered up the rest of the gear. "Are you hungry?' he asked, helping her on with her jacket. He glanced at his watch. "I know it's late, but how about Aunt Chilada's?" She knew the place, a small café that served fast, fresh Mexican. And they wouldn't feel self-conscious in sweatshirts there either, she knew.

"Sounds good to me." Rachel was glad she had climbed the wall on an empty stomach, especially remembering how dizzy she had felt a few times looking down. She really hadn't been hungry at the fancy restaurant— maybe because she had been so nervous—but she was ravenous now.

A short time later, over guacamole, chips, and messy burritos, they sat talking, mostly about their adventure at the climbing gym.

"Thanks again for taking me there," Rachel said. "It was really fun, especially because I never thought I could do it."

"I'm glad I didn't give in to those looks you were giving me in the car," he admitted with a smile.

"Did I give you looks?"

"A few. Like I was crazy and you wanted to just . . . bolt."

She started laughing. "I'm sorry. Being hit with that free-range salad threw me off."

"After the salad fiasco, I figured, rock climbing is going to work big time . . . or it's going to be the worst date either of us ever had."

"I was thinking the same. That was a hard call, Coach. You went for the risky play," she teased him.

"I guess I did. But I knew you had the right stuff."

Rachel smiled, appreciating his vote of confidence. She hadn't been nearly as sure.

"And you're a very good sport. A lot of women would have insisted on going home."

"That was my first impulse," she admitted. "But you're very persuasive . . . and a good coach," she granted him. "What was that you kept telling me?"

" 'Don't think, just climb.' Just figure out your next move, your next hand- and foothold. It's a pretty good method to get you where you need to go."

"It worked for me." She shrugged and bit into a chip loaded with guacamole. Rachel had never imagined a date like this in a million years. But maybe God was trying to show her something. *Once you realize that you have to move on, that you must go up or down, some surprising—even amazing—things can happen.*

A little over an hour later, Ryan pulled his car up to the front of Rachel's house. It wasn't that late, but it wasn't nearly as early as she had expected to come home. She suddenly felt awkward again.

Ryan shut off the engine. That made her feel even more nervous. "It's okay, you don't have to walk me to the door or anything."

He glanced at her. "All right . . . if you don't want me to. I think you know I had a great time tonight. I hope we can do this again . . . Well, not *this*, exactly," he added, making her smile.

"I know what you mean."

"Good. Because I know you had some reservations about going out with me. Because of your loss," he added.

"That's true. I did." She wasn't sure if she should be entirely honest with him, then decided he might as well know everything. "Will felt uncomfortable about it, too. He didn't exactly say he was upset, but I could tell."

"And?"

"We talked about it—as much as I could get him to talk. I think he's working through it."

Ryan looked concerned. "I'm sorry it upset Will," he said. "But I'm not surprised. I know I can't compare my divorce with what you've been through. But when a family breaks up, it's a loss. And kids take it the hardest. Andy was very frightened for a while. He didn't want me or his mother to date. It upset him."

Rachel appreciated Ryan being so honest about his own experience. He hadn't said much about his divorce, and she was curious to know more. "How many years have you been divorced, Ryan?"

"About three years now. Andy's mother, Michelle, and I were married very young, right out of college. We just grew apart, I guess. We're very different people. She's remarried and happy now. She and her husband live in Cape Light, right near Rowley. They run an interior design business together and travel a lot. They're both seriously into French cuisine, chamber music, and Art Deco furniture."

Michelle sounded very sophisticated, Rachel thought. Then again, Ryan's ex-wife didn't sound like the type of person who would go rock climbing in boy's sweats.

And maybe that's a good sign, she realized. *Because you are that type of person.*

"So it's been three years. But you said you haven't dated much?" she asked. She couldn't understand that. He was so attractive, she imagined women must be asking him out all the time. "Is that too personal?"

"Not at all," he assured her. "And no, I haven't dated very much. I was seeing someone for a while. But that didn't work out. She took a job in Texas. Besides, Andy keeps me on my toes," he added. "He's growing up fast. Soon he'll be in college and I won't have much chance to spend time with him."

"I know what you mean," she said. "I think about that, too. Right now, Will and Nora fill my life. But time goes by so fast. It won't be that long before Will is out of the house, and Nora, too."

"We'll both be empty nesters," he said with a laugh. "That's not the reason why, but I'd like to see you again, Rachel. I'd love it, actually. Still . . . it's your call."

Rachel was touched by the way he asked the question—and glad that she had been honest with him. And she was relieved that he understood what she was going through with Will. She decided a little more honesty was in order.

"All I know is that I had a great time tonight," she told him. "I'm really enjoying getting to know you better, Ryan. Maybe I'll feel different later," she admitted. "But . . . so far, so good. So, yes. I would love to see you again."

He smiled gently and touched her cheek, pushing back a strand of her hair. Then his head dipped close to hers and she closed her eyes, expecting a kiss. She felt him kiss her softly on the cheek, and pull her close for a moment in a warm embrace.

She pulled away, feeling a little light-headed and confused.

"Sure you don't want me to walk you to the door?"

"No, that's okay. My mom must have noticed the car. I can see her standing in the foyer. Good night. Thanks again."

She jumped out of the car, grabbed her discarded dress and boots from the back, and ran up to the front door.

She was glad Ryan had not really kissed her. She had not been ready for that yet. But when she searched for feelings of guilt and sadness about Jack, she felt just a twinge, a whisper. She knew in her heart that her husband loved her and would never want her to be lonely.

Still, the date had been a big red line in the road, marking passage to some new, uncharted territory—and marking the place she was leaving behind. But she knew that every ending marked a beginning, too. Something inside her had subtly shifted tonight.

She would always feel the deep sadness of losing Jack, their future life together stolen from her. But now, coming forward even stronger, was a feeling of gratitude for the years they had spent together. The children they had raised. The love they had shared. Such a great blessing, such an amazing gift. Rachel felt deeply thankful, and sensed she was moving forward to a new perspective, a new phase of her widowhood.

It was just this scary moment of reaching for the next hand rung and foot peg. That was the tricky part.

"So far, so good, Jack," she whispered to herself. That was all she knew for now. And all she needed to know.

December 15, 1978

BEN KNEW HE COULDN'T BLAME CAROLYN. HE HAD ONLY THE SWEET-est love for her in his heart, and she was the last person he would ever hold responsible for his sadness and frustration. Even if she had been more available lately to at least talk in the evenings, he probably still would have sought out the counsel of Reverend James Hascomb, his mentor and friend, who had encouraged him to come to Cape Light.

But with his in-laws visiting and Rachel's demanding schedule, Carolyn had little time or energy to listen to his problems with the congregation. In a way, Ben was almost embarrassed to admit to her the level of disrespect he had encountered—and his shaky state of confidence and the questions that now loomed in his mind about his ability to have a church of his own and truly lead it.

On Wednesday night, after the news of Oliver Warwick pleading guilty had broken in town—and the pipe in the basement had broken in the parsonage—Ben realized he was in over his head, completely overwhelmed. He wasn't going to make it through the holidays without venting to someone who could understand his plight. He would end up like the worn-out plumbing—exploding without warning.

He had called Reverend Hascomb Thursday morning, first thing, and made an appointment to see him. He hadn't gone into detail on the phone about the problems troubling him, but the older minister didn't press him for details. "Come by around ten tomorrow. We'll have a talk, Ben. It will be good to see you."

"Yes, Reverend. It will be good to see you, too," Ben had replied sincerely.

And here he was. Reverend Hascomb had answered the door of his neat little cottage before Ben had knocked. He never changed; he was a large man with a fringe of curly salt-and-pepper hair, bald on top. His round face always wore a peaceful, almost beatific, expression. But his small blue eyes remained sharp, bright with keen intelligence.

They greeted each other warmly, and Ben followed Reverend Hascomb into his study, a cozy room with a small couch and two armchairs facing each other in front of an old hearth, built of rough, flat stones—the same sort of rock you might see in a typical stone wall running along the New England countryside. A large oak desk near the window was piled with books and papers, and more piles of books were stacked on the coffee table and on the floor nearby.

Ben took a seat in an armchair, and the Reverend shooed a big orange cat off the sofa and then sat down there.

"Make yourself comfortable, Ben. Are you sure I can't bring you a cup of coffee or tea?"

"Thank you, I'm fine. I don't want to put you out." Ben sat back, feeling ready to unburden his darkest fears and doubts.

A low-burning fire warmed the room, along with the sweet scent of Reverend Hascomb's pipe smoke.

"What's troubling you, Ben? You don't look yourself. Has the baby been keeping you up at night?"

"A little. She's not a great sleeper and is teething now, too. But it's not that. There are . . . tensions in the congregation. I'm sure you've read about Oliver Warwick's legal problems?"

"Yes, of course. He's a member of your congregation, as I recall."

"A very prominent one. Or was, until recently. Oliver was on the search committee and was a big advocate of calling me to the church. We've always gotten along very well. He was also the church treasurer— until recently," Ben clarified. "What's happened is, the entire town has been affected by this. Everyone seems to know someone who has either lost their job or their pension, or has been injured in some way by Oliver's poor choices. Which he is certainly responsible for, no question of that . . ." Ben's words trailed off. He wasn't sure he was explaining this clearly.

"Go on. I'm listening."

"Well, he has a few stalwart friends who, even now, are standing by him. But his mistakes have resonated throughout the town." Ben paused. "This is causing a great deal of tension in the congregation. I'm sorry to say this, but many members of my church seem happy to see him fall. As if he 'had it coming to him.' Or as if it's divine retribution of some sort. I've tried to navigate the situation as best as I could. I've encouraged compassion for all—for the families who have lost their livelihood and are suffering, and for the Warwicks, who are truly facing their darkest hour. But all my spiritual efforts and well-crafted sermons . . . and impromptu sermons," he added, thinking of the Christmas fair meeting, "don't seem to be swaying anyone's opinion. Many don't seem to listen to me . . . or even respect me. Their minds and hearts are set against the Warwicks, and there doesn't seem to be anything I can do to influence them. To encourage them to be better Christians. It's been very frustrating. And deflating," he confessed.

He paused and leaned forward in his seat. Reverend Hascomb was still listening to him, puffing on his pipe, in his familiar attitude of total, but effortless, focus.

"That does sound daunting," Reverend Hascomb said finally. "And during your first Christmas there, too."

"Yes, that's definitely part of it. I had high hopes for the last few weeks: special services, special sermons. Now that's all been overshadowed by this issue. But the bigger problem is that I just don't feel I'm a spiritual leader there. I don't feel I'm a shepherd leading my flock. I'm floundering, Reverend. I have little or no influence with them. I feel like a windup doll rolled out on Sundays to run the service, say my little sermon, make everyone feel good. But whatever I say goes in one ear and out the other. They go on with their lives, feeling they did good to attend church on Sunday. But they may as well have stayed home and read the funny pages."

"I understand what you're saying, Ben. I do." Reverend Hascomb tapped his pipe out in an ash tray and put it aside, then brushed some ash off his large hands. "It is the perennial frustration—or shall I say, challenge?—of our work. Crying in the wilderness. It's practically a cliché."

Ben cringed, thinking he must have sounded as if he was whining. But he didn't think he was a chronic complainer. He had been speaking the truth of his heart.

"Imagine how God feels when He looks down and sees us making the same mistakes over and over again. Ignoring all the wisdom in the Old Testament and everything Jesus and His disciples tried to teach us. For goodness' sake, it's all written out. In black-and-white. And we've had the instructions at hand for well over two thousand years. From His point of view, not too much improvement in our behavior since then, wouldn't you say?"

Ben didn't answer; he knew he wasn't expected to.

"You've only been at that church, what . . . six months?"

"Just about," Ben confirmed. "Since May . . . I know you have a point. Maybe I haven't been there long enough to have any influence. Or to have earned their respect. I do believe they would be paying more attention to their former minister, Reverend Bingham, on these questions, and not just brushing him off," he admitted. "But this situation also seems to me to be a test. A moment when I should be winning their respect. I should be reaching them. And I'm failing. I'm failing miserably. I'm starting to think I really don't have what it takes to be the head minister of a church."

It was hard to say those words out loud, though he had thought them many times in the last few days.

"I see. Your doubts are that serious, Ben?"

"They are, sir. Maybe I've taken on this job too soon. Maybe I just don't have what it takes to be a real spiritual leader, and not just a well-educated student of theology who can write a good sermon. And the sermon isn't even that wonderful every week," he admitted.

Reverend Hascomb sat back and tilted his head. "Are you considering leaving this church? Is that what you're saying?"

Ben couldn't answer. His thoughts hadn't gone that far. Well, perhaps, once or twice. But they always jumped back to a safer place.

"I don't know, Reverend," he answered at last. "It's hard for me to say that for sure at this point. Maybe because it would be hard to admit I've failed. I was so excited to be called to this church. I was thrilled. It was the answer to my prayers. Right now, it seems like the most difficult job I've ever had. I'm not a quitter. I've never quit anything, my entire life. I've never left a job half done, or just walked out on a mess. But I have to be honest with you, of all people. Yes . . . I am considering it. I don't know what else I can do. I'll never feel happy or satisfied just being a figurehead at a church, a prop the congregation wheels out on Sundays for an hour or two."

Reverend Hascomb shook his head. "I'm sure it's not that bad. There must be a few out there, maybe in the back pews, who are listening to you?"

Ben felt as if the reverend was coaxing him to get some perspective. Perhaps he had been exaggerating a little to get his point across.

"Yes, there are a few. But they would be open to the words of any minister, because God's spirit is already in their hearts," he pointed out.

Reverend Hascomb smiled and nodded but quickly grew serious again. "I can see you're in very deep turmoil about this, Ben. When we're in pain, it's only natural to reach for some fast fix. Even if it means biting off your own leg to get out of the trap. But don't make any hasty decisions. Don't do anything you'll regret later. I have a feeling that this situation is still unfolding, and . . . and, well, it's hard to say this, but I must."

"Please go ahead. I'm very interested in any insights you can offer, Reverend."

"Well, I know you're very sincere in your desire to lead your members to a greater spiritual understanding and attitude. But I must suggest you examine these frustrations you feel carefully and look for any part of your reaction that might merely be a bruised ego. What I'm trying to say is, I know you had a certain image or expectation of how Reverend Ben Lewis was going to relate to his congregation. And that has not gone anywhere near the way you expected. In fact, you've gotten some negative feedback that's hurt your feelings, insulted you, undermined your confidence. Hurt your pride," he concluded in a soft but serious tone.

Ben cringed inside. It was true. "Yes, my pride has been hurt. It's been a blow to my own image of myself. That's part of it. But not all of it," he insisted.

"Yes, I know. I know you have sincere intentions here. But make sure they are entirely pure intentions, coming from the highest place," Reverend Hascomb advised. "Especially before you make any big changes . . . Were you thinking of leaving before Christmas?"

"I would never do that. That would be totally irresponsible. I would never leave them without a minister for Christmas. I'd announce my decision after the holidays, then wait until they replaced me—or found an interim."

"That would be the responsible thing to do. I guess you've thought this through."

"I have. Somewhat," he admitted.

Yesterday morning, right after he had made the appointment with Reverend Hascomb, Ben had the impulse to draft a resignation letter. But he decided to hold off on that effort. He had wondered about other churches in New England that might need a minister. Then he wondered if he would ever get called again and, if so, whether he would have the courage to try with a new congregation. Maybe as an associate or a youth minister? Or perhaps he could piece together a living as clergy at a hospital, or counseling somewhere.

If I do leave this church, he thought, *it will unsettle and uproot my family all over again. We've hardly unpacked. But Carolyn will understand. She would be shocked at first, but she would never want me to feel unhappy and frustrated. We would find a way, somehow, with God's help.*

Reverend Hascomb set his pipe down. "I know you've tried preaching to them, even praying with them. But let's remember what the apostle Matthew advised: 'You will know them by their fruits.'"

Ben nodded. "Yes, that's true. I'm trying on that front, too." He thought of his idea for collecting funds for the families of workers who were losing their jobs, and of Sophie's idea for the toy collection. For all the conflict, he and his congregation were actively helping others, making a hard time just a little better.

"Good, then. Give it time, Ben. Even Jesus and his disciples didn't expect to win over everyone they encountered," Reverend Hascomb reminded him. "We must recognize and respect where each soul is in its spiritual journey. Maybe that's why we used to call ourselves Pilgrims." He smiled, reminding Ben of the deep historic roots of his church. "You can't force people to believe. You can't shame them into compassion. It has to come from the heart, authentically. Maybe our role is just to plant a seed there. Even one as tiny as the mustard seed."

Ben easily recalled that verse, also from the book of Matthew. "'So Jesus said to them, "Because you have so little faith. Truly I tell you, if you have faith as small as a mustard seed, you can say to this mountain, 'Move from here to there,' and it will move. Nothing will be impossible for you.'"'"

"Have I helped you sort this out at all?" Reverend Hascomb asked, his tone kind and concerned.

"Yes, you have, Reverend. I have a few things to think about now. And a little more gas in my tank to get through Christmas," Ben added, forcing a smile.

"All right, well . . . I'm here if you need to talk again. Anytime. I have a feeling there's more to this situation that has yet to play out, Ben. Maybe . . . well, almost certainly . . . God has placed you at that church for a reason, an important reason. You may soon find out what it is. Or you may never know. But we are all part of a plan. When you feel low and discouraged, try to remember that."

"I will, Reverend. Thank you," Ben said, shaking his hand.

As Ben walked to his car, he noticed how clear and sharp the blue sky looked today. He felt a little brighter inside, too, as if some clouds had lifted. His talk with Reverend Hascomb had renewed his energy and spirit and helped him put the situation in perspective. As always, Reverend Hascomb's advice was sound and true.

Even pointing out that my ego might be getting in the way, Ben admitted to himself.

It was some comfort to be reminded that his dilemma was endemic among his profession, dating all the way back to the apostles. But was that truth comforting enough to keep him running at this wall? For that's what it felt like at times. Other ministers might get used to this feeling, might take it in stride, as part of the territory. But Ben still wasn't sure he could go on this way indefinitely.

CHAPTER ELEVEN

Present day, December 18

R ACHEL DIDN'T HAVE LONG TO WAIT TO SEE RYAN AGAIN.
The day after their climbing wall date was a Thursday,
which meant there was a basketball practice that night. *No time to be
nervous,* Rachel told herself. Still, during her breaks between patients
that day, Rachel found herself both nervous and eager to spend time
with him, even in a frantic, noisy gym.

When she got home from work, she spent a little more time than
usual on her appearance, though hopefully not so much that it would be
obvious to him. Will was quiet on the ride over, listening to music on his
iPod. Nora was about to be dropped off at her grandparents' house again
and talked enough for all three of them.

"Grandma and I are building a *real* gingerbread house. It's going to
be awesome. We made all the walls and the roof and even some elves
who live inside last night when you went out, Mommy. And now we're
going to start putting it together. Right after I do my homework."

"Wow, that sounds great. I had no idea you two were so busy."

Rachel knew they had been baking something last night. The pleasant, sugary scent had filled the house when she walked in. But she had been in too much of a post-date daze to focus on the details.

"Sara's grandma made one with her. But they used a kit. Grandma said we can eat ours after Christmas, and we'll know it's homemade."

"Very true," Rachel agreed. "I can't wait to see it . . . and eat it, too."

Nora sounded so happy. Rachel had to remember to thank her mother for taking on this special baking project. It surely took a saintly amount of patience. Most grandmas *would* buy a kit.

Rachel hadn't had much time so far to do Christmas things with the kids. She had barely started her shopping. But they did plan to visit Sawyers' Tree Farm on Saturday, which was always fun, then put up their tree on Saturday night. Maybe she and Nora could do some cooking or baking before Christmas, too.

Although she had been very busy with work and all the time spent on basketball, Rachel knew that was not the only reason she had put off her Christmas preparations. She knew it was time to decorate, to put up a tree and have a real Christmas again. But it was still hard. She knew the kids felt it, too, though they hadn't talked about it openly. Not yet, anyway.

WHEN THEY REACHED THE GYM, MOST OF THE TEAM WAS ALREADY starting to warm up, running laps around the court. Will didn't run ahead to pull off his fleece and join in, as he usually did. He loped alongside Rachel, his earphones still firmly in place. She wondered if he was tired, or maybe just more relaxed about his place on the team.

Damion, who was the starting shooting guard, had pulled his hamstring again in a game and was out for the season. Will was not a starter yet, but first reserve for the spot and getting a lot more playing time. His skill on the court had improved considerably now that he was playing in this higher-level league. Rachel knew that Jack would have been very proud. Will was really maturing as a player this season, just as his father knew he would.

When Rachel arrived at the benches, Ryan met her gaze and held it, his smile making something inside her light up. "Hey, long time no see. Where's your climbing gear? I thought you might want to scale the scoreboard while the kids were working out."

"Maybe later. I have to figure out who didn't get their Falcons sweatshirt." She took out her clipboard full of lists and sat down on the bench near him. It felt good just to be around him. Everything was easy between them. *Maybe it was because she felt as if he was also a friend, as much as . . . well, a romantic interest,* she told herself. Even in her mind, she couldn't say the word "boyfriend" yet.

"Hey, Sam, pick up the pace. You're not picking daisies out there," Ryan urged a boy who tended to lose focus.

Jason, the trainer, walked up to them, nodding a greeting. "What do you want me to start them with?" he asked Ryan.

"I was thinking over and under. They all need to work on their passing skills."

Over and under, a drill for speed and agility, was not Will's favorite. The boys lined up in groups of three and had to hand the ball along, going up over the head of the player in front of and down between the legs of the player behind them, back and forth, faster and faster.

"Sounds good to me," Jason agreed.

The boys came in from their laps and gulped down water. Will looked a little winded and Rachel felt a twinge of concern, but he seemed to catch his breath quickly.

"Over and under, guys. Break into squads of three," Jason called out. There was some grumbling, but they headed back to the court with their basketballs. Jason clapped his hands briskly. "Let's move it! We don't have all day."

Will was one of the foot-draggers, stalking out slowly to find partners. "I hate over and under," he muttered. "What a stupid drill."

Ryan's eyes narrowed. "What did you say?"

Will looked alarmed for a moment that Ryan had actually heard him. Rachel expected her son to say "Nothing" or maybe even apologize.

Instead he said, "This drill is stupid. I don't get the point."

"I think you know the point," Ryan said in an even tone. "But if you're not into the drill, take a few more laps."

Will stared at him. He couldn't believe he was being reprimanded.

"Well? The laps or the drill, it's your choice," Ryan told him.

Finally, Will put his head down and set off to run around the gym again.

Rachel stared at Will, but he wouldn't meet her eye. He had broken an ironclad rule: No sassing the coach or the trainer or Rachel. She had seen Ryan enforce breaches this way before and had never thought much of it.

Now it was her own son, who rarely, if ever, talked back to any adults—well, to other adults. But he had, and this was the consequence. She glanced at Ryan, knowing he was doing the right thing, but she was still a little worried about Will, who had just caught his breath after all the laps he'd run during the warm-up.

Ryan looked back at her, an unspoken question in his expression. Rachel heard Will's big sneakers slapping the wood as he made a turn around the court. He was panting a little, but nothing unusual.

Get a grip, she told herself. *Don't fly off the handle, like you did at the first game. Your son will be all right. He needs to be put back in line once in a while. He sasses you back all the time now. You keep saying he needs a male role model. Well, this is what a male role model does.*

She looked back at Ryan, then down at her clipboard. He did understand that she was backing him up on this, she felt. That was the main thing.

Will survived his extra laps and even took a few turns at over and under. The team practiced hard and played a fierce scrimmage. Ryan commended Will a few times on shooting some fast, strong baskets under pressure. Will took the praise in stride.

"Great practice, gentlemen," Ryan said as parents began to appear. "Remember, the game on Sunday is early, ten a.m. So get to bed early Saturday night. I want to see you all well rested. It's the last game before the break for the holidays, so we want to come out strong."

As the boys headed out, Rachel stood with Ryan, packing up their duffel bags. "Want to grab a bite to eat with me and Andy tonight? There's a place in Rowley called American Burger we've been wanting to try."

Rowley was a small town between Cape Light and Newburyport and not very far from the gym. "That sounds good. What do you think, Will?"

Will shrugged. "I don't know . . . whatever you want. I have all this science stuff to study. There's, like, a test tomorrow."

Rachel had to smile. There either was a test or there wasn't one. There couldn't be "like" a test. But she didn't bother to correct his grammar.

She looked over at Ryan. "Thanks, but I guess we'd better get straight home. We still have to pick up Nora. You'll have to give me your review."

"I will. I'll call you later," he promised, meeting her eyes in a way that made her blush.

Rachel just smiled and headed out of the gym. Will was walking a few steps ahead with Andy, and she wondered if he had heard Ryan's parting words.

What if he had? *He needs to get used to the idea of me seeing Ryan,* she reminded herself. She wasn't sure if his surliness at practice was a reaction to Wednesday night—or what she called a U.T.M., an unidentified teenage mood.

Maybe a little of each. She decided to talk to him later. Just to get a handle on what was going on.

There was a time to leave Will alone to sort through things on his own, but also a time to talk about things openly. "A time for every season," as one of her favorite Bible verses said.

IT WAS GETTING CLOSE TO ELEVEN. RACHEL HAD COME UPSTAIRS TO check on Nora. She was a restless sleeper and always kicked her covers off. Rachel found her sleeping soundly. She kissed her head and pulled her blanket up, then headed downstairs to fold some laundry and set the coffeemaker for the morning. When she came back upstairs, a stripe of yellow light at the bottom of Will's bedroom door told her he was still awake.

She knocked lightly. "Will, can I come in?"

"Yup," he answered.

Rachel opened the door and found him sitting on his bed, his long legs dangling off one side, his back against the wall, which was covered with posters of NBA players. His ever-present earphones dangled around his neck, and his computer was open on his lap. School papers covered his bed on one side, an open textbook and binder on the other.

"Earth science?" she said simply.

"Yeah, I'm sunk. I don't get any of this." He stared at the screen without looking up at her.

"I thought Grandpa was going to help you study for that class."

Then Rachel felt instantly guilty. She should have done more to push that idea along. She had been so busy lately, helping the basketball team and being distracted by Ryan.

"Yeah, well, that didn't happen. Maybe we could study for the next test. And he could just pray for me this time."

Rachel wasn't sure if Will was serious or not. He sounded serious, but she had a feeling he was just being sarcastic. She let it slide—and tried not to smile and encourage him.

She walked into the room and stood near his bed, then pushed some papers aside and sat down on the corner of the quilt. "Can I help you? Test you on terms or something like that?"

He shook his head. "I don't think so . . . thanks."

Rachel waited a moment, hoping he would look up at her, but he kept his gaze glued to the computer screen. "Anything you want to talk about with me?"

She waited. He shook his head. "Nope."

"How about the practice? What happened there?"

He shrugged. "I just said what everybody says about those dumb over and unders. Coach must hear kids say that all the time, but he just, like, totally comes down on me."

"Will, you were disrespectful. You know the team rules."

He shrugged again. "Whatever. I guess he gets his kicks showing us he's boss. That gets old real fast."

Rachel's inner alarm system sounded. Barely a week ago, Coach Coop could do no wrong. Will's attitude had definitely soured. Rachel had a feeling she knew why, too.

"Will . . . are you upset that I went out with Mr. Cooper the other night? You can be honest with me. I'm not going to be mad at you . . . I really just want to know."

Will twisted his mouth to the side and shook his head. "No big deal. It is what it is," he said flatly.

"I have a feeling that you're saying that, but you don't really think it's true."

He sighed and finally looked up. "Mom, I get it, okay? It's not about that at all. Cooper just gets under my skin sometimes. He thinks he's Phil Jackson or something . . . but he's not. Okay?"

Will had named one the most famous coaches in the history of the NBA. Ryan didn't act as if he thought he was a superstar. Will was being unfair. He was angry, she realized, and didn't have the first clue of how to express it. Or maybe he just wasn't ready to.

"Okay," she said finally. "How late are you going to stay up? You can't do well on the test if you don't get enough sleep."

"Not too much longer . . . if I can get back to studying and stop talking?"

"Yes, you can stop talking. You said an entire . . . twenty words in a row. I should be grateful." She shrugged and kissed his cheek, finally making him crack a small smile.

When she got downstairs, she found she'd missed a call from Ryan on her cell phone. It was getting late, but she decided to call him back.

He picked up on the first ring. "Hey, thanks for calling me back. Did you hear my message?"

"Did you leave one? I just saw the missed call and tried your number."

"I just wanted to say that I'm sorry I had to come down like that on Will today. I'm sure it was hard for you to watch. But I can't treat him any differently than the rest of the team if he breaks a rule."

"I wouldn't want you to," Rachel said quickly. "I saw what he did. He deserved a reprimand. I just tried to talk to him about it, but he sort of stonewalled me."

Rachel didn't feel free to tell Ryan that Will had complained about him. She didn't think that was the real reason he was being ornery anyway.

"What did he say?" Ryan asked. She could tell he cared about Will and would be concerned if Will felt unhappy.

"He said all the kids hate that drill," she admitted. "But . . . I really don't think it has anything to do with over and unders. I'm pretty sure what's bugging him is that you and I went out on a date. He just doesn't know how to express that."

Ryan was quiet for a moment. "Yeah, I can see that. You told me on Wednesday night he was having trouble dealing with it."

"I thought he was dealing with it. He claims it's all okay and 'it is what it is,'" she quoted. "But I don't think I'm getting the whole story. I'm going to talk to him again. Before the game on Sunday," she added.

"I know the symptoms," Ryan said. "Andy's like that, too; never wants to discuss his emotions. He's a genius at changing the subject. Listen, is there anything I can do? Do you think I should ask him about it? A man-to-man thing? I don't feel good about Will feeling bad. Maybe I can help him see there's nothing to feel scared about."

Rachel appreciated that Ryan felt so concerned, and cared about Will's feelings. But she didn't think it would do any good for him to get involved directly. It might actually make things worse.

"Thanks but . . . I think it's better if I deal with it for now. I think he is trying to work this out. It's just hard for him."

"I'm sure it is," Ryan said. "Does that mean you don't want to go out again until he's all right with it? I was wondering if you wanted to get together this weekend, Saturday night or Sunday?"

Rachel felt suddenly anxious. As if all the oxygen had been sucked from the room. She didn't think he would ask to see her so soon. One date a week was enough for her . . . or even every other.

And asking her about how Will's feelings affected their relationship . . . well, she had to give him an A-plus for being direct.

But she actually hadn't even gotten there yet in her own mind.

"I just don't know about Will," she said honestly. "And I can't get together either of those nights anyway. I promised the kids we'd get our tree Saturday night, and we're going to see my folks on Sunday."

"All right. I didn't mean to pressure you. How about 'so far, so good'? Does that still stand?"

Rachel laughed, thinking it was sweet of him to remember that. "Yes, it still stands. I guess we'll see you Sunday anyway, at the game."

"Oh, yes, big game coming up. Better not go out the night before anyway," he added. "I hear there's some snow coming tomorrow, but it should all be over by Saturday afternoon."

"I hope so. I wouldn't want to have to call all those parents if the game is canceled." Another one of her manager jobs.

He laughed. "That would be annoying. But I would help you," he promised.

They chatted a few more minutes and finally said good night. Rachel found herself left with the same warm feelings she'd had after their date. She liked him . . . she liked him a lot. No matter what other bittersweet, or even guilty, thoughts rushed in like clouds in front of the sun, she couldn't deny that she liked Ryan Cooper. He seemed to be smart, kind, and funny—all the qualities she admired.

Will's issues seemed to shift into the background. Wouldn't he be bound to have issues whenever she started dating? Maybe she shouldn't press him so much to talk about it. Maybe he had to process this on his own awhile longer and he would be able to accept it.

She very much hoped so.

SNOW FELL STEADILY ON FRIDAY NIGHT AND ALL THROUGH SATURDAY morning, just as predicted. Rachel and her children woke to a world of pure white outside their windows. It was not the first snowfall of the winter, but the first real blizzard. The branches and rooftops were outlined with a thick coating of white, and the snow kept falling and falling, mounding up in the backyard until every distinguishing feature—the rosebushes and birdbath, the shrubs and even some trees—was practically indistinguishable.

"It looks like the frosting we used on our house," Nora said, staring out the window with Rachel.

"On your house?" Rachel didn't understand.

"Me and Grandma. On our gingerbread house."

"Oh right. It does look like that," Rachel agreed.

Pancakes were a high point of the morning and kept the kids cheerful for a little while. But it was too cold and snowy to go outside, and they soon became bored.

Will shut himself in his room, playing video games with his friends online. Rachel read to Nora from a chapter book about a lost dog and his adventures while he was far from home.

Nora seemed able to listen for hours. Rachel loved the story but was feeling tired of reading, and her legs felt cramped from sitting so long.

"What do you think? Maybe we should save some of this for later?" Rachel asked.

Nora shrugged. "What else can we do?"

"Why don't we take out some Christmas decorations? Maybe we can still get the tree later. We're getting a really late start this year," she added.

Last Christmas had been just under a year since Jack's death, and they hadn't decorated at all. This year the kids agreed they wanted a tree and decorations inside. But so far, they hadn't done much about it. This was partly Rachel's fault, she knew. It was another hard, but necessary, thing to do: trim the tree without Jack.

"What do you think?" she asked Nora. "Shall we find a few special ones?"

Nora nodded. "I like the snow globes and the carved wooden bear. Can we take those out?"

"Absolutely. Let's go up to the attic and look around."

Nora loved to go into the attic but wasn't allowed on her own. Her eyes lit up at the mention of this adventure. "Great. I'll get my flashlight."

There was a light in the attic that went on with a switch. But Nora liked to take the flashlight she kept in her room for emergencies. Rachel's father had given it to her right after Jack died when she was having nightmares. Somehow, it had really helped.

They were just coming down with some boxes—more than Rachel had expected to unpack—when Will came out of his room. "Can I go snowboarding with Andy at the golf course?"

"Has the snow stopped?" Rachel looked out the window. She hadn't realized it, but the snow had tapered off considerably. It was light enough to go outside now.

"Just about. Coach Cooper is going to take us and a bunch of kids from the team."

"All right, fine with me. Just make sure you dress warmly, and take your waterproof gloves and helmet," she added.

Will nodded and pulled out his phone, texting Andy, she had no doubt, that he could come. He went back in his room to get changed. And then the home phone rang.

Nora was already downstairs and picked it up. "Mom, can I go to Sara's house and play in the snow?"

"Um . . . sure. I'll get you dressed and walk you over there in a little while."

Rachel brought the decorations downstairs and left them on the dining room table. It seemed an accomplishment just to have taken a few things down from the attic. She and Nora would unwrap them later, and maybe tonight she would take the kids to Sawyer's. Or tomorrow after the game.

She opened one of the boxes and pushed back the tissue. The carved bear wearing the Santa hat. She looked down at it but didn't take it out. It was so hard to have Christmas without Jack. It had been his favorite day of the year. But maybe that was more of a reason for them all to enjoy it—for his sake—not lock it away in the attic forever. He would have never liked that, she realized, gently taking out the wooden bear.

While both her children were out in the snow, Rachel made a big pot of chili and corn bread. She loved to cook during a snowstorm, filling the house with warm, delicious smells.

Just before she set out to pick up Nora, she got a text from Ryan.

On our way back. Hope you weren't worrying.

Rachel had not been worrying. But she had wondered. They had been out a long time and she'd sent a text to Will. But it was so cold, she doubted he was taking his phone out to check messages.

Thanks. Was just going to text Will. You must be frozen!

She waited. Finally a text came back.

Uh . . . a little. :)

She laughed. He must have really meant "a lot" if he was willing to admit it. It had been good of him to take the boys out and stay with them. It was the kind of thing Jack would have done.

Thanks for taking Will. Bet he had a great time. Made some chili and corn bread. Dinner here with Andy?

Rachel had typed in the words before she'd totally thought it through. Maybe Will wouldn't like the idea. He had been so down on Ryan the other night. But Ryan had had them over to dinner, and she needed to return the invitation at some point. Tonight seemed as good a time as ever, and doing it on the spur of the moment spared a lot of anxiety, she reasoned.

She heard the beep of a text coming in and saw Ryan's reply:

Love to. What can I bring? PS: Boys are starving. Hope you made a ton.

She quickly texted back: Enough for an army. I have everything.

She signed off and set out to get Nora, then found herself breaking into a big smile as she walked up the snowy street. Everything looked so fresh and new, so soft and white. The tree branches looked as if they'd been covered with lace, and the houses and front yards on her street seemed to have been tucked beneath a soft white blanket for the night.

She was happy to be spending the evening with Ryan again. She couldn't deny it. It had worked out just by chance, and Rachel had a good feeling about the evening ahead.

CHAPTER TWELVE

⌒✎

*R*YAN AND THE SNOWBOARDERS STOMPED INTO HER HOUSE, pulling off big boots, wet jackets, hats, and gloves, and looking red-cheeked and weary but cheerful.

The boys headed upstairs to Will's room, and Rachel told her son to loan Andy some dry socks and maybe some dry jeans, too.

Ryan had taken off his boots at the door, and she could see that his socks were very wet, as well.

"Would you like some dry socks? I'm sure there are some that will fit you in the laundry room." Without waiting for his reply, Rachel found a pair of Will's big gym socks and brought them out.

Ryan rewarded her with a grateful smile. "I knew I came to the right place. Dry socks, hot chili, and fresh corn bread. And a lovely hostess," he added. "Who could ask for more?"

Rachel felt herself blushing and focused on the salad she had just started making.

"How can I help?" he asked.

"A fire would be nice." She had been meaning to make one all day but hadn't gotten around to it. "There's plenty of wood and kindling in the basket."

"I'll get right on it." He headed for the fireplace in his stocking feet. Rachel couldn't help noticing again how handsome he was. His shoulders looked very wide and strong in a light blue ski sweater, and his worn jeans hugged his hips and long legs as if they were made for him.

A fire was soon crackling in the hearth, and he returned to help finish setting the table.

"I'm glad you came for dinner tonight. We were going to get our tree today and decorate, but that didn't work out with the snow."

"My luck, then," he said happily. "I'm glad to see you, too—and not on a dressy date that makes us both so self-conscious and crazy," he added with a smile.

Rachel felt the same. Just hanging out at home in their stocking feet, and maybe watching a movie after dinner—that was her idea of a great evening.

Everyone had a good appetite after being out in the cold all day, and Rachel was glad she had made plenty of chili. Nora put on her pajamas early and wanted to watch *The Wizard of Oz*, her favorite video lately. Ryan sat with her while Rachel loaded the dishwasher. She heard them talking over the exciting moments of the story. Nora still liked to hide her eyes when the Wicked Witch came on the screen, and Rachel peeked in and saw Nora burying her face in Ryan's sweater.

By the time Dorothy and her friends reached the Emerald City, Nora had drifted off to dreamland. Rachel shut off the video. "I should wake her so she can walk up to bed," she said quietly.

"You can't wake her when she's sleeping like a little angel," Ryan protested. "I'll carry her upstairs." He did, and laid her gently on her bed, then went downstairs while Rachel tucked her in. When she came down a few minutes later, she found him sitting by the fire. She sat next to him on the couch, and they gazed at the glowing flames together.

"How are Andy and Will doing? They must be exhausted," Ryan said.

"They're still pretty lively. I heard them Skyping with a school friend. They seem to have a lot of energy left."

"They'll need it for tomorrow's game. We just have to win the next three and we'll be in the play-offs."

She detected a quiet note of pride in his tone. He had earned it, she thought. He did a great job coaching the team, no matter what Will thought.

"I can't believe the season is almost over," Rachel replied, staring into the flames. "Didn't it just start?"

"Well, the travel league plays a short season," Ryan said. "Really, it's just a month or so, and then we're into the play-offs—if we make it."

Rachel shook her head. "Is it just me or does time go faster and faster as you get older?"

"It does go fast. Too quickly sometimes." He turned and looked at her. "I hope we can still see each other after basketball season, Rachel. I keep saying I don't want to pressure you but . . . I'm afraid I keep doing that, don't I? The thing is, I know I'd regret it if I wasn't honest."

"It's all right." She did appreciate his honesty. "I don't feel rushed . . . Well, maybe a little," she admitted. "I'd like to keep seeing you, too."

He slipped his arm around her shoulder. "That's good enough for me. That's plenty," he said happily.

Rachel felt very conscious of his touch and his nearness. She also realized she didn't want to move away. There didn't seem any reason to pull apart. She felt so relaxed with him. Everything was so easy. He laughed at her jokes and really listened to the things she said. He took her thoughts and opinions seriously. She liked what she knew of Ryan Cooper and wanted to get to know him better.

They heard heavy footsteps on the staircase. Will and Andy appeared. "Are there any more brownies?" Will stood in the doorway, staring at his mother and Ryan. His expression didn't change, but something about his eyes gave away his reaction to seeing Ryan's arm around her shoulder. Rachel was sure he was upset but doing a good job of masking his feelings.

"I wrapped up the pan. I'll get them for you." She started to get up as Will turned and walked into the kitchen.

"Chill, Mom. I can find them."

Rachel sat back down again. This time, at the end of the couch, an arm's length from Ryan. He looked over at her with a small smile. But she had a feeling he thought she had overreacted.

A short time later, Andy and Ryan were ready to go. Ryan thanked her again for dinner and turned to Will, patting his shoulder. "Bring your A-game tomorrow, Will. It's all hands on deck."

"Got it covered," Will said, avoiding Ryan's gaze.

Rachel noticed that Will had not said, "Got it covered, Coach." But at least he hadn't pulled away when Ryan touched him.

Later, after she had straightened up and turned off the lights downstairs, Rachel came up and passed the door to Will's room. It was open, but she knocked anyway. When he turned to look at her, she walked in.

He was taking out his uniform and basketball sneakers, making sure he had everything he needed so he wouldn't be running around hectically in the morning. Just the way his father had taught him.

"It was nice of Mr. Cooper to take you and Andy out all day. Did you thank him?" she asked.

"Yeah, I did."

"Did you have a good time?"

He nodded. "Yeah, sure . . . Did you have a good time with Mr. Cooper, watching TV?"

Rachel bristled at his tone. "What do you mean by that?" She knew very well what he was getting at, but this wasn't the way to talk about it.

"Nothing. I guess he likes *The Wizard of Oz*, that's all. He seemed really into it, watching it with Nora."

"We all liked watching it . . . Are you angry that Mr. Cooper and Andy came for dinner?"

He gave her a look, as if she had grown an extra nose. "Why do you think that?"

"Something seems to be bugging you, Will. I wish you'd just tell me what it is. Did it bother you when you came down and saw Mr. Cooper's arm around my shoulder? We were just talking."

He shoved his Falcons sweatshirt into the duffel bag. "I told you before. It is what it is. I wish you'd stop asking me how I feel about it, okay?"

Rachel held on to her patience. She was doing something wrong here. Trying to talk to him about this seemed to be making it worse, not better.

"All right . . . It's okay if you don't want to talk about it now, but I really think we should. I don't think you're so fine about it."

"I'm just tired. I don't need all these questions. I just need to go to bed. Coach Cooper said to get a good night's sleep. I'm just trying to follow team rules."

Rachel heard a mocking tone when he mentioned Ryan. But she didn't call him on it. He wasn't ready to talk about this. He was probably nervous for the game. Maybe after the game was over, they could talk. She hoped so.

"All right. Good night. See you tomorrow."

Rachel walked into her bedroom feeling deflated. Will really had issues about her dating Ryan. There was no getting around that or trying to minimize it. And she had just told Ryan that she would like to keep seeing him, that there was a future for their relationship. With his gorgeous blue eyes gazing at her so adoringly, what else could she say? What would anyone say?

She had forgotten all about her children. Particularly Will. Not forgotten, but minimized the problem. *Because being with Ryan feels good.* Now she just felt guilty and selfish.

Maybe I'm actually ready to slowly dip my toe in the water. To date someone as kind and patient as Ryan. But Will isn't ready to see that.

She had thought Will was processing this, dealing with it in his own way. But now she could see he really wasn't. This was not something Will could accept.

She had felt so lighthearted a few hours ago, anticipating Ryan's visit. Light as a snowflake. But now, as she climbed into bed, her heart felt heavy. She felt stuck and didn't know what to do.

THE NEXT MORNING, THEY HEADED OUT TO THE GAME ON TIME. WILL seemed to be in his usual pregame mood, jumpy and excited and a little absentminded. Her parents were sorry they couldn't go to the game, but the timing conflicted with the service at her father's church. Rachel rarely missed church on Sundays, but she knew they couldn't do both today.

She dropped Nora at her parents' house at half-past nine. She and Will would come back to the house later that afternoon to help her parents trim their tree. It was a family tradition that both her parents and her kids loved.

Only a few parents were in the bleachers when Rachel reached the gym with Will. She lugged her duffel bag over to the Falcons' side of the court. Once again, Will took his time getting to the bench, wearing his iPod until the last possible second. Jason gave him a look and he finally took it off, then loped out onto the court to do laps with his teammates.

He's not exactly hustling, Rachel thought. *But maybe he's tired from all the snowboarding. He'll perk up once the game starts.*

"Hey." Ryan greeted her with a warm smile that showed his deep dimples to advantage. "How are you doing?"

"I'm good. How are you? Nervous for the game?"

"Just pumped up. We're going to win this. I have a good feeling," he said, gazing at her.

His warm look made her heart skip a beat. She turned and took off her jacket, trying to hide her reaction.

"Hey . . . Will . . . Charlie . . . stop horsing around, okay?"

Rachel turned at the sound of Jason's voice. Will was on the other side of the court and should have been practicing layups at the basket, but was fooling around with a boy named Charlie.

Rachel looked over at Jason. He waved his hand. "They're all pumped for the game. They'll burn it off."

Rachel glanced at Ryan. He was reading over his lists and play sheets and hadn't seemed to notice.

A short time later, the bleachers were filled with fans. The opposing team had arrived and was finishing their warm-up. Ryan called the boys into a huddle to review their plays for the first quarter.

Will sat on an upper riser, not out of range of hearing but not in close and totally focused either, Rachel noticed. He had put his sweat-shirt back on after the warm-up, and she noticed him slip his phone out and check a text, then text back.

Ryan noticed, too. "Will. What does the post do during the five-three-nine play?"

Will shrugged. "I'm not sure . . . I'm not the center."

Ryan fixed him with narrowed eyes. "Right, you're not. You can sit out the first quarter and look over the plays with Jason to refresh your memory."

Will stared at him. "You're kidding, right?"

"You know the rules," Ryan said calmly. "No phones during a practice or a game. I'm surprised we're even having this conversation."

Rachel felt alarmed to see them confront each other, but once again, Will had been disrespectful—and had intentionally broken a rule he knew Ryan was very strict about.

Will looked sullen but put his phone away. Then he moved over to sit next to Jason, who already had out a stack of play sheets.

The starters soon took their positions, and the game began.

Will had finished reviewing plays but didn't come to sit down on the lower bench with the rest of the reserve players, Rachel noticed. He was sulking, but maybe he'd get over it once he went into the game. She hoped so.

In the second quarter, Will sat down with the reserves and the first-string players who were resting. Ryan soon called him up. "Will, you're in . . . go get 'em."

Will ran out to his position, looking determined and calling for the ball. But he lost his focus when blocking passes to the player he was guarding, who made two baskets in a row for the opposing team. Will finally got hold of the ball and started dribbling. Two seconds later, the other team's point guard stole the ball from him.

Rachel felt her heart fall. She knew Will would feel humiliated by having the ball stripped from him. No one wanted to cause a turnover. But it happened, even to huge stars; she remembered Jack saying that. Besides, basketball was such a fast game, a player could redeem themselves seconds later. "Go, Will . . . Go!" she cheered when he finally got the ball again.

He took a wild shot, and the opposing team easily caught the rebound. Will raced after them to the opposite end of the court but was unable to guard his man, who sank a perfect three-pointer.

The other team called a time-out—and Ryan called Will to come off the court. Rachel could tell from Will's expression that he was frustrated and ashamed of the way he had played.

"It's okay, Will. Cool down a few minutes, have some water." Ryan touched his shoulder, but Will shook him off.

He put his hands on his hips, and glared at Ryan. "Hey, let me play. I was sitting down the whole first quarter."

"Sorry, Will. I think you need a break. Your head's just not in the game. Sit here and watch awhile."

"I was on the bench the whole first quarter!" Will protested. "How can I get my head in the game if I'm just sitting here like a lawn statue or something?"

Rachel felt stirrings of alarm again. *Will, please don't do this!* she thought.

Ryan remained cool, not taking offense. He glanced at Will, then back at the players on the court. Will's replacement had just scored.

"Relax, you'll play," he told Will again. "There's a whole second half. This team plays hard. We'll need fresh horses by then."

Will didn't like that answer either. In fact, he seemed even more upset. "You're not playing me until the second half? You're kidding, right?" Will was actually yelling now. Luckily the gym was loud, and with everyone cheering, his voice didn't carry very far.

But Rachel could hear him. She wanted to get up and intervene but knew she shouldn't. This was between a player and his coach. Ryan finally reacted to Will's tone with a stronger voice, but still didn't sound mad at him. "Cool down, Will. I'm not kidding. I know this is a big game. I know you can do us some good out there. But you have to cool down and sit down . . . or you won't play in the second half either. Okay?"

Ryan turned and looked at him. Will stared back. "No, not okay." He shook his head and seemed about to say more when he started to wheeze, his chest inflating and his head tilting back as he tried to suck in more air.

Rachel jumped up, recognizing the beginning of an asthma attack. Ryan ran for his duffel bag, too, but Rachel got to Will first with his inhaler and made him take it.

Finally, Will sat down on the end of the bench. Jason took over coaching the boys on the court, and Ryan came over to them.

"Are you okay, Will? What's going on?" Ryan crouched down in front of Will, looking genuinely concerned.

Will turned away and Rachel couldn't help it—she shielded her son like a protective mother hen. "He's all right. I've got this. You'd better keep your eye on the game."

It wasn't her words, but something in her tone that warned Ryan off; that made him look at her as if their own relationship had taken a sudden shift. She felt sad inside, but she couldn't help it. She had to think of Will now, not worry about Ryan's feelings.

She watched Will while his breathing slowly returned to normal. "Are you all right?" she asked him finally.

He shook his head, and he looked very pale . . . and very downcast. "I still can't breathe that well. Can we go home? It might come back."

Rachel wasn't sure what to do. She was sure that if he had scored a few points, or blocked a few, he wouldn't be so eager to leave—even if he had needed the inhaler when he came off the floor. But she couldn't make him stay if he said he felt sick. She had no choice but to take him at his word.

"All right. We'll go. Get your things. I'll tell Coach Cooper."

She walked over to Ryan, who was intently focused on the game again. She was inches from him before he noticed her. "I have to take Will home. He doesn't feel well."

Ryan looked surprised. "Is he that sick?" He looked over at Will, who had his sweatshirt on and held his duffel bag.

"He says he's having trouble breathing. I think it's better if I get him out of here," Rachel said.

"All right . . . But let me talk to him a minute. Jason can take over." Rachel could tell he was concerned and didn't want Will to leave angry at him. But she didn't think Will wanted to talk to him right now. She was sure he felt embarrassed about walking out on his team.

"That's all right. I don't think he wants to talk to anyone right now," she said honestly. "You need to watch the court. I'll have him call you later. Good luck with the game."

Ryan seemed dismayed but didn't argue. She saw him wave good-bye to Will, but Will didn't wave back.

As they walked along the sidelines, heading for the exit, the other players loped up and down the court, shouting directions to each other. "Over here, man. I'm open! I'm open!"

The buzzer sounded as baskets were scored. Will hunkered down, his hood pulled over his head, his eyes straight ahead. Rachel put her arm over his shoulder. She wondered if Jack would have let him leave a big game like this, even if he had sassed the coach and been left on the bench for the duration. Maybe he would have made him stay for that reason alone, she thought.

But her son was hurting inside. This wasn't any time to teach him a lesson, she decided. She was doing the right thing. It was time to pay attention to Will's feelings and put her own aside. Wasn't that the message he was sending her?

When they got home, Will went straight upstairs for a shower and then took a nap. He was still sleeping a few hours later, in the early afternoon, when Rachel went into his room and raised the window shade.

"Hey, Will. I think you need to get up. We're going to Grandma and Grandpa's soon."

He rolled over and squinted at her. "What time is it?"

"After two o'clock. Are you hungry? I'll make you a sandwich."

He nodded and sat up. "Sure, that'd be good. Thanks."

She sat on the edge of his bed and gazed at him. "Do you feel better? How's your breathing now?"

"I'm okay. It went away," he said. "I think I just freaked when Coach said I wasn't going in again until the second half."

Rachel was glad he had some insight into his reaction. "Yeah, you seemed pretty steamed. You know that stress sets off the asthma as much as anything, right?"

"Yeah, I know."

"So . . . what else? Are you ready to talk to me yet? Or do I need to keep asking questions?"

He sighed and looked down, pulling at the threads on his quilt.

"I don't know."

"What don't you know?" she asked, confused. "You don't know what's bothering you?"

Will scowled at her. "I told you. He shouldn't have taken me out of the game. Especially after he kept me out of the first quarter."

She knew it would only make Will defensive if she defended Ryan's reasoning. She shrugged. "It was a coaching decision."

"Well, maybe he's not such a great coach," Will said heatedly. "That was a stupid decision. I just had to get into my rhythm out there, and he didn't even give me a chance."

"And that's why you're upset?"

"Yeah, of course."

Rachel hesitated. Should she name the elephant in the room? She had to, she realized, or this situation would just get worse. "So you're not upset about the fact that Ryan and I . . . like each other?"

"How could you like him?" Will demanded. "He's not even a good coach. And all the other guys are going to think it's weird that my mother is dating him. Besides, what about Dad? Did you just forget about him?"

There it was. He'd said it. Will's eyes were glassy with unshed tears.

She shook her head. "It's not like that, Will. It's not like that at all. I think about your father all the time. You have no idea."

"I used to think you missed him, the way Nora and I do. But now, I guess I don't know," he said. "Maybe it's wrong to say that, but it's just the way I feel. You keep asking me how I feel, so now I'm telling you the truth. Okay?"

Rachel nodded. "Okay. I hear you. I have been asking you, and now I hear what you just said."

But it was all she could do to get those words out with the wind almost knocked out of her. *What have I done?* was all she could think. She had fallen for Ryan Cooper, and in the process she had hurt her son. She knew Will was still grieving for Jack, still grappling with that loss, and now she had made him feel as if Jack didn't matter to her anymore. No wonder Will was confused and furious.

Will sighed. She heard his breath sound wheezy again and started to worry. "I'm sorry, Mom," he said quietly. "Are you mad at me?"

"No . . . I'm not mad. Not at all. Thanks for telling me the truth. I wanted to know what you were thinking, and now we're square. You wash up and I'll make a sandwich. Then we have to get over to Grandma's."

When Rachel got down to the kitchen, her phone was beeping, signaling a text message had come in. She checked the screen and saw it was from Ryan.

How's Will doing? Better I hope. Pls tell him Falcons won. We missed him.

Rachel felt so sad seeing the message, she felt tears well up in her eyes. But she knew what she had to do. She texted back: Will is much better. Off to my parents' house now. Can you meet for coffee tomorrow sometime?

Ryan replied quickly: Would like that. Where and when?

She texted him back: Three o'clock. The Beanery.

She would be done with patients by then, and the kids weren't home from school until four thirty. Ryan quickly agreed and she put her phone away.

It would be hard to tell him she couldn't see him anymore. Especially after Saturday night, when it had all felt so right, so possible. But it was best to get this over with, she thought.

She had been fooling herself to think she was ready to get out in the world again. It was going to take some time before Will could get past his loss, and she wasn't going to rush him and hurt him for her own selfish needs. What kind of mother would she be? Hadn't he been hurt enough already?

WHEN RACHEL AND WILL ARRIVED AT THE PARSONAGE, NORA RAN TO answer the door. She looked excited, her big brown eyes bright, and Rachel felt her spirits lift at the sight of her little girl.

"The gingerbread house is almost done . . . but you can't see it yet." Nora was practically hopping up and down with excitement.

Rachel leaned over and kissed her cheek. "I can't wait. I bet this is a real work of art."

"Oh, it is," her mother promised as she walked out of the kitchen, pink and green frosting streaking her apron.

Rachel kissed her mother hello, and Nora took her hand. "Don't go in the kitchen. You're not allowed to look yet."

Rachel was dragged toward the living room, and Will and her mother followed. Her father stood among an array of big green plastic containers and seemed tangled in a length of tree lights.

"Will, go help Grandpa," Rachel urged him. Will took the other end of the string of lights and helped unravel them.

"Thank you, Will. That is a help. Every year I try to put them away neatly. I think elves get in there and tangle them," her father said. "How was the game? Sorry we couldn't make it. Did you play much?"

Will shook his head. "Only a few minutes. I sort of stunk up the place and my coach took me out . . . Then I had an asthma attack."

"Oh dear, that's not good. But maybe that's why you didn't play well when you were out there. You didn't feel right," Carolyn said quickly. Rachel could see her mother's comment made Will feel better. "How are you now? You look okay."

"He's all right. He got winded and needed the inhaler. It wasn't a full-blown attack," Rachel clarified.

"We wouldn't want that," her father said. "How did the team do? Did you find out?"

"They won," Rachel said. Will gave her a look. "Coach sent me a text. He asked how you were and said they missed you."

Will stared at her a second but didn't say anything.

"Can you take the other end of these lights and get them all the way up on that top branch, Will? You're taller than me now." Her father laughed. "I don't feeling like taking out the stepladder."

"And we don't even need one this year, with a tall young man on hand," her mother added.

"I can do it, Grandpa. Don't worry." Will stepped over and fixed the lights while her father directed him and draped the lights around the lower branches.

"I don't know why we're always the last ones in town to decorate our tree, Carolyn," Ben said. "You would think a minister could do a little better than that."

"It's like the shoemaker's children going without shoes," her mother answered. "We always have good intentions, but we never do it much earlier, Ben."

She opened one of the plastic containers and took out a shoebox. It had old-fashioned printing on it, from the 1960s or 1970s. Rachel vaguely recognized it. It was one of the special boxes that held her mother's favorite ornaments.

Carolyn opened it carefully and took out a delicate glass angel that wore a gold halo, filmy wings, and a long, sparkly white robe.

"Isn't this beautiful? Your grandfather gave it to me the year your mother was born," she told Nora. "A lot of our ornaments were ruined when we moved here. A pipe broke in the basement right before Christmas, and it ruined practically everything down there. Remember, Ben?"

Rachel saw her father sigh and shake his head. "I remember. That was not my favorite Christmas," he said quietly. "Not by a long shot."

"Oh, there were bright spots. It was Rachel's first Christmas, and you gave me this angel and said it reminded you of our baby," her mother said fondly.

Rachel had heard that story many times before, but could never see the resemblance.

Nora held the ornament up and looked at her mother. "It does look like you, Mommy . . . a little."

Her father came around from the back of the tree. "When she was a baby, it looked exactly like her," he insisted. He leaned over and plugged the lights into the wall socket.

They lit up instantly, making the tree look brighter even without any ornaments.

"Good job, Grandpa," Will congratulated him. He held his hand out, and his grandfather looked confused for a moment. Then he slapped him five.

"That looks pretty," Nora said.

It did look pretty, and Rachel felt better now in the company of her family. She decided to put her worries about both Will and Ryan aside for a few hours and just enjoy getting ready for Christmas.

CHAPTER THIRTEEN

December 17, 1978

*B*EN RETURNED TO THE PARSONAGE MUCH LATER THAN HE expected on Sunday afternoon. After the service and coffee hour, he had to stay at church to rehearse the children in the Christmas pageant, which was very much like trying to herd a bunch of cats dressed in Biblical costumes. *But cute cats,* he thought.

He also stayed to help the music director rehearse the chorus and special soloists, who would be lending their talents on Christmas Day. There had also been more cleanup from the Christmas Fair, which had been held the day before, mainly in Fellowship Hall. But there had been booths and activities all over the building. Sophie and her committee were still gathering leftover supplies and putting away folding tables.

The fair and the toy collection had both been smashing successes. A good-sized fund from the fair—and from the collections made at shops in the village—was building. There was also an impressive pile of gifts for the families of workers who were going to lose their jobs when the canneries closed down—probably next week, from what Ben had heard.

It would be a sad Christmas for so many. But at least the church was trying to help them. Ben didn't even feel he was still trying to prove a point. He could see now that was wrong thinking—as wrong as vilifying Oliver Warwick. Reaching out to the families was simply the right thing to do, and he took some comfort in knowing that.

As he entered his home and took off his coat, he forced himself to shake off his heaviness of heart and leave his worries about church matters at the door. Carolyn and her parents had already started putting up a Christmas tree. Ben could hear them in the living room. He was late and needed to catch up. He took a package from his briefcase and walked into the living room to greet them.

"Well . . . there he is," his father-in-law said. "We heard you coming up the walk. We thought it might be Santa. Shouldn't he be here about now?" Charles theatrically checked his watch.

Ben forced a smile, but the jibe did not go unnoticed. For the past two weeks, his father-in-law had not missed an opportunity to point out how many hours Ben spent at the church.

"Oh, Charles, enough of that," Louisa scolded her husband. "This is Ben's busy season. If he owned a shop in town, you wouldn't tease him like that for working long hours right now, would you?"

Ben appreciated his mother-in-law's defense—though he would hardly compare being a minister to owning a shop. Well, maybe there were some similarities.

"Hi, honey." Carolyn emerged from the kitchen carrying Rachel, who was already in her soft pink pajamas. "We waited awhile but then just went ahead and started on the tree. I hope you don't mind. We wanted Rachel to see it."

Ben leaned over and kissed them both hello. "That's all right. I didn't want to hold everything up." He finally took a long, appraising look at the Christmas tree. It wasn't just started; it was done. Even the star at the very top was firmly in place. "Hey, that's my job!" he wanted to say. But he hadn't been here, and his father-in-law had taken over, obviously.

"The tree looks beautiful," he said finally. "You all did a great job. Sorry I missed it. I want to take a picture of you and Rachel standing right in front there," he told Carolyn, "to send to my mother and sister."

Ben's father had died years before, and his mother lived with his sister in Vermont. Ben hoped to visit them after the holidays with Carolyn and the baby.

"Not right now, honey. I look a mess." Carolyn smiled and shook her head. "You can photograph us on Christmas, when both of your girls are dressed up." She smiled at the baby and fluffed her soft hair with her fingertips.

Both of his girls looked perfectly beautiful to him right now, but he didn't argue with her. "Here . . . I have something for you." He had left the package on the lamp table when he walked in and now gave it to Carolyn.

"A present? You didn't have to do that, Ben. It's not even Christmas yet."

"I think it was a good idea," his father-in-law mumbled.

Louisa gave her husband a look as she stood up to take the baby. "I'll take her a minute. You sit and open your gift."

"It isn't much," Ben warned Carolyn as she pulled open the bow. "Just a trinket, really."

Charles loudly cleared his throat and rolled his eyes. Ben ignored him.

"I'm sure I'll love it, whatever it is." Carolyn ripped off some paper and opened the box, then carefully removed a glass ornament from its nest of tissue paper.

"Oh, it's beautiful, Ben," she said, showing it to everyone. "You know how I love angels."

"I did remember that, dear. But this one reminded me of Rachel. I bought it to remember our first Christmas with her."

"Oh, Ben . . . that's so sweet." Carolyn jumped up and gave him a big hug, then hung the ornament at eye level, right in the middle of the tree where they could all see it.

"Very thoughtful," his mother-in-law praised him.

"Yes . . . very nice," his father-in-law agreed, though there was something of "What's the big fuss about? I expected jewelry" in his tone, Ben thought.

Ben didn't care. The gift had been sincerely given. He had several other, more lavish gifts for Carolyn hidden away around the house. Little luxuries he knew she wanted, like a cashmere cardigan and her favorite French perfume.

But the ornament was his favorite. It had caught his eye in a shop window, reminding him so much of their daughter. The soft reddish-brown curls painted on her head, the blue eyes and sweet smile. The gold halo, gossamer wings, and pearl-white gown were accessories he could only imagine on his daughter, though he didn't doubt Rachel wore them daily, along with her onesies and diapers.

"Well . . . guess I'll work on those outside lights if we're done in here," his father-in-law announced.

"Don't bother; I'll do that tomorrow," Ben said.

"Better to get it done and out of the way. Tomorrow will bring its own chores," Charles replied. *And you won't be around for those either, I expect,* Ben heard him add silently.

"Hold your horses, Charles," Louisa said. "Ben just got home. He must be hungry. Here, have a sandwich and some cocoa before you go out again." She held out a platter to him. There were a few half-sandwiches left, looking a little soggy and passed over. And the pitcher of hot cocoa was now cool to the touch.

Ben took a small triangle of bread, ham, and Swiss. "Thanks. That will do. It's almost dinnertime. I don't want to spoil my appetite."

He ate his late lunch in two bites, then dutifully followed his father-in-law outside. Once again, celebrating this Christmas season was not living up to his expectations or daydreams. For one thing, he didn't expect to have his in-laws here for so much of the time.

But the house was looking neater, and Carolyn's mother had been doing a lot of cooking and baby relief, so Carolyn had more energy and was much more cheerful, Ben reminded himself. *You must count your blessings and not always be measuring the moments against some idealized scenario—at home or at church.*

CHARLES CLEARLY DISAPPROVED OF BEN'S LONG HOURS AT THE church. But as Ben left the parsonage on Monday morning, he felt like telling his father-in-law, "You ain't seen nothing yet."

Driving toward the church, Ben braced himself for the week ahead, with so many projects to complete by Christmas and more rehearsing and preparations for the special services. This year, since Christmas Eve fell on a Sunday, he was committed to two services in a row, instead of just the Christmas Day service the church usually celebrated.

He reached the church at eight a.m., instead of his usual nine, but still found cars in the parking lot. Some dedicated church members were there before him, Sophie Potter among them, of course. She greeted him as he came through the glass doors closest to Fellowship Hall.

"We're just setting up for the toy giveaway, Reverend. The parents should start coming around ten o'clock. There are plenty of toys and other gifts for them to choose from. You would be amazed at what people donated."

Ben glanced into the room. Rows of tables were covered with toys, games, and all kinds of things children loved to play with. There was even a row of shiny bikes and skateboards along the windows.

"It looks like a toy store in here," he said in awe.

"Doesn't it? I was thinking Santa's Workshop. That's what we're calling it." She showed him a big poster board sign she was about to hang up outside. "So people don't feel so . . . well, so self-conscious because they need a handout," she said honestly. "We thought the name helped a little."

"It helps a lot," he agreed, amazed once again by her thoughtfulness and sensitivity.

"I can help, too, if you need me." His schedule was packed, but this effort was important.

"Don't worry, Reverend. We have plenty of volunteers today. People are eager to help if you show them the way. We can do a lot with a little, with God's help," she added.

"Very true, Sophie." The reminder lightened his heart and his step. He could accomplish all the work set before him when he called upon heaven to help.

The day went by quickly, but as darkness fell and Ben was left alone working at his desk, he still was not free to leave the church. A trustees' meeting was scheduled for seven o'clock that evening, and it didn't make any sense for him to rush home and come back again.

He walked over to the Clam Box and ordered a container of chowder and a sandwich to go. He planned to eat at his desk and get a little more paperwork done before the meeting.

A man walked in and sat near him. He looked Ben's way and nodded. "Reverend. How are you tonight?"

It was Peter Blackwell, the church member who had walked out on the prayer at the Christmas Fair meeting. Ben had looked for him at church since then but hadn't seen him.

"I'm all right, Peter. Good to see you," Ben said sincerely.

Peter shrugged. "I've been working overtime at a big construction job the last two weeks. Even on the weekends. But I've got to thank you for helping my son. That was good of you, all things considered."

Considering how confrontational I was at the meeting, Ben translated. Ben had heard about a job that Peter's son, Jacob, was qualified for—at the diner, in fact—and he'd put in a good word with Otto and sent Jacob over to the diner. But he had never heard how that all turned out.

"Did Jacob get a job here?" Ben asked curiously.

"Oh, yeah. Otto hired him on the spot. He's back there cooking right now," Peter said proudly. "He likes it even better than the cannery. It's real cooking, what he was trained for. So him losing his factory job turned out for the best," Peter said with surprise. "I'm grateful to you, Reverend. What you did shows real . . . Christian spirit."

A waitress brought out Ben's order from the kitchen in a paper bag, and he paid her for it. "I'm so glad Jacob got the job, Peter. I hope to see you back at church sometime."

Peter nodded. "I'll be there on Christmas with my family. We're looking forward to it."

Ben said good night and headed down Main Street and across the green. There were bright spots here and there, like the lights out on the water. Who was it who said what you focus on tends to expand? If you focus on good, you will see more good in your life, and if you focus on the negative situations . . . well, you'll see more of the same.

Ben wasn't sure, but it seemed true. Finding Jacob Blackwell a new job was a small gesture in the big picture. But the change in Peter Blackwell's attitude was a positive ripple, some evidence that these small efforts had a larger effect. That was the way God worked, showing us we are all connected—another reason to love your neighbor as you love yourself, Ben reflected.

THE TRUSTEES' MEETING WAS FAIRLY ROUTINE. EACH YEAR THE churches of Ben's particular sect of Protestantism were bound by charter to present an annual report of all activities to their members. That meeting was always held in January, and many important issues were discussed and voted on, and new officers were elected. There was always a rush of last-minute preparation, so it was worthwhile to get as much as possible done before the holiday break.

Walter Tulley had stepped in as interim treasurer after Oliver's resignation. A new treasurer would be nominated and elected in January. A commercial fisherman, Walter was very competent and organized in this job, Ben thought. Walter gave short, but detailed, reports and was explaining the past year's accounts.

"That last figure is the sum of member pledges collected so far this year," Walter said, discussing a sheet he had passed out. "That doesn't include the next two weeks, up until January first, of course. It also doesn't include the special collection taken at Christmas Eve and Christmas Day services."

"And we've earmarked that money for the workers who have lost their jobs at the canneries," Ben reminded them.

"Oh, right." Lester made a note on his sheet. "I forgot about that."

"A good idea, I thought," Ezra said.

Lester glanced at the wiry doctor. "It won't be a million dollars, goodness knows. But I suppose it will help."

"Warwick's lumberyard is being sold, I hear. So those folks won't lose their jobs," Joe Morgan told the others. "Though I hear the buyer has got Warwick over a barrel and he's practically stealing the business from him."

"No comment there," Lester murmured, staring down at the papers in front of him.

"There's also the Christmas Fair profits." Walter looked down at his records. "That's going to the families, as well. A tidy sum—several thousand—and the Christmas collection should match, or even beat, that figure."

"A little here, a little there. It adds up," Ezra said cheerfully.

"Yes, it does. A lot of church members worked very hard on the fair," Ben said, then added, "Sophie Potter in particular. It was a very successful effort."

Lester loudly cleared his throat. "Well, everyone should be thanked then. The donations will be some solace for the families . . . Let's go on with the reports for the annual meeting, shall we?"

It was Joe Morgan's turn to report on costs for repairing the building over the past year, and the discussion turned in that direction.

But Ben felt encouraged to hear the fund was growing. Lester was right. It wouldn't be a million dollars, but he knew it would be some help to the families and was pleased that members of his church had worked together to accomplish this. It was impossible to change this dire situation in a radical way. But it was possible to accomplish small acts with kindness and compassion. At the very least, they were doing that.

Present day, December 22

WHEN RACHEL ARRIVED AT THE BEANERY, SHE FOUND RYAN WAITING for her at a table near the entrance. The café was not very busy at this hour. She was thankful for that. The conversation was going to be hard enough without having to raise her voice over other customers. Right now her only competition was the occasional hiss from the cappuccino machine.

Ryan greeted her with a heart-wrenching smile as he stood up and kissed her cheek. Rachel did not kiss him back, though she couldn't help but smile. There was something so lovely about being kissed by this smart, kind, incredibly good-looking man. She slipped off her coat and sat down. The table was very small, and she suddenly felt so close to him, she wasn't sure if she could follow through with her plan.

A waitress came by, and they both ordered cappuccinos.

"How is Will?" Ryan asked. "No aftereffects yesterday or last night?"

"He's fine. It wasn't a total, all-out asthma attack. But I'm glad we caught it quickly."

"Of course. He seemed upset to leave the game."

"He was. But it was his choice," she added. "He was upset about a lot of things. That's probably why he didn't play well . . . and why he's been so difficult with you."

"Testing me, you mean?" Ryan looked at her with a curious expression.

"You might say that. I've been talking to him and . . . well . . . he's upset about us dating. He's tried to act as if he doesn't care, but he's actually very disturbed about it."

Ryan's expression grew serious. "I see. I wondered about that myself," he admitted. "I mean, after you told me that you'd had that talk with him. I'm sure it's hard for him to get used to the idea."

"What about Andy?" she asked, suddenly curious. "Has he been upset by it?"

"Not that I can tell," Ryan said. "But his situation is different. His mother is very much alive. He spends lots of time with her, and she's happily remarried, so he's gotten used to how things are. What Will's going through—losing his father so suddenly—has got to be harder."

"Very hard," she said, relieved that he understood. "In fact, I think it's best for him . . . and everyone involved . . . if we stop dating, Ryan."

Ryan's eyes widened with surprise. She realized he had assumed she just wanted to talk over the situation. Not break up. Well, they were never really going out. *One date doesn't make a relationship,* she reminded herself. Still it felt as if that's what she was doing. She was breaking off something real, and it hurt far more than she had expected.

"Really? I mean, do you really think that's the best way to handle it, Rachel? Maybe if we just take it slower and give him time to get used to the idea . . ."

Rachel shook her head. "I'm sorry. I don't think that would work— or be the right thing to do. Especially for Will." She looked up and met his gaze. "Please believe me, it has nothing to do with you. Will really likes you. He looks up to you, honestly."

Or he did before we started socializing, she wanted to add.

Ryan sighed and shook his head. She could tell he wasn't going to give up on this easily. "Listen, I can't tell you how to handle your kid. I know that's your decision. But it seems to me that Will is very young, and maybe he needs to try to think a little differently. To consider you, your feelings."

He was sounding a bit like her mother now, she thought. She had agreed with Carolyn, at first. And going out with Ryan had felt good and right. She had felt as if a whole new phase of her life might be opening up. But she had done a one-eighty turn after seeing the look on Will's face the day before, the anger and the tears in his eyes.

"I'm sorry," she said. "I don't see it that way. Just the opposite, in fact. I'm really certain that I need to put my own feelings aside for now. That's what a good parent does. I'm certain this is the right thing to do—for Will and for myself. I couldn't be happy knowing that I was making him unhappy," she added quietly.

"I'm not saying you shouldn't be sensitive to his feelings, Rachel, believe me. Or that I'm not sensitive to them. But there are ways of working this out. It's normal for him to have this reaction. But you need to see he's a little stuck. You need to help him through it."

Rachel didn't need to hear any more. Nothing he said was going to persuade her.

"I'm sorry we're even having this conversation. I wish it were different"—she met his gaze only briefly; it was too hard to look at him—"but I can't just . . . coach him through this," she said. "I don't even want to try. I can't talk Will into feeling something he just doesn't feel. I have to respect what he does feel. My children are my priority and always will be. I'm sorry. That's just the way it is."

Ryan sat with his head bowed, stirring his coffee. Rachel's had gone cold, the foam deflated. She hadn't even taken a sip.

"I do know that. I knew it from the first minute I met you. I won't say anything more about Will. But I have to tell you, honestly, that I'm very sorry this didn't work out. I know we only had one real date, but . . ." He paused, as if he felt he was going to say too much. "Well . . . it was a really good one," he added with a small, wistful smile. "A sign of good things to come, I thought. I'm sorry we'll never find out for sure." He paused and gazed at her.

Rachel knew what he meant. She felt sorry, too. But she couldn't be nearly as honest about her own feelings. If she told Ryan how much she cared, how he had started to change her life, how he had made her feel hopeful and happy again . . . well, none of that was what you said when you were breaking up with someone. It wouldn't be fair.

"I respect your decision, Rachel. And I understand if you don't want to help the team anymore," he added. "You don't have to tell me now. Why don't you think about it over the break?"

Rachel had been thinking about her role on the team, and imagining that she would feel horribly uncomfortable continuing. She wasn't even sure right now if Will wanted to play with the Falcons anymore, though he hadn't said that outright. She just got a feeling he might feel awkward around Ryan and had been thinking of quitting the team. But Ryan was right. Nothing had to be decided right now.

"Okay, I'll think about it," Rachel said.

He forced a smile and nodded. Then he suddenly stood up and dug his hands in the pockets of his leather jacket. "Well . . . have a Merry Christmas. I guess we'll talk after the holidays."

"I guess so. I hope you have good holidays, too. So long . . ." Rachel nodded and blinked as she watched him leave the Beanery. She felt her eyes fill with tears and was glad she hadn't started crying in front of him.

For goodness' sake . . . you really aren't ready for this if you're getting so upset after just one date.

But it had been more than that, she knew. They'd seen a lot of each other these last few weeks. She knew she was going to miss him.

She felt sad and confused and wondered if she really was doing the right thing. But what she'd told Ryan was true. Her children came first and always would. She had to do it for Will.

December 24, 1978

BEN'S ALARM CLOCK WAS SET FOR SIX THIRTY A.M., BUT RACHEL'S whimpers woke both him and Carolyn even earlier. "I'll get her. I have to get up soon anyway," he told his sleepy wife.

Carolyn's head dropped back onto her pillow, and she smiled with her eyes closed. "Thank you, Ben . . . Call me if she fusses too much," she whispered. She was asleep again before he had slipped on his robe and slippers.

He stumbled down the dark hallway to the nursery and looked down into the crib. "There, there . . . What's going on with you, little one?"

He picked up his daughter and cuddled a blanket around her as he pressed her to his chest. The parsonage was chilly in the morning, despite the repairs to the heating system.

Talking to her quietly the whole while, he changed Rachel's diaper and carried her downstairs for a bottle. He was quite proud that he could now balance the baby on his shoulder while filling a small pot with water, setting it on the stove, taking a bottle from the fridge, and dropping it in to warm.

Rachel wasn't fussing too much, but he bounced her around and hummed a bit. "Jingle bells, jingle bells, jingle all the way . . . Oh what fun it is to ride in a one-horse open sleigh-ehhh!" He dipped up and down as he sang, just to see her blue eyes widen and the surprise on her baby face.

"Oh my . . . look at that. We had some snow last night, Rachel. I'd better call the deacons and make sure they come early to shovel the parking lot."

He held her near the window so she could see what he was talking about. "When you're a little older, we'll build a big snowman together, and I'll pull you on a sleigh," he promised. "We can have a snowball fight, too. If we're careful."

He was looking forward to doing so many things with his little girl. She was getting bigger and stronger every day, and as he held her in his arms like this, the peaceful, white world outside seemed an echo of her purity and innocence . . . and of his unlimited love for her. Ben stood quiet and still, focusing on the moment, feeling steeped in the true beauty and meaning of his life. No matter what happened with his position at the church or any of his worries, he felt a connection to something much deeper and much more powerful. A connection that gave him peace and equanimity—and the energy to do what he had to do these next few days.

"Do you know what today is?" The water had simmered, and he took the bottle out and tested the formula on his wrist. Just right. "Christmas Eve. Baby Jesus is born tonight. He was a baby, just like you," he murmured, cradling her in one arm and offering the bottle. She sucked hungrily and smiled.

"Not so fast. You'll get gas, and I'll be in trouble with Mommy . . ."

Watching Rachel drink, Ben braced himself for his challenging schedule of back-to-back services today and tomorrow. But he was grateful for this precious moment with his daughter, reminding him what it was all about, essentially, at the very heart. About love. The greatest commandment of all . . . the greatest power . . . the highest expression a being could aspire to. That is what Jesus came here to teach us, ultimately.

That was all you really needed to know, Ben decided.

BY THE TIME BEN ARRIVED AT THE CHURCH, A CREW OF CHURCH MEMbers had already shoveled the walkway. They were now working on the parking lot and seemed perfectly cheerful. Luckily, only a few inches of snow had fallen, light fluffy stuff that didn't faze hardy New Englanders.

Ben had worked the day before as well, but had left before the mail delivery. Now he picked up the bundle of envelopes on his way inside and dropped them on his desk. It looked like the usual assortment, mostly bills and junk mail. One envelope caught his eye—cream-colored, watermarked stationery with embossed printing on the return address. It had come from Lilac Hall. He quickly opened it and unfolded a single sheet.

Dear Reverend Ben,

Thank you for your thoughtful note. I so appreciate your kind words. Such are few and far between these days, for myself and my family.

Yes, there are many challenges ahead now for us, and many decisions to face. Many I never expected. Lillian and I do our best to weather the storm. She's been a rock. A man could never ask for a better wife.

We will be moving soon and are quite busy packing. I hope that you and I can meet again when our situation is settled.

Thank you for your prayers. I have appreciated your help during this difficult time. And God's help, too.

Yours truly,
Oliver Warwick

Oliver's sincere message made Ben feel sad. Decisions he "never expected." The man had a gift for understatement. But Ben was heartened to find a note of faith as well and hoped that meant Oliver did not feel as dismal and hopeless as he had at their last meeting. Ben knew there were many families with lives upturned due to Oliver's errors—upturned as completely as the Warwicks' lives were now. But he felt again that Oliver and his family were deserving of compassion as much as any.

Every seat in the sanctuary was filled that morning, despite the snow. The choir sang beautifully, and three musicians from the congregation played "God Rest Ye Merry Gentlemen" on flute, oboe, and cello. It was a lovely touch, Ben thought.

When it was time for Joys and Concerns, Ben did not see many hands up. Perhaps people didn't want to mar the holiday with realistic concerns.

But he did spot Ezra Elliot, sitting in his usual spot toward the back. "Yes, Ezra? You have something you would like to share?"

Ezra stood up. Ben could tell by the set of his jaw this was going to be a concern, not a joy. "I just drove over to church from Southport Hospital. Oliver Warwick had a heart attack last night, and he was taken there by ambulance."

Ben felt a shock wave move through his body; he could tell the congregation was shocked, too.

"He's out of the woods," Ezra said, "but in serious condition. I was staying with the family, helping them deal with the medical issues," he explained. "I ask for your prayers for his recovery . . . and for his family. They've had a lot to shoulder these last weeks. This blow seems almost too much."

Ben couldn't find words for a moment. He wondered why Lillian or even Emily had not called him, but he knew how proud and stubborn Lillian was, and they surely must have been overwhelmed last night, waiting to see if Oliver would survive.

Ben continued with the service, trying to maintain the Christmas Eve mood of joyful expectation. The choir closed the service with "O Come, All Ye Faithful" and a section of Handel's "Hallelujah Chorus," which was Ben's favorite.

But an image of Oliver drifting between life and death in a hospital bed shadowed his mood like a cloud. There was no question. He had to go see him. Whether the family had reached out or not.

After the service, he went straight to his office, though he knew the congregation would be looking for him and wondering what had happened to the usual greeting line. Especially on a holiday. He pulled off his robe and scarf and grabbed his coat. Then he thought to take a case from his closet that held sacred items used to minister to the sick—what he called his traveling sanctuary.

Carolyn was waiting outside his office in the hallway, holding Rachel, who wore a red velvet dress, white tights, and tiny black patent-leather shoes. Carolyn looked beautiful in a black velvet top and long red wool skirt. He suddenly remembered he had forgotten to tell her . . . or take their picture by the Christmas tree, as he had promised.

I'll take their picture later, he promised himself. *Or maybe tomorrow.* Then he felt the familiar pang of guilt as he once again parked his family life on a back burner. He hoped it wouldn't always be like this.

Carolyn glanced at his coat over one arm and the clerical case hanging from the other. "You're going to Southport to see Oliver," she said.

"I think I ought to . . . I'm sorry," he apologized quietly.

"I think you *should* go. Poor Oliver. I'm sure he wants to see you."

Louisa and Charles walked up to them. They both had their coats and gloves on and looked ready to find the car. "We'd better get back to the house, Carolyn, and start the roast," her mother said. "It takes a while. We don't want to serve dinner too late."

Ben and Carolyn usually celebrated on Christmas Day, but since his in-laws were visiting, they had decided to have special dinners both days. Carolyn and her mother had been preparing all week.

"Ben has to go to Southport. To see that man who had the heart attack. He was mentioned in the prayer requests?" Carolyn said to her mother.

"Oh yes . . . Oliver something . . . that rich fellow who got into all that business trouble," Louisa added in a hushed tone. Even the La-Fontes, who had only been in town two weeks, were up on all the news about the Warwicks. "Do you really have to go there today, Ben? Surely they don't expect you to—"

"Mother? . . . Ben has to help them. That's what ministers do. Even on Christmas Eve . . . Especially on Christmas Eve," Carolyn explained boldly.

"I am sorry. I'll try to be back for dinner," he told them.

"I understand. They need you now. Much more than we do," Carolyn replied sweetly. "Please tell them all I'm praying for them. And I'm very proud of you," she whispered in his ear, reminding him of why he married her in the first place.

His father-in-law had not said a word; he just took in the scene with his usual grumpy disapproval.

Finally he said, "You probably want some company or help. It's a long drive to Southport."

Ben stared at him. "If you want to come along, I guess it would be helpful. You don't have to, though, Charles," he added quickly.

"I'll come. Let's get going. A job begun is half done."

Carolyn met his glance and gave him a sympathetic look. She kissed his cheek and made him promise to call when they were heading back.

Once on the road with Charles, Ben felt trapped in an awkward silence. He was rarely, if ever, alone with Carolyn's father and didn't know what to talk about. Sports? The news? There hadn't been much time for him to keep up on either lately.

He was also quite distracted, thinking more about Oliver and his family, and the battles they were fighting on so many fronts now.

"Would you like me to turn on the radio?" Ben offered, reaching for the dial when the silence seemed oppressive.

"Suit yourself. Not much music on the car radio these days that I enjoy."

Ben decided he didn't need the radio either. "Not much traffic on the highway. There might be more tonight," he noted, just for something to say.

"I have no idea. Hard to say if you don't live in the area."

At least he was honest, Ben thought. His bluntness of speech was a certain category of sincerity. No one would ever call Charles LaFonte a people pleaser, that was for sure.

Neither man spoke for a long time. Finally Charles said, "I have to admit, you are dedicated to your calling. If you're half as dedicated to my daughter, I'd say she's in good hands."

Ben was so surprised by the compliment, he nearly swerved into the next lane. He glanced at Charles to make sure he was serious.

"I'm doubly dedicated to Carolyn. And to Rachel. Never fear, sir," Ben promised him.

"I think you know you're not the man I expected her to marry," Charles replied, sounding agitated about the issue all over again.

"Yes, I know that," Ben assured him.

"But it's clear to me she wouldn't have it any other way. Even with that drafty old parsonage, busted pipes, and you practically living at that church." His big shoulders shrugged under his wool jacket. "So, what do I know? What does anyone know, when you come right down to it?"

Ben nearly laughed with relief. "I feel the same. And I've heard it's a good thing. The beginning of true wisdom."

Charles gave him a doubtful look, then a very small, almost undetectable, smile.

When they reached the hospital, Ben was given a pass and allowed to go straight up to Oliver's room, even though Oliver was being closely watched and visitors were limited. Ben didn't want to leave his father-in-law alone in the crowded waiting room. There wasn't even a vacant seat. He'd had no idea the holiday would be such a busy time here.

"Come with me," he told Charles.

"Am I allowed?" his father-in-law asked him.

"Carry this case. It makes you look official."

Charles took the case, and they walked to the elevator and got in. The security guard didn't even ask where they were going.

"What's in this?" Charles asked, glancing down at the black case.

"It's like a doctor's bag, for ministers."

"I see." Charles nodded. He seemed to be thinking about that.

They walked down a quiet hallway and soon found Oliver's room. There was a chair just outside the door to the room. "I guess you can wait for me here. I won't be long."

"All right. No rush. I'm not going anywhere." Charles put the bag down carefully beside his seat and sat down.

Ben knocked lightly on the door and walked in. The room was dimly lit, but he could see that Oliver was in a bed near the door. Lillian stood beside him, gently adjusting his pillows. "Is that better, dear? Do you want me to adjust the bed? I can call a nurse," he heard her say.

Oliver looked very sick. Ben could hardly recognize him. His long, slender body was sprawled at awkward angles under the sheet and thin blanket. A bare foot stuck out from under the bottom of the bedding. He was clearly too tall for the bed.

He wore a blue hospital gown that tied in the back. Several tubes extended from his arms, and monitors were attached to his chest. His skin was very pale, the bluish-red veins showing on his neck and forehead. His thick, dark hair, which always looked so perfectly cut and combed, was pressed back flat from his forehead.

Ben visited with many people who were sick, in hospitals and at home. But Oliver looked worse than most, and Ben's heart was pained at the sight. He knew he had to force his personal reaction down and summon up some brighter energy.

"Hello, Oliver. Hello, Lillian," he greeted them. "I hope you don't mind me stopping by without calling first."

"Reverend Ben, good to see you," Oliver said, extending a pale, limp hand.

"Hello, Reverend." Lillian seemed very surprised. "I suppose Ezra told you what happened?"

"Yes, I heard it from Ezra this morning. What an awful thing," Ben said sincerely. He stood next to Oliver and gazed down at him. "How are you doing, Oliver? Ezra says that you're coming along well."

He hadn't exactly said that, but it did patients good to hear they were improving.

"He's hanging in there," Lillian answered. "We thought we'd lost him for a moment. It was terribly frightening."

She took out a tissue and dabbed her nose. Ben could see she was very shaken. So could Oliver, though he could barely turn his head. "Now, now, Lily. Don't cry. It's all right. I'll be okay. I'll live to fight another day." Ben could see him trying to smile, but that was a painful effort as well.

"Yes, you will, dear," she said, returning to her usual definite tone. She stroked his forehead with her hand. "I won't lose you now. After all we've been through, that would not be right—or fair."

Ben glanced down. He felt privy to a private moment between husband and wife. If he had ever doubted Lillian's love for her husband, or that she had a softer side, he would only have to recall this scene.

Ben could finally see that she felt deeply for Oliver, had sympathy for all he had gone through, and understood that he was much more, and much better, than the foolish, careless mistakes he made. Though it had to be hard to forgive him completely for risking their lives, and their daughters' welfare, too.

"It's funny how troubles are relative, Reverend," Oliver said, turning his gaze to Ben. "So many things that weighed me down yesterday seem less important today. I'm just glad to be alive, I guess. We take so much for granted. Especially in tough times like this. Your health for instance. No matter how much money you have, you can't buy good health. Or a good friend," he added.

"That's very true, Oliver. Very true," Ben agreed, feeling touched by his wisdom—a sort of "death's door school of wisdom" that he'd heard before from other patients in other sick beds. They often forgot these lessons as soon as they had the power to get up and walk out of their hospital rooms. But Ben had the feeling Oliver would not forget so soon.

Oliver gripped his hand. "You're a true friend, Reverend. You and a handful of others. Digger Hegman and Bates. And that upstart Elliot."

Ben smiled. Oliver and Ezra had a funny relationship—a devoted rivalry, you might call it. Oliver couldn't help talking about Ezra with a few friendly jabs. And Ezra was the same.

Oliver met his gaze, leaning his head forward a tiny bit. "You know what I was thinking when I thought it was the end? In the back of the ambulance when they couldn't keep me awake? I was thinking how my father had always secretly wished that I had died in the war, not my older brother, Harry. His namesake, his firstborn, Harrison Warwick the second . . . My father wanted Harry to take over the business, not me. He didn't want me near those canneries or the lumberyard . . . or any of it. My father always expected me to be a failure . . . and so I am. I've proved him right."

Lillian patted his shoulder. She looked pained to hear this story, though Ben guessed she must have heard it many times before.

"Now, now, Oliver, none of that. We don't have to talk about all that right now," she said.

"No, Lillian. It's true. Why not talk about it? These are the things a man thinks about, and talks about, at his mortal hour. Reverend Ben knows that," he added, glancing back at his minister. "I was the one that should have died in Italy, not Harry. He would have handled everything perfectly. Not run the companies my father worked so hard to build into the ground. Now my father is looking down, saying, 'See, Oliver. I was right. It should have been you who died. Not my favorite son. My firstborn. My namesake.'"

Ben cleared his throat. He felt moved to tears by Oliver's confession. "I don't know what your father thought, or what he would say right now," he replied quietly. "I do know that your heavenly Father, your *true* Father, who breathed divine life into you the moment you were born, is looking down at you, Oliver, with love and compassion and forgiveness. *You* are His favorite son, and He's very proud of you for telling the truth and doing all you can to make amends to those you wronged. He knows you're not perfect," Ben added, his voice rising a bit. "He knows He didn't make you that way. None of us are. He will take you up to be at His side when it's your time to go. Not a moment sooner. You're here, in this room right now, because He wants you to be. Because He still has work for you to do. You still have a lot to live for," Ben reminded him. "Your wife and daughters, for one thing. You'll get through this. Don't give up. Know that you are loved, by your family, your friends, and God above. You are forgiven for the mistakes you've made, and and you are infinitely loved, Oliver."

Oliver nodded; he couldn't speak. He was crying, but a smile formed on his cracked lips. Lillian was crying, too, but took tissues and gently dabbed her husband's eyes, unmindful of her own tears.

"Thank you, Reverend. For those . . . those words. I will remember them the rest of my life," Oliver promised.

Lillian glanced at him and nodded.

Ben felt gratified. God had allowed him to be an instrument of hope and a channel for His message. He knew why he had been sent here today and knew his work was done.

"Shall we pray together a moment? The Lord's Prayer?" he suggested.

Lillian and Oliver joined hands with Ben and he led them in the short but most important prayer, the cornerstone of Christian theology. ". . . and forgive us our debts, as we forgive our debtors. And lead us not into temptation, but deliver us from evil: For Yours is the kingdom, and the power, and the glory, for ever. Amen."

Ben said good-bye to the Warwicks moments later. Oliver was tired; his eyes were practically closing as Ben walked out of the room.

When Ben stepped out into the brightly lit hallway, he felt as if he were suddenly in another world. A world of light and activity; a very different world than the dimly lit sickroom.

Charles stood up from his seat and faced him. "Ready to go?"

"Yes, I am. He's a sick man. I hope I didn't wear him out, visiting too long," Ben said as they walked toward the elevator.

"I don't think you wore him out. I think he wanted to talk. Get some things off his chest," Charles said.

"Yes, I think he did," Ben agreed. "I'm sorry you had to wait so long, and now we have a long drive back."

"I offered," Charles reminded him as they stepped into the elevator again. "It was important that you came. I think you really helped that man. And his wife. I saw his face as you were leaving, and heard a bit of what you said to him . . . My daughter is right; you do have a gift that way."

Ben turned to him. He had been so down on himself lately about his calling and his spiritual gifts, or lack of them, that he was surprised to receive this compliment, and from such an unlikely source.

"Thank you, Charles. It means a lot to me to hear you say that," Ben said honestly.

"Well, it's true," Charles replied in his matter-of-fact way.

Ben just smiled. They left the hospital and walked to Ben's car. The sun was almost at the horizon, though it wasn't quite dark outside yet. On the far side of the sky, Ben could see a few small stars. Was God trying to send him a message by sending praise through such a begrudging, unlikely source? Ben had been trying to focus on small signs of progress. But he really had to frame this one and put it up on a shelf somewhere.

CHAPTER FOURTEEN

⌒

Present day, December 24

RACHEL STOOD BACK AND TRIED TO GAUGE IF THE CHRIST-mas tree was standing straight in its holder. "A little toward the windows, guys . . . That's it . . . Right there."

Her children were stretched out on the floor under the lower branches, frantically turning the screws in the tree holder that secured the trunk.

This had always been Jack's job, dragging the tree inside, sticking it in the holder, making sure it was straight. The tree was a lot heavier than it looked, even though they had not chosen a very tall one this year. But it was full and nicely shaped, Rachel thought, and one of the last at Saw-yers' Tree Farm. But just right for them.

"Mommy, can we stop now? My fingers are falling off," a little voice complained from under the pine boughs.

"I'll do it," Will said, taking over from his sister. "You need to really dig into the trunk at the end."

Will had been acting very manly today, she had noticed, taking the stepladder up from the basement, along with a hammer, string, and nails to make a safety line so the tree wouldn't fall down. He had helped Mr. Sawyer lift the tree onto the hood of the SUV and tie it down, then helped carry it to the back door and into the house.

"That looks great. I think you've got it," Rachel said finally.

"I'll put the lights on." Will stood up and brushed himself off. "I found an extra power strip. We'd better use that. It's safer."

"Oh . . . right." Rachel nodded, trying not to smile. Even Jack hadn't been that careful.

Will needed a little help to drape the lights, but he was so tall now, he didn't even need the ladder. While Rachel helped him, Nora started taking out the ornaments and setting them on the coffee table, which was covered by a soft towel.

"You know, Mommy, Mrs. Ledo said that in some countries people always wait until Christmas Eve to put up their tree. Like in Austria," Nora said knowledgeably. She had found a box of ornament hooks and was carefully fitting them on the ornaments.

Rachel had to smile at her brave attempt to make this very, very late tree trimming somehow seem normal.

"Well, we've been so busy the last few weeks, it just got away from us," Rachel explained. "But I think Christmas Eve is a nice time to decorate a tree. It does get you in the spirit."

Will didn't say anything. He stood back and admired his handi-work, then plugged in the lights. "Presto . . . it's showtime," he announced, seeming pleased that the lights went on without any further adjusting or fiddling.

"Good job, Will." *Even better than your father,* Rachel almost added. Instead she reached out and patted his shoulder.

"Okay, who wants to start?" Rachel gazed at the ornaments. They each had their favorites and quickly began to find special spots for each on the tree.

Rachel's mother bought each of her grandchildren a new Christmas ball every year, representing some special interest or hobby. Nora had a ballerina, a fairy, a soccer ball, Hello Kitty, and a whole bunch of dogs. Will had many bearing the colors and emblems of favorite teams, like the Red Sox and Celtics, and some Harry Potter characters. Rachel had a funny angel-and-reindeer couple who looked like they were dancing.

Jack had bought her that one. "You and me, honey," he said with a grin when she opened it.

Rachel had laughed. "Yeah, you do dance as if you had four feet," she had teased him.

She felt wistful as she attached the hook to a soft pine bough. The reindeer duo spun as if they really were dancing.

"Mom . . . look. Should I hang it?" Will held up Jack's favorite. Rachel recognized it instantly. The ornament showed the all-time-great Celtics star, Larry Bird, making a jump shot. Though it was late in Bird's career, the star center had been Jack's hero when he was Will's age. Jack had rarely been at a loss for Bird-wisdom while teaching Will the game. Rachel felt an ache in her heart and knew Will was feeling the same.

"Let me see . . ." Nora raced over to him, but he wouldn't let her touch it.

"Be careful. It's already wearing out a little."

"Your Dad loved that one so much. It was the only one he really cared about. I think we should hang it, don't you?" Rachel asked them, wondering suddenly if the memory was too difficult.

Will nodded. "Yeah . . . he did love it. But let's save it for last. Like he always did. Remember?"

She did remember. Jack was happy to set up the tree, fix the lights, and then have a beer while he watched his family do the rest. Except for Bird, which he hung himself: the very last ornament on the tree. "Some people save the treetop star for last. Our family saves Larry Bird," he would tell them, making the same joke every year.

"It is tradition," she agreed.

Both children were misty-eyed, and so was Rachel. "I know you miss Daddy. I do, too," she said quietly. "But he loved Christmas so much. It was his favorite day of the year. He would be happy to see us putting up a tree again this year," she reminded them. "He wouldn't want us to ever stop doing this. Even if he can't be here with us."

"I know," Will said. "But . . . it's just sort of weird without him."

It was different; Rachel would never deny that. Nora didn't say anything, just hugged her around the waist, commanding her attention. Rachel thought she might be crying. But when she looked down, Nora was staring up at her, not quite smiling, but almost.

"I think Daddy is here," she said quietly. "Where else would he be?"

Rachel smiled at her and nodded, though she felt tears filling her eyes. "I think so, too."

"Grandma said when I miss him, I can just talk to him. And he can hear me," Nora explained. "She said he's always nearby, helping and protecting me, and if I miss him, to just say a prayer."

Rachel stroked her daughter's soft hair. "Do you want to say a prayer now?" Nora nodded. Rachel looked over at Will, and he shrugged.

"Okay, honey. You start," Rachel told Nora.

Nora squeezed her eyes closed. "Dear God . . . Thank you for this excellent tree and all our Christmas balls. But we miss our Dad. Sometimes it feels like he's right here with us again. So maybe you can let him visit. Please take care good care of him in Heaven and let him know how much we love him . . . Amen."

She opened her eyes and looked at Rachel and Will.

"Good job," Will said in a thick voice.

Rachel forced a smile. "I think God does let him visit."

"I think so, too." Nora threaded a hook on a big polar bear wearing skis. "I think he would really like this tree and . . . could I be the one to hang up Larry Bird?"

She looked at Rachel and then at her older brother with big, pleading brown eyes. Will just laughed. "Yeah, sure. You called it."

Rachel smiled to herself, feeling the sad moment lift and disperse. This first time had to be the hardest time, she reasoned. She did feel sad, but . . . accepting. And grateful, too, for all the wonderful, sweet, funny memories. She had a feeling her children felt the same.

As Nora and Will searched the branches for empty spots and tried to fit in the last few ornaments, Rachel stepped back, watching them.

"Right there," Nora said, pointing to a spot above her head. Will grabbed her around the waist and hoisted her up and, and with laserlike precision, Nora hooked Larry Bird to the very front and center of the Christmas tree.

"Good job," Will said, dropping her down. He held out his hand, and she slapped her brother five.

Rachel watched them and said a prayer, thanking God for her two wonderful and amazing children. *I'm so proud of them, Jack. Aren't you?* she asked silently.

There was no way to change what had happened. No way to go back to the past. They could only accept it and move forward, feeling grateful for the time they had all been together. That was the way she saw it now.

Christmas Day, December 25, 1978

BEN WOKE FEELING TIRED DOWN TO HIS BONES. DOWN TO HIS VERY soul. The drive back and forth to Southport and a late, heavy dinner weighed him down like a pile of bricks in his bed. He felt as if he could sleep a week. But after a few moments of lying there, his eyes slowly opened and the excitement of Christmas morning slipped through his veins—a tingling feeling he found he had never outgrown.

I am blessed that way as well, he thought with a chuckle as he pushed himself out of bed and prepared to get ready for church.

When Rachel was older, they would get up even earlier, he suspected, to see what Santa had left for her under the tree. He could already imagine her tiny hand tugging his along, down the stairs into the living room. They would have some fun unwrapping toys and gifts—before he dashed off to get ready for the service.

But in the meantime, he and Carolyn and her parents had opened a few gifts on Christmas Eve and would open a few more today at a leisurely, adult pace.

He did spot many colorful boxes under the tree that had not been there last night when he had gone to bed. He suspected Carolyn had been tiptoeing around the house while visions of sugarplums had danced in his head. He was curious now to see what was there, but knew that he had to wait.

When he reached the church, he rushed into his office and slipped on his white robe and the gold scarf that was especially for Christmas. Then he took out the folder with the sermon he had prepared. He liked to practice it once or twice in the empty sanctuary, if there was time. The chorus was rehearsing, but he hoped they would be out with a few minutes to spare. Out in the narthex he found families already arriving, greeting each other happily.

"Reverend Ben, Merry Christmas!" Otto Bates walked up and heartily shook Ben's hand. He looked very dapper today in a dark gray suit and burgundy tie—more like a business executive than a short-order cook.

"Merry Christmas, Otto. I hope you have a wonderful day," Ben said sincerely.

He greeted church members all around, feeling encouraged by their warm wishes for the holiday. Perhaps he had been building things up in his mind, their indifference to him and his lack of authority here. Perhaps Christmas melted these petty squabbles and tensions away.

He shook hands with Peter Blackwell and admired his grandchildren. As he gazed around, he realized the day was indeed living up to his expectations of his first Christmas at his own church. The colors and sounds, the organ music and voices drifting from the sanctuary. The feelings of goodwill and peace toward all.

The realization gave him hope and encouragement. He had been at such a low point when he visited Reverend Hascomb, but was glad now he had heeded his mentor's advice and taken things slowly, putting his own feelings aside.

Doris Hegman walked toward him. "Merry Christmas, Reverend. I came early to get a seat. Funny how you don't see half these people all year, but everybody comes to church on Christmas."

"As it should be," Ben answered with a mild smile.

"Too bad about Oliver Warwick in the hospital and all that," the old woman added. "But you reap what you sow, as the Good Book says."

The words pierced Ben's heart like an arrow. Was she really suggesting that Oliver was being punished with a heart attack for his misdeeds? Ben had no words to express his shock and disappointment.

Digger suddenly appeared, looking remarkably presentable in a tweed jacket buttoned over a thick gray sweater. His dark, wiry hair and long beard were neatly trimmed and combed. Ben had seen him enter earlier with his wife, Ruth, and their little girls.

Digger took his mother's arm and gently steered her away. "We've found some seats, Mother. Come along. Merry Christmas, Reverend."

"Merry Christmas, Digger," Ben replied, "and to your family."

He quickly walked back to his office. Instead of rehearsing his sermon, he decided to take some time alone, to calm himself and clear his head. Had the congregation learned anything? Made any progress at all? Or was it just sugary Christmas cheer covering over the same old cruelty? Had anything at all changed if someone could walk right up to him on Christmas morning and say a thing like that?

The words of his mentor came back to him. *We must recognize and respect where each soul is in their spiritual journey. . . You can't force people to believe. You can't shame them into compassion. It has to come from the heart. Maybe our role is just to plant a seed there.* Ben tried to take comfort in that thought. It would do no good to judge and lash out now, he knew; to make Doris—or anyone—feel guilty for their wrong thinking. That was not the way to plant a seed. Teaching God's ways should be freeing. Learning to love and forgive should not be a penance but lighten one's load. Jesus said, "My yoke is easy and My burden is light."

Somehow, he had to get this message through in his sermon today, in his teachings about the meaning of Christmas. Ben suddenly felt he was facing his true challenge, his true test as minister of this congregation. It was as if all that had happened in these past few weeks had been leading up to this moment.

Perhaps that was not really true. Perhaps he was overreacting and blowing things out of proportion. But it felt true. Ben said a quick, silent prayer, asking God to fill him with the Spirit and bring the right words to heart and mind.

A sharp knock on the door caught his attention. "The choir is ready, Reverend. It's time," Gus Potter called to him.

"I'm ready, too," he answered, more forcefully than usual. He checked his appearance in his mirror, smoothed his hair and scarf, and picked up his sermon again.

"God, give me the will and grace to carry out this Christmas service—honoring the birth of Your son—in all the glory it deserves."

Ben took his place at the back of the choir and followed them into the sanctuary, singing "Joy to the World." But even the beautiful harmonies and lilting voices could not take his mind off the sermon. He moved through the service in a rote manner, following his notes and the program, and stumbling a moment or two, though fortunately, no one seemed to notice.

When it came time to give his sermon, he took his place at the pulpit and set out his neatly typed pages. He noticed Vera and Lester Plante sitting up front. Perhaps they had felt some sympathy for Oliver and his family at the news of his heart attack . . . and perhaps not. Perhaps they shared Doris Hegman's opinion. Ben knew it was not his place to judge them, either.

But it is your place to lead, a small voice reminded him. *To remind people like Doris and the Plantes of what the Good Book* actually *says.*

He cleared his throat and looked out at the congregation, sitting quietly, waiting for his words.

"Good morning, everyone . . . Merry Christmas. Today we gather to celebrate the birth of Jesus Christ, our Lord and Savior. A miracle among miracles, it's been called down through the ages.

"But what does this holiday mean to us every day of the year? How should this day resonate in our lives, every hour, every minute? Because it's not just a single day out of three hundred and sixty-five—one that we cook for, decorate for, shop for, and then enjoy in a whirlwind of opening gifts, eating rich foods, and visiting with friends and family . . . though that is all certainly part of it.

"But I'd say that wild frenzy of activity is just the wrapping paper and bow on the gift. I'd say it's the gift inside we must focus on . . . and cherish. The miraculous and divine gift that is perfect for everyone on our list. That fits all and suits all individual styles. A gift we cannot just make use of here and there . . . but must absorb into our very beings, until this gift has truly become a part of us, taken into the fabric of our natures and temperaments, our hearts, our very souls . . ."

His voice trailed off. He looked across the sea of faces. They were listening to him, thinking about what he was trying to say.

"Recently, I heard someone say that a man we all know, whose fortunes, future hopes, and even his bodily health are now in ruins, is lying sick in a hospital bed because God is punishing him . . ."

He caught sight of Doris Hegman's face toward the back of the sanctuary. She sat up, looking shocked, then had the good grace to cringe a little.

"It doesn't matter who said this. It could have been anyone. We've all thought, if not said, such things," he added, trying not to single Doris out. "But the words did pain me. And they seemed so at odds with the meaning of Christmas and what we've all gathered here to celebrate. And at odds with the essence of the most blessed, precious gift you've ever been given."

Ben felt something in his heart shift. Any residue of anger or frustration with Doris—or anyone in his church—evaporated like mist, leaving behind pure love for these people who gazed back at him, hungry for the word of God, the spiritual message he so wanted them to understand.

He put his carefully typed pages aside and moved forward, into his ideas, into his words, feeling himself lifted by a higher spirit, one of forgiveness and compassion.

"What is the message of Christmas? Why was Christ, the Messiah, the King of Heaven and Earth, born in a humble stable? Why did one so great and powerful come into this world so modestly?

"To show that we cannot judge one another's worth by material appearances in this world. We cannot judge and compare and say some are better, some are worse. We can't view the world and live through our egos—our 'small' earthly selves—motivated by fear and a drive to simply survive.

"We must strive to see and experience this earthly life with a higher consciousness, an awareness of the divine. The divine essence within all of us. We must strive to connect with our hearts, our higher, spiritual selves that offer unconditional acceptance and love . . . and forgiveness. Not judgment and exclusion . . . and rejection."

He paused, gazing across their many faces, all different, but all enlivened by the spark of the divine, deep within their souls.

"Just as the sun shines down on all of us, the light of God shines within us all. The kingdom of God is within us, and without us, just as the Scripture says.

"So often you get a Christmas card that says, 'Peace on Earth. Goodwill toward men.' How many of us stop to think about that greeting card slogan? But it is also the deep, abiding message of Christmas.

"It's not enough to cultivate a good relationship with God. God wants us to cultivate good relationships with one another; even with total strangers."

Ben had not intended his voice to rise so loudly, but suddenly he realized it was echoing through the sanctuary. His audience sat in perfect silence, all eyes upon him, all ears listening. No one fidgeted in their seat. They barely seemed to breathe.

He paused, then spoke in a quieter tone. "God wants us to recognize that we are all His children, all divine, made in His image. And we must respect and treat each other with the same reverence and respect we give to our Heavenly Father. That's why He sent His son, Jesus, down to earth on Christmas morning: to walk among us as an ordinary man. A man with human frailties and imperfections that are unconditionally forgiven. Unconditionally loved.

"'What is the greatest commandment, Lord?' Jesus was once asked. 'Love your brother as you love yourself.' What was Jesus trying to teach us? That every transaction with another person on this earth, in this lifetime, is a spiritual opportunity, a spiritual choice. You can treat that person from your earthly, small-minded self. Or you can relate to them with love and acceptance. With kindness, forgiveness, and gentleness; as you would a sister or brother, or one of your own children. You can treat them in the image of the divine power that created you, offering complete love and acceptance.

"We are here to love and support one another. Not ridicule or humiliate. Not judge and punish. We are here to look through our hearts and hold out our hands to the ones who are injured and to those who make mistakes and cause the injury. Which includes all of us, I must add.

Who among us has never said a harsh word? Told a lie or lashed out in anger? Everyone deserves prayers and compassion, and aid—living proof of our faith in action."

Ben took a deep, centering breath. He could tell by the expressions of his audience that he had, at the very least, surprised them. He saw his wife's face, shining like the sun, her blue eyes filled with pride. That was enough encouragement for him.

"On Christmas Day, let us all be renewed and reborn in the birth of Christ, down to our very cores," he concluded. "Perhaps this miraculous gift is, in a way, a compass, always pointed in the right direction. In a way, a light, always shining within and without, making our paths clear. Let it be as a pair of glasses that makes us see one another in a new way. Let us treasure this gift and use it—to set out on a new path, one of love and compassion, the path of our Lord and Savior, born this day. Bless you all and your families. Enjoy a blessed Christmas," he finished quietly.

Everyone sat perfectly still for a long moment. Even Quentin Digby, the music director, seemed awestruck, forgetting to cue the chorus for the next hymn, "Away in a Manger."

Ben saw Doris Hegman sitting with her hands folded in her lap, staring straight ahead. He hoped he hadn't been too hard on her. But perhaps she was now thinking about what she'd said in a different light.

Ben sang along as he returned to his seat beside Carolyn and his in-laws. He was not sure if he had helped or enlightened his congregation. But he knew his intention to lead them to a higher place had been sincere, and he trusted the impromptu words that felt as if they had been given to him.

After the service, Ben took his usual post by the rear doors of the sanctuary, greeting the congregants as they walked out. Many lined up to wish him a Merry Christmas. "Fine sermon, Reverend. I wish I had a copy of that one," Walter Tulley said sincerely. "It's the type of thinking you'd like to read from time to time. To keep you on track."

Ben felt very gratified by the compliment. "Thank you, Walter. That is music to a minister's ears," he admitted with a laugh. "As it happens, I didn't actually write that one down beforehand. I did write a sermon for today . . . but it wasn't the one I just delivered. Perhaps I'll use those thoughts in an essay soon, for our church bulletin," he added.

"That would be swell, Reverend. I think a lot of people would appreciate it."

Others in line offered similar reactions along with good wishes for Christmas. There were also those who simply rushed by, avoiding eye contact with him, Vera and Lester Plante among them.

Ben sensed this message had been too strong for some, making them uncomfortable. But hadn't Reverend Hascomb once told him, "If you don't see your congregation fidgeting in their seats from time to time, you aren't doing your job"?

He knew that he had spoken from his heart, from his very spirit. He had told the truth as he saw it and he had spoken from a place of compassion and love. And wasn't that, after all, what God asked of him?

Ben went home shortly after the service. There was nothing left to do at church except tally up the special offering that had been collected over the last two days. Walter had promised to call with that figure once he had finished the calculations.

Ben felt happy and relieved to return to the parsonage, and looked forward to a quiet day with his family. He was even glad for the company of his in-laws. As much as he loved his little family, it was nice to have Carolyn's parents there on Christmas. It made the holiday feel more festive. Carolyn and her mother were cooking a very special dinner—roast goose, which smelled divine.

He sank down on the couch for a quick nap, with a fire in the hearth and the Sunday newspapers that he'd never read all around him.

A time to plant, a time to reap. A time to work and to rest, he reminded himself. This was his time to be at peace. *You've done all you can do. You've gone to the mat. Left it all on the field. Or on the pulpit,* he clarified. *Let it go now, Ben. Let it go, and let God do the rest.*

Hours later, Carolyn's parents had gone up to bed and Carolyn had put Rachel to sleep as well. Ben had shut off all the lights, except for the Christmas tree, and a fire still burned in the hearth, though it was just glowing embers now.

"Come sit with me. Let's look at the tree," he called as Carolyn came down the stairs again.

"Gladly. The house is so quiet now. I love it," she confessed.

He opened his arms and she slipped in beside him and rested her head on his shoulder. "Do you like your presents?"

He felt her nod, her cheek rubbing on his new flannel shirt.

"I love them. They're all perfect. But this is the best one—some quiet time with you. I hope you can slow down now with the holidays over."

"I can and will," he promised, kissing the top of her head. "If only because I'm a bit exhausted. I think I've preached myself out," he said with a laugh.

"Your sermon today was wonderful, Ben, truly inspired. I know I told you before, but I'm so proud of you. This congregation is blessed to have found you."

"I'm glad you think so. But I don't know if they all agree."

He was thinking specifically of Lester Plante, who could rally a group of like-minded congregants, especially if Doris Hegman complained about him.

"There will always be people who don't understand you, Ben, no matter who you are or what you do. I believe the thing is to be your most authentic, honest self in this world. That's what God wants us to do," Carolyn replied. "And you are doing that. So it will all work out, one way or the other."

"Yes, that's true. I'm glad I have a wife who is so wise—and so full of faith. That's my blessing," he added, smiling down at her. "Carolyn . . . I've been worried lately that maybe I'm not cut out to have my own church, to be holding this position. Maybe it's just not the right place for me now," he said quietly, half-afraid of what she might say. He wouldn't blame her at all if she said she wasn't ready to pack up and leave Cape Light.

Carolyn didn't answer at first. "There are other things you can do as a minister, Ben," she said finally. "We both know that. If you're not the right minister for this church, so be it. That means God has something better in store for you. We both know that, too."

Ben tilted his head so he could meet her eyes, as brilliant as the lights on the Christmas tree. "Thank you for saying that. Thank you for being you," he added. "I love you more every day. Honestly, I don't know what I'd ever do without you."

He smiled softly at her, thankful to have married someone who could boost his faith when it sagged so sadly. Someone who could always shine a light on his steps when he stumbled.

He kissed her, and the world around them melted away in the crackling fire and the soft haze of the colored lights on the Christmas tree.

Present day, Christmas Day, December 25

OF COURSE THERE WERE PILES OF PRESENTS TO OPEN, DELICIOUS foods—that both Rachel and her mother had cooked and baked—a fire in the hearth, and a sing-along with her mother playing the piano and her father handing out the worn pamphlets of carols they had been using since Rachel was a little girl.

But everyone in her family would agree that the highlight of the day had to be the unveiling of Nora and her grandmother's magnificent gingerbread house. More than a house, really.

"A confectionary architectural masterpiece!" her father had proclaimed.

"What's that mean, Grandpa?" Nora asked, with a puzzled expression.

"It means it's awesome," Rachel translated, walking around the little table where her mother had set it up for viewing.

The house wasn't all that large, though it was larger than most of the gingerbread houses Rachel had seen. What made it so amazing was that the decorations were so intricate and detailed. Every chocolate shingle on the roof was set with care, as were the tiny chimney built of jelly beans and the jelly bean "stone" fence around the snowy white-icing yard. Every window, and shutters, too, made with squares of chocolate-covered graham crackers. Every edge of the walls an icing border of different colors. A path of peppermint wheels led to the door, which had cut-out windows covered with thin squares of apricot sheets so that a small light glowed from within. And of course, the occupants of the mini-mansion were a gingerbread woman and a gingerbread man. He wore a striped stocking cap, and she had on a polka-dot dress and green boots.

"I think we should take a picture and send it to the newspaper," her father said excitedly. "Doesn't someone give prizes out for this sort of thing? There are contests for sand castles."

"Oh, Ben . . . we just had fun making it. It's the experience of these things," her mother replied wisely. "Something Nora will always remember," she added, stroking her granddaughter's hair.

Even Will was impressed. "That is totally awesome," he said to his sister. He had actually taken his earphones off to give the house his full attention, and now took a picture with his phone. "I'll send a photo to Uncle Mark at least," he said to the others. "He's got to see this."

They hadn't called Mark yet, but planned to in a little while.

"Yes, show Uncle Mark," Nora agreed happily. "We'll make another one next year, Grandma, even better."

Carolyn laughed. "It will be hard to top this . . . but I'm game, honey, if you are. Maybe we started a new family tradition."

"Yeah, I think we did," Nora said with a happy note of surprise in her voice.

Rachel smiled but didn't say anything. She didn't want to ruin the moment. Maybe they had started a new tradition, one that she would carry on with Nora and Will's children, she reflected. Life went on after losses. Families went on. It was good to preserve the memories and the traditions, but good to make new ones, too.

Not just good, she realized. Inevitable.

A short time later, they enjoyed their special desserts: cheesecake for her father, classic Southern pecan pie for her mother, and chocolate cake for the children. The gingerbread house had been spared, though Nora couldn't resist picking off a few chocolate shingles.

Rachel helped her mother in the kitchen with the last of the cleaning up. Everyone was tired; it was time to pack up and go home.

"How is your friend Ryan? What is he doing for the holidays?" her mother asked in a casual—but not really—tone.

Rachel was drying a china platter and hung on tight to it, careful not to let it slip. She had expected her mother to ask about Ryan, and tried to keep her true emotions out of her reply.

"I'm not really sure. We don't talk very much if there aren't games, and the schools are all on winter break now."

"Really? I thought you were getting to know each other. Aside from the basketball team," her mother hinted broadly.

"We were, but . . . we decided not to date anymore." *I did,* she silently corrected herself. "It was just too complicated. It wasn't working out."

Carolyn seemed surprised, and then disappointed. "I'm sorry, honey. Sorry I said anything," she added. "You looked so happy that night after you came back from your date with him. I assumed it was working out."

"It's all right, Mom. It's just that . . . it didn't." Rachel placed the platter down on the kitchen table. "He's a very nice man. I have nothing against him."

"Of course not. I guess you weren't ready, dear," her mother replied, letting her off the hook.

It was hard for Rachel to lie. Since breaking it off with Ryan, she had come to see that maybe she *was* ready. More than she had realized.

"Something like that," she finally replied. She didn't feel right telling even her mother the whole story. She didn't want to be disloyal to Will.

But she still felt a wave of sadness each time she thought of Ryan. She had wondered where he was today. If Andy was with his mother and Ryan was alone. Will had mentioned something about Andy going to New Hampshire to ski, so maybe they were celebrating together there, with Ryan's sister and her family. She hoped so.

She missed him in a way. But she was also thankful for the break in the basketball schedule and not having to see him. She hadn't talked to Will yet about returning to the team. But she sensed he felt uncomfortable now about Ryan, for obvious reasons.

Rachel wondered if Ryan was thinking of her today. If he ever thought of her—or was too angry or maybe indifferent—now that she had told him it couldn't work. She had to admit that she did think of how things could have been. She thought about it every single day. She remembered how comfortable they'd been together the night he came over for chili. She hadn't really dated much before she married Jack and knew she was no expert on romance, but she had a feeling that what she'd had with Ryan was rare. It didn't happen very often——maybe twice in a lifetime if you were lucky—and she had walked away. She understood now that it would be a long time before her feelings for him faded.

If she could tell her mother anything right now, Rachel knew she would have said that she wished things were different . . . but didn't see how they could be.

CHAPTER FIFTEEN

~᙭~

Present day, January 2

THE HOLIDAY BREAK FROM SCHOOL WENT BY QUICKLY. Rachel rearranged her schedule with therapy patients and was free to spend most of the week with her children. She took them ice skating, bowling, to a game arcade with go-carts, and to the movies twice. But by Friday—the day after New Year's Day—her suggestions at the breakfast table were met with shrugs and bored stares, and Will and Nora didn't have any idea of what they wanted to do, either.

Rachel had an inspiration. "How about indoor rock climbing?"

Her children stared at her, this time with disbelief. "You're goofing on us, right?" Will said.

"I'm totally serious. So what do you think?"

"Can I come, too . . . please?" Nora's eyes were bright with excitement. "Even if I don't get too high."

"I think you'll do fine, honey. It's not very hard, once you get the hang of it. Not much different than the climbing structure in the playground."

It was a little different, but that was no reason to discourage her, Rachel thought.

Will gave her a curious look. "I thought you said it was too danger-ous? Remember that party I wanted to go to there?"

Rachel did remember, and felt a little embarrassed now about the way she had held Will back. "I had to find out a little more about it. It's not dangerous if you follow the rules, and it's not that hard, either. It's fun."

Now Will really looked surprised. "It's fun? How do you know? Did you ever go?"

Rachel smiled and avoided his gaze. Her son hadn't seen her return from her date with Ryan, and she had kept that little adventure to her-self, barely even giving her mother the details.

"I did. Once. I just wanted to try it," she added hastily. "So do you want to go? If you do, I'd better call and reserve a time. I bet it's crowded during the school break."

"Can we bring Charlie?" Will asked, mentioning a boy on the bas-ketball team.

"Sure, you can bring a friend. You can, too, Nora." She looked back at Will. "What about Andy? Isn't he your best friend now?" She tried to ask as if she wasn't prying.

"Andy's still in New Hampshire, visiting his aunt and snowboarding and stuff. His dad shot a video of him coming down this huge hill and he put it on Facebook. Guess I'll see him when he gets back."

Will definitely sounded envious. Rachel made a mental note to take him snowboarding some time . . . when she worked up a little more courage.

"Sounds like they're having a good vacation," Rachel replied while looking up the number of Summit Rock Climbing on her laptop. She had been curious to know if Will felt awkward with Andy now, since he was so uncomfortable about her seeing Ryan. But that didn't seem to be the case. *You've also been wondering what Ryan is doing this week,* she admitted to herself. *So now you know.*

Rachel heard no more about Andy or Ryan until the vacation was almost over. Andy called Will on Sunday morning, the day before school was to start. Will was in the kitchen and Rachel heard his side of the conversation while she was emptying the dishwasher.

"Really? Cool," he said, for about the hundredth time. "Wait, I'll ask." Will put his phone down and turned to her. "Andy got home from vacation last night. Can I hang out at his house awhile today?"

Rachel focused on stacking bowls in the cabinet above the sink. "Sure. I'll drive you over after church."

"Cool," he said, then turned back to the phone, making more plans with Andy as he left the room.

Rachel put away the last of the flatware and slid the drawer closed. She was glad that Will and Andy were still friends. She wouldn't have wanted her son to lose a good friendship over this situation with Ryan. But that didn't mean she had to see a lot of Ryan. She would drop Will off and then stay in the car when she picked him up.

So what's with the nervous knots in your stomach at the mere idea of driving to his house? Get a grip, Rachel. You'll have to face him again sooner or later.

Rachel knew that was true, though she wasn't at all sure if that was a moment she dreaded—or looked forward to.

Will's delivery and pickup went smoothly. Rachel didn't even catch sight of Ryan at the front door . . . or through the living room window. Though she did look carefully.

Will started talking about him almost as soon as he got in the car to go home, so she knew he had been there.

"Coach Cooper said practice starts again on Tuesday. We have a big game next Saturday, January tenth," he added. "Coach said he's sending out an email."

So Will was calling Ryan "Coach" again, and talking about practices and games. That was a good sign. And Ryan was sending out emails to parents. That must mean he just assumed she didn't want to be involved with the team anymore, she realized.

"So . . . you're going back to the team?"

Will shrugged. "Yeah, I guess. I got a little bent out of shape at the last game," he admitted. "But there were a few guys from the team there tonight and they're all acting like I absolutely have to come back. Or they'll die or something. And Coach Cooper asked me to come back, too. As long as I feel okay. Which I do," he added emphatically. "There aren't too many games left, and he said if we can win a few more, we might be in the play-offs."

Rachel had a feeling Ryan knew just the right thing to say to Will to let him know he harbored no hard feelings and make her son feel like he was an important member of the team.

"It's all good, then. I'm glad you're going back." She meant it, too. Now that Will was sure Ryan wasn't "a threat," he seemed to like his coach again. But she did hope the team didn't play any extra games. It was going to be hard enough to see Ryan again as it was. Even across a crowded gym.

On Monday morning, Rachel found an email from Ryan. It was addressed to all the team members and parents, confirming the information he'd told Will the day before. Practice would resume on Tuesday and Thursday of the coming week, and the next game was Saturday, January tenth.

At the top of Rachel's note, however, she found an extra message.

Rachel—I understand that continuing as the team manager may be inconvenient right now. As you can see below, we're close to the end of the schedule, and Jason has agreed to take over the job. So, no worries. Best wishes for a Happy New Year.

—Ryan

Rachel stared at the words a minute. Part of her was relieved that he had figured out this graceful exit strategy. She knew that she could no longer casually hang around on the bleachers with him a few afternoons a week—though she had been dreading telling him that.

But now that it was final, she wondered if he had decided things for them because he didn't want to be around her anymore either. That made her feel sad. She didn't like thinking he might be angry at her, or that she had hurt him with her decision. It also made her feel that her decision not to see him anymore was truly final.

It was easy to get Will back and forth to practice without seeing Ryan, though on Thursday, when Rachel drove over to pick him up, she was tempted to get out of the car and peek into the gym a minute. But she valiantly hung on, and instead texted Will to say she was in the lot, waiting.

But there was no avoiding Ryan at the game on Saturday—at least, no avoiding the sight of him. The gym was already crowded when she arrived with Nora. Will had left earlier, picked up by a teammate, so he would be in time for the warm-up and pregame practice.

Rachel could tell from the parking lot that they were running late. Uneasy about seeing Ryan, she had left the house at the last minute.

Even Nora noticed. "It's so crowded, Mommy. What if we don't get a seat?"

Rachel was wondering the same thing. "Don't worry, honey. I think Grandma and Grandpa came early. I'm sure they saved us a space." She hoped so, anyway.

She entered the gym and looked for her folks . . . and found herself meeting Ryan's gaze instead. He was all the way on the other side of the court. The team was dribbling and shooting, and it seemed about twenty basketballs were in the air at once. But when she met his gaze, all the noise and motion faded, and she was lost in the blue of his eyes—like staring up at the clear winter sky.

Rachel turned away, pretending she hadn't seen him. Had he nodded at her in a silent greeting? She wasn't sure. She was only sure she couldn't look at him anymore. Not that way.

"Grandma . . . Grandpa . . ." Nora started waving, and Rachel saw her dart up to the next aisle in the bleachers and then run up the steps about halfway. "They're here, Mom! They saved us seats," she called back.

Rachel saw her father stand and wave and she waved back, making her way through the crowd.

There wasn't much time for conversation before the game began. In the first quarter, it looked as if the Falcons were going to be overpowered. They started the second quarter with glum expressions, down twelve points. But they came out scoring big, with two three-point shots in a row and some great rebound points as well. When halftime came, the teams were tied, and the opposing team, the Badgers, looked tired and dismayed.

The Falcons looked tired, too, Rachel thought, but encouraged. Will hadn't played the first quarter, but was in for a few minutes in the second. The rest of the time, he sat on the bench, close to Ryan, intensely watching the action on the court.

"I hope Will gets more time on the court this half," her father noticed. "He's playing excellent defense. He's blocked quite a few shots."

"Yes, but I love to watch him score a basket," her mother said. She turned to Rachel. "How does it feel watching from up here, instead of with the team?"

Did she mean with Ryan? Rachel wasn't sure.

"A little different. I can enjoy it more. I don't have to be worried about team issues . . . like who lost their jersey or forgot some permission form. Or warn everyone about the time-outs."

The whistles blew, signaling that halftime was over. Rachel was relieved not to have to talk anymore. Her mother had been one awkward question away from asking about Ryan; Rachel felt sure of that.

The rest of the game flew by. Rachel and her family sat on the edge of their seats as the lead bounced back and forth between the two teams, always within a point or two.

With seconds left to play, the Falcons gained the lead by two points with a spectacular jump shot by Andy. The Badgers then took possession of the ball, and Ryan called a time-out. Rachel watched him huddle with the boys and go over some strategy on his clipboard. She hoped they weren't all too nervous to focus. There was enough time on the clock for the Badgers to score. It was still anybody's ball game. Especially if it went into overtime.

As the Falcons ran back onto the court, she saw Will had come off the bench for the final seconds of the game.

"Will is in," her father practically whispered, his gaze glued to the court.

"I know," Rachel replied, practically holding her breath as the Badgers inbounded the ball then pounded down the court, aiming to tie it up or win.

The Badgers pulled off some quick, hard passes that the Falcons were unable to block. Their star forward took possession and drove toward the basket in the two-point zone. But right in the middle of his layup, he faked a shot and passed the ball to a teammate in the three-point zone— a dangerous shooter, with nobody guarding him.

Rachel saw Ryan wince and cover his eyes as the boy took his look and gracefully shot for the game-winning basket.

The entire crowd seemed to be holding their breath, watching the ball arc toward the basket, seconds left on the big clock. Rachel watched with her eyes half-closed. She was about to close them all the way . . . when she suddenly saw Will leaping up with one arm extended, actually airborne, as his hand came between the ball and basket and he slapped the shot away, protecting the Falcons' slim lead.

Rachel jumped to her feet screaming and cheering. Will's big sneakers had barely touched the boards again as the buzzer sounded. Rachel saw him catch his balance as he landed in a crouching stance. But before he could stand up again, his teammates piled on top of him like a pack of hysterical puppies, hugging and slapping each other on the back with high fives all around.

"We won! We won!" Nora cheered, jumping up and down.

Rachel's entire family cheered insanely, making the row they sat in rock like an amusement park ride. Her usually calm and staid father looked dumbstruck. He grabbed her mother's arm and practically danced around.

"Did you see that? Will *won* the game. He won the game for his team!"

Her mother nodded, looking teary-eyed. "What a thrill." She shook her head and wiped her eyes. "I'm so proud of him."

"I am, too," Rachel replied, feeling choked up.

"Can we go down and see him, Mommy?" Nora tugged on her hand. "Look, everyone is going down there. Can we go, too?"

Rachel looked down at the spot where the team was still jumping up and down in an excited circle. Now they were surrounded by parents and well-wishers. She had not figured on this, thinking she would wait for Will in the parking lot.

"Let's go and congratulate the team," her father answered before she could. "They deserve a front-page headline for pulling that iron out of the fire."

Indeed they did, Rachel had to agree. She had to put aside her dread of facing Ryan. Will would feel hurt if they were the only family that walked out of the gym without saying congratulations.

Her parents and Nora led the way. It was like swimming against the tide to get through the crowd, but finally, they reached the team bench. Parents were crowded around the team, who mostly sat on the benches, still catching their breath.

Ryan was addressing the team. "You were phenomenal out there, guys. There's nothing else I can say. You all gave one hundred and ten percent, pulling with real teamwork to create this victory. Except for Will," he added with a sly smile, "who gave us *two hundred* percent, coming off the bench and blocking that last shot. That was epic," he added, speaking the native language of his players.

Everyone laughed, and Rachel saw her son smile and duck his head, seeming proud but embarrassed to be singled out. Andy gave him a friendly punch in the arm.

"If you keep up this level of play, we definitely have a shot at the play-offs. Maybe even the championship. Then we'll really celebrate. Right now, I'm inviting you all to Village Pizza for a small victory party."

Rachel stood at the edge of the crowd, practically hidden by her parents. Ryan caught her gaze, looking surprised to see her. He seemed to forget for a moment what he had been going to say.

"Hope to see you all there. Parents, siblings, and grandparents are included," he added. Her folks weren't the only ones in the crowd, and everyone seemed pleased to hear that open-ended invitation. "So grab your gear and I'll meet you in a few minutes."

Will already had his duffel bag and jacket in hand. He pounded down the bleachers and jumped the last few steps to meet them.

"Bravo, son. Bravo!" Her father greeted him with a huge hug.

"You were wonderful, Will. You looked like a real basketball star out there," her mother said.

"You were awesome, honey. Honestly," Rachel added. "So cool under pressure. We're so proud of you." Tears suddenly sprang to her eyes, thinking of how proud Jack would be right now. But she was sure Will already knew that. She didn't want to shadow the moment with sad thoughts.

"You looked like . . . LeBron James," Nora said, making him laugh.

"Right . . . one of these days. Thanks, everyone," he added. "I didn't even know what I was doing," he admitted. "It was like my body was just on automatic or something. Totally in the zone."

They began walking out of the gym to the parking lot with the tail end of the crowd.

"How about the pizza party? We're going, right?" Nora asked eagerly.

Rachel tried to sound casual about it. "If Will wants to."

"Of course I want to go." He looked at her as if she were crazy. It was a crazy question to ask, she had to admit. How could he miss this celebration that he had earned?

"Okay, then, let's all go," Rachel suggested. "You're invited, too," she reminded her folks.

They looked at each other in that long-married way they had of communicating without even speaking.

"Maybe for a minute or two, to congratulate the team," her father said. "We know where it is. We'll take our own car."

"Can I go with Grandma and Grandpa?" Nora asked.

Rachel wasn't sure why she liked to ride with her grandparents all the time, but didn't see any harm in it. "Sure, if they say it's okay."

"Of course it's okay. Come on, honey, take my hand. There are a lot of cars out here. We have to be careful." Her mother offered her hand, and Nora took it eagerly.

Rachel had to smile. If she had done the same thing, Nora would have skipped off in the opposite direction.

She and Will soon found her SUV, and Will got into the front seat beside her, clicking on his seat belt. He did look a little bushed, but excited and happy, too.

"Looks like you're the team hero." Rachel glanced at her son with a smile. "Coach called that last play 'epic.'"

Will shrugged. "I was just lucky and in the right place on the court. Coach has been working with us on that stuff. Everybody worked hard for us to win. It's never just one guy," he said in a more serious tone.

Rachel was heartened to hear his modesty. "That's true. You all played very well."

"And Coop had good strategy to beat those guys. He called some good plays," he added, giving Ryan his due.

Rachel didn't answer, just nodded.

They were both quiet a moment. Then Will said, "You know, Mom . . . how you and Dad always told me that if I did something wrong, I should just be honest about it and tell you?"

Rachel took in a sharp breath. What now?

"Yes . . . we always said that. That's what you should do." She feigned a calm tone she didn't feel. "Is there something you want to tell me?"

Maybe he drank some beer with his friends one night over the vacation? Or lied to me about where he was going?

"Yeah. I do. I've been thinking this week about a lot of stuff. What I said a while ago, about you and Coach Coop. I—I made it sound like I didn't want you to go out on dates with him."

Rachel stopped for a red light and glanced over at him. "Yes, I remember."

He met her gaze a moment, then looked straight ahead again. "Well . . . I've been thinking . . . that was sort of stupid. I shouldn't have acted like that."

Rachel glanced at him, then pulled over to the side of the road and parked. "Why do you say that, Will?" she asked calmly. "Do you feel differently about it now?"

"Yeah . . . I guess I do. I mean, I did feel a little weird going back to the team. But all the guys seemed to want me there. And Coach Coop . . . he was, like, so cool about it. He never made me feel like I was a jerk or he was mad at me or anything like that."

Will seemed surprised, but Rachel wasn't. She knew Ryan was a mature, kind man who would never take out his personal feelings on any kid.

"So, you like him again? Is that what you're trying to say?"

"Yeah . . . well . . . I sort of always liked him. But I was mad at him. And I was mad at you, too."

Rachel nodded. "Yeah, I noticed that."

He smiled at her, then looked serious again. "I guess what I'm trying to say is, I won't be all scared and all bent out of shape if you want to date him. Or date some other guy. Because you seem sort of sad sometimes. And Dad wouldn't have wanted you to feel like that either."

Rachel felt overwhelmed; she wasn't sure how to respond.

"I've been thinking about Dad a lot," Will went on. "And what I think is, no one is ever going to replace him."

"No," she agreed, "no one ever could. And in a way, he's still with us. I see him all the time in you and Nora. He was definitely in you tonight when you made that winning basket—and then just now, when you gave all your teammates credit."

Will just stared at her for a long moment. Then he nodded. "I know what you mean. So I don't think it's right for me to say, like, hey, you have to be lonely and not have anyone around to have fun with and do things for you, like Dad used to. I'm sorry about what I said, Mom. And sorry I screwed everything up for you and Coach Coop."

Rachel smiled and shook her head. She leaned over and hugged him. "It's all right, honey. I'm just so glad you feel better about Dad." She had no idea how this might—or might not—change things with Ryan; she would have to think about that. But she was grateful that Will had come so far in his grieving for Jack.

"You always told me that everyone makes mistakes, and if I screwed up, the best thing is to admit it and apologize." He sighed. "I was thinking of telling Coop, too."

Rachel felt alarmed to hear that. "Did you?"

He shook his head. "I wanted to tell you first."

"I'm glad you did," she said. "You can tell him sometime. Or I can, if you want," she added. "Thanks for being so brave, Will. It's hard to admit when you've made a mistake and ask for forgiveness. It's one of the hardest things to do. I know that no one can ever replace your father in your heart. Or in my heart, either," she promised. "But hearts are like . . . outer space. There is no limit to the number of people we can hold in there."

"Thanks, Mom."

"For what?"

He shrugged. "For being . . . I don't know . . . pretty cool, I guess."

If Rachel had been wishing for a video recorder at the end of the basketball game, she wished even more for a sound recorder now. She started the car again and pulled out onto the road.

"*Pretty* cool? I am *totally* cool . . . You just never noticed," she told him with a laugh.

VILLAGE PIZZA WAS OVERRUN WITH CELEBRATING FALCONS AND their families. Rachel felt a sense of safety in numbers, especially with her parents and Nora there. Ryan was on the other side of the restaurant, sitting with Jason and his girlfriend. But he waved to them as they walked in and found a table. The excitement of the game had worked up everyone's appetite, and the pizza was a welcome sight.

While everyone was eating, Ryan walked around to the different tables and spoke to the players and parents. But by the time he reached Rachel's table, she was sitting there alone. Will had left to join his teammates and relive the game again play by play. Her parents had only stayed a short time, as they had planned, and Nora had left to sit with some other little girls she knew from school.

Rachel noticed Ryan getting closer, only a table away. It was too late to bolt for the door, so she pretended to be checking messages on her phone.

But moments later, he hovered over the table. "Hi, Rachel. I'm glad you came."

She looked up at him and couldn't help but smile. "I *am* the team manager . . . or was," she corrected herself.

"That is true. You definitely contributed to the glory," he added with another charming grin. "Mind if I sit down?"

Rachel found she didn't mind at all. "Please do."

He looked encouraged to hear that, and took the chair right next to hers. They were suddenly so close, she nearly forgot all the small talk she had cued up in her head for just such an emergency.

"So . . . how was your vacation?" she asked. "Will said you and Andy were in New Hampshire, skiing."

"We went up to visit my sister. We had a lot of fun. I couldn't get Andy off the snowboard. How was yours?"

"It was fine. I took some time off from work. I did a lot with the kids. Including rock climbing," she added, daring to meet his gaze for a moment.

He smiled but didn't look surprised. "Yes . . . Will told me." He paused. "I have to admit . . . that gave me a little hope."

Now it was Rachel's turn to feel surprised. So he wasn't angry at her after all. That gave *her* hope. But before she could say anything more, Ryan added, "I was so glad that you were there today to see Will play. You must be so proud. He came off the bench cold and made the winning play for us. He showed so much character."

"I was very proud of him. But I was even prouder of him after the game. We had a talk in the car on the way over here. Partly about you," she admitted.

"Really? What did he say?"

"I can go into the details some other time, when we have more privacy. But . . ." She thought a moment about her answer and what had changed. She knew now that dating Ryan wouldn't hurt Will. But she also knew how much she had missed him, how much she hadn't wanted to give him up. "But if you ever want to go rock climbing again, feel free to call me?" She met his gaze with a hopeful smile.

"Really?" His expression lit up, looking so pleased at her words,

Rachel would have thought the Falcons had just won the championship. "Tell you what," he said, not giving her a chance to say no. "Let's skip the rock climbing for now. I still want to take you out for a real date . . . How about tonight?"

Rachel felt a rush of joy at his reply. "Right. Dinner and skydiving, maybe?" she teased. "Hey, that's okay. I'll just leave some sweats and a helmet in the car. Since I met you, I feel sort of . . . fearless."

He gazed at her, his eyes shining. "I feel so lucky," he said quietly. Then he glanced around a moment and gave her a swift, sweet kiss. "I have a feeling the best is yet to come, Rachel."

Ryan reached for her hand across the table, and she returned his gentle touch, treasuring all that had passed in her life. But suddenly looking forward to the future again, too.

CHAPTER SIXTEEN

⌒⌒✕

December 28, 1978

EN FOUND THE CHURCH QUIET AND EMPTY IN THE WEEK
between Christmas and New Year's. Even Mrs. Guilley had
taken time off to visit with her family in Worcester. After all the demands
of the holidays, Ben relished the time alone and the easy schedule. His
in-laws were heading home to North Carolina tomorrow, so as not to
miss their annual New Year's Eve bridge game with their neighbors. Ben
had enjoyed their stay more than he had expected, but he looked forward now to heralding in the new year with just his wife and their baby.

He glanced over a few papers on his desk. Walter Tulley had added
up the special collections. Including the collections made around town
at various businesses and the profit from the Christmas Fair, there was a
sizable sum to disperse to the unemployed families. Ben was surprised at
how the many small efforts had added up to so much. Members of the
church continued to reach out in the community, as he had reached out
for Peter Blackwell's son, and several of the unemployed in the congregation had found new jobs. That was heartening news, too.

As he headed out for a bite at the Clam Box, he wondered how the Warwicks were doing. Since Oliver's heart attack, he had spoken to Lillian twice over the phone, and she had reported that her husband's recovery was coming along slowly but surely. So far he had not been able to speak to Oliver directly. He hoped he could soon.

He walked into the diner and spotted Otto at the grill.

"Hello, Reverend. What will you have today?" Otto turned in his agile way and set down a glass of ice water and a fresh place setting at Ben's spot.

"Let's see . . . a bowl of Rhode Island chowder would be fine. I need something light. I've been eating much too well these past few weeks."

"If it's any comfort, you're not the only one who says that, Reverend," Otto replied with a laugh. "I think my business slacks off by half the week after Christmas."

It did look quiet in the diner for the lunch hour, Ben noticed. Otto stepped over to the chowder pot and filled a bowl for Ben.

"You're one of the only fellows in town who orders the Rhode Island. I'm not sure why I keep it on the menu," Otto remarked as he set down the bowl of clear clam broth filled with chunks of quahogs, potato, onion, and celery. "It's Oliver's favorite as well," he remarked wistfully. "I dropped off a big pot at the mansion when he came home from the hospital. We had a little visit."

"That was good of you, Otto. How are the Warwicks doing? I spoke to Lillian a couple of times, but she hasn't said much."

Otto dropped two cellophane packs of oyster crackers by Ben's soup dish and dipped his head. "Not too much to say. It's a sad situation. They're selling everything off. Anything that ain't nailed down," he added. "All the antiques and paintings and fancy rugs and such his parents bought in Europe, that was all packed up when I got there, being loaded in a big truck. Oliver said it was being sent up to Boston to be sold. At South-bee, or something like that."

"Sotheby's?" Ben asked, naming one of the world's most famous auction houses of fine art, antiques, and jewels. The Warwicks had owned plenty of things in all categories.

"That's it." Otto nodded. "Says he sold his boat, too. *Lady Luck*. Not that she brought him much of that. She's a beautiful sloop, forty-two foot, all fine wood inside and out, teak cabin and brass trim." Otto sighed and shook his head. "They don't make them like that anymore, believe me."

"I did hear Oliver's boat was a real showstopper."

"He was some sailor, too," Otto quickly added. "He didn't just have a showy boat and the outfits, like some of these club sailors. Oliver crewed in big races all around the world."

Ben had heard of Oliver's sailing expertise and adventures. But that part of life was over for him now, Ben guessed. Unless he was invited to crew on someone else's big boat. Had his yacht-club friends remained loyal? That was another question.

"I guess the family will be moving soon." Ben's soup was cooling off, but he had lost most of his appetite.

"This coming Sunday," Otto told him. "They found a nice house on Providence Street. Most folks would say it's pretty grand. But coming from that castle they live in, I suppose it seems small potatoes."

Providence Street was one of the nicest streets in town, with beautiful old Victorians, so Ben felt sure the house was impressive. But he got Otto's point. Everything is relative. Lilac Hall had been palatial.

"How were they able to buy a new house?" Ben asked curiously. "I thought Oliver was using all of their assets to repay the pension fund."

"He is, pretty much. The strange thing is Lillian's family is mighty well-heeled, could have bailed them out easily. Her father's a big banker in Boston and her brother is a judge," he added. "No help from that quarter. Her parents hated Oliver before they even laid eyes on him. Forbid Lillian to see him, no less marry him. They disowned her when she did. She hasn't seen her people since."

Ben had heard something about that breach; how Lillian was raised on Beacon Hill, a true blue blood, a Boston Brahmin. But she had been swept off her feet by Oliver and had given up everything to marry him.

"I have heard some of that. It's a sad story," Ben said.

"Sure is. Personally, I don't understand how parents can turn their backs on a child like that." Otto shook his head, looking baffled. "But Lillian is a strong one. She came up with this idea of selling Lilac Hall to the county, as a museum. And she persuaded Oliver to set the proceeds aside for the family. She told him the girls shouldn't have to suffer because of what he'd done. I think that's true," Otto said. "He'd already put aside money for their college. So they can both make something of themselves. They're both smart girls."

"Yes, they are." Jessica was only eight but quite bright, and Emily, a high school junior, was at the top of her class, certainly destined for great things if this family setback didn't throw her completely off track.

It was some comfort to know that the Warwicks had a place to go to after Lilac Hall. Though Ben wondered why they stayed in town. It seemed it would have been easier to relocate, to go where people didn't know you. But there were drawbacks to starting over again somewhere new, as well.

"You know what galls me, Reverend?" Otto wiped an invisible spot on the counter with considerable effort.

"What's that, Otto?"

"Where are the reporters now? Where's the front-page story about Oliver selling every last stick of furniture to pay back the folks he wronged? He doesn't have to do that, you know," Otto added. "Some of his money was protected, in a big family trust or something legal like that. Old Harry Warwick knew all the tricks, wasn't taking any chances, especially knowing Oliver would be handling things once he was gone. But Oliver insisted on giving it all away. As much as he can. Why isn't anybody writing a big headline today about that?"

Ben had to agree. "Yes, it rarely makes headlines when someone does the right thing."

"Ain't that the truth," Otto agreed, stalking off with his jaunty walk to wait on another customer.

After lunch, Ben decided to drive out to Lilac Hall. He wasn't thinking of dropping in on the family unannounced. He guessed they wouldn't like that, especially Lillian. But for some reason, he just wanted to see the place.

As he approached the estate, he noticed a long row of cars parked along the shoulder of Beach Road, and even more leading up the lilac-lined drive to the house. The lilac bushes were bare now, but Ben could picture them in bloom, as they had been the first time he had come here.

He parked near the open gates and watched some people walking up to the house, and some coming back carrying lamps and knickknacks. Some held paper cartons, looking very pleased, as if they had won some valuable prize. He could only imagine the contents.

While the most valuable furnishings had been sent to Sotheby's to be auctioned, there had been plenty of fine things left—china and vases and books—that were being sold off right now, Ben guessed.

The sight saddened him. He recalled the last time he had been inside the great house, bringing Oliver those papers to sign—was it only a month ago?—and he'd gotten a hint of the scandal that was so soon to come.

Funny how he didn't realize then that it would be the last time he would see Lilac Hall in all its glory, or probably the last time he would ever visit the Warwicks there.

He bent his head and closed his eyes and said a quiet prayer for the

Warwicks, asking God to help them handle all they were going through, and all they would face in the months to come.

December 31, 1978

BEN DID NOT EXPECT MANY CHURCH MEMBERS TO BE AT THE SERVICE on Sunday. The service after Christmas was traditionally low in attendance, with so many people visiting relatives out of town—or simply tired out from the holidays. But perhaps because it was New Year's Eve, he found the pews nearly full. To reflect, pray, and ask for God's forgiveness and blessings, to start the New Year in the right direction, he thought.

The second reading for the day was from the New Testament, from Matthew, Chapter 25, verses 31 through 46, one of Ben's favorite passages. He read the final lines with emphasis, hoping his audience was paying attention; he had based his sermon on these simple words.

" '. . . then the King will say to those on his right hand, "Come, you blessed, of My Father, inherit the kingdom prepared for you from the foundation of the world: for I was hungry and you gave me food; I was thirsty and you gave me drink; I was a stranger and you took me in; I *was* naked and you clothed me; I was sick and you visited me; I was in prison and you came to me."

Ben paused a moment and gazed at the congregation. " 'Then the righteous will answer Him,' " he continued, " 'saying, "Lord, when did we see You hungry and feed *You*, or thirsty and give *You* drink? When did we see You a stranger and take *You* in, or naked and clothe *You*? Or when did we see You sick, or in prison, and come to You?"

" 'And the King will answer and say to them, "Assuredly I say to you, inasmuch as you did *it* to the least of these My brethren, you did *it* to Me." ' "

The parallel to Oliver Warwick's story was stunning. At least, to Ben it was. But he didn't need to point that out specifically, and knew that was not the lesson he wished to draw.

It was a much bigger notion: Oliver could be anyone in the congregation or even the community. Oliver could be anyone at all who had fallen, suffered, and needed help. Ben hoped the Scripture would remind his audience that we are all the same in the sight of the Lord, all asked to love and care for each other, and to treat one another as we would treat Jesus Himself, if He walked among us again.

During Joys and Concerns, Sophie Potter stood up. "I just wanted everyone to know that the Warwicks are moving today. I think they need some help. Gus and I are going over to Lilac Hall directly after church. Anyone who wants to help ought to come. Many hands make light work," she added with a small smile.

The church was very quiet for a long moment.

Ben lifted his chin and met Sophie's gaze. "Thank you for sharing that news, Sophie. I'll go. I'd be happy to help them."

Sophie smiled back and sat down. Another long silence followed. No one raised a hand to offer a joy or a concern. And no one responded to Sophie's announcement either.

Ben was just about to start the Morning Prayers when Otto Bates stood up. "I'll go help the Warwicks. I'll bring my truck."

Joe and Marie Morgan got to their feet. "We'll go, too," Joe said. "It's a cold day to be carrying boxes."

Digger Hegman and Ezra Elliot simply raised their hands. Ben already guessed they would volunteer, or may have even planned on going already, without announcing it.

But he was surprised when Peter Blackwell stood up. "I'll go help. I'll bring my tools. Maybe they need some new washers and such in their new place."

Walter Tulley volunteered next, offering to bring his toolbox. Ben had noticed that commercial fisherman were unusually handy; most could double as carpenters or electricians.

Many more people offered to help in different ways—to bring over food or help the family unpack. Even some of Oliver's former employees, who had lost jobs at his factories, spoke up, wanting to do what they could.

Ben was so surprised, he could barely speak. His heart was full of gratitude, witnessing the bounty of love and goodwill that had grown in these hearts and spirits, sprouting up from tiny seeds planted by God's hand.

After the service, Ben followed a caravan of cars and trucks that wound down Main Street to Beach Road and headed toward Lilac Hall. The Potters led the way in their red pickup truck that said POTTER ORCHARD on the side. Ben was not far behind in his sedate gray sedan.

As he drove along, he reflected on this surprising group effort. Perhaps the hardest hearts had not been touched. But so many who had criticized and judged Oliver were literally lining up today to help or had at least voiced a new attitude, one of real sympathy for the Warwicks, acknowledging their mutual human frailty. Putting their judgment aside and treating the Warwicks at they would a member of their own family who had made a grave mistake and was suffering the consequences.

Ben knew it was God's work in their hearts and God's will that they should feel this way. But he felt encouraged, as if he might truly be an instrument of God's divine love and wisdom.

This Christmas season had been nothing like he had expected. He had been tossed into the fire, tested like tempered steel. Tested just as Oliver Warwick's character had been. And they had both come through wiser and stronger—and deeply changed.

Ben had a sudden thought about Reverend Hascomb. It was high time to give his mentor a call, to wish him a happy New Year, and to thank his old friend again for his advice. He must tell Reverend Hascomb he felt sure now that he had not made a mistake by choosing this calling and this church.

Ben could see the road ahead clearly, and though he knew now it would not be without its bumps and even a few roadblocks and detours, he knew he would be able to continue his path as a minister—at this church, or wherever God called him.

The parade of vehicles proceeded up the long, lilac-lined drive that led to the mansion. A small truck was parked out front, the kind with a big orange "Rent Me!" sign painted on the side. Lillian must love that, Ben thought.

A servant was loading boxes in the back. There were many more boxes piled haphazardly outside the big front doors, along with a few suitcases and a big black steamer trunk. Too much to fit in the rental truck in one trip, or even . . . three, Ben thought.

Lillian, dressed in black trousers and a wool jacket, came out of the house carrying another box.

She stared at the cars and trucks that kept rolling down the drive and parking in the circle around the fountain, her mouth agape.

Ben had already parked and climbed out of his car.

"The sale is over . . . The rest is not for sale," she announced in a loud voice.

Sophie was the closest to her. She gazed at Lillian with pure kindness. "We heard you were moving today, and we've come to help. You can't fit all this in that tiny truck. I bet there's even more inside."

Lillian stared at her, her head pulled back at an odd angle.

"Well . . . there is," she admitted stiffly. She seemed wary, even suspicious. "I don't quite . . . get it," she said bluntly.

Ben stepped forward and joined them. "Otto told us you were moving today. We thought you could use a hand. Some other friends from the church are going straight to Providence Street with groceries and such."

"Friends from the church?" Her tone challenged him.

Ben was not intimidated. Neither was Sophie. She reached out and took the box from Lillian's hands. "You still have friends, Lily," she said mildly. "Lots of them."

" 'Real friendship is shown in times of trouble; prosperity is full of friends,' " another voice cut in before Lillian could reply. "Euripides said that. I daresay it's true."

Ben turned to see Oliver walking out of the house with another large suitcase. He wore a plaid wool jacket and khaki pants, looking a lot like one of the workers in the factories he used to own.

Ben walked up to Oliver and took the suitcase. "We've all come to help you. I think deeds speak louder than words; louder even than those of the ancient Greek poets."

"Indeed they do," Oliver agreed with a smile. He looked out at the large group that had assembled in the drive. Many still stood beside their vehicles, perhaps wondering if they were welcome.

He gazed around and cast one of his legendary smiles. "Thank you all so much for coming," he said sincerely. "This is . . . a miracle. Isn't it, Lily?"

"I'll say," she agreed drily.

He put his arm around his wife's shoulders and looked down at her, his eyes beseeching her to let her guard down and be thankful for this show of concern.

Lillian finally nodded, her head tilted to the side. "We really had no idea how we were going to get through this today, but . . . I can see now that God has heard our prayers. At least one of them," she clarified. "And sent you all here to lighten our load. And I thank you."

Perhaps because she was notoriously spare with praise and appreciation, Lillian's few words of recognition carried great weight. Everyone in the group seemed to feel welcome and ready to spring into action.

"That's what we're here for. To lighten your load," Sophie agreed loudly. "Now you just tell us what you need us to do. Get all these boxes into trucks and take them to the new house, I guess, is the first order of business."

"But please be *very* careful," Lillian insisted. "There are many boxes marked 'Fragile.' I couldn't bear it if I found precious things had been broken."

After Sophie assured her everyone would take extreme care, Lillian had no problem at all issuing orders and managing the loading of all the trucks and cars.

Still, it was hours later when they finally finished unloading at the new house, unpacking essentials, making up beds, and taking care of all the necessary moving-in-day tasks.

Otto arrived around dusk with a truckload of food from the diner, and everyone sat at the Warwicks' dining table, which was almost too long for their new dining room.

With the help of a few other women, Lillian hurriedly located the thick table pads and a long cloth so that the fine wood would not be marred or stained by the impromptu meal. Ben could tell from her pale expression, she considered this maneuver a narrow escape from catastrophe.

Finally, Otto was permitted to unpack the food he had brought from his diner. The scents were tantalizing and brought everyone to the table, tired and hungry from their hard work.

"And I brought some beer," he added as he set out the many take-out containers, paper plates, and plastic utensils. "After all, today is New Year's Eve," he reminded everyone.

"So it is," Oliver replied, sounding as if he had forgotten.

Ben suspected that Oliver and Lillian's tradition had been to ring in the New Year with the most expensive champagne. But Oliver stood up and raised a bottle of beer. "I'd like to make a toast in our new home. To all of you. With deep gratitude for your help and the kindness you've shown my family. And my gratitude, hopefully, for your forgiveness," he added quietly. "I wish you all sincerely a very happy, healthy New Year. May God bless you for what you did today."

Ben stood by his side and bowed his head. "Amen," he said quietly.

"Amen," Oliver replied.

Present day, January 11

THE CHURCH SEASON HAD MOVED FROM CHRISTMAS INTO EPIPHANY, and Sunday's service celebrated the baptism of the Lord. Ben read a beloved passage of Scripture, from the Gospel according to Mark, about the prophet John the Baptist, who roamed the desert.

Ben delighted in John's description, a man so filled with the spirit, so dedicated to his message, that he shunned all possessions, all comforts and niceties of mainstream society.

" '. . . Now John was clothed with camel's hair, and with a leather belt around his waist, and he ate locusts and wild honey. And he preached, saying, "There comes one after me who is mightier than I, whose sandal strap I am not worthy to stoop down and loose. I indeed baptized you with water; but He will baptize you with the Holy Spirit . . ." ' "

Ben enjoyed preaching about baptism at this time every year and took care to remind the congregation that even though the common practice today in their church was to baptize little babies, who had no choice in the matter, the tradition had originated in a far different way. Early Christians were baptized as adults to publicly proclaim their faith, often risking persecution and even death. But it was more important to them to acknowledge their fellowship—their ties to God—and to other Christians.

". . . and that is the aspect of baptism I consider the most important. A person saying 'I am not just a lone believer, but part of God's family.

And part of this church family, too.' For we are a family. United by our ties of faith and fellowship, as strong as any. Have no doubt," he added sincerely.

When it came time for Joys and Concerns, Sophie Potter was eager to be the first to speak, waving her hand wildly. Ben quickly recognized her and she came to her feet.

"I'm so happy to announce that the church history is complete and the books are in print. Here's the first copy. Isn't it wonderful?" She held up a large book with a dark blue cover and turned it so that everyone could see.

Ben had seen the rough design of the cover, but the book looked far better in print. The front cover was decorated with a very old photograph of the church and attractive gold type.

Ben gazed at the volume with pleasure and awe. "My, my . . . this is a big surprise. I had no idea it was going to be ready so quickly."

"Dan had us on a tight deadline." Vera Plante, who sat beside Sophie, filled in that detail. She must have been telling the truth; she still looked a bit stressed, Ben noticed.

"And he did a lot of work himself to get us there," Claire North added.

"This book has so many wonderful stories and photographs. I know you're all going to love it." Sophie opened up the book and showed a few pages. "You'll recognize a lot of familiar faces. Maybe even your own," she added with a laugh. "You'll learn a lot about our church that you never knew. I guarantee it," she added. "I hope everyone will step up at coffee hour and buy a copy or two—and help us fund all the great programs we have going on here."

"Thank you, Sophie. I'd like to thank everyone on your committee who worked so hard on this project—you and Vera Plante, and Claire North. Carolyn Lewis, of course." He turned and smiled at his wife. "And everyone who helped us get our facts straight . . . And of course, Dan Forbes. And Mayor Emily Warwick, for loaning us the town records—and her husband," he said, making everyone laugh. "I already know I'll take at least two copies," Ben added, thinking he would definitely send one to Mark in Portland. His son would relish the historic inside stories, especially when Ben told him that his own father had written the section about Oliver Warwick.

"You've got it, Reverend," Sophie promised as she sat down again.

Ben smiled to himself, gazing out at his congregation—at Lillian and Ezra Elliot, sitting in a front row, holding hands. At Lillian's daughters, Jessica and Emily, all grown now, with families of their own seated nearby. At Joe Morgan, once the youngest man on the board of trustees, and now a well-respected church elder and grandfather. He smiled to see Digger Hegman and his daughter, Grace, as quiet as her mother Ruth had been and just as devoted to Digger.

Then there was Sophie Potter, a widow for many years now, and in her eighties but full of energy and life, full of love and kindness for everyone she met. Full of ideas for the congregation, keeping it rich in history and rich in fellowship and love.

How could he ever have known, as a young man who had just arrived here so many years ago, the trials he would face? How much he would learn? How so many years would roll out as they had . . . and he would still be here, as well liked and respected as any minister might hope to be?

He continued the service, reciting the Morning Prayers, and silently adding one of his own.

Thank you, God, for my many years of service in this wonderful congregation—for all the friends and strong ties I've made here. For all the lessons I've learned, and the blessings I've known. The very greatest of all, Your call to be a minister and the gift You gave me—a gift that I once so foolishly doubted. The gift of bringing others closer to You, to know and trust Your great love for us all.